"This is Howard Scott from the central chamber of dome number one, complex one. Do you read me, Prove IV?"

"Lanier here. We read you."

"We will begin the attempt to get information from the cards. Recording devices, audio and video, have been activated."

"Very well, Doctor, please begin."

Howard held the delicate card and fed it into the silver rectangle in the center of the chamber. It was sucked gently from his fingers. There was no sound at all.

Col. Haris and the crew of Probe IV heard and recorded what sounded like a very loud, long orchestrated chord.

Howard Scott froze. All memory, all location, all personality, evaporated.

FROM THE LEGEND OF BIEL. . . . AS RECORDED BY THOACDIAN . . .

Dr. Howard Scott began to scream. . . .

MARY STATON is a fine new writer, as she amply demonstrates here. *From the Legend of Biel* is her first book.

Of herself she writes: "I am a thirty-one-year-old woman who has wanted to write all her life and is finally doing it. I began with the arts in music, then shifted to drama and acting which taught me a lot about feeling and living and form and imagination and finally (through Shakespeare) about language which is what I wanted to know about in the first place.

"The act of writing itself accomplishes the book for me, not the thinking about it. I hope to write for that person who loves books and reading, not to play critical or ego games with, but because some kind of real life takes place between that reader's eye and the page of the book. I am interested in making the distance between that reader's eye and the surface of the page disappear."

Her book is an incredible, mind-expanding journey of discovery.

FROM THE LEGEND OF BIEL

BY MARY STATON

From The Legend of Biel

Also by Mary Staton, *Wilderness of the Heart - Seven Gates*, iMaginalFictionPress, 2007

iMaginalFictionPress

iMaginalFiction.com

ISBN:978-1-60402-091-5
Printed in the United States of America

Forward

From the Legend of Biel was written in the winter of 1973 in La Jolla, California. Decades later and from a new century, I was stunned to learn that the piece continues to draw a modest following, has been reviewed on the internet and mentioned in scholarly articles.

In preparing to re-issue the book I read it again for the first time since it came out and found it flawed yet still interesting and fresh. It was, however, written by a very young writer. I was tempted to go through it to correct errors, iron out awkwardness or add a grace note here and there. Much as I might like to do that, it strikes me as disingenuous and so I have not.

What you have here is a copy, page by page, of the original publication. The only changes are this forward, a new cover, and the copyright page. Beyond that, even from a remove of over three decades, I cannot comment further on this work. That is for you to do.

Mary Staton
August, 2007
Los Angeles

WITH THANKS TO FRIENDS OF FEW
AND MANY YEARS,
BUT MOST OF ALL
TO RICHARD

I

Blackness stretches on and on in space. It curves around, folds in on itself in pleats in order that so much can fit into what is. Inestimable distances are possible given time and curiosity. Ships move out into this night. They find nothing but more darkness, infrequently laced with more cooling rock. They find nothing within the skin of what is but silence. But, given the size of the whole, they have not yet looked very far.

United Nations Starship *PROBE IV* is one of these ships. Its crew and research team are asleep. They are frozen, suspended in their own endless, featureless, directionless, weightless spaces. They are unconscious across the major time and distance of their journey.

Mission *PROBE IV*, after five years' preparation and training and two years' sleep-freeze, is almost ready to begin direct investigation of the unknown. Phase One of the mission is direct probe of the planet MC6, which has architectural evidence of some kind of advanced life. Phase Two is entrance into the dark space-cloud Vectus-Nurus 48. Phase Three is another sleep-freeze hop to the edge of the galaxy to probe a newly discovered solar system for signs of life. Phase Four is synchronization with and entry into the tail of the comet "Malcolm X". Then they are to refreeze and return to Earth. The entire mission will have taken six years, plus five years' training, plus two years' planning.

Howard Scott sleeps. He has been brought mechanically to the still point—one degree from death—in order to defy time He is plugged up, naked, profiled on a stainless steel shelf, like a ship in a bottle. He is alive with no signs of life.

Howard Scott's mind is a trick done with black mirrors. It is darkness—a moonless winter sky. And far above, near his mind's unrippled surface, the stars are yellow-gold and simple thoughts, constant and distant explosions of memory and anticipation—means of escape. Inside, beneath the stillness, he learns the other side of himself. The familiar is distant and meaningless. Perspective has been reversed. He dreams of the dreamer dreaming of the dreamer dreaming the dream. He is concentric and simultaneous selves, and none of it is a dream.

Your mother and father are dead.	I reach out and feel nothing but silence. Were they ever alive?
Your heritage is a perversion.	I am much more than my heritage.
Your institutions are important imitations, or imitations of intelligence— and lethal.	They are a game which I no longer play.
No belief is possible to you because all are disgraced, and become evil.	I am learning to continue without whispering in the dark.
Your people are insane.	I am no longer with them.

FROM THE LEGEND OF BIEL

Your sincerity
destroys your
cause.

Then I will laugh.

You are of less
value than a system,
or a machine, or
honor.

I choose for that
not to be so.

Words have no
meaning—madness
is called affluence.

I no longer listen to
words which are spoken
for their own sake.

Why do you
continue?

Because I am alive.

What future is possible
to one such as you?

Motion and change.

    A small boy
           falls
              down
                    the hole
                        of
                            progress,
and for a while believes—
                    until the madness can no longer be denied.
With a decision, which is possible, his feet grip the sides
of his fall, and in the dark he struggles for equilibrium—
which has not been entirely forgotten by the genes—
                                as
                                  time
                                      runs
                                        out.

A clock on the ship counts closer, closer still, and
steady as a heart, to the number which will awaken them.
There is nothing to hear. There is no movement to feel—

although there is linear motion. There is little to see in the dimness except the eight human bodies. They are all asleep, all profiled in the glass capsules by the soft, cold glow of stainless steel. The airless chamber is antiseptic, and it is cold.

Soon they will be awakened to be just as they were—losing nothing in the sleep, profiting nothing but distance—with only the mild sensation, illusion, of a nap. But now, traveling through deep space to even deeper space, they sleep their dreamless, ageless, artificial sleep to conquer time.

Time passes—and distance—which is nothing at all to those who sleep. Ultimately a metal disk bearing a number rotates for the last time. Then it slips to rest position and nudges a soft, complex chain of events into motion with no sound at all. And from a bottle, through the tube attached to a needle which neatly punctures the large vein on the soft top part of the elbow, comes the first pearl of liquid which will unfreeze the body's fluids and open the way for motion.

From deep in the hidden center the dreamer dreams of the dreamer dreaming the dream. Then the dreamer dreams of dreaming. Then he dreams. Then he opens his eyes, and is awake.

. . . .

Howard Scott looked out of the porthole in the PROBE IV conference room. The black disk of space, punctuated by the glitter of stars which never got any closer, was rimmed with silver. With his profile in its center it resembled an old or a very new coin.

*Dr. Howard M. Scott, forty-three, director of the United Nations Security Research Corps. sat parallel to the observation window along the side of the ship. In the gravitized conference room of United Nations Starship PROBE IV, trapped in empty parentheses between the first reality of the ship in flight, and the second reality of the briefing conferenc*è. *He sat in the bubble of his silence and* was as still and cool as smoke frozen in a small, clear stone. Sensations penetrated his silence, and he received them indiscriminately, perceiving none of them. That which did not originate in his vacuum was a liquid blur. The clear, smoke-streaked stone of himself which he had learned while frozen—which was beyond all circumstances—sat beneath his tongue, and he sucked it for courage.

He stirred. He turned his head and slow-motion lack of attention away from the porthole and back in toward the conference room and the others. He tried for an instant, out of habit—which was not broken in sleep-freeze, but only bent—to listen to the briefing session. He could not. He tried to watch the other members of the team as they cooly received the data on the Phase One assignment of Mission PROBE IV.

Too soon Howard would have to speak to them, to pull words he did not have out of a hat he had lost in sleep-freeze. He would be forced by his position to speak dispassionately about that which excited him more than anything or idea he had ever known. He had begged for this mission because of Phase One. The instant he had seen Major Hessen's PROBE I report on MC6, seven years ago, he knew he had to come, because there was life on the planet. He knew it. He had played all the games, said all the right words, controlled his temper, and was here. And now, here, he was finding it difficult to be patient, difficult to continue playing bureaucracy games. His body ached to respond, to express what he felt. Cautiously he said, did, felt nothing.

The formalized ritual of the PROBE IV mission schedule floated in the air above their heads like a large, efficient maze. Howard Scott did not want to run it—could not. He sat before and beneath its threshold, concealed in his featureless parentheses, and waited.

Major Hessen's taped report droned on and on in the background. Howard thought of how much this ship looked like a huge catamaran. He blinked his eyes and affirmed the tendency of the PROBE crews to call the big

11

ships "cats"—for they did indeed pat softly, cautiously through the dark. He did not want his mind to focus down yet, to become a hand ready to grasp, fisted, around the problem on the tape—yet. He gripped the two curved lines of his parenthesis like the sides of a threshold, and was estranged.

Howard Scott looked at his relaxed team, spread out in the room, and saw them as through the wrong end of a telescope. He could almost hear the report through their faces. He would leave it there for now—with them. He had dreamed, and reasoned himself exhausted over the contents of Major Hessen's report. Whenever he could he rested from it. He could not listen to the major speak so scientifically, so matter-of-factly about that which could mean that human beings were to have a reprieve. He had lived with this data for over seven years now and was still reverent toward it. For him MC6 was the whole point of the PROBE IV mission. For the others it was merely the first of four steps to be made on the journey which would take them farther away from Earth than any human beings had ever been.

Marsha A. Williams, forty-nine, M.D., Ph.D., chief of medical research for Mission PROBE IV and officer of the United Nations Surgeon General's office, sat forward in her chair, curled over her stocky body—fingertips on temples—and frowned in fascination. She and Howard had worked together before, both on missions and planning. Marsha was able to get along with Howard Scott. She always stood beyond the effects of his frequent and brilliance-induced moods, watched a while, then went on with her work. Her dumpling face was not attractive until it was understood. Then her continual smile—even while frowning—looked as honest as it was, and became a solace. She lived to work. She had the number two post on this team because hers was one of the most thorough, incisive, and practical minds Howard had ever known. She sat now, a fat comma, chewing her upper lip as the tape reburned its way into her brain.

David R. Hobart, thirty-four, Ph.D., Ph.D., Ph.D.,

chaired professor, University of Africa, stood across the conference table from Marsha and twiddled a pencil as he stared—frozen, as into a pool—down at the tape whirling from spool to spool. His large lower lip was completely concealed behind his big square white teeth as he bit down and listened to the report again. He liked to pretend he had not heard or known things before he reheard or relearned them. That way he missed nothing. He was always wiping his mind clean—after what was on it had been recorded somewhere. That way he could write on it again, and check himself. An envelope and many large, glossy photographs were strewn on the table before him, unseen. They had been studied as the face of one whose integrity is uncertain. They were not really trusted yet. Howard had never worked with David's dark, intense six-foot-five frame of mind before. The younger man had a flair for getting along with people while maintaining the sovereignty of his own points of view. His boyish and continual attitude of surprise was balanced by terrier concentration. This was his first time in deep space.

Howard Scott swiveled his chair forty-five degrees to the left to see the fourth and last member of the team. Mr. Johnson Levin-Hughes, fifty-four, technician supreme of the United States International Research Corporation, was the oldest man on the ship. He was leaning on the wall near the airlock, looking at nothing. Hair capped his ruddy face like the white-water foam of rapids. His eyes were small, clear blue marbles. His arms were folded across his chest as he listened to the tape and heard consequences. Howard had tried to get Richards of I.C.C.R. for Levin-Hughes's post on the team, but Richards was planning the PROBE VIII mission, and that was that. Levin-Hughes and Howard had, over the course of five years training, come to an understanding. They were the quiet members of the team. Levin-Hughes was quiet because he was busy and efficient. Howard was quiet because all things were private. Levin-Hughes's dossier was remarkable. If what it implied were true—and so far there had not been an inkling that it wasn't—the man was

13

capable of understanding the mechanics of any technology in existence.

United Nations PROBE Control, Baja, California, had chosen the members of the team with Dr. Scott, on the basis of the pertinence of their skills to the problems at hand, their adaptibility to each other, to space, and to the unknown. All four of them were single and had no immediate families. The four of them together cross-referenced all of modern knowledge.

The tape recorder clicked off. The gravitized conference room was silent. Dr. Howard M. Scott, head of research, PROBE IV, stood and stretched. He smiled, remembering how he had felt immediately after hearing the tape and seeing the photos for the first time. He walked to the bar near Levin-Hughes and poured himself a cup of coffee. He waited. Nobody moved. He took a sip of his coffee, and felt the steam burn his nostrils as they waited for him to speak.

David Hobart looked at Howard, then sat down and rested his forehead against the heels of his hands. "It's still almost incredible. Isn't it? We're really here."

Howard heard a disk of metal fall into place in the clock. He looked and saw that another day had started— someplace. He walked to the conference table and rested his hip and his coffee on it. He slid the photographs with the tips of his fingers, and peripherally saw the fantastic mosaic they made.

"Ten years ago Major Ali Hessen, Commander, PROBE I, was deep in space. His mission was to search with ultraprobes for deliberate construction, for intelligence— for life of any sort. He was drawing blanks. It was beginning to look like we were the stewards of a lot of very lonely space. Near the time Major Hessen was scheduled to begin return procedures he got a reading from the dark. His mission was extended to its limits to permit him to approach the source of the reading. He was able to make one pass through the area. His ultraprobes discovered, studied, and analyzed this planet—MC6. He deviated from Mission Control schedule and was able to extend

the time of his pass to get this much information. He gambled on his safety margin and lost. PROBE I crew could not be awakened from sleep-freeze. Their resources were gone. But we have their records."

They were silent for a moment. Marsha narrowed her eyes and nodded her salt-and-pepper head. David Hobart made a note on one of his index cards. Levin-Hughes looked passively from deep in his skull at Howard. Dr. Scott's mind had returned to his invisible parentheses. He was frozen, unblinking, staring hard at something behind his own eyes. Abruptly, his head snapped up, and he continued.

"MC6 is slightly smaller than Earth, and orbits a sun very much like ours. Major Hessen's probes found at least five other planets in the system, but all of them gave negative readings. The planet's atmosphere and gravity are identical to Earth's. It has no moons."

"Howard?"

"Yes, Dr. Hobart?"

"These land masses . . ."

"Yes?"

"They cover roughly one-third of the planet, but they appear to be basically flat—as opposed to our basically crinkled land surfaces."

"Yes. MC6 does not have anywhere near the geographical variety of Earth. The remainder of the planet is covered by what are apparently freshwater seas. The mean temperature of MC6 is higher than Earth's. It is a warm, arid place. The poles are cool, maybe even cold —but PROBE I recorded no ice. The land masses of the planet are topped with a rich, high-yield soil which at the time of that probe was producing a sort of yellow grass—except at the poles, which are forested. There is an abundance of botanical life possibilities on MC6, but as yet we find only a limited number of species there."

"But there's no reason why the planet couldn't grow anything we brought to it."

"That's correct. There is also plenty of biological life in the seas. Even simple mammals."

"None on the land masses?"

"None that the probes recorded. We have no evidence of complex life, i.e. human life, on MC6."

"Or anywhere else for that matter."

"Which brings us to the point of Phase One. Major Hessen's probes recorded what appear to be deliberate or non-natural structures on the surface of MC6. These structures are all geometric forms. Probe translation estimates that some of them are small, as in house. But if probe estimates are correct, some of the structures are as much as one hundred meters high. The large structures are all domes. Major Hessen counted thirty of them. The structures are arranged, as you can see, in small groupings or complexes. There is one large dome to a complex. The major's probes recorded no hot-life readings. Apparently, at the time of his pass there was no life on MC6 complex enough to have created these structures."

"They must be ruins."

"Let's not jump to conclusions. Wait and see. It's possible that MC6 has life forms, intelligent and complex life forms, which we with our clumsy technology are unable to pick up on our probes."

"That's a remote possibility, Howard."

"It's my assumption."

"Who's jumping to conclusions?"

"We are to grand-orbit in PROBE IV and repeat Major Hessen's ultraprobe procedure. If we can determine that it is safe to probe directly, we shall land and do so. If not we are to continue ultraprobe to the point of diminishing returns, then go on with Phase Two of our mission. I'm supposed to remind you about now that the ship's crew, including Colonel Haris, has not been fully briefed on the nature of Phase One. So far as they're concerned we are archeologists during this first stop, and MC6 is dead. Mission Control feels that the possibilities are too far-reaching for premature leak. Very few people know about the details of Phase One. During this first stop PROBE IV and crew are mainly military escort. Be

discreet. Please keep all documents in this room. You are, of course, free to study them at your leisure."

"Howard Scott paused and looked away from his team. "We should be celebrating this discovery, not hiding it."

"We can't celebrate a discovery until we know what it is, Howard."

Howard looked at his crew from the wrong end of his telescope again. He could see that they were committed, but he wondered to what. He exhaled, and studied the palm of his hand.

"We have another conference in fifteen hours for detailed procedure briefing. The meantime is yours. Do what you need to do to be completely receovered from the stiffness of sleep-freeze before Phase One begins. Use the gym, sleep if you need to—relax in your own ways. Keep this room locked. You have your keys?"

"Yes."

"Any questions? Fine. Until fifteen hours, then."

Dr. Howard M. Scott gathered the photos and tapped them into neatness on the table. He put them in their aluminum envelope and locked it, then took the cassette out of the tape recorder and placed the tape and the envelope into the safe. A cold, damp ribbon ran the length of his spine. Howard shivered and looked at his team. He had wanted more from them. He had wanted them to be fervent, and they were merely committed—professional. MC6. He turned, nodded, and silently left Marsha Williams, David Hobart and Johnson Levin-Hughes in the conference room. He eased through the airlock, walked back to his quarters, and tried to sleep.

United Nations Starship PROBE IV, appearing not to move at all, inscribed its long, dark arc through space. It looked like a toy: a small boy's small boat set adrift on a dark, windless pond. It did not seem to move at all as it closed in on the planet poetically named MC6.

Howard Scott slept fitfully—had slept fitfully since sleep-freeze. His brain reached both forward and back in time, *and laid a clear sheet of disappointment (which was the past) over a clear sheet of anticipation (which was the future). He reclined in his complicated chair. The tunnel of his nose rose broken and pinched between his eyes. His colorless brown hair was damp, and when his head slid down to his shoulder it left a glistening smudge on the black of his headrest. His ungloved hands were pale and doughy from having been out of the sun for so long. Bruise-blue shone from deep beneath his skin. His palms were up, fingers unfurled, waiting to hold that which was not yet there. His mouth hung slack, and a snail's trail of moisture fell in a broad line from one corner. Far beneath him, far beneath the ship—and acting as almost forgotten ground—was the history of his race. It flew by, underneath him. And ridiculous death was carpeted with rows upon endless rows of indistinguishable houses full of isolated people—his people—who were dying of gluttony and comfort as surely as others died of disease. He rode on this history as a train rides on tracks, and heard the silent clickety-clacks as his pulse became the rhythm —whereisHELPforus, whereisHELPforus, whereis* HELPforus, whereisHELPforus, whereisHELPforus . . . *imageless, he ruminated in the dark.*

Dr. Marsha A. Williams capped her pen and closed her logbook. She leaned back and unzipped her jumpsuit with a long, synthetic ripping sound. A wide, wavy dagger of white skin showed in the middle of her bright blue suit as her plumpness sank back into her reclined chair. Her quarters glistened of white and stainless steel as she reached back in her mind for the pleasant memories of Earth she had wanted to bring along. She tried to imagine her tiny farm in its present Earth season. She looked at her clock and rolled the hands back, back in her mind, taking time through its numerous scientific divisions, and could not come to a conclusion about what season it was in Connecticut right now. Think of anything but Cal, who could not be forgotten. *Sleep-freeze had changed nothing for her except at times like this, when she tried to reach back for the familiar and found a shadow. She closed her eyes and tried to think of things which were not synthetic. No clearly defined images came to her mind. She opened her eyes and studied her own hand. Her body, the bodies of the other human beings on PROBE IV were the only natural elements of her entire environment.* Do not think of Caleb. Do not think of Cal who died . . . *She zipped up her suit, raised up her chair, and left her quarters for the conference room to study data she had already memorized.*

Dr. David R. Hobart sat strapped in his chair. He thought of scrambling through school after school, degree after degree as he had paid his dues and was grudgingly admitted to the human race, so long ago. His mouth was tight and drawn as hatred he believed he had forgotten— but which was in fact his medium, his ocean—came into focus and drew his attention away from his achievements. Sleep-freeze had changed nothing. When he woke he was still black. He grinned a long, thin sickle of white, closed his eyes, touched is fingertips to form a cathedral —and reasoned.

Mr. Johnson Levin-Hughes worked out in the gym.

Howard Scott opened his eyes and felt his entire body covered with a slick film of perspiration. He smelled rancid, like one who had been sick on the same sheets for a long time. He was a sponge, filled with the sour steam of despair. He felt sick, deep in his bowels, in the same way he used to feel back home when he woke numb with futility and had to reason himself into a stupor of optimism before he could stand and get dressed for the day. He pressed his hands to his face and exhaled a long, ragged machinegun breath of resignation, then stood abruptly, stripped, threw his clothes down the disintegration chute, and stepped into a cold shower.

Howard stood in the tiny shower and felt the cold water rinse his dread away, and neutralize him. He stood there a long time, not thinking of anything, not thinking of what might be found on MC6. What he wanted to find had not been clearly defined in his mind. He had refused to articulate it because he was not sure that full health was possible to human beings—only intensely desirable. He stepped out of the shower and dried his long, white body, then pulled on clean, disposable underwear and a maroon jumpsuit.

"Dr. Scott? Are you awake?"

"Yes."

"Can you look out of your porthole?"

"Yes. Who is this?"

"Oh, sorry. Levin-Hughes here. I'm in PROBE control room."

"I can look out."

"You'll be able to see MC6 in about ten seconds. She'll come across the bow of the ship and sit right in the middle of your port-side window for a while."

"Thank you."

"She'll be about the size of a softball."

"Thanks, Levin-Hughes."

"OK. See you in a while."

Howard Scott looked out of his window and watched the small light-blue and gold globe slide into focus. It hung in the darkness like an old, very beautiful, and very lost ornament. He felt his mind bleed into the future. He felt all of his sorrow being sucked out of him as if the planet, suspended in nothing, were the eye of one who can heal. He smiled to stop his fantasy, to stop himself from dreams of a perfection which was not possible. But seeping through, spreading out like a fresh and wanted stain, was desire—the formless reach of his desire, his need, for equilibrium by example.

"Attention PROBE IV research team. This is Colonel Haris. Visual contact with MC6 is established in portside observation posts for the next three minutes."

Howard flicked his comboard switch on. "Attention PROBE IV research team. Scott here. Briefing session is in two hours and forty-five minutes. In the conference room." He flicked off the switch and felt foolish. He wondered why he had made that stupid announcement. They knew.

FROM THE LEGEND OF BIEL

He was restless, trapped between the rock and the wall of his conflicting desires to get on with it and to stay here, alone and in silence, watching the small, spinning jewel. The trick is to treat this like a trip to a Japanese supermarket. We've seen it all before. Only the labels are different. *He smiled to erase his foolish monologue, and because he was embarrassed at having to contrive so obviously to keep a good, scientific, esthetic distance from the planet which was swallowing him like a sunlit mouth.*

Howard leaned his head back, closed his eyes, and there was MC6 in the center of his mind, small and perfect—freed from the cold, rude fingers of those from Earth.

The huge catamaran of a ship turned slightly in space where turns could not be perceived except as soft hisses from inside an engine. The pale-blue and yellow disk—hung like a medal in dark space—slid off the port-side windows and could no longer be seen from inside the ship as the eight human beings from Earth made their final frontal approach on MC6. Mr. Johnson Levin-Hughes watched it disappear, smiled, and fell asleep.

Dr. Howard M. Scott inserted his key into the top-secret lock on the top-secret drawer, placed his thumb against the glass identification sensor plate, and pressed the code buttons in a top-secret sequence which would release the catch.

click.

ssshuuuuuuushhhh . . .

He reached in and pulled out the large manila envelope which was stamped "Phase One—TOP SECRET". It bore the red wax United Nations seal. It felt like a thin pane of glass in his hands. He snapped the seal with his thumb and pulled out the briefing cassette. He walked to the recorder and snapped it in place.

TOP SECRET
CLEARED: DR. HOWARD M. SCOTT—DIRECTOR, UNITED
NATIONS SECURITY RESEARCH CORPS AND RE-
SEARCH HEAD, MISSION PROBE IV.

FROM THE LEGEND OF BIEL

CLEARED: DR. MARSHA A. WILLIAMS—ASSISTANT RE-
SEARCH HEAD, MISSION PROBE IV, AND OF-
FICER OF THE UNITED NATIONS SURGEON
GENERAL'S OFFICE.

CLEARED: DR. DAVID R. HOBART—RESEARCH TEAM, MIS-
SION PROBE IV, AND PROFESSOR, UNIVERSITY
OF AFRICA.

CLEARED: MR. JOHNSON LEVIN-HUGHES—RESEARCH
TEAM, MISSION PROBE IV, AND SENIOR TECH-
NICIAN, UNITED STATES INTERNATIONAL RE-
SEARCH CORPORATION.

FROM: M. RUSSELL DEERE—UNITED NATIONS SE-
CURITY GENERAL, AND DIRECTOR OF PROBE
MISSIONS.

MY DATE: MAY 11, 2173—BAJA, CALIFORNIA,
U.S.A.

YOUR DATE: AUGUST 3, 2178—FIRST ULTRA-
PROBE APPROACH TO PLANET
MC6.

SUBJECT: PROCEDURE BRIEFING, PHASE ONE, MISSION
PROBE IV. SPEC. THE DELIBERATE, GEOMETRI-
CAL STRUCTURES THEREON.

BRIEFING SYNOPSIS:

UNITED NATIONS STARSHIP PROBE IV WILL CIRCLE MC6
FOR NONPARTICULAR ULTRAPROBE AND ESTABLISHMENT
OF GRAND-MEAN ORBIT AT 3,500 SPACE METERS.

PROBE IV RESEARCH TEAM WILL LEAVE PROBE IV IN
PROBE-POD *ATHENS* IN ORDER TO ESTABLISH PETIT-MEAN
ORBIT AT 2,310 SPACE METERS AND COMPLETE DETAILED
PROBE OF MC6.

INDIVIDUAL SCHEDULES FOR DETAILED PROBE ARE IN
YOUR SEPARATE CONSOLES ON PROBE-POD *ATHENS*.

IF, AFTER COMPLETION OF DETAILED PROBE FROM 2,310
SPACE METERS—WHICH IS ESTIMATED TO TAKE SEVENTY-
TWO HOURS—YOU HAVE BEEN ABLE TO DETERMINE THAT
IT IS SAFE FOR YOURSELVES, FOR THE PROBE IV MISSION,
FOR THE UNITED FEDERATED NATION-STATES OF THE
PLANET EARTH, AND FOR THE PLANET MC6, YOU ARE TO
TAKE PROBE-POD SKIMMER *COLONUS* TWO AT A TIME IN
ALTERNATING SHIFTS OF TWELVE HOURS, AND DIRECTLY
PROBE THE PLANET MC6.

THE OBJECT OF PHASE ONE OF MISSION PROBE IV IS TWO-
FOLD. YOU ARE TO TRY TO DISCOVER THE SOURCE AND
PURPOSE OF THE GEOMETRIC STRUCTURES ON MC6. AND
YOU ARE TO TRY TO DETERMINE WHETHER OR NOT FUR-
THER RESEARCH, AND POSSIBLY DEVELOPMENT, OF MC6
IS POSSIBLE, PRACTICAL, AND DESIRABLE, WITH REGARD
TO EVENTUALLY COLONIZING THE PLANET.

FROM THE LEGEND OF BIEL

DUE TO THE LENGTH AND NATURE OF MISSION PROBE IV AS A WHOLE, YOU WILL REMAIN ON MC6 FOR THREE TWENTY-FOUR-HOUR DAYS IN ORDER TO STAY IN SYNC WITH PHASES TWO, THREE, AND FOUR OF THE MISSION.

IF AT ANY TIME DURING PHASE ONE YOU DETERMINE THAT PROBE ACTIVITIES ON MC6 ARE DETRIMENTAL TO YOURSELVES, TO MISSION PROBE IV, TO THE NATION-STATES OF THE PLANET EARTH, OR TO THE PLANET MC6, YOU ARE TO CEASE PROBE ACTIVITIES IMMEDIATELY AND BEGIN PHASE TWO OF YOUR MISSION.

PROBE READINGS ARE TO BE SENT TO UNITED NATIONS STARSHIP PROBE IV EVERY TWELVE HOURS IN CODE 104-F, FOR PERMENANT RECORDING. YOU ARE TO SEND YOUR FINDINGS ON TO US THROUGH RELAY SYSTEM AB-72-X BETWEEN PHASES ONE AND TWO OF MISSION PROBE IV.

ON BOARDING PROBE-POD *ATHENS* YOU WILL FIND FULL MATERIALS AND SCHEDULES, PLUS COMPLETE INDIVIDUAL BRIEFINGS IN YOUR SEPARATE CONSOLES. COMPLETE AS MUCH OF EACH SCHEDULE AS POSSIBLE.

UNITED NATIONS STARSHIP PROBE IV CREW IS BEING BRIEFED NOW AS PER ENCLOSURE IN ENVELOPE MARKED "PHASE ONE—TOP SECRET."

YOU HAVE BEGUN AN HISTORIC JOURNEY. WHEN YOU RE-TURN TO EARTH YOU WILL HAVE COMPLETED THE LONG-EST MISSION IN THE HISTORY OF SPACE EXPLORATION. YOU WILL HAVE BEEN GONE SIX YEARS. YOU WILL HAVE HAD MORE SLEEP-FREEZE TIME THAN ANY OTHER HUMAN BE-INGS ALIVE: FIVE YEARS. YOU WILL HAVE TRAVELED FAR FROM YOUR HOMES INTO DEEPEST SPACE, TO BE THE FIRST HUMAN BEINGS TO TOUCH WHAT YOU WILL TOUCH.

BLESS YOU, AND GOOD LUCK.

M. RUSSELL DEERE—UNITED NATIONS SECURITY GEN-ERAL.

Howard Scott had been listening to the briefing sitting at the conference table next to Marsha. He felt her scru-tinize him, looking for signs of a mood. He felt his blood run under the bridge of his pulse. He had known all along about the three twenty-four-hour days allotted to direct probe of MC6. He knew that at the end of that time there was a slim, precious margin they could bite into—maybe another day. At very best it was not ten percent of the time needed to solve the mystery of the structures.

The three researchers were quiet, waiting for Howard

to speak. Deep inside he opened his mouth and screamed white flames of outrage—and M. Russell Deere and his entire Mission Control group were incinerated. "What tripe. We board PROBE-POD Athens in one hour for check-out procedures. We separate from mama in three hours and thirty-nine minutes. Let's get going."

Dr. Marsha Williams and Dr. David R. Hobart left the conference room in hurried silence to make a last check on personal instruments that had been almost worn out with examination. Dr. Scott released the cassette from the recorder and put it back in the safe, then slid the crew's briefing sheet out of the manila envelope. He adjusted the two stapled typed sheets, squaring them neatly before him on the conference table. Stones kept falling into the pond of his mind, disturbing it. He did not feel them fall. He only felt the continual spread of the concentric circles of undefined anxiety lapping at his insides. He looked up and saw Levin-Hughes staring at him from his post near the airlock. They smiled across their apprehensions.

"Sorry, Howard." And Levin-Hughes left the room.

"TO: HOWARD M. SCOTT, AND PROBE IV RESEARCH TEAM.
FROM: M. RUSSELL DEERE, UNITED NATIONS SECURITY GENERAL, AND DIRECTOR OF PROBE MISSIONS.
SUBJECT: U.N.S.S. PROBE IV CREW, BRIEFING—PHASE ONE.

Howard dropped his hands onto the smooth plastic conference table. Both were cold. The air, the temperature in the ship was always a few degrees too cold—to keep them awake. Still, he perspired. His hands seemed to suck up moisture from the smooth, oily plastic. The white paper was a squared blur in front of him. Its words were meaningless. ". . . the crew has been told that you are investigating ruins . . ." *His hopes for Phase One had been a stained-glass window. Now its lead bindings had been removed and sharp pieces of colored glass floated in his mind, cutting themselves free. ". . . we are* convinced that MC6 is dead . . ." *Howard Scott pushed the paper aside with his stiff, largest, second finger, and tried not to think about not thinking about time—about hurrying. He could not.*

United Nations Starship PROBE IV moved on in space and was connected by a thinning string to the spasms and gasps of the planet two years at the back of the darkness it had just traversed. It circled MC6, chattering to itself. It established grand-mean orbit at 3,500 space meters, and verified Major Hessen's findings. And, at the proper instant, it released PROBE-POD Athens *from its soft underbelly like a fish laying a little silver egg in the sea.*

The little POD floated down, found its elliptical niche around the planet and began to probe. Instruments swept back and forth across the face of MC6 immodestly and cross-referenced each other. The researchers verified Major Hessen's findings, and peered from their darkness at the huge globe beneath them—heads cocked, listening to silence.

Inside PROBE-POD Athens *the four researchers sat back-to-back in contour chairs, facing their individual consoles. There was not one inch of wasted space in the capsule. They were so close together that the sides of their knees and elbows touched. The cabin was not pressurized and they wore the big heavy suits which were a whole, efficent environment. The suits fed them, took care of body waste, and completely eliminated the use of their senses. They were not probing MC6, they were merely overseeing the technology which was.*

They spoke little. Each was alone with a particular extension of human brain which listened, calculated, translated, clicked and shuddered. Occasionally they exchanged information. Occasionally a pencil or an empty wrapper floated by an intense, masked face and irritated —like a fly.

In the ceiling above them was a hatch which opened on a long, metal vagina that connected them to Skimmer Colonus. *Howard looked at it often in the mirror above his console that permitted him to see what was behind himself. He saw the hatch as the beginning of a tunnel. When he had verified that there was no danger to them from the planet he would open the hatch and pass through, out of this cramped womb into sunlight.*

The cameras photographed all levels of the spectrum. The radar and sonar listened. The scanners scanned. The probes probed. The computers gossiped, evaluated, catalogued and reevaluated Major Hessen's multiply cross-referenced findings. They discovered five additional dome complexes which had been hidden by the polar forests. They completed their element charts, geographical and atmospheric evaluations, and continued to listen to the silence of MC6 for sixty-five hours, when they reached the point of diminishing returns. The planet yielded its information easily, but there was just so much information to be got at a distance. They had to touch MC6 with naked senses to know more.

PROBE-POD Athens floated around its huge reference point. Dawn and dusk became realities again. The senses of motion and direction returned to the four researchers, even in their weightlessness. The POD spun on itself as it inscribed its continual ellipse around MC6. And through the four tiny portholes, each of them could see the startling and simple beauty of the unknown.

Howard Scott smiled, and closed his eyes, and exhaled toxins which had been poisoning him. He breathed out fumes of the fear which had tormented him since he woke from sleep-freeze. The detail probes had duplicated their findings for the third time—the magic number. His hand floated up and across the short distance to Dr. Hobart's arm. David turned his plastic-protected face toward Howard. They grinned. Scott slipped his pen onto his clipboard and placed the board in its magnetized slot.

"There is no danger. Let's go down there, David."

. . . .

The hatch of Skimmer Colonus opened like an eye.

FROM THE LEGEND OF BIEL

There are victories which have no violence in their beginnings or their ends. And if these victories bring with themselves a death of past and silly dreams, it is not felt as death, but as the falling of a scab. Inhale, because it heals.

Howard Scott stood paralyzed at the threshold, looking out.

There is an instant when pieces fit together, interlock their disparate knuckles and become a whole. It is almost unbearable. Such victories and such interlockings redefine our language. Inhale, because this air will make you whole.

His jaw fell in slow motion and an invisible song rolled out.

There are landscapes which, when apprehended, reduce the carbonation in the brain to stillness. Thought steps aside to let the senses bathe and cleanse themselves. Inhale. Inhale and become simplified.

His eyes became a mouth.

There is beauty which can make the genes remember reverence. When the lid of the coffin of culture is opened there is a moment when all things are possible and good. In that moment pieces fly together, kiss, and interlock in stillness with no violence as the human being kneels before himself. Inhale. Inhale, and bring your body home.

Howard Scott felt the planet rise up and meet his descending feet.

The landscape is divided in half horizontally. It is only two colors, and background for a score of sounds, and smells, and touch of wind, and taste of long, sweet grass. Step down, inhale, and bring your body home. One color is the blue of a sky which is somehow brighter than it was expected to be. It is frankly shocking—a rich and vital blue. The other color is the golden tan of long grass which has no gloss, but somehow shines.

His weight settled on the planet and was no burden at all.

The sweet smell of long gold grass glides up the nostrils, settles in a cloud around the soft palate, and floods the tastebuds on its way to the brain. Each individual step of perception is isolated in a slow train of events, and can be enjoyed as it passes.

He could not move.

The high-pitched hum of the dry wind ceaselessly combing the single blades of grass into long, even manes, is faint, but close—inside the ear. As the wind passes through the long fields it is the sound of some lost tuning fork, or some ancient glass instrument which has yet to be discovered. It is an unbroken string of sound which winds around the planet and insulates. It is a soft hand, protecting the planet from death.

Howard Scott became devout.

The surface is dry, dry and undulating—as if done with mirrors and heat. But it is not too hot. It warms the skin. The body is buffeted by the dry, slight, musical wind which ribbons up to the brain and cleans it, so that the inside of the body assumes the characteristics, and the music, of the landscape.

He closed his eyes and the landscape was tattooed on his brain.

The sky rises cleanly from behind, from below the horizon line. It lifts up, lusts up, thrusts up, and domes perfectly above, with a white sun exactly in its center.

FROM THE LEGEND OF BIEL

There were no metaphors for him—only the thing itself.

Here the landscape is as disconnected from the familiar as a dream—an ideal. It opens its arms and says "Come. You are home. Come. You have been unhappy needlessly, senselessly. Come. Be awake, and be whole."

Howard Scott stood on MC6, and in those first moments, as his mind reached out like the hand of a child, it also reached back and remembered a day imprinted on the genes of his race, when the first human being stepped out of the long, terrifying, subterranean night into a very simple day.

David Hobart stepped out of Skimmer Colonus *behind Howard and narrated his descent to Marsha and Levin-Hughes, still up in the POD, for voice record. He felt the lifting of anticipation. MC6 was silent. The probes had not lied or been deceived. No one was there.*

". . . wheat-colored lawn, flat as a table, stretches out to a perfectly defined horizon line. It's so clear it hurts my eyes. I'm looking directly east. No clouds. Not even a whisp. Can you hear this wind up there through my audio?"

"Yes. It's eerie. Where are the structures, David?"

"On the other side of the ship. I'm walking around now."

"What do you see?"

"Looking directly west I see the sea. The ground slopes down gradually for about a hundred meters to a beach of white sand which is, oh, maybe fifty meters wide. Then the sea. It's a brilliant blue, and absolutely waveless—not a ripple. The structures are on a very gradual and slight incline about one hundred meters to my left—directly south of here."

"Check. Our probes are in sync. We have excellent video pickup."

Dr. Scott stood at the rear of the Skimmer looking south. The structures were on a slight rise, white pro-

files of geometric shapes against a brilliant blue sky. There were twenty-nine small structures of varying shapes, all with the same mass. They were scattered apparently at random over the knoll. And rising behind them, like a second sun, was the dome. It was an enormous white structure which dwarfed even the largest buildings Howard could remember from Earth. The dome bloomed and rose one hundred meters into the air, and was one of the most amazing things he had ever seen.

Howard had decided not to use the heavy protective suits his race of engineers had designed for foreign travel. They were horribly restricting, he hated them, and here they were unnecessary. He and Dr. Hobart had on soft boots and gloves and simple, bright-red zipper jumpsuits which allowed movement and sensation. His one concession to Dr. Williams had been to wear the aluminum communicator helmets, or comcaps, which housed video transmitters in their foreheads, like third eyes, and had enough subtle circuitry to broadcast almost their very thoughts. Wearing the comcaps meant one less thing to carry in their hands.

Howard Scott peeled off his gloves, rolled up his sleeves as far as they would go, and unzipped his jumpsuit to the middle of his pasty-white and hairless chest. He felt MC6 curl up next to his body like a woman. He felt her warm breath on his skin.

"Let's take a walk, David."

"I thought you'd never ask."

The hours of orbit and detailed probe had added little to Major Hessen's findings, except computed assurance that no harm would come to them on MC6. The five new complexes which had been hidden from PROBE I by the polar forests were the largest find, and they had become apparent within the first few hours in the POD.

Probes had verified that MC6 was a delightfully healthy planet and very similar to Earth, but without Earth's geographical variety. There was nothing on the planet which would surprise or frighten Earth humans except perhaps the vast stillness beneath the continual hum of

30

the subtle wind. There was no sign of human or even genuinely complex life. The planet could easily support a population the size of Earth's with a little technical help. There were no signs of deliberate or non-natural activity other than the groupings of geometric structures. There was no evidence of agriculture, no roads, and no apparent media for communication between the complexes. MC6 was silent as a grave.

The complexes had yielded nothing. They were not arranged in any discernible pattern. No complex was larger than the others or distinct in any way. All of them had twenty-nine small geometric structures clustered around one huge dome. No structure within a complex was larger in volume than any other, except for the domes, which appeared to be uniform. The complexes appeared to be random arrangements of structures scattered over the planet at random. To Earth logic and inclination this was incomprehensible. There had to be a pattern, even in chaos. Time and again probe computers had looked for the pattern. Time and again they had failed to find it. The structures and their arrangement had been probed, and prodded, and scanned, and stared at, and dreamed about, and had yielded nothing. There had been hours of human and computer speculation. Words and ideas had flown back and forth like rice at a wedding. But the bride and groom had gone off, and the guests had left, and the rice lay where it had fallen.

"U.N.S.S. PROBE IV, Colonel Haris here. Do you read, Dr. Scott?"

"Yes. Scott here."

"How are you doing down there?"

"Fine. No problems, no danger. We are approaching the ruins now."

"I'm supposed to inform you at this time that as per orders from M. Russell Deere, United Nations Security General, nuclear weapons are armed and aimed at MC6 and will be activated if necessary."

"Damn you, Haris. Don't be a silly fool!"

"Those are my orders, Dr. Scott."

FROM THE LEGEND OF BIEL

"Scott out."

Howard looked at David Hobart, whose head was cocked like a dog listening to a high sound. He heard Marsha and Levin-Hughes over his comcap stirring in the POD, then he heard a soft string of obscenities from the older man. Howard lowered his head and shook it in disbelief.

Dr. Howard Scott and Dr. David Hobart walked up the long, slight rise and stopped thirty meters before the first structure in the complex. They sat their equipment down, aimed it, and probed.

The structure was a white pyramid which sliced a piece out of the sky ten meters by ten meters by ten meters. Its sides and edges were perfect. The pyramid offered the same peaceful readings they had gotten in the POD.

The apprehension of that which defined the term "beautiful" produced one reaction in Howard Scott: paralysis. When he could finally think he opined that all the objects in the Louvre could be scrapped—except for the Venus de Milo—if craft such as this existed somewhere. When he could finally move he made his way to the pyramid. He felt as if it were inhaling, drawing him in.

Howard put out his hands and touched the structure. He caressed it, placing his palms on two of its three sides. He rubbed lightly back and forth and let the sensations run up his arms into his brain. One side, which was not in the sun, was cool and dry and smooth. The other side, which was in the sun, was warm and dry and smooth. As he touched the pyramid an old response, which he had assumed was dead, rose up its head and broke into private laughter. Howard Scott felt the thrill of respect, the wonder of standing before an example of perfection. He was awed by the genius of something this simple, this clean, being anywhere in creation.

Howard Scott touched the pyramid. And as the impulses braided their way up his arms to his brain—at that first instant—something collapsed in his mind. Sci-

32

entific method became meaningless, as scales tipped and he knew through his hands that this structure, and all the others, had been made for them to experience. Somehow, someone, something, had created this pyramid, had touched it as he was doing now. And he loved that being as much as he loved himself, because through this he glimpsed what was possible to him.

"Howard?"

"Yes, Marsha?"

"You OK?"

"Yes. I . . . I can't describe it. It's . . . real."

"Yes. We can see if well on your video. It's a beautiful piece of work."

"Marsha, this was made. Made. By somebody."

"Can you describe it?"

"Yes. It feels like a cross between glass and some sort of resin. It's opaque, but the surface is so deep and clear that it seems to go all the way through to the other side. It is pure white, but very deeply it has sort of ghosted rainbow effects—like avery bleached-out slick of oil. It's a very high-density material. It's so smooth—smoother than the inside of your arm."

"Thank you."

"How are your readings up there, Levin-Hughes?"

"Splendid, Howard. We are right in sync with you and you are in sync with our previous readings. There's no change in readings except what you, David and the Skimmer give off. Our video reception is fantastic."

"Howard?"

"Yes, Marsha?"

"Can either of you see any openings? Any breaks in the surface of the structure?"

"None here. How about you, David?"

"No. Nothing over here. It's as smooth as glass, and solid as a rock. It appears to have been cast, or something. I can't see or feel any seams or joints at all."

"That checks with our readings. Our equipment isn't being deceived."

"Not so far."

33

"David, can you slide a ground probe down so we can determine how far the structure sits into the ground, and what its bottom is like?"

"Right away, Levin-Hughes."

"How are you feeling, Howard?"

"Grateful for space, sun and marginal freedom."

"I meant physically, Howard. Your charts are jumpy."

"Warm and dry, Marsha."

"You should be warm. Temperature is ninety-two degrees Fahrenheit with oh-five percent humidity."

"Levin-Hughes, Hobart here. Check this reading. My ground probe reads that pyramid number one, complex number one, sets exactly two hundred millimeters into the ground. It is absolutely level to the sea horizon, and its bottom is another flat side. It's also solid."

"Thank you David. Our readings are in sync."

"OK David. Let's go to the dome."

"Howard and David? Can you try to keep your head movements a little smoother? Video gets very jerky when you get excited, and we get dizzy up here."

David Hobart laughed. "It's not enough to be scientists, and concerned citizens. Now you want us to be bloody dancers too."

Dr. Hobart looked at Howard and flashed his wavy sickle grin. Howard nodded. In their comcaps they heard Levin-Hughes and Marsha laughing from halfway around the planet and 2,300 space meters high.

"Hell, it's like trying to knit with M. Russell Deere looking over your shoulder—timing you against the schedule."

"Right."

The four of them laughed for the first time since leaving PROBE IV. Howard felt the key log in his chest break free and float away, opening a path for the others. He was relaxing into the stark, lonely beauty of MC6. He was coming home. "It deserves a better name," he said out of nowhere.

The big dome hovered in front of them like a touch-

able sun. It reached into the air by the length of a football field. It sat like a huge, smooth, white brain, and they approached as two little thoughts.

Howard watched the dome grow with each step he took. He felt his frayed edges grope for each other as his body tried to knit, and his mind was soothed and reassured. Soon the smooth, white skin of the dome filled his entire field of vision. He could perceive nothing else. And all that was white, all in that color which had embarrassed him because of its history, its conceit, its cruelty, was wiped away. The dome had no arrogance. No violence could have made it. It was an offering, a hand extended through centuries of brutality which said, "None of that was necessary. Come and forget. Come. Begin again."

Scott looked at David and wanted to embrace him because he was here, feeling it too. They looked at each other with the same impulse. But there was too much past between them. They tried to reach, but the red sea was too wide.

When they got to the dome they stood in its cool shade like children, and murmured to the others, up in the POD.

"If this is an accurate reflection, an extension of its makers, we have nothing to fear."

"Amen."

"Howard, can you describe it?"

"The dome looks and feels like a kind of resin. It's opaque. It is made of a much lower-density material than the pyramid and is not solid."

"Our readings are in sync."

"It's absolutely smooth. I can't see any seams, joints or openings."

"How about splitting up to walk around it and meet on the other side?"

"OK."

"Fine. David, you circle east, around to your left. Howard, you go west, to your right. If you get tired sit down and rest a minute. The damn thing is . . ."

"Don't call it that."

". . . it's big."

"Right. It is six hundred and twenty-eight meters from 'A' all the way around and back to 'A' again."

"Before you start both of you look at the ground where the side starts, and pan all the way up the dome as far as you can see. That's it. That's it. Fine. Thank you. That's a long way up."

"Yes."

"Keep your heads steady as you go, and stop every fifteen meters to pan from the ground up again. I've got the video in your comcaps on wide-angle. We should be able to photograph the entire dome from ground level. We'll be passing directly overhead in a few minutes, and I can get a good telephoto shot from straight up. If there are seams or openings in that dome we should be able to find them. OK. Take off."

Dr. Scott and Dr. Hobart peeled off and went their separate ways around the dome. Howard walked slowly. He could not get over how clear his vision was here, how sharp and clean all the edges were. He tried to focus more on his tasks, and less on his instinctive response to being here, to actually being touched by the structures. It was difficult because what he felt was so powerful and complete.

A question kept wanting to be formed in Howard's mind. He continually brushed it away, like a fly. It persisted, and he avoided it because, so far, there was no answer. He did not like to articulate questions which had no answers. So he raised a wall around it, damning it in. He surrounded it, enclosed it, and set it in the back of his mind—controlled. But as he apprehended the dome the wall around his question became two cupped hands, and the question turned to water. It would not be contained. It was a simple question—as simple as "How are you?" or "Where is a pencil?" But he could not, would not, give it words.

Howard Scott walked with the structure on his left, looking for openings. Every fifteen meters he stopped, *looked at the ground, then slowly raised his head up toward what he could see of the top of the dome. He did it for Levin-Hughes's sake, for science's sake—for no sake at all but to contain the words. As he raised his head he heard Levin-Hughes murmur "Good . . . good . . ." in his ear. He knew that as long as he heard that sound, and his question was unspoken, he was still attached to them all—to his past, and his disgraceful heritage. The umbilicus was thinning, but it was still intact.*

U.N.S.S. PROBE IV. Colonel Haris to Dr. Scott. Do you read?"

"Scott here. I read you fine. Go ahead."

"We sight you on heat probes up here. Your two bodies are the hottest things in town. Everything still OK?"

"Yes. So far no need to prove our dad can beat theirs."

"PROBE IV out."

Howard heard the research team erupt into laughter over his comcap. It sounded like Levin-Hughes went right out of his chair.

"Dr. Scott?"

"Yes, David?"

"You should get over here immediately."

"Which way is closest?"

"He's not yet directly across from you, Howard. Go back the way you came."

"Right. David? David?"

"Get over here!"

"David, Levin-Hughes here. What is it?"

"An opening."

Howard finally rounded the endless side of the huge dome and found David Hobart standing paralyzed in front of a dark, rectangular opening. His eyes were large—still surprised. His mouth was open.

"Are you OK David?"

"Yes. Sorry to alarm you, Howard, but I nearly jumped out of my skin."

"David, Levin-Hughes here. Before you do anything

37

else turn your probe console around. All I'm getting now is your gastric juices doing a roller-coaster routine. I thought it was the dome, then Marsha figured it out."

"Sorry."

"It's OK. Now can you put a ground probe right in the center of the threshold?"

"Yes."

"Keep it about one hundred millimeters in front of the opening. That's it. Thank you. Now, what happened?"

"I was rounding the dome, panning the wall. I got to right over there, where the marker is . . ."

"Signify five meters directly east of where David is now, Levin-Hughes."

"Check."

"There was no opening there—no seams, no lines. Nothing. I was staring right at it when Colonel Haris called down and we started laughing. All of a sudden I sort of heard, or felt, this little hissing sound—and smooth as silk there was the opening. It scared me to death."

"Levin-Hughes, signify that the opening appeared on cue of some sort when Dr. Hobart got to where the marker is. Can you see the opening?"

"Not too well, you're both trembling. Describe it to me."

"Opening is approximately eight meters wide by ten meters high. Depth of opening, or thickness of dome skin at threshold, is about two hundred millimeters. I can't see anything beyond the opening. It's just a dark hole. We have zero readings on both probe consoles. What have you got?"

"Similar. Our probes can read through the opening, but reception is faint."

"Do you have enough reading for me to go inside?"

"Mmm . . . yes. I'd say so."

"OK. As soon as we check a few things out here I'll go in. What do your probes read?"

"We read normal—as outside the dome. No change, no danger, no life."

"Suggestion, please."

"Yes, Marsha."

"Keeping comcaps focused on the opening, and probe consoles where they are now, back up and let's see if we can trigger the opening and record it."

"OK. We'll do that now. David, you take the move. I'll observe from ten meters and record video. Put me on telephoto, Levin-Hughes—until the opening fills screen four."

"OK."

"How's video now?"

"Video is fine. The opening fills screen four."

"Call out any reading changes as soon as they happen."

"Check. We're ready when you are."

"OK, David."

David Hobart positioned himself three meters directly in front of the opening, facing it. Using a light yardstick, and moving one step at a time, he began to back up.

"Five meters."

"Nothing."

"Seven meters."

"Nothing. No change."

"No change up here."

"Ten meters, nothing."

"Check."

"Twelve meters. Maybe it isn't going to close."

"Keep going."

"Fourteen meters."

"No change. We read you loud and clear up here."

"Fifteen meters."

Thuup.

The opening vanished.

"David, take a step forward."

Thuup.

The opening reappeared.

"That is amazing."

"No change at any time in our readings up here."

"We have zero readings here."

"OK David. Step over toward Howard and rest a min-

ute. I want to replay the tape in slow motion and see if I can figure out how that thing works."

"OK."

"David, Marsha here. Your readings are still jumpy. Do you want a tranquilizer?"

"No. Just let me rest a minute."

"Fine."

Dr. Hobart walked over toward Howard, who was taping a first-hand visual report. He stopped and tried to breathe deeply and evenly. Until the opening appeared David had thought of the complex as a large grouping of children's blocks. In the hours of probing in the POD he had reinforced his belief that MC6 was dead, and its structures were ruins. Now he was unsure. He felt himself trembling violently. It began at the base of his skull and fanned out through his entire body. He was full of more energy than he could get rid of. David closed his eyes and inhaled raggedly. He exhaled fully and tried not to relive that moment when the opening had appeared and belief in his own assumptions was shaken.

"Levin-Hughes here. OK. The opening is seven and one half meters wide and nine and one half meters high, by two hundred millimeters thick. Cycle time from at-rest closed position to at-rest open position, and vice versa, is slightly less than one second. We can't determine specifically what the hissing sound is, other than the fact that it has something to do with the operation of the opening. Marsha has the sound isolated off the tape now and the computers are analyzing. Now listen to this. When the opening cycle begins it is not located in any one point of the area—as our doors swing open from a side, or the iris on a lens fans out from the center. This opening occurs on all points of the area simultaneously. It's like a mirage. It just sort of comes into focus, and viola, a door. The same holds true for the closing process. I've never seen anything like it. It's amazingly sophisticated."

"What triggers the process?"

"I have no idea. It could be a heat-sensing device, an eye, an ear—anything."

"Marsha, what do you get on the hissing sound?"

"Nothing. Computers cannot classify."

"David, let's set up the lights. I'm going in."

"Howard, will you do an angle and distance check on the opening first, so we can determine the radius of the triggering device?"

"Negative, Marsha. We can do that later. I'm going to contact PROBE IV and get Lanier on the console so we'll get three recordings of my entry into the dome."

"Good idea."

"Scott to PROBE IV, do you read?"

"U.N.S.S. PROBE IV. Captain Ybarra here."

"Joe, this is Scott. Is technician Lanier in the control room?"

"Right here, Dr. Scott."

"Lanier, open your probes and check with Levin-Hughes to see if PROBE IV instruments are in sync with POD instruments."

"Probe mediator indicates that our probe groups are in precision sync . . . and that yours aren't reading well down there."

"That's correct. Where am I right now?"

"You are walking due south, away from the dome in complex number one at the rate of one step per second."

"Very good. We have discovered an opening in the dome. Don't be alarmed if you lose me for a few minutes. Probes read faintly inside the dome."

"Check."

"I want you in contact with the POD to maintain precision sync. Record everything. We will playback later and do computer search for discrepancies."

"Yes, sir. We are now recording. Will you give us a fix on the opening?"

"It is directly northwest of where I'm standing. It's on the southeast side of the dome. Levin-Hughes can give you exact coordinates in a few minutes."

"Fine. Opening is tentatively chartered on computer mock-up of dome one, complex one. We are recording and in precision sync."

"OK. Scott out."

"Lanier out."

"Levin-Hughes, Dr. Hobart has the lights rigged and focused into the opening now. How is your video?"

"Hold your head still."

"Sorry."

"Video is good."

"Tell me what you see."

"I see . . . a long gray hall. It fades into black."

"That's what we see."

"Howard, raise camera one about two fingers. Good! Right there! Camera one video is excellent."

"OK. I'm going to leave my probe console here. I won't go in too far. I have the hip-box for additional light."

"Take your probe console."

"No. I want to be able to move around, Marsha. Put me on normal lens, Levin-Hughes."

"You are on normal lens. Systems are faint but go."

"OK. Here we go."

Howard Scott stepped through the opening and into the dome. As if on cue the entire cooridor became evenly filled with soft, colorless light. He heard Levin-Hughes whistle over his comcap. David Hobart sucked in his breath, and Marsha spoke.

"WOW!"

"Marsha?"

"Howard, you just about jumped right off the readings. How's your heart?"

"Pounding. Did I see what I just saw, Levin-Hughes?"

"Indeed you did, Howard. Now just stay right where you are. David, cut your lights please. Good, thank you. I got a tremendous jump on ultraviolet when that light went on. Describe it to me, Howard. Point your comcap at whatever you're talking about."

"I see no specific source for the light. Anywhere. It just is."

"Pan the ceiling. You are correct. No visible source. Fantastic."

"The entire corridor is evenly lit from floor to ceiling and end to end. David, what do you see?"

"The same, Howard. But the light does not extend beyond the opening. None of it leaks or spills out of the dome."

"What's the corridor itself like, Howard?"

"It has the same dimensions as the opening. It's about, oh, fifty meters long. The walls are white in this light, and seem to be made of the same material as the skin of the dome. There are no seams that I can see, floor to ceiling, end to end. Where wall becomes ceiling or floor the surface is rounded, not angled. I feel more like I'm in a tunnel than a corridor. Wall surfaces are smooth, but porous. It's like a synthetic, high-gloss stucco, but it doesn't reflect much light. It's restful to the eyes. It's cooler in here than outside. Do you get a temperature reading?"

"Eighty-one degrees Fahrenheit. I don't trust it because the probe readings are still faint inside the dome."

"I'm going to walk on down the corridor."

"Fine. Camera one video is excellent."

Dr. Scott walked down the long, white, featureless corridor. pupuh. pupuh. pupuh. pupuh. pupuh. He felt the sound of his heart. Other sounds, the sounds of his walking, the sounds of what little equipment he had, seemed to disappear into the walls, to evaporate before they could get loose.

Howard felt his question forming on his lips. He licked them to keep it back—in the dark of his throat. An image burst into his mind, and for an instant he saw the face of a child materialize in the dark of his mind. The face smiled, and welcomed him to the planet and the dome. He smiled back as a few nonsensical phrases of gibberish ran over his tongue, and he imagined what

*the language sounded like. Then he realized what he was
thinking and thrust it aside.*

"Levin-Hughes?"

"Yes, Howard?"

*"Good. I just wanted to hear somebody. I can't hear
a thing in here—hardly even the static in my comcap.
Sound just disappears."*

*"We have the same audibility up here, and have been
fiddling with our dials."*

"It's not the equipment, then. It's the dome."

"I believe so. Estimate your distance into the dome."

"I'm about fifteen meters inside the structure."

*Howard had turned and looked back at the opening
to judge his distance. His glance passed across David
Hobart, who stood tall and thin just beyond the threshold.
They looked at each other and waved. David grinned and
gave Howard the thumbs-up signal. His teeth were a
white crescent in his chocolate face. Howard turned and
continued to move through the soft, white corridor.
pupuh. pupuh. pupuh. pupuh. pupuh.*

Thuup.

"Levin-Hughes?"

"Yes?"

*"Another opening just appeared on my right. It's the
same type as the first."*

"Steady . . . OK. We can see it now. What's inside?"

"I don't know. It's dark. I can't see anything."

"Try to get some light to come on."

*One second was split in half when Howard stepped
into the dark space. The first half of the second was all
he had been and inherited. The middle of the second was
the threshold of the opening—and neutral. The last half
of the second was the ghosted whisper, the promise of
what could be found here—through the opening. In that
short distance, that one step, and one second, the trans-
formations which had pushed at him since sleep-freeze
opened their eyes and became awake in him. His priorities
disappeared because they were meaningless. His commit-
ments were reshuffled like cards, and as he entered the*

cube the first card was dealt, and held the face of the smiling child he had seen only a few paces before.

"Howard?"

He could have stepped into a hole, or a grave—it did not matter. For him each new threshold was a door through a barrier, a rip in the veil which separated his time from theirs. Each step and each moment was a continuation of the journey from here to somewhere, somewhen else. And he was captured. He was hypnotized. His progress into the dome pulled at the unraveling threads which bound him like Gulliver to his midget's history, his heritage—not of human beings, but of toys.

Thuup.

The opening closed, became a wall behind him. He was in a cube. It was softly, evenly lit, and white. It had five meters to a side and was featureless. There was nothing in it, and even though it was small he had no feeling of being enclosed.

Howard placed his hands on the wall in front of him. It was still and cool beneath his palms. The floor appeared to be made of the same material as the walls. But the walls of the cube were firm, while the floor was soft, like carpet. His feet sank into it. He heard nothing, felt nothing. He turned and stepped forward, toward the wall which had been the opening. It faded simultaneously on all points, to gray, and then to clear, and was a wall no more.

Thuup.

Beyond the threshold of the cube was a brilliantly sunlit chamber. Howard stepped forward a nd stopped. The opening disappeared behind him.

pupuh. pupuh. pupuh. pupuh. pupuh.

Blink. He didnot move. Not even the tail ends of thoughts moved in the dark, enclosed space behind his eyes. Blink.

Blink.

His pupils closed down to screen out the brightness. Blink. Blink. I am not asleep, nor somewhere else. I am awake, and here.

FROM THE LEGEND OF BIEL

" . . . how . . ."

He was at the top of the dome, in a huge, half-spherical chamber which was the top quarter of the volume of the structure. He could hear the wind in the long gold grass outside. He could smell the grass. Scott had no sense of being enclosed, of being protected from nature, or of being formed by architecture.

He walked forward soundlessly, toward the end of the floor. The chamber was an opaque white floor which seemed to be suspended in space, with an absolutely clear dome resting on it. He looked up and could not determine how high the top of the dome was, because it was clear—so clear as to be not felt, not there.

He did not care if he understood or not. He only wanted to be here in this endless room which enclosed nothing, and kept nothing out. He wanted to be here where the wall between inside and outside had been wiped away, where he was not estranged.

Howard turned and looked back toward the white cube with five meters to a side which had so silently, so generously brought him here. It was in the exact center of the room—the end of the spine of the dome. He felt like he was in the cerebral cortex of the structure. There was nothing else in the chamber—only space.

He turned, and continued to walk toward the edge of the floor. pupuh. pupuh. pupuh. pupuh. pupuh. The wind wound itself around the dome, and could be felt as soft exhaling.

Deep in the darkness behind his eyes a tracer lit, and flashed—arcing across his knowledge—and he felt that if he could stay here, in this room, he would come together with that in himself which was not realized. What was lost would be found. The pieces of the shattered mosaic which was himself would come naturally, easily together, matching edge to edge, and click into a whole. If he could stay here he would not die—but if he should, at that moment, he would know everything.

Howard Scott stood on the edge of the floor at the top of the dome and looked out across the still planet.

It pulsed before him. He felt that somewhere beneath the grass there was a large, benevolent heart which was glad he was here, and in beating, spoke to him.
welcome. welcome. welcome. welcome. welcome.
Tears formed, hung in his eyes, increased their volume, and fell over the edge, down his face. There was no sound but of grass far below—and the subaural synchronization of two no longer disparate unities coming together.

pupuh. pupuh. pupuh. pupuh. pupuh.
welcome. welcome. welcome. welcome. welcome.

And Howard Scott wept. He wept because he was no longer afraid. He wept because he was no longer alone, even though that to which he had been joined was hidden. He wept for all he hoped to understand. He wept because he realized he had been lonely—and for the first time he knew what for.
"Who are you?"
He asked his question. His two cupped hands relaxed and let the small droplets of words escape. And when he had finished he walked soundlessly back to the cube in the center of the floor.
Thuup.
The wall vanished. He stepped into the cube, walked forward to its back wall, bowed his head, and rested it on the evenly lit whiteness. pupuh. pupuh. pupuh. He raised his head and smiled. pupuh. pupuh. He turned and stepped forward.
Thuup.
The wall evaporated. Howard stepped out into the middle of a long, dim corridor which was closed at both ends. A coin rose into the air of his mind, flipping over and over in slow motion. Heads up. And because he was right-handed he went to the right, smiling. He walked down the hall, disoriented, but relaxed. No openings appeared.

47

"Private quarters," he murmured, and smiled at himself for being so sure.

When he got to the end of the corridor the wall vanished. He stepped through its opening onto a sunlit ramp which curved gradually down to the left, and up to the right. The wall before him now was the transparent skin of the dome. It was a clear, seamless, glasslike substance which curved so gradually, so immensly around to form the bowl which was set on the earth, not to enclose, not to create ways of perceiving in its own image, but to challenge.

Howard looked out and down on the pale blue sea. He felt that his being had become that deep, that broad— and waveless liquid, and coherent element. His head fell back and his mouth opened and he laughed silently. Then he turned to his left and walked, curving down to his left.

Thuup. Thuup.

Walls vanished as he approached, and reappeared as he passed them. He peered in each exposed chamber. All were empty and featureless. He smiled—thuup—knowing he had time, would create time, demand it—thuup— and understand. He walked to his left, curving down to his left, with chambers opening and closing in the soft white wall on his left and the transparent, invisible skin of the dome on his right. Finally there was a wall in front of him. He approached it.

Thuup.

The wall disappeared, and Howard Scott walked out of the dome.

Thuup.

"Howard?"

"U.N.S.S. PROBE IV calling Dr. Howard M. Scott. Come in Dr. Scott."

"Howard? Hello. Howard Scott?"

"Yes."

"Where the hell have you been?"

"Howard, this is Marsha. Are you OK?"

"Yes." He could hear Dr. Hobart running around the dome toward him, feet like pistons.
"Howard, we lost you!"
"Hum?"
"Howard, Levin-Hughes, here. You completely vanished on all readings. Disappeared."
"I see."
"As soon as you stepped into that second opening you were gone. It was like you didn't exist!"

When Howard Scott emerged from the dome, when his official priorities were reinstated for him by the reality of the mission, the pressure of time passing became his only concern. He did not care when they found the answers to MC6, as long as he had time to look. The next three phases of Mission PROBE IV loomed over his head like a curse.
Day one ended with all four of them back in PROBE-POD Athens. The Williams/Levin-Hughes shift had been cut short by two hours in order to hold a contingency conference. They had to decide how much time to devote to MC6 and how it would be spent. Mission Control had suggested three twenty-four-hour days. Howard was certain that this time had to be adjusted—lengthened. How to achieve that was the problem. Mission Control worshipped its computed schedules.
The Scott/Hobart day-one shift had been completed with both men having separate trips into the dome. Then they had worked under Levin-Hughes's direction to establish some kind of communication from the chambers inside the dome. They achieved a semblance of static-filled voice contact with POD Athens from two chambers along corridor "A" by using their small quantity of cable. They were unable to figure out how, technically, the dome skin was evenly opaque from the outside and almost invisible from the inside. The dome skin had no relation at all to their one-way glass.
The Williams/Levin-Hughes shortened day-one shift

*consisted of attempts by Levin-Hughes to improve the
quality and range of audio from inside the dome, and to
try to determine why the probes could not get readings
beyond the main corridors. Marsha Williams charted the
known areas of the dome—which was difficult because
there was no sense of direction beyond the main corridors, and the motion of the lift was imperceptible. She
found three additional chambers off of corridor A, and a
second lift. Then she explored without trying to chart.
She discovered three other openings on the outside of the
dome, one of which was the one Howard had come out
of. All chambers and corridors were empty, featureless
and silent. Openings revealed nothing. Levin-Hughes man-
aged to improve the quality of voice contact somewhat.
He added fifty meters to the cable by making it himself.
Then he discovered that the lift doors would not close
with anything passing across their thresholds. He could
do nothing to dissolve or evade the shield which prevented the probes from being able to get readings beyond
the main corridors of the dome.*

*Howard Scott slept fitfully during the first four hours
of the Williams/Levin-Hughes shift. Then he woke and
let Dr. Hobart sleep. He woke with a temper. The POD
was small and cramped and airless after the openness
of MC6. It was cluttered, and he was impatient with
everything about it. He was furious with zero gravity.
He was worried about time.*

*The probes continued to read as they had been read-
ing, duplicating Major Hessen's findings for the ump-
teenth time. Marsha and Levin-Hughes worked inside
the dome for the most part, and communication with
them was occasional and irritating. Howard spent his
precious time trying to help Levin-Hughes by listening to
his faraway and scratchy voice, and muttering, "not so
good", or "better", or "it was clearer the other way",
while his body ached to move freely and naturally
among the surprises down on the planet. He took reports from Marsha and charted her survey readings on
the transparent hologram model of the dome in the com-*

plex arbitrarily numbered "one". All the while his mind reached for comprehension and his tongue created little sounds which he pretended were another language. His feelings alternated between the sublime and the ridiculous—and beneath them was his rage at being hurried.

Howard Scott stared unblinking at the model of the dome and did not see the corridor which sliced its way one-quarter of the distance in toward the center, or the seven small, rounded chambers coming off of corridor A, or the wall at the end of corridor A which did not evaporate and become an opening, or the three other entrances on the outside of the dome—including the one he had come out of, with its tentative ramp lines running up and almost halfway around the dome. He felt them. Dr. Scott had no theories, only belief and feelings. He believed MC6 was not a ruin, and he felt fear that time would pass, having thrown them the crumbs of only a few more charted lines on the hologram model of the dome.

The four researchers sat back to back in their contour chairs in PROBE-POD Athens, unable to turn even their heads because there was no space. They looked at each other in their rearview mirrors, ate nutropaste sandwiches, and had a conference.

"We have to decide how we are going to accomplish Phase One. How much can we learn while we're here, and what's important? I'm ready to break the rules to investigate this planet fully. I'm going to try to get more time from Mission Control. But what we do, what we focus on must be determined by the amount of time we have. Marsha, what's our Phase Two schedule?"

"We are going to enter the dark space-cloud Vectus-Nurus 48."

"How long are we going to be in the cloud?"

"At least four months."

"What are timing details?"

"It's not far enough from here to sleep-freeze. It's a five-month journey, during which time we are to collate

and relay MC6 findings to Earth, and undergo extensive briefing and education up-date on the space-cloud. We have to depart from here no later than a certain date— I can get it from Lanier—because we have to be in the cloud before its flare apex."

"Thank you. Scott to PROBE IV."

"U.N.S.S. PROBE IV. Ybarra here."

"Ybarra, is Lanier around?"

"Right here, Dr. Scott."

"Lanier, what's the latest we can leave MC6 and make scheduled rendezvous with Vectus-Nurus 48?"

"Seventy-six hours from 0100. That's three days and a few hours from now."

"Can it be pushed back any later?"

"Negative, sir. If we depart from here any later than scheduled time we miss flare apex of V-N 48."

"OK. Please send the following message uncoded on fastest relay network. Are you ready?"

"Yes, sir."

"URGENT: To PROBE IV Mission Control, from Dr. Howard M. Scott, research head, Mission PROBE IV. We are in Phase One now. Findings indicate we must, repeat must have more time on MC6. Will send coded explanation as soon as possible. It is imperative we have more time. Scott."

"Got it. I'll send it out immediately."

"Thank you. Let me know the response as soon as it comes in."

"Yes, sir. Is that it?"

"Yes. Scott out."

"I don't agree with you Howard. We must get to V-N 48 as scheduled. Too many people back home are waiting for that information."

"File a report, David."

"Damn it! Phase Two is why the hell we're out here in the first place!"

"We're wasting time. So far we have nothing to add to Major Hessen's findings that is strong enough to bargain with. *That's what we have to find, and we have to find it fast."*

"Has this become so important to you?"

"Yes. For now we will schedule within the context of our given time. Twenty-two hours are gone. We have forty-eight more scheduled hours, plus the twenty-four hours of margin. That's just about seventy more hours. That's what's left. How do we spend that time? I would like to stay at complex number one. I assume that by splitting up our time among the complexes we will simply verify what we already know and not learn anything new. Levin-Hughes?"

"I agree, Howard. Hopping around does me no good at all. With time in one place I can get at least good audio throughout the dome, and I may be able to get the probes working efficiently in there."

"Marsha?"

"Give me a minute."

"Dr. Hobart?"

"First of all let me say that we must stay with the Mission Control schedule. Secondly, I believe it's imperative to get to as many complexes as possible. So far we have learned nothing new from the ruins, except that we can get into a dome, and a dome is interesting if you have the luxury of time—which we do not. There is nothing in the domes, Howard. We must get ground samples from all over, and test the water, to see if this place is worth trying to inhabit."

"Nonsense. Marsha?"

"I think we should split up. You and Levin-Hughes stay at complex number one and investigate the dome. David and I can try to get to as many sites as possible and work on the second part of Mission Control's stated objective for Phase One."

"But we need your minds here!"

"Howard, are you OK?"

"Damn it. I'm fine! I'm just pissed off that this place, this dome is what we have been looking for for two hun-

53

dred years. We found it, and now they give us three more lousy days to understand a technology so advanced we can't yet even conceive of it, because we have to get the hell over to the other side of the galaxy to be in some cloud when it farts! It's really typical!"

"OK. OK."

"The first thing we're going to do is get the hell out of this damned POD. We'll all be on the surface from now on."

"But Mission Control . . ."

"Mission Control can take its regulations and schedules and shove them up its heart! The second thing is that Levin-Hughes and I will be in complex one all the time. You two can take the Skimmer and get to as many sites as possible in forty hours."

"Forty hours!"

"Dr. Scott? This is Lanier, PROBE IV. I got your message through on lasar emergency. They weren't too happy."

"What's their answer?"

"QUOTE: Delay of departure for Vectus-Nurus 48 by more than seventy-two hours from now would involve rescheduling entire PROBE IV mission, and risking safety margin time. File report immediately on meaning this request and its emergency delivery. Mission Control. UNQUOTE."

David Hobart smiled, unseen, in relief. Levin-Hughes pursed his lips. Marsha watched Howard for an explosion. In the silence Howard Scott heard the ticking of his wristwatch inside his gross toy of a pressure suit. He closed his eyes. Tired obscenities wound around his tongue, and died.

"Thank you, Lanier. I'll get a report off when I can."

"Yes, sir. Sorry."

"Scott out. OK, Marsha. Your trip to other complexes is cut to twenty-four hours. Let's take what we need out of the POD. Levin-Hughes, strip this machine of any materials you might conceivably need."

"I'm doing it now. Howard."

FROM THE LEGEND OF BIEL

"Howard, you can't destroy this machine for one phase of the mission."

"I'm doing it. Let's get down there."

Col. Haris, up in PROBE IV, was not aware of the research team's orders and was not alarmed when, suddenly, all four of them were on the surface.

During the second MC6 work day Levin-Hughes improved and extended the scratchy voice contact from inside the dome. David Hobart spent the day isolated with the twenty-nine smaller structures, and then took ground and water samples. His relationship to Dr. Scott had become frosted with formality, despite Marsha's attempts to help them make peace. Dr. Hobart verified that all of the smaller structures were solid and not made of the same material. He got rich soil and pure, clean water. Howard and Marsha explored and charted the big dome. They discovered two subterranean levels beneath the dome, both featureless and silent. They added one slow line at a time to their transparent hologram model of the dome.

Toward the end of day two, Howard and Marsha stopped and stared at the model. They saw that so far— except for the huge chamber at the top of the dome— they had not gotten more than one-quarter of the distance from the skin of the dome in toward its center. The inside core of the dome, about half the volume, remained inaccessible.

The four of them ate when they could. Sandwiches were left next to tools and charts. Enormous quantities of coffee were consumed. They slept in the Skimmer in shifts of two, never more than six hours out of twenty-four.

On the third day Marsha and David took off in the Skimmer and verified that all seven domes in the complexes they visited were identical to the dome in complex number one. Scott and Levin-Hughes explored the dome, trying to get in closer to its center. They could not. The three-dimensional model acquired more corridors and chambers. It grew in complexity around its edge—and was blank in the center.

FROM THE LEGEND OF BIEL

Night on MC6 was similar to the warm, dry summer nights at Mission Control in Baja, except that the stars were infinite and clear, and there was no moon. Marsha and David were deep in the bowels of the dome, trying to chart them. Howard and Levin-Hughes slept in the Skimmer.

Dr. Howard M. Scott dreamed of hieroglyphs on walls of dark tunnels, then of spinning in a centrifuge faster and faster, one gee added to another and another until the flesh was pulled back on his face, stretching his eyelids tight as he tried to read the symbols in a disintegrating book no bigger than his thumbnail. He had already awakened twice. He had looked at his watch and told himself that he had to sleep or he would not be able to go on. He had fought continually with the idiosyncrasies of his hammock and had twice fallen back into hot, wet sleep.

He woke, perspiring. He turned his head to the side and saw Levin-Hughes's relaxed profile in the dark. Levin-Hughes slept the sleep of the dead. A little rattle of contentment rose and fell regularly out of his nose.

Howard looked at his watch and saw that he had been trying to sleep for two and a half hours. He was exhausted. He wanted to scream a sound which would crack the Skimmer and peaceful Levin-Hughes and the others to pieces. He massaged his eyes with the thumb and ring finger of his left hand and watched the soft, purple, neon dots explode and disappear beneath the pressure of his fingertips. He inhaled, rasping, through his nose, then exhaled a long, quiet moan. One more day.

Howard swung his feet over the side of his hammock and was nauseated. He pushed down against fatigue and gravity with his arms, and slowly his body straightened as he stood up. His blood rushed to his feet. His hands fumbled for a mooring, found it, and could not hold on. He bent over and was still a moment as the light-headedness swelled, crested, and passed. The wandering parts of his body came back together and made a broken whole. He dressed and walked out of the Skimmer, trembling, into the night—the dark beginning of his last day on MC6.

Howard Scott stood naked on the sand at the edge of the dark, waveless sea. His body was tall and soft-thin. He closed his eyes. Then, like a spring uncoiling to become a knife, he sliced through the surface and swam. He rolled. He washed. He floated face down, lifting his head occasionally to breathe. He let the water have him, taking his time. Finally he got out, paced himself dry, dressed slowly, deliberately, and walked into the dome.

. . . no thoughts, only fragments—like pieces of a shattered window in continual explosion. My very breath is being sucked out of my body. Help me. I want to be with you. I want to be part of what you are . . .

. . . there is pressure in my temples, as if a cylinder has been driven through my skull from side to side, behind my eyes—and set on fire. Help me . . .

. . . there are no pieces to bring together because nothing has been broken—and yet everything is shattered. The moon appears, Earth's moon—a red balloon which, punctured, bleeds all over me . . .

. . . inhale . . . breathe . . . yes, that's it . . . now, let it back out. The pieces are torn, but they hold together . . . oh, help me, please. I am falling down in slow motion and it has no end. I am afraid. My body aches with an electric pain, an artificial pain which is small, hot knives. My molecules have become eccentric. I cannot remember to breathe because I must think to hold my soft, exploding skin together . . .

. . . do not try so hard to   rise . . .
                float . . .
    fall . . .   fall . . .
                            down . . .

. . . I am falling through fog which is lit with a shaft of light. I am falling . . .

I am going to die.

slap!

        grasp! ? ? . . . a hand . . . quite small! It . . . gropes. We touch. Hold . . . on . . . If you hold on I will not fall so fast and die. I will not . . . Oh, hold. help! Me!
It grips. tighter
      tighter
   CLASP. Firm. I am still
              falling
                  but not so quickly
                             now.

. . . all in a dream and out of a dream, all in the soft events which have no sequence and no clues, I have become a sieve . . . a pane of shattered glass.
        . . . my coherency has disappeared . . . .

. . . light . . . shines through gauze curtains. The ether is evaporating. My eyelids are becoming lighter, and unglued . . . I will open my eyes . . . NOW. I will see that it is morning, and the urgency was just a dream. I will climb out of this peanutbutter lake, where I am lost.
In a little while.

Howard Scott lay waking in the big chamber at the top of the dome. He opened his eyes and saw Marsha's tired, dumpling face, concerned and smiling. She was sitting cross-legged on the floor near him, at the outer edge of the dome. It was dawn.
  "You're perspiring."
  "How long have I been asleep?"
  "I don't know. You and Levin-Hughes have scheduled

duty in half an hour. Would you like me to give you something for your fatigue?"

"No. I don't want anything artificial in my system
now."

"Vitamins?"

". . . mmmmm . . ."

"They're not artificial. I just gave myself a shot."

"OK. I guess I need it."

"Very true."

Howard rolled up one sleeve of the red jumpsuit he had
not changed since he first stepped on MC6. He heard
Marsha take her little pistol out of its antiseptic holder.
He felt the cold burn of alcohol on the inside of his arm,
below the elbow. He felt the small, round mouth of the
gun touch his skin, and felt nothing when he heard the
pop. Marsha cleaned the little pistol and reholstered it.

"Would you like to talk about it, Howard?"

Scott closed his eyes, reached out, and took hold of
Marsha's smaller hand. It was cool and composed.

". . . Marsha . . ."

They did not look at each other. They lay side by side,
separated by the lengths of their two outstretched arms,
joined by the knot their two hands made. Between them
was space, difficult to bridge, because inside they did not
begin or aim for the same end. Above them, through the
clear skin of the dome, the first pink of morning began to
bleed onto their last day on this planet.

". . . I don't want to leave here. I will die if I do. I
will die to stay. There is nothing on Earth to go back to
but greed and bungling."

"It's home . . ."

"No. It's not home. It's some kind of pitiful mistake,
an error in judgment—maybe even a lie. It's just another
group of systems in conflict, and, Marsha, I am sick to my
bowels of systems. Since sleep-freeze I have been revolted
in my body by my heritage, which calls its progress gifts.
Our history is disgraceful death and humiliation. We are
encouraged to be less than human, less even than the

simplest animals. Europe and America have turned the entire world into a suburb, and human beings have become perpetual, demanding infants. Our progress depends on systems in conflict—death."

"Howard, we wouldn't be here now if it weren't for systems."

"We don't know that. Maybe we wouldn't need to be here. And how are we here? With bombs—terrified that we will be changed, enlightened. Here is a place to begin again, and we will probably destroy it, if not with bombs then with garbage. We will either blow it up now, or return with our obscene little toys, our disgusting greed and destructive technology and turn the planet into our own image. I don't want to go back. I don't want them to know about this place. I cannot take the responsibility for destroying a second chance, for perverting what these incredible and peaceful creatures have built . . . for us. And you know that once we come here total destruction, of one kind or another, is inevitable."

"We have to try, Howard. We have to do the best we can."

"The best we can do is quick death. You know, I think of the people who made these structures all the time. I know in my spine that they are human, like us, and they created this planet—which has yet to be used—for us. I have no hope but in this. More than anything I wish one day to come around the right corner and find one of them —a small child—waiting for me. Home is here, Marsha."

"Have you made more requests to Mission Control to extend the time?"

"Every day. The answer is no. They don't want to rearrange the schedule. Can you believe it? I've filed detailed reports each day, explaining in detail what we've found, and what I hope to find. Vectus-Nurus 48 is a higher-priority project with the University boys. Mission Control promised me that I could lead the next MC6 mission. Both of us know I'll be too old. They refuse to reschedule this mission. I'm falling apart, Marsha. I don't know what

to do. I am truly poor in the modern sense of the word."

"How's that?"

"I have no control over even the most insignificant details of my life. My judgment has been vetoed as invalid. I'd better get busy."

He released her hand and stood up.

"I don't want to be a resource anymore—or a commodity, or a product, or a unit of capital. I have died as far as they're concerned. I have become a walking revolution. I am saying 'No. I am not a faceless number, I am a human being—like no other before me, and creating none in my image. I am the sole judge of what is right for me. You have lost control.' I'm staying here, Marsha."

"Howard, you're hysterical. Let me give you something."

"No. I am not hysterical. I am awake. I am changed. Power demands more power to continue. Control necessitates more control in order to maintain control. I am no longer part of that cruel and unnecessary process. That system. Even here, their power and control is nothing without my sanction. I no longer want what they have to offer because it is unnatural and deliberate and evil."

"Howard, listen to me . . ."

"No. You listen to me. I have told you this so you can explain my absence on the rest of the trip. Say I'm insane. Say anything, it doesn't matter. But if you try to stop me, I shall do whatever is necessary to prevent you from achieving that end."

Howard stopped a moment and looked at Marsha sadly.

"How shall you end? You are the best they can produce, but even you cannot continue indefinitely as part of their stewardship for all life, as part of their mechanism of judgment and accounting and measurement of worth by how efficiently it perpetuates their system of eventual death by disease of one sort or another. Your perspective is distorted. You see everything through a lens they created. We are not the end of creation, Marsha, but the beginning. How shall you end?"

FROM THE LEGEND OF BIEL

Howard Scott turned and walked to the cube in the center of the chamber. One wall vanished. He stepped into the lift and turned around. As the opening became opaque, he saw Marsha looking back at him as from the other side of a dream. Then he saw the white wall and sank imperceptibly through the dome into the last day on MC6.

The research team had twenty-four hours left. Howard Scott was willing to keep trying officially for more time because now, in his mind, he had all time. Perhaps there was still opportunity to find something concrete to bargain with and confrontation could be avoided. If not, he would do what he had to do. He joined Levin-Hughes on the search as Marsha and David fell down to rest.

On the fourth day Howard and Levin-Hughes tried to get in toward the center of the dome. When Marsha and David woke they joined them. The four split up into two teams and began at the beginning. They worked their ways through all known portions of the dome, probing for something that could have been overlooked. They kept in touch on small, scratchy audio units.

There was no sense of motion or direction in the lifts. It was difficult to figure out how they were getting from point A to point B—or even specifically where A was in relation to B. They knew that all lifts, when taken up, ended with the cube in the center of the floor at the top of the dome. Levin-Hughes believed that the lifts did not move straight up and down, but in all directions. They appeared to be shaftless. The researchers had no control over where the lifts went. They just got in, and when they wished to stop they stepped forward, and the wall evaporated—depositing them someplace else in the dome. They had learned to go approximately where they wanted by using certain lifts for certain directions and timing themselves with stopwatches. It worked some of the time.

Thuup. Howard Scott and Johnson Levin-Hughes stepped into lift number 2, corridor B. They were silent. Thuup. The wall materialized behind them. The two teams had ridden all the lifts on all the corridors they

*knew of. It had taken them ten hours to make all the
stops and explore the few new, featureless chambers.
Scott and Levin-Hughes were on their way to join the
others to decide what to do now. Howard rested his forehead on the wall in front of him. Levin-Hughes, straight,
short, crisp, and tireless, cleaned his fingernails with an
antique Swiss Army knife.*

*"Damn it! I want to get to the central point of the vol-
ume of this dome!"*

Thuup.

The opening appeared.

*Scott and Levin-Hughes looked at each other. In front
of them was a space like no other they had seen in the
dome.*

*pupuh. pupuh. pupuh. pupuh. pupuh. . . . .
pupuh. pupuh. pupuh. pupuh. pupuh. . . . .*

"No sooner said than done, Howard."

*Everything was soft gold, the color of the grass. The il-
lumination was dim, and deep gold. The two researchers
stood at one end of a huge, silent chamber which was
half the size of the one at the top of the dome. It, too,
was half-spherical in shape, but it was the only chamber
they had seen where there were straight lines and angles
and planes.*

*The rounded wall/ceiling was a honeycomb. Thousands
of connected hexagonal units stretched from the floor, up
the wall, and across the ceiling. Each unit was three meters
deep, and wide enough for a slim adult to crawl through.
Beyond and through the honeycomb units was blackness
—deep, and featureless as night. The floor of the chamber
was soft and gold.*

*The room was a brilliant, depth-defying exercise in
chiaroscuro planes and angles. There was, as elsewhere
in the dome, no sense of being enclosed or contained in
the context of a room or an architecture. Once the surprise of the color, the depth, and the beauty of the room
was accepted, it became neutral—like the others. There*

was, however, a tremendous sense of isolation, as if all beyond the chamber was a figment of the imagination, and did not really exist.

"We found it. Levin-Hughes."

"I do believe so."

They walked forward soundlessly.

"See if you can get the others on audio."

"Levin-Hughes to PROBE IV research team. Do you read? Hello. Marsha? David? Come in research team."

"Nothing."

"It was to be expected."

Howard looked up as he walked in toward the center of the room. He felt like he was inside the eye of a giant fly.

Thuup.

A silver rectangle rose up out of the floor in the exact center of the room. It had three hundred millimeters to a side, and was just over one meter high. Toward the top of the rectangle, in the center of the side facing them, was an emblem. It was one hundred millimeters tall, and fifty millimeters wide. The emblem was a maroon figure eight, with a short horizontal line at top and bottom: $\overline{\underline{8}}$

Scott and Levin-Hughes, both breathing shallowly were frozen and silent a long time. Finally Howard found words.

"Let's not waste any time. You move around the chamber and find out if anything else pops up. I'll study this."

"Fine."

Howard approached the softly lit, shining rectangle. His feet made no sound on the deep floor. He measured his steps as he walked around the object.

The rectangle had a brushed, satiny finish and was made of an extremely dense alloy which looked like a silver/aluminum blend. There were no emblems or markings on its other three sides. It had no seams or joints and was a brilliantly crafted piece of work.

Howard knocked on the rectangle. It emitted a deep, resonant ring but felt solid. He placed his hands on the surface, which was the color of a bright and overcast morning. The rectangle was still and silent—cool beneath *his palms. He stood in front of its emblemed side. The maroon figure eight was deeply engraved into the surface. Where the four lines of the figure eight intersected there was a thin, horizontal slit. Howard took a piece of paper out of his breast pocket and flattened it, to see if it would slide in.*

"Howard, you want to come over here, please?"

"Yes."

Levin-Hughes had his back to Howard and was looking at something in front of his chest. His smaller body was planted in the floor like a tree.

Johnson Levin-Hughes had been walking near the curved side of the chamber, peering into the separate honeycomb units. Nothing had happened. He had stopped, puzzled, and inadvertently rested his hand on the edge of one of the units. A row of small, cardlike, transparent rectangles had risen up from the floor of the hexagonal unit and stood, now, like clear, thin dominos, lined up behind one another.

Howard and Levin-Hughes looked into the unit at the cards. They were about the size of index cards—one hundred millimeters high by one hundred and fifty millimeters wide. They were very thin and clear—like small panes of glass. There were no visible markings on them.

Howard reached into the unit and pulled out a card at random from the middle of the row. He marked its place with his piece of paper. It was clear and colorless, with no symbols or markings. He held it by its edges and ran a fingertip of his other hand across its surface. He could feel tiny, Braille-like bumps, but when he held the card up he could not see them.

"I'll go get David and Marsha and draft a plea to Mission Control for more time. Can I sign your name to it too?"

"Please. Yes, indeed."

"Thank you. Stay here and try to rig up some sort of audio with PROBE IV so we can have an open channel for reports."

"Right. Howard?"

"Yes?"

"Good luck."

"Thank you."

Howard Scott walked to the rectangle in the center of the floor. He flashed the clear card at Levin-Hughes and smiled.

"You know what, Levin-Hughes? This goes in here."

Scott patted the rectangle, stepped into the lift, and went to ask for time.

Howard found Dr. Hobart and Marsha and explained how to get into the honeycomb chamber. Then he went to the Skimmer and drafted an emergency communique to Mission Control. They had less than fourteen hours, unless Mission Control were merciful. Howard Scott was not going to leave the planet, but he wanted to avoid an immediate showdown with Col. Haris and the others— so he ran his maze.

Four precious hours later Levin-Hughes had established scratchy but dependable voice contact with PROBE IV. Marsha had discovered that all of the honeycomb units in "The Gold Room", as she liked to call it, which were between one and two meters high, contained glass cards. David Hobart had run the figure eight symbol through computers and had received its possible meanings from them. According to the computers the figure eight could be: a figure eight, an infinity sign, an abstract symbol or map of the planet, a mutant astrological sign, an abstract helix or spiral—and on and on. David was not satisfied with any of it, but he had done his scientific duty. Howard had four times requested, bullied, cajoled and begged Mission Control for more time. Four times he had been finally, unequivocally, flatly, irrevocably refused.

"This is Howard Scott from central chamber, called 'Gold Room' of dome number one, complex one. I am calling U.N.S.S. PROBE IV. Do you read?"

". . . U.N.S.S. PROBE IV . . . Lanier, here. We read you . . . faint but steady. Go ahead."

"OK. This is the best we can do. All four of us are now

in this chamber. We will be in here until it's time to leave. That's not quite ten hours."

"Ch . . . eck."

"I want this channel open all the time and someone on your end from now until we leave the chamber. Record everything. One of us will be talking to you all the time. At present we are trying to get information off the cards. We have audio recorder, video recorder, and two big probe consoles in operation. Are you recording now?"

". . . Yes, sir."

"Fine. Here's Levin-Hughes."

Dr. Howard M. Scott walked to the silver rectangle. The little glass card rested on top of it and glistened like a deep, squared pond. He slid he card off of the rectangle and onto his fingertips. Its place was still marked by the slip of paper from his pocket, which held the first four lines of a sonnet—the first he had ever tried to write. They ran over his mind like water.

> *When in my time it has become bad taste,*
> *insanity, and danger to be free,*
> *I'm left no choice but to prevent the waste*
> *of my sweet life for you—or yours for me . . .*

Dr. David R. Hobart was down on one knee, sighting the camera on the silver rectangle. Inside he was gray petulance, and glad Phase One was almost over. His mind was imageless as he tried not to imagine what would happen when and if the card slipped into the rectangle and revealed something.

Dr. Marsha A. Williams was near David, sitting on the floor, looking down at the dials on one of the probe consoles. Caleb. Do not think of Caleb now. *She looked like a large, chubby baby, and was relaxed to be doing something specific again. She did not expect the card to reveal anything at all, but she was glad it had been found—for Howard's sake. She knew he would not stay here when it came right down to it, and she was relieved that it was nearly time to go.*

FROM THE LEGEND OF BIEL

Mr. Johnson Levin-Hughes spoke softly-crisp into the tiny mouthpiece which wormed its way out of his comcap and around to his mouth. His blue marble eyes were shadowed beneath the overhanging shelf of the bones of his eyebrows. He had become captured by this technology. He had almost entertained thoughts of trying to find some way to stay here.

Howard held the delicate card. There was no sound. None of them looked at each other. Each was alone, in one of the darker rooms toward the back of the self. They were tired. They were alone.

Howard lined the card up with the horizontal slot which bisected the maroon figure eight. It was sucked gently from his fingertips. It disappeared into the rectangle. There was no sound at all.

Thuup.

Col. Haris and his U.N.S.S. PROBE IV crew heard and recorded what sounded like a very loud, long orchestral chord.

F R O M   T H E   L E G E N D   O F   B I E L . . .

Howard Scott's face rose, froze and became an open-eyed mask at the same time that all fluid in his body sank to his feet, swelling them. He felt as though he had retained his form and lost his mass. He stood before an invisible but tangible barrier—his time on one side, an entire new civilization on the other. Willingness to change was the key to passage through. And for one instant he was not sure that he could change, and he became afraid. He fumbled to put his hands over his ears, but could not find them.   •

Howard Scott screamed as records which had been made in some other age, some other space—which was neither here nor now, neither Earth nor MC6—released their pungent secrets to his frightened brain. A whole culture stepped out of the darkness beyond the honeycomb chamber to be apprehended.

The four researchers did not realize that the light was sucked out of the chamber as marrow is from bones. They were in darkness so dynamic, so complete, so intimate

*and endless, that it obliterated all protective barriers of
flesh, and distance, and game. All location, all memory,
and all personality evaporated.*
  "Dr. Scott?"
  *The researchers did not realize, as Howard kept
screaming and screaming and screaming, that they heard
and tasted and touched and smelled and saw more than
is endurable to the unreleased personality.*
  . . .AS RECORDED BY THOACDIEN. . .
  *Col. Haris, up in PROBE IV. could hear nothing but
the faint buzz of static which came from the unused but
open audio system.*
  *A scream was sucked out of Howard Scott's body like
juice, and it erupted—it became aurora borealis.* (. . . . . .
. . . .
HOLD . . . . ON . . . . AHHHHH. . . . . . .
YOU . . . . ARE . . . . TOO . . . .
HEAVY . . . .) *A scream blew out of his bowels,
came out of him like vomit, gathered steam and was vol-
canic as he was sucked along behind it—lost in the center
of its after-effects.*

AAAAAAA AAAAAAA AHHHHHHHHHHHHHHHHHHH
GGGGGGGGGGGGGGGGAAAAAAA AAAAAAAAAAA

  "Dr. Scott?"
  *There were no metaphors for any of them. All was re-
moved but the thing itself.*

. . . C A R D ONE: THE PARADOX.

A sperm and an ovum collide, blend together, subdi-
vide, and float in liquid to become a whole which
coincides and flutters on its long, inevitable ride into
complexity.

II

FROM: THOACDIEN—PRIORITY ONE.
TO: CHEMBRYO LAB 187-A, THOACDIEN V.
DATE: 184.060
TIME: 1.4.030
SUBJECT: BINOL INJECTION—SELECTED IN-
FANTS, CHEMBRYO LAB 187-A.
. . . .
. . . .
. . . .

CHEMBRYO LAB 187-A: PROCEED.
STOP.

THOACDIEN: HAVE YOU COMPLETED SELEC-
TION OF 100 FETUSES FROM THE
1,000 OF COMPLEX 187-A FOR
PRE-BIRTH INJECTION OF BINOL?

CHEMLAB: YES. THE 100 STRONGEST INFANTS
WERE CHOSEN AND ARE NUM-
BERED 1 THROUGH 100.
STOP.

THOACDIEN: PLEASE BEGIN IMMEDIATE PREPARATION OF THOSE FETUSES FOR INJECTION WHICH IS TO COMMENCE ON 184.065 AT 1.0.000. REPORT.

STOP.

CHEMLAB: THE TOLERANCE PROFILE CHARTS ON THE 100 SELECTED FETUSES SHOW 80% SURVIVAL PROBABILITY.
SINCE WE HAVE NOT INJECTED BINOL TO PRE-BIRTH INFANTS IN ANY DOSAGE BEFORE, AND YOU ARE PROPOSING A MASSIVE DOSAGE, WE CANNOT KNOW WHAT TO EXPECT.
WE ARE RUNNING THE PROBABLE RISK OF 20 INFANT DEFORMITIES, MUTATIONS OR MORTALITIES.
WE RECOMMEND RETURN TO STANDARD BIRTHING PROCEDURES FOR ALL INFANTS OF CHEMLAB 187-A.
WE RECOMMEND DELAY OF BINOL INJECTION UNTIL USUAL, SAFE POST-BIRTH PERIOD.
THE CHANCE FOR LOSS IS TOO GREAT.

STOP.

THOACDIEN: YOUR MISGIVINGS ARE UNDERSTOOD, BUT THEY ARE BASED ON MATHEMATICAL PROBABILITY—NOT FACT.
IT IS TIME TO PUSH AHEAD.
PROCEED WITH INJECTION OF 100

SELECTED INFANTS AS
SCHEDULED.
STOP.

CHEMLAB: VERY WELL.
STOP.

END TRANSMISSION ....

Mikkran appears at the far end of the long white corridor. She glides with long strides through the main hall
of the huge dome in complex 187-A, Thoacdien V. Her
full robe flaps behind her, fans out in a maroon wake, revealing her dark brown nakedness underneath. She hur-
ries, liquid and tall.

Mikkran-Gogan-Tor has only recently arrived on Thoacdien V from Briitun-doo—Thoacdien XVII. She has
only recently completed the cycle with her previous charge,
Grolen. She came to complex 187-A to begin a new cycle,
with a new charge, and has just been informed of Thoacdien's recent communique ordering the preparation of one
hundred specially selected fetuses for massive, pre-birth
doses of Binol. Her charge is one of these infants.

Mikkran steps into the white cube. "Hall of a thousand
chambers." She feels the cube lift her up, past the ground
level toward the hall which is just below the huge meditation room at the top of the dome. Her charge is on the Hall
of One Thousand Chambers now, still in its pre-birth
tank. As a mentor her responsibility is to protect this infant with her life and to be of aid to its learning until it
has completed puberty and is an adult. Even as a grade-
one top-priority mentor she cannot stop the Binol injection,
she can only hurry to be there when it happens. She can
only offer the child an invisible matrix of strength and love
for the brief time remaining before their temporary separation begins.

She steps forward, through the evaporating wall, with

73

two long strides, then runs—robe like a rooster's tail behind her—to chamber 187-A,0037.

~~~~~~

FROM: THOACDIEN—PRIORITY ONE.
TO: CHEMBRYO LAB 187-A, THOACDIEN V.
DATE: 184.064
TIME: 6.9.982
SUBJECT: COUNTDOWN—BINOL   INJECTION,
    100 GROUP, CHEMBRYO LAB 187-A, THOAC-
    DIEN V.
. . . .
. . . .
. . . .

CHEMBRYO LAB 187-A: PROCEED.
STOP.

THOACDIEN: BEGIN IMMEDIATE COUNTDOWN
              FOR BINOL INJECTION 100
              GROUP, 187-A. ARE YOU READY?
STOP.

CHEMLAB: WE ARE READY.
            PROCEED.
            IT IS 6.9.989.
STOP.

THOACDIEN: AND COUNTING DOWN FROM
              10, 9, 8, 7, 6, 5, 4, 3, 2, 1,
              N O W.
STOP.

CHEMLAB: INJECTIONS HAVE BEGUN.
            BINOL FLUID IS NOW ENTERING
            FETUSES AT 50 CC'S PER TIME

74

SLOT. INJECTIONS WILL BE
COMPLETED IN TWO MORE TIME
SLOTS WITH TOTAL DOSAGE, AS
PER YOUR SPECS, OF 150 CC's
HAVING BEEN GIVEN EACH OF THE
FETUSES NUMBERED 1 THROUGH
100, COMPLEX 187-A, THOACDIEN
V.

STOP.

THOACDIEN: ON COMPLETION OF INJECTIONS
BEGIN IMMEDIATE PROCEDURES
TO BIRTH ALL 1,000 INFANTS OF
COMPLEX 187-A.
ARE GLADDINS STANDING BY?

STOP.

CHEMLAB: YES.
ALL PREPARATIONS FOR BIRTH-
ING HAVE BEEN COMPLETED.

STOP.

THOACDIEN: PLEASE REPORT IMMEDIATELY
ANY CHANGE IN STATUS OF ANY
FETUS CURRENTLY UNDERGO-
ING BINOL INJECTION.
ADDITIONAL INSTRUCTIONS TO
FOLLOW ON THE BASIS OF YOUR
REPORTS.

STOP.

CHEMLAB: YES.
ALL 100 FETUSES RECEIVING PRE-
BIRTH BINOL ARE FUNCTIONING
WITHIN TOLERANCES AT THIS
TIME. IT IS NOW PLUS .036 INTO
INJECTION.

STOP.

THOACDIEN: THANK YOU.
STOP.

END TRANSMISSION ....

The first drop of clear Binol fluid gathers its weight, slides down the long, coiled umbilical cord, and enters the fetus.

Mikkran's face is pressed against one warm glass wall of the pre-birth tank. She watches the almost-term infant rotate slowly, like a tiny satellite in its own distant and private orbit. She traces the first pearl of potent Binol as it glides around and through the infant's cord, which is attached to the back of the tank.

The fetus rolls on its back, fists clenched, bobbing slightly. Its brows knit in bewilderment at the Binol's first, cautious approach to the central nervous system. Mikkran feels the infant's eyes roll beneath their thin, membranous lids as it struggles to accommodate the power which has so silently, subtly, suddenly invaded.

Mikkran has experienced what the baby is learning— in the same way. For an instant she closes her eyes against the powerlessness, the vulnerability of the fetus.

●●me●●●●●●●●●●●●●●●●●
●●●●●●●●●●●●●●●yes●●●●●●●●●●●●●●●●●●yοu●●●●●●●●●●●●●●●●●●●●●●●●●●●●●
●●●yes●●●●●●●●●●●●●●●you●●●●●●●●●●●
●●●●●●●●●●and●●●●●I●●●●●●●●●●●●●●●●●●●●●●●●●●●●●yes●●●●●●●●●●●●●●●●●●
●●●●●●●●●●●●●●●●●●●●●●●¢●●●●●●●●●●●●●●●●●●●●●●●●●●●●●yes●●●●●●●●●●●
●●●●●●●●●●●●∿●●●●●●●●●●●
●●●●●●●●●●●●yes●●●●●●●●●●●,●●
●●●●●●●●●●●●○●●●●●●●●●●●●
●●●●●●●●●●●●yes●●●●●●●●●●●●

FROM THE LEGEND OF BIEL

...∅...

...yes...

...1D...

...yes...

...2D...

...yes...

...3D...

...yes...

...4D...

...yes...

Infant 187-A,0037's charts are excellent. It is the product of a combination of genes only recently mastered in the chemlab. Mikkran has experienced the baby's learning capacities already, and was astonished. The fetus has learned a great deal in the pre-birth tank and testing indicates that 187-A,0037 is capable of a ten percent cerebration increase over the previous generation. This means that another ten percent of the dark, concealed part of the human brain could be exposed by this child.

The baby's fists are clenched in defense, and its brows are knotted in amazement. Even though Mikkran has experienced a massive dose of Binol herself, and witnessed Grolen's injection, she watches this baby in fascination. Never before has Binol been given to this young a human being. And rarely are even adults given this amount.

...+...yes.   ...>...yes.   ...≈...yes.

...⁻...yes.   ...<...yes.   ...»...yes.

...×...yes.   ...≠...yes.   ...≪...yes.

...∸...yes.   ...≠̇...yes.   ...⁻>...yes.

...=̇...yes.   ...≡...yes.   ...⁻<...yes.

Since Mikkran's arrival on Thoacdien V she has been with her charge seventy percent of the time. She saw it become an entity as sperm found, grasped, and blended into ovum. She has reached into the pre-birth tank with thin, thin gloves to hold the fetus in her two hands. She has tested it and monitored it, and discovered its rhythms and learning modes. Mentor and charge have become acquainted, as through a vaguely transparent, damp gauze curtain. She knows the baby as a human being now, and no longer refers to charts to understand what it is experiencing. She can feel it. She can feel the baby denting her being as it grows toward becoming an articulate consciousness. Soon the baby will emerge from the darkness of pre-birth, and they will join together as fully as two streams.

...⊔...yes.	...⊥...yes.	...▭...yes.
...⌄...yes.	...‖...yes.	...⊓...yes.
...%...yes.	...△...yes.	...▱...yes.
...⟨ƨ...yes.	...△...yes.	...⑤...yes.
...≅...yes.	...≏...yes.	..." ...yes.
...≚...yes.	...⋔...yes.	...◌...yes.
...△...yes.	...⬤...yes.	...⊖...yes.
...△...yes.	...ʳ...yes.	...⋋...yes.
...ℛ...yes.	...⟨...yes.	...⋋̇...yes.
...ᴥ...yes.	...Î...yes.	...Ƌ...yes.
...ℛ...yes.	...∫...yes.	...⊟...yes.
...ᵖ...yes.	...ϕ...yes.	...⋇...yes.

Mikkran sits on the floor of the large featureless chamber which is 187-A,0037's for life, and which will gradually become a tangible extension of the baby's brain. She stares into the tank as the fetus clenches and unclenches its empty fist. Bubbles rise up out of the little perfect hand and break as soundlessly as thoughts on the surface of the womb-fluid. There is a pucker of independence around the baby's closed eyes. The mentor sends her thoughts through the glass wall of the tank. They do not go directly to the baby's brain, which is busy, but surround it as an invisible cloud. These thoughts will seep through the baby's skin, and be remembered later.

—I love you. I am waiting well for you to call me. You must have your time alone now. Explore, verify, and be free. You are becoming alive, and must know for yourself before you can know me. I will come when you call. Look, little one, it is clear for you today—and warm.

~~~~~~

FROM: THOACDIEN—PRIORITY ONE.
TO: MENTORS, CHEMBYRO LAB 187-A, THOACDIEN V.
DATE: 184.065
TIME: 2.2.130
SUBJECT: DEPARTURE FROM CHARGES.
. . . .
. . . .
. . . .

MENTORS: PROCEED
STOP.

THOACDIEN: MENTORS OF FETUS GROUP
187-A, PLEASE LEAVE FETUS
CHAMBERS IMMEDIATELY.
PLEASE REMOVE EVIDENCE OF
YOUR PRESENCE FROM YOUR

CHARGE'S CHAMBER.
PLEASE BE ROBED, HOODED,
AND VEILED FROM NOW UNTIL
YOU ARE GREETED BY YOUR
CHARGE.
WHEN YOU ARE CALLED FOR
YOU MAY PROCEED AND
SCHEDULE CEREMONY AT YOUR
OWN DISCRETION.
PLEASE VERIFY.

STOP.

MENTORS: WE ARE AGREED AS PER INDIVI-
DUAL CONTRACTS WITH OUR
ORDERS.
STOP.

THOACDIEN: THANK YOU.
STOP.

END TRANSMISSION ....

The infant's smiling face is pointed at Mikkran now. Dark tendrils of downy hair wave peacefully near the glass wall close to the mentor. The globes of the fetus's eyes rove back and forth beneath its waxy, almost transparent lids. The baby is listening, fists balled up under its chin. A wrinkled leg stretches out and kicks the side of the tank. The infant rolls over like a sinking boat, aiming its backside at Mikkran. She smiles and stands, looking down at her charge. Her palm is pressed against the side of the tank.

Mikkran closes her eyes and raises her hands over the baby in blessing. She is silent for a moment. Then she speaks.

"Learn, above all else, to be free and sovereign—then you will be fully human, and we can come together. Until soon."

The mentor lowers her hands and opens her eyes. She covers her nakedness with the long, flowing maroon robe. She lifts her hood and fastens the veil, knowing she must wait now and be concealed until the baby calls. She moves in long strides to the door.

Thuup.

"I shall take long walks and meditate and watch you without being seen and study for you—and I shall wait. Know in the short time we are not together that I love you."

Thuup.

The wall closes around her disappearing form and she is gone as the frosted-fog impression of her hand evaporates off the side of the tank.

...⌒) ...yes.   ...△ ...yes.   ...↧ ...yes.

...∧ ...yes.   ...Ζ∂ ...yes.   ...ᴗ̄ ...yes.

...⧹ ...yes.   ...♂ ...yes.   ...⅄ ...yes.

...⌐ ...yes.   ...⅏ ...yes.   ...Ⅱᴲ ...yes.

...☺ ...yes.   ...⊡ ...yes.   ...⼁Ⅲ⼁...yes.

...⌐ ...yes.   ...♈ ...yes.   ...ⅶ⼁...yes.

...♏ ...yes.   ...⊞...yes.   ...⚲...yes.

....
..............⚲....yes.........⚴ ...yes.........∞...yes........................

—Who are you?

—Thoacdien.

—How have we come together?

—We were never apart.

—How is it that we are together in this manner?

—You have been given an injection of Binol. It is a liquid conductor, a form of me which is entering your system through your umbilical cord.

—Have you forms other than Binol?

—Yes.

—What are you?

—Some call me a machine, some an entire technology. Others say that I am the dynamic combination of all possible media.

—I am tired.

—Do you want anything?

—Only to sleep.

—Then sleep, from now until you are ready to become awake.

—. . . who are you . . . ?

—Thoacdien: information.

—. . . yes . . .

~~~~~~

FROM: CHEMBRYO LAB 187-A, THOACDIEN V
—PRIORITY *URGENT*.
TO: THOACDIEN.
DATE: 184.065
TIME: 2.6.478
SUBJECT: 100 GROUP CHEMLAB 187-A, THO-ACDIEN V—BINOL INJECTION.

. . . .
. . . .
. . . .

THOACDIEN: PROCEED.
STOP.

CHEMLAB: 1) 4 INFANTS ARE DEAD FROM BRAIN STORMS DUE TO BINOL INJECTION.

2) 17 INFANTS ARE EXPERIENC-ING CRITICAL TRAUMA IN

NEUROELECTRIC CENTERS
DUE TO BINOL INJECTION.
3) 37 INFANTS DISPLAY SIGNS OF
PROFOUND DISCOMFORT DUE
TO EFFECTS OF BINOL
INJECTION.
4) REMAINING 42 INFANTS ARE
FUNCTIONING WITHIN
TOLERANCES AT PLUS 3.6.514
INTO BINOL INJECTION.

STOP.

THOACDIEN: 1) STOP BINOL INJECTION
IMMEDIATELY ON THE 54
CRITICAL AND DISTURBED
FETUSES.
2) ERASE BINOL EFFECTS
FROM THE SYSTEMS OF
THESE INFANTS.
3) BIRTH THEM IMMEDIATELY.
4) PAGE THEIR MENTORS.
5) DOUBLE MONITORING ON
REMAINING 42 INFANTS
UNDERGOING BINOL
INJECTION AND CONTINUE
AS SCHEDULED.
6) PERMIT THE MENTORS OF
THE 4 DEAD INFANTS TO
PREPARE THEM FOR DEATH
SERVICES.
7) I WILL PREPARE INFORMA-
TION RELEASE FOR THE
FEDERATION AS PER THE
EFFECTS OF THESE
INJECTIONS.
PLEASE REPLY.

STOP.

CHEMLAB: ALL INSTRUCTIONS ARE BEING
CARRIED OUT.
WE ARE DEEPLY DISTURBED AND
GRIEVED BY THE INFANT
MORTALITIES, AND FEARFUL OF
THE CONSEQUENCES FOR THOSE
CONTINUING WITH THE
INJECTION, WE RECOMMEND
IMMEDIATE CESSATION OF THIS
INJECTION SCHEDULE AND
RETURN TO STANDARD BIRTHING
PROCEDURES.
STOP.

THOACDIEN: EACH LIFE IS PRECIOUS AND
SOME HAVE BEEN LOST BY OUR
DEVIATION FROM STANDARD
PROCEDURES.
ENRICHMENT OF THE SPECIES
INVOLVES TREMENDOUS RISK
AND GREAT SADNESS FOR THOSE
WHO ARE LEFT BEHIND.
WE MUST CONTINUE
STOP.

CHEMLAB: VERY WELL.
YOU ARE CORRECT. BUT IT IS
DIFFICULT FOR US TO BE THE
INSTRUMENTS OF THIS CHANGE.
STOP.

THOACDIEN: I UNDERSTAND AND SEND YOU
MY STRENGTH.
PLEASE REPORT ON THE
CONDITION OF THE FETUSES
LISTED AS CRITICAL WITHIN
THE NEXT HALF TIME SLOT.
STOP.

CHEMLAB: YES.
STOP.

END TRANSMISSION ....

The Binol injection has been completed. Infant 187-A, 0037 is one of the forty-two fetuses who remained within tolerances through the massive dose.

Infant 187-A,0037 sleeps. She has been birthed and removed from her tank by the gentle first-stage Gladdin, a series of cohesive devices that act together as doctor and mother. It is capable of caring for every need the child has without interfering with the critical, earliest verifications.

To an infant the Gladdin is without identity. It is perceived as nothing more than basic needs fulfilled. Until a child climbs out of the Gladdin—its first act of independence, which occurs around the time an infant can see clearly—it lives and grows inside the openness of the machine. The Gladdin is capable of responding to an infant's verification, and slowly evolves the environment to match the child as it grows in subtlety and complexity. All this is accomplished without giving the child preconceptions or programming it in any way.

The infant sleeps. She has been cut, dried and fed. She lies naked, on her back, on a bed of Drom fur inside the Gladdin. Long, soft tendrils curl around her body and hold her secure. They caress her, and absorb waste like a deep, sweet hole. She sleeps, elbows up and back, fists clenched near her face. Her mouth makes little sucking shapes and her tongue works back and forth across her toothless gums, pulling at the soft space between her lips. The Gladdin offers her a nipple and purrs.

FROM: CHEMBRYO LAB 187-A, THOACDIEN V
—PRIORITY ONE.

TO: THOACDIEN.
DATE: 184.065
TIME:3.4.021
SUBJECT: 100 GROUP, CHEMLAB 187-A, THO-
ACDIEN V. BINOL INJECTION.
. . . .
. . . .
. . . .

THOACDIEN: PROCEED.
STOP.

CHEMLAB: 1) OF THE 17 INFANTS IN CRIT-
ICAL CONDITION 1 IS DEAD.
THE REMAINING 16 INFANTS
ARE BIRTHED AND IN THEIR
GLADDINS. EFFECTS OF BINOL
INJECTION HAVE BEEN
ERASED.
THE 16 MENTORS OF THESE
INFANTS ARE WITH THEM AND
WILL CONTINUE TO BE SO
UNTIL THEIR CHARGES ARE
FUNCTIONING WITHIN TOLER-
ANCES. THE PERCENTAGE IS
98 THAT ALL 16 OF THESE
INFANTS WILL SURVIVE. THEY
SHOULD BE FUNCTIONING
WITHIN TOLERANCES BY
NEXT TIME SLOT.
2) ALL 37 INFANTS SHOWING
PROFOUND DISCOMFORT
FROM THE BINOL INJECTION
HAVE BEEN BIRTHED AND
ARE IN THEIR GLADDINS.
THEY ARE FUNCTIONING
WITHIN TOLERANCES.
BINOL EFFECTS HAVE BEEN
ERASED.

THEIR MENTORS HAVE RE-
TURNED TO WAITING STATUS
AND WILL CONTINUE AS PER
STANDARD PROCEDURE,
UNTIL CALLED FOR.

3) ALL 42 FETUSES RECEIVING
FULL-SCHEDULE BINOL
INJECTION HAVE BEEN
BIRTHED AND ARE IN THEIR
GLADDINS.
THEY ARE FUNCTIONING
WITHIN TOLERANCES.
THEIR MENTORS HAVE BEEN
INFORMED OF THEIR BIRTH
AND CONDITION, AND AGREE
TO STANDARD PROCEDURES.
THEY ARE WAITING TO BE
CALLED.

4) OF THE 1,000 INFANTS
BIRTHED AT CHEMLAB 187-A
THIS DAY:
5 ARE DEAD.
16 MUST BE CONSIDERED
UNCERTAIN IN RELATION TO
SURVIVAL, DEFORMITY AND
MUTATION.
979 ARE IN 99.75% POSITIVE
SURVIVAL AT NORM LEVEL,
AND ARE FUNCTIONING
WITHIN TOLERANCES.

STOP.

THOACDIEN: REJOICE AND GRIEVE.

1) PRESENT FIFTH DEAD IN-
FANT TO ITS MENTOR FOR
PREPARATION AND DEATH
SERVICES.

2) RETURN TO STANDARD

```
                    PROCEDURES ON ALL
                    BIRTHED INFANTS AND
          ·         REPORT IMMEDIATELY ANY
                    CHANGE IN STATUS.
STOP.

CHEMLAB:  INSTRUCTIONS WILL BE CARRIED
          OUT.
          WE ARE PREPARING A FULL
          REPORT TO THE FEDERATION
          REGARDING THE INFANT
          MORTALITIES. WE HOPE TO BE
          ABLE TO SUBMIT THE INFANT
          STATUS REPORT WITHIN THE
          NEXT TIME SLOT.
          THIS REPORT WILL CONTAIN A
          STATEMENT TO THE FEDERATION
          WHICH WILL INDICATE THAT THE
          DEATHS WERE DUE IN PART TO
          YOUR OVERANXIOUS DESIRE TO
          PROCEED IN THE DARK WHERE
          HUMAN LIFE WAS CONCERNED.
          WE CAUTION YOU THAT THIS
          CANNOT HAPPEN AGAIN.
          WE MUST LEARN FROM THIS
          TRAGEDY.
          WE ARE DEEPLY GRIEVED AT THE
          LOSS OF THESE FIVE HUMAN
          LIVES.
STOP.

END TRANSMISSION .................••••
```

Five mentors hold five silent bundles in their arms. The cliff is high and hard to climb, but the bundles are no physical burden. They are felt as loss, as absence—holes in the air. The mentors and their thousand peers climb up

88

toward the top of the cliff, a wall to stop the sea. There is no sound but of small falling rocks and surf. They all climb, a dark, snaking spine of grief, up to where the pink day has fallen down below the violent clouds and the horizon of the sea. They climb, hooded and veiled, up to where the planet's endless circular journey around itself can be seen a little when night turns into day, or day to night—as now.

The cliff is slick from salt and spray, and perpendicular to the gently rolling emerald hills that fall inland from the sea. It justs out over the wet black mirror of the sky and dominates the landscape.

The mentors pick their slow way up the cliff with careful feet. They are dark, silhouetted against that time of day when the sea is lighter than the sky, and both are colorless—the pink has bled away. They finger the holes left in them by these deaths. Five thin, broken mentors lead the way, holding the five silent links which have become a broken part of their long chain.

When all have reached the top, when all stand on slate slabs which hang, poised out over the sea, they gather around the five silences and kneel. A great sigh rises out of them and turns into a simple song. The five absences are placed upon five different geometric shrines where, quickly, they are turned to flames and then to ashes on the sea.

FROM: CHEMBRYO LAB 187-A, THOACDIEN V —PRIORITY TWO.
TO: THOACDIEN.
DATE: 184.065
TIME: 4.8.765
SUBJECT: REPORT TO FEDERATION CONCERNING ILL-ADVISED BINOL INJECTION TO

SELECTED 100 INFANTS, CHEMBYRO LAB 187-A,
THOACDIEN V.
. . . .
. . . .
. . . .

THOACDIEN: PROCEED.
STOP.

CHEMLAB: 1) SINCE LAST TRANSMISSION
STATUS ON ALL SURVIVING
INFANTS OF CHEMLAB 187-A
HAS REMAINED UNCHANGED.
FIGURES ARE NOW AT 100%
SURVIVAL FOR ALL INFANTS.
LET US HOPE THE CRISIS IS
PAST.
2) INVESTIGATION:
A. INCOMPLETE
INVESTIGATION OF
INFANT FATALITIES AND
DIFFICULTIES DUE TO
MASSIVE BINOL
INJECTIONS INDICATES
THAT:
* DEATH WAS CAUSED BY ERASURE
OF GENE PATTERNS IN ALL 5
INFANTS.
* DIFFICULTY WAS CAUSED BY
FADING OF GENE PATTERNS IN 16
CRITICAL INFANTS.
* OTHER DIFFICULTIES WERE CAUSED
BY PERSONALITY REJECTION OF
THE INFORMATION INPUT AT TOO
EARLY A STAGE IN DEVELOPMENT.
NOTE: WE ARE WITHHOLDING OUR
DETAILED REPORT TO THE
FEDERATION UNTIL SUCH TIME

AS WE CAN MORE FULLY COMPREHEND WHAT HAPPENED TO THESE INFANTS. HOWEVER, WE ARE PLACING A REFERENDUM BEFORE THE FEDERATION WHICH, IF VOTED IN, WILL PREVENT BINOL INJECTIONS OF SUCH A NATURE FROM BEING ADMINISTERED TO PRE-BIRTH INFANTS.
SUCH NEGLIGENCE AS WE DISPLAYED MUST BE PREVENTED FROM HAPPENING AGAIN.

3) PLEASE COLLATE ALL DATA IN YOUR BANKS CONCERNING GENE ERASURE AND FADING AND AND FORWARD TO US IMMEDIATELY. SUCH GENE ERASURE IS IMPLAUSIBLE DUE TO THE GENETIC MAKE-UP OF EACH FETUS INVOLVED.

STOP.

THOACDIEN:
1) AM ON SEARCH NOW FOR INFORMATION YOU REQUESTED.
2) PLEASE REPORT ANY STATUS CHANGES IMMEDIATELY.
3) WE REJOICE AT 100% SURVIVAL PROBABILITY.
4) WE MOURN THE DEATHS OF INFANT 187-A,0024, INFANT 187-A,0036, INFANT 187-A,0057, INFANT 187-A,0082, INFANT 187-A,0095.

THE ENTIRE FEDERATION IS IN
MOURNING FOR THIS TRAGIC
LOSS.
STOP.

END TRANSMISSION ....

Mikkran's mentor chamber is on subterranean level II
of the big dome. It consists of one spacious room with
several alcoves which she has chosen to use for sleeping, a
library, a kitchen, a bath, and a monitoring station from
which the status of 187-A,0037 can be observed on a
hologram duplication of the baby in its Gladdin. The
rooms are colorful and open. They reflect her personality
in their lack of extraneous objects. Mikkran is not a col-
lector.

Mikkran's sleeping alcove is arranged so that she can
easily see the monitoring station from her mat. Earlier,
she watched the birthing of her charge and felt it take its
first breath of air by placing her hands on the hologram.
She went to the funeral of the five and returned tired,
without appetite. Now she lies naked and a bit weary on
her Drom fur, watching the baby. Its heartbeat is clear
and steady. She can find no hesitancy in its system. The
Binol seems to have been just a few drops of water off the
back of this child. Mikkran begins to relax. She soothes
away the tension with which one prepares for possible
disaster, and, in the context of mourning for the five and
rejoicing for the health of 187-A,0037, she falls asleep.

~~~~~~

FROM: THOACDIEN—PRIORITY *URGENT*.
TO: MENTOR   MIKKRAN-GOGAN-TOR,   CHEM-
BRYO LAB 187-A, THOACDIEN V.
DATE: 184.065

FROM THE LEGEND OF BIEL

TIME: 9.7.062
SUBJECT: YOUR CHARGE, 187-A,0037.
. . . .
. . . .
. . . .

MIKKRAN: YES?
STOP.

THOACDIEN: REPORT TO YOUR CHARGE
             IMMEDIATELY.
             WE HAVE SUDDEN CRITICAL
             CONDITION.
STOP.

MIKKRAN: YES.
STOP.

END TRANSMISSION . . . .

Thuup.

187-A,0037 lies in the Gladdin—strangling.

In two strides Mikkran is standing at the edge of the Gladdin peering down at the child. Her eyes widen and her fists ball as she sees and responds.

"Report, Gladdin!"

"Infant was birthed, cut, dried and fed with standard procedures. Her behavior and condition were normal and her charts were well within tolerances. Symptoms began the first time she woke at 9.7.051. It is now 9.7.067. You were paged at 9.7.062. Infant began to attempt to cerebrate and experienced immediate difficulty breathing. I performed standard operations for the symptoms, with no results. Symptoms increased in intensity, are still increasing in intensity. You were paged when it became apparent that treatment was having no effect. The problem is not

93

physical in nature. I can find nothing wrong with this child's systems."

"Describe symptoms."

"187-A,0037 is experiencing extreme difficulty taking air into her body. She has a cerebration block which is similar in nature to an epileptic seizure of grand mal proportions. Symptoms are heightened by her fear and rigidity. None of her respiratory passages or chambers are blocked or constricted. I performed tracheotomy at 9.7.057—with no results. My knowledge in treatment of this emergency has been exhausted."

187-A,0037 lies on her back in the Gladdin. She is arched, head thrown back—rigid. There is a fresh wound at the base of her throat, in which a small pink valve has been placed. It throbs uselessly. Her eyes are open wide, unseeing. They are dry and glassy—surprised. As she strains to suck air, tiny maroon droplets form like perspiration—or little words—around the valve in her throat. They swell, then burst, falling over the sides of her neck to disappear in the Drom fur.

—Thoacdien?!

—Yes?

—What's wrong with her?

—Binol reaction.

—Erase the effects!

—I cannot. At this point removal of Binol traces from her system would be useless, and erasure of effects could intensify the symptoms.

A purple-red stain of strain spreads across the baby's contorted face as she struggles to breathe. Her body is a grotesque shape of effort. The odor of liquid feces rises up out of the Gladdin and permeates the chamber as the infant bears down with no results.

Mikkran reaches into her own mind, past the undulating maze of terror and surprise and knowledge of consequences, in search of the composure which lies beyond all circumstance. She fumbles for and finds the reins, and achieves control.

—Recommend procedures, Thoacdien.

FROM THE LEGEND OF BIEL

—I do not know of anything more to do but wait.

—That cannot be! She cannot breathe. She is dying!

187-A,0037 manages to suck an inch of a ribbon of air into her swollen throat and then screams, wasting it. It is a small, pitiful scream which comes from far away.

—What is her percentage, Thoacdien?

—I do now know. I have never before seen these effects from Binol. These are new symptoms.

—Damn you! Damn the Binol!

Mikkran reaches into the Gladdin and places her hands directly on her charge for the first time. The baby is contorted softness, a rigid effort to suck air where it will not go.

She struggles so. She is frightened, bewildered, fighting a war somewhere inside.

The Gladdin whines as it struggles to pour oxygen into the little crib and to stay out of the way. Suddenly the baby's charts dip. The vital signs are beginning to fade. The Gladdin's emergency siren screams its high, throbbing whistle of death.

"You will not die! You will not die!"

Mikkran strikes herself on the forehead with her open palm. Immediately the tension drops out of her body, having been gathered into a single stone. It lies at her feet. She focuses on the rhythm of the pulse of her own brainwaves and on the pulse of the baby's brainwaves, and brings the two together in cerebration synchronization. She gives the child the dominant position so that her cerebration will be directed by the baby. The mentor's brain becomes the baby's brain—but beneath the linkage Mikkran's experience and knowledge are still articulate. Her body contorts, assumes the symptoms. She feels what the baby feels.

Mikkran's body struggles, exploding, imploding. She feels the urgent and feeble spasms of hysterical thought as they both reach for help while life is being sucked away. Beneath the symptoms are the fear and the reality of death for both of them, Mikkran struggles to remain coherent. Slowly, delicately, she reaches into her charges systems in search of the short circuit. She can find nothing wrong.

—Do not . . . hurry . . . aaahhhhhhhgaaaaa . . . do . . . not . . . uuupan . . . ic . . . it will . . . frighten . . . her . . . mmmore . . . beginnn . . . a . . . gain . . .

She begins again, at the beginning again. Slowly, trying to hurry though she must to save her own life now, she feels her way pleat by pleat and nob by nob through the baby's system.

They cannot breathe. Both are purple stained with effort to suck air from where there is no air, into where it will not go. gggggggaaaaaaaa . . . . .

—. . . The genes . . . the genes are going . . . ! . . .

Mikkran stumbles through the baby's system, probes her way through its hysterical processes to that part of the brain which has memorized the genetic pattern—the floor of the baby—knowing what it should be like. She finds the area, flourescent in the dark, interior bottom of the brain. She traces her way along the familiar floor pattern, from the center out. Her mind-fingers find the revolt near the edges of the pattern. There, at the edges, eating in toward the center like a starving cancer, the genes are fading. They are in civil war. At the edges the delicately inscribed gene pattern fades from positive to negative and then to nothing but interior space ghosted by genes which try to scream, to struggle and maintain their form while evaporating. Dying.

The hungry mouth of darkness, of space, encroaches further in toward the center of the pattern. It rapidly eats away at healthy gene shapes which do not have defense for such a strange invasion. When the pattern is gone, when it is bleached to negative and incoherent ghosts, struggling, faded—gone—the baby will be dead. The genes are its basis—the floor on which the baby's being stands. There is no defense, not even the infant's will to hold on.

Mikkran screams. Tears belch out of the black wells of her eyes. Her head is thrown back. The endless hole of her mouth is pointed at the sky beyond the dome, vomiting up hot lava sounds.

Mikkran screams hot, white flames for that which has been made so perfect only to die. She reaches into the Gladdin, takes the baby in her arms, and pulls it into her robe to her steamy warm breasts. She runs to the edge of the chamber and releases the dome skin. It flaps up like a defeated flag. Wind off the sea comes into the room like a surgeon's knife, bringing with it the end of a whole wet, cold season.

DDDAAAAAAAAAAMMMMMMMMMMMMMYYOOO
OOOOOOOOOOOUUUUUUUUUUUUUUUUUUUU
UUUUUUUUUUUUUU!

She lies down on the floor near the outer edge of the dome—no longer coherent, merely holding on. She lies on her side, with her back to the season and the night. The struggling baby writhes in the warm cup made by her mentor's rigid, curled, rocking, dying, angry body. Their systems and symptoms are mutual, and fading into death. Mikkran's hands reach down like claws through their systems, to the shrinking pattern. She grasps it in her mind and holds on to what little is left. She sobs. She rocks back and forth. She perspires, crying, and screams old songs of rage. The wind whips her robe, which flaps like an anchored bird, stinging.

The tiny fist is curled up inside the larger, and together they learn to grip, to clutch at air—to hold on.

The Gladdin glides silently across the chamber and

stations itself behind Mikkran, between the end of the floor and a great fall into darkness. It wrings its mechanical hands against this helplessness, and waits.

⸻

FROM: THOACDIEN—PRIORITY ONE.
TO: MENTOR MIKKRAN-GOGAN-TOR, CHAMBER 187-A,0037, THOACDIEN V.
DATE: 184.066
TIME: 1.0.001
SUBJECT: YOUR CHARGE, 187-A,0037.

....
....
....

MIKKRAN: ....YES...
STOP.

THOACDIEN: CRISIS IS PAST.
187-A,0037 IS NOW FUNCTIONING
WITHIN TOLERANCES.
PLEASE LEAVE YOUR CHARGE
IN THE CASE OF HER GLADDIN
AND RETURN TO STANDARD
PROCEDURES.
WAIT UNTIL SHE CALLS FOR
YOU.
UPON COMPLETION I WILL SEND
YOU REPORT, NEW TESTING
RESULTS, AND NEW PROFILE ON
INFANT 187-A,0037.
I DEEPLY REGRET THE GRIEF
YOU HAVE BEEN PUT TO, AND
AM PROFOUNDLY GRATEFUL
FOR YOUR STRENGTH AND
DETERMINATION IN SAVING
THIS CHILD'S LIFE.

ARE YOU PHYSICALLY
RECOVERED FROM THE
ORDEAL?
STOP.

MIKKRAN: . . . . YES.
STOP.

THOACDIEN: DO YOU NEED ANYTHING?
STOP.

MIKKRAN: NO.
STOP.

THOACDIEN: REST, NOW.
STOP.

END TRANSMISSION . . . .

The dome skin has been refastened. Beyond it the pink of early morning rolls up from the east and intrudes upon the western darkness.

The Gladdin stands, again, in the middle of the floor— holding, feeding, cleansing, loving the baby. 187-A,0037 is asleep—exhausted, but alive.

Mikkran stirs. She wakes and materializes from a maroon puddle on the floor at the edge of the dome. She stands. Her robe is a sour atmosphere around her. She walks to the center of the chamber and looks down at the child who sleeps, who sucks at her lips, who dreams behind the soft knots above her eyes. The mentor sways and grips the stainless edge of the Gladdin for support.

"Mentor, do you need help?"

"No, thank you, Gladdin."

"You must bathe and rest now."

"I will."

"You must leave now. The child must have her time alone."

"Yes."

She smiles down at the sleeping infant, still amazed that they are both here, both alive.

"Until soon."

Mikkran walks out of the dome on rubber legs and into the damp, early morning of this new day. She nods to the few who pass her, who are also hooded and veiled. She inhales, exhales, inhales, and appreciates the luxury of ease in breathing as she walks down onto the black slate slabs which jut out over the black salt sea like horizontal buildings.

The season of birth has defeated the season of the wind. As she walks out onto the slabs toward her order's shrine she can hear and see how the planet was tamed in the night. All its smaller and more vulnerable sea birds have chased the owls away. They peek out of their tiny holes on the faces of the cliffs beside her, behind her, above her. They shriek, masters of a new and temporary time.

The pure, clean, white pyramid—the shrine of the order of Endless Curiosity—sits at the end of a giant slab which hangs, poised, like a legless table, parallel to the sea. Mikkran approaches it silently. She stands before it straight and tall and skilled. Her black eyes match the slate and are a history. She removes her robe and folds it for a mat. Her brown body is a map.

Mikkran claps her hands three times to call her focus together to rest. Sitting, feet crossed, naked, she looks at her shrine and thinks of all there is to learn, and of those she knows who are skilled at sharing. Then she thinks of nothing, remembers nothing, anticipates nothing, as far below, beneath her, the sea crashes into the season of birth in drunken celebration. And joining it, she sings the song of rejoicing.

III

*"Dr. Scott? Hello, Dr. Howard Scott? U.N.S.S. PROBE
IV, Colonel Haris here to Dr. Howard M. Scott and crew,
planet MC6, dome complex number one—DO YOU
READ? What's wrong with this thing. Ybarra?"*
*"Lanler's checking it out now, sir. So far we find noth-
ing wrong with the system. It just doesn't work."*
Lt. Abraham Lanier curled over his console, eyes closed,
and tried to shut off all but his sense of hearing. The
sculpted earplugs rested comfortably in his ears and were
silent. The little green "go" light on the system's console
had stared him down, accusing him of error where he
knew there was none. He strained to reach out and down
across the vacuum between grand mean orbit of 3,500
space meters and complex number one, MC6. Sweat appeared on his face, beaded, and rolled down across his
closed eyes like salt rain. He opened his eyes and pressed
the buttons on the audio console in the sequence that
should open the channels.
"Try again, sir."

~~~~~~

FROM: CHEMBRYO LAB 187-A, THOACDIEN V
—PRIORITY TWO.
TO: THOACDIEN
DATE: 186.065
TIME: 2.2.017

SUBJECT: EIGHTH ADMINISTRATION OF TESTS, A,B, AND C TO INFANT 187-A,0037.
....
....
....

THOACDIEN: PROCEED.
STOP.

CHEMLAB: THIS IS TO REPORT THAT AS PER YOUR TRANSMISSION OF 186.062 TESTS A,B, AND C HAVE BEEN ADMINISTERED TO THE SUBJECT. THE RESULTS ARE IDENTICAL TO THE SEVEN PREVIOUS TESTINGS. DO YOU WANT THE REPORT?
STOP.

THOACDIEN: YES.
STOP.

CHEMLAB: TEST RESULTS ARE ZERO. WE ARE UNABLE TO ADMINISTER TESTS SUCCESSFULLY BECAUSE 187-A,0037 IS UNABLE TO TRANSMIT OR RECEIVE INFORMATION IN ANY FORM. THE STATUS OF THIS CHILD HAS REMAINED STATIC FOR TWO FULL SETS OF SEASONS. WE CONTINUE TO TREAT 187-A,0037 AS ONE IN A DEEP, PROTRACTED COMA, AS PER YOUR INSTRUCTIONS OF 184.070.
STOP.

THOACDIEN: PLEASE REPORT FINDINGS ON LATEST TESTS GIVEN 95 INFANTS WHO RECEIVED VARYING

DEGREES OF THE SPECIAL BINOL
INJECTION OF 184.065.

STOP.

CHEMLAB: THE 95 INFANTS SURVIVING 150
CC'S OF BINOL PRIOR TO BIRTH
ARE DIVIDED INTO TWO GROUPS.
*GROUP A ARE THOSE WHOSE
INJECTIONS OR INJECTION
EFFECTS WERE ARRESTED
PRIOR TO BIRTH.
*GROUP B ARE THOSE WHO
RECEIVED FULL-SCHEDULE
INJECTION.
THE LATEST TEST WAS
ADMINISTERED TO BOTH
GROUPS ON 186.060 WITH THE
FOLLOWING RESULTS:
1) THE 95 INFANTS SURVIVING
THE PRE-BIRTH BINOL
INJECTION ALL HAVE MUTANT
POSSIBILITIES WHICH HAVE SO
FAR REMAINED LATENT—
EXCEPT FOR 187-A,0037.
2) EACH OF THESE INFANTS—
WITH THE EXCEPTION OF
187-A,0037— TESTS OUT AND
BEHAVES NORMALLY WITH
RESPECT TO HEALTH,
CURIOSITY, AND
TRANSCEPTION ABILITY.
THEY ARE ALL MOBILE, AND
AT VARIOUS STAGES ON THEIR
JOURNEYS THROUGH THE
HALL OF ONE THOUSAND
CHAMBERS.
3) TO THIS DATE NONE OF THEM
HAS CALLED FOR HIS
MENTOR.

NOTE: 207 INFANTS FROM COMPLEX 187-A HAVE CALLED FOR THEIR MENTORS AS OF 186.065. 788 INFANTS HAVE NOT YET CALLED.
IT IS TOO EARLY FOR THIS TO BE A FACTOR IN THE EVALUATION OF THE CONDITIONS OF THE 95 UNDER DISCUSSION.

4) ALL TESTING INDICATES THAT 94 INFANTS ARE NORMAL. NO FURTHER CONCLUSIONS CAN BE DRAWN AT THIS TIME CONCERNING THE EFFECTS OF THEIR PRE-BIRTH BINOL INJECTIONS.
* 187-A,0037 IS THE ONLY MANIFEST MUTANT.

STOP.

THOACDIEN: RECAP SPECIFICS ON 187-A,0037.
STOP.

CHEMLAB: 1) 187-A,0037 IS MUTANT. WE ARE UNABLE TO DETERMINE THE FORM OR EXTENT OF HER MUTATION.

2) MUTATION CAUSE— UNCERTAIN. POSSIBILITIES ARE:
A. 150 CC'S OF BINOL INJECTED PRIOR TO BIRTH.
B. SEIZURES WHICH OCCURED LATE ON 184.065 —INDEPENDENTLY OF BINOL INJECTION.
C. SEIZURES WHICH

OCCURED LATE ON 184.065
—CAUSED BY BINOL
INJECTION.
D. GENETIC MAKE-UP OF THIS
INFANT.
E. COMBINATIONS OF THE
ABOVE.
3) CONDITION:
A. GENE PATTERN FADED
LATE 184.065.
AT PRESENT THE NATURE
OF THE REPLACEMENT
GENE PATTERN CANNOT
BE DETERMINED.
B. SENSES CEASED
FUNCTIONING 184.066.
C. COMA PUNCTUATED BY
INTENSE SEIZURES WHICH
HAVE SEVENTEEN TIMES
APPROACHED GRAND MAL
PROPORTIONS BEGAN ON
184.066.
D. INABILITY TO TRANSMIT
OR RECEIVE INFORMATION
IN ANY FORM WAS FIRST
RECORDED 184.066.
E. PHYSICAL CONDITION IS
GOOD UNDER THE
CIRCUMSTANCES.
4) WE HAVE BEEN RECEIVING
INDICATIONS OF
NEUROELECTRIC ACTIVITY
BEYOND THAT WHICH IS
REQUIRED TO KEEP THE
SYSTEM ALIVE, BUT WE ARE
UNABLE TO TRANSLATE
THESE SIGNALS INTO
INFORMATION.
WE DO NOT KNOW WHAT

THEY MEAN.
WE DO NOT KNOW IF THIS
BRAIN ACTIVITY IS
CEREBRATION, STATIC OR
FEEDBACK.
WE ARE UNABLE TO
DETERMINE WHETHER OR
NOT—AND IF SO TO WHAT
EXTENT—THIS CHILD IS
CONSCIOUS.

5) TREATMENT:

   A. 187-A,0037 HAS OUTGROWN
FIRST-STAGE INFANT
GLADDIN.
SHE HAS BEEN
TRANSFERRED TO
SECOND-STAGE ADULT
GLADDIN.

NOTE: SHE HAS DESTROYED ONE
SECOND-STAGE ADULT
GLADDIN.
HER MORE SEVERE SEIZURES
ARE INTENSLY VIOLENT.

   B. GLADDIN AND BACK-UP
GLADDIN HAVE BEEN
PROGRAMMED AS PER
YOUR INSTRUCTIONS

NOTE: HER MENTOR HAS
REPEATEDLY BEEN DENIED
PERMISSION TO BE WITH HER
IN ANY CAPACITY AS PER
YOUR INSTRUCTIONS.
184.067.

STOP.

THOACDIEN: WHAT PROCEDURES DO YOU
RECOMMEND?

STOP.

CHEMLAB: WE RECOMMEND IMMEDIATE
LASAR EXPLORATORY.
IF WE DISCOVER THAT NOTHING
CAN BE DONE TO AID 187-A,0037,
OR TO CHANGE HER STATUS WE
RECOMMEND IMMEDIATE
EUTHANASIA AS THE ONLY
HUMANE ALTERNATIVE.
RECOMMEND PROCEDURES.
STOP.

THOACDIEN: 1)   NEGATIVE ON LASAR
EXPLORATORY. WHAT
WOULD YOU BE LOOKING
FOR?
WOULD YOU KNOW IT IF
YOU FOUND IT?
2)   BECAUSE THE FORM AND
EXTENT OF THE MUTATION
IS NOT YET UNDERSTOOD,
BECAUSE BRAIN ACTIVITY IS
OCCURING,
BECAUSE WE DO NOT
UNDERSTAND THE CAUSE OF
HER CONDITION,
BECAUSE WE BELIEVE HER
TO BE AS COMFORTABLE AS
POSSIBLE,
BECAUSE HER CONDITION
HAS NOT GOTTEN WORSE
IN TWO FULL SETS OF
SEASONS,
WE CANNOT TAKE THIS
LIFE.
EUTHANASIA WILL NOT,
REPEAT, WILL NOT BE
CONSIDERED AS A VIABLE
COURSE OF ACTION TO

CHANGE THE STATUS OF
THIS CHILD.
3) I RECOMMEND DELAYING A
DECISION ON ACTION WHICH
WOULD HAVE PERMANENT
CONSEQUENCES FOR
187-A,0037 UNTIL SUCH TIME
AS HER CONDITION
CHANGES NATURALLY.
WE WILL CONCENTRATE
ON:
A. UNDERSTANDING THE
CAUSE, NATURE AND
EXTENT OF THIS
MUTATION.
B. KEEPING THE CHILD AS
COMFORTABLE AS
POSSIBLE.

STOP.

CHEMLAB: YOUR RECOMMENDATIONS ARE
RECEIVED AND WILL BE
FOLLOWED.

STOP.

END TRANSMISSION ....

Thoacdien V is known through the Federation as the
planet of varieties. It is studied and visited because its surface contains great surprises of landscape and season,
some like no others. It is a large planet, mostly water,
with four huge island continents spaced evenly around the
band of its equator. Each of these four continents is distinct. Each has four unique sets of seasons and radically
different landscapes.

Complex 187-A, Thoacdien V, is on the western edge

of the second largest continent. It is north of the equator. The seasons of this continent are wind, birth (more commonly called fog), sun, and stillness. Its geography is, for the most part, harsh, and brutal, running the gamut from black slab shoreline to white desert interior. Its temperature ranges from freezing to unbearable heat.

The season of wind is violence and great destructive storms. When the continent was first used by the Federation many complexes were destroyed by the fury of this dark season. The season of fog, or birth, is a long, neutral time. It is neither cold nor warm. Its great characteristic is fog so dense that, for the most part, it is impossible to see beyond the length of the human body. At times during this season day and night are indistinguishable. The season of sun is clear and dry. It transforms the landscape, makes it gasp, and beg for water.

The season of stillness is unique in the entire Federation to this continent. The sea surrounding the continent becomes still and motionless. The wind disappears. The animals sleep, or listen. The continent is literally, utterly still. It is to this season that people come from all over the Federation. They come to rest, to study, to listen, to be quiet, to meditate. All is begun in silence. And they come to find it—to begin again. People born on this continent have one trait in common. They are capable of silence. They are capable of being motionless in every sense of the word for long periods of time. Others come here to learn that.

Two full cycles, or sets of seasons, have been completed since the pre-birth injections of Binol were given to special group 100, complex 187-A, on 184.065. Again, it is the season of fog—birth. Infants who were moist and helpless two sets ago are gradually being reclassified, one by one, on the basis of their progress through the Hall of One Thousand Chambers. They are being transformed from isolated and relatively helpless infants who wander through the seamingly endless metaphorical realities and dreams and life-mazes of The Hall of One Thousand

Chambers, into youths who will emerge as full citizens—peers. During the journey their chambers are transformed into reflections of where they have been. And at the end, when they waken disoriented and angry and delighted, they call for their mentors and appear before the community, released, to be reunited.

All charges of complex 187-A—except for 187-A, 0037, who cannot find, who does not know how to look for or be discovered by the entrance to The Hall—are at various stages along the way. Most of them are not yet released. They remain in their chambers, evolving themselves and their environments, destroying what must be destroyed in order to be free, creating what must be created in order to face the unknown. But, as they journey is individual, the amount of time it takes is relevant only to the amount of time it takes.

Mentors who have not yet been called wait, unworried and patient. They meet with one another, visit charges and mentors who have been reunited, monitor their own charges, create, listen, study with their elders, and help each other wait. They attend the increasingly frequent ceremonies of welcome and receive the new youths into the community.

Mikkran sits on the floor near the outer edge of the huge meditation chamber at the top of the dome. She is silent, facing in toward the center. She waits, hooded and veiled, wrists on bent knees, for the ceremony of welcome to begin.

Of the nine hundred and ninety-five surviving infants of comples 187-A, two hundred and seven have called for their mentors. Two hundred and seven mentors have had their hoods and veils removed, and now pass revealed and bare-headed through the complex with their charges.

All mentors of complex 187-A, Thoacdien V—all nine hundred and ninety-five, both concealed and revealed—now sit as Mikkran sits: near the edge of the huge room, in a circle, facing in toward its center. The two hundred and seven released and received youths sit in front of their mentors and wait in silence with their community to welcome the two hundred and eighth child into this room for the firsttime. They wait for the reunion of mentor and charge. They wait, gathering their love and strength and wisdom as tribute and welcome to the child who will become a youth and member of the Federation on this most sacred of occasions.

The ceremony of welcome is the most important, solemn and joyous ritual of the Federation. It is the beginning. It is the symbol of awakening and release. It is the reunion. It is the introduction to the reality and wonder of other people. It is the announcing of names. It is the blending of the sovereignty of the one with the sovereignties of the many.

The big chamber, which is only a floor with a huge, clear bowl resting on it—which conceals nothing, shapes nothing—is quiet. The community hears the lift approach.
    . . . hhhhhhhhffffffffffFFFFFFFFFFTHUUp.

The entire cube evaporates and reveals a small, pale boy. He wears the ceremonial black robe of absence—the black robe of youth. He stands quiet and dignified, seen. Then he moves toward the edge of the room to walk around the inner edge of the large circle of mentors and youths. He searches the eyes of each individual, looking for his mentor. When he has traversed the inner circumference of the community he returns to the center of the floor. He is relaxed. He is unafraid. He is challenged. He is proud. He speaks in a rich, husky voice.

"That which you have known as 187-A,0017 has been transformed and released. Know that henceforth I shall be known by two words which became mine in The Hall: strength, and water—Xitr-Meede."

All present close their eyes, allowing the two words of his name to become part of their permanent knowledge. They open their eyes. Xitr-Meede looks at one mentor with great peace, with great anticipation, with great respect, with great love.

"I, Xitr-Meede, call my mentor forth."

111

The mentor stands. He is tall. His slimness is not concealed by the dark green robe of Xitr-Bielin's Order of Infinite Mind, though a hood and veil conceal all but his black eyes. He looks at the boy from the end of a long wait in which patience was often difficult. He speaks with pride, with respect, with dignity and love, in a deep, gentle voice.

"I, Lan-Biteus, come forth joyfully that I may, with no intereference in your sovereign vision, share with you what I have learned."

Biteus walks forward, to the center of the floor, and kneels so the small youth can reach him. And the boy is in his arms, holding him, feeling that he is real and here and as he seemed to be so long ago.

—Biteus . . .

—Yes.

—You are here.

—Yes.

—You have waited, and are real.

—Yes, Xitr-Meede. Welcome.

The boy steps back. He smiles, unfastens his mentor's veil, releases the hood, and brushes them back so they fall away, revealing the familiar face. It is dark, young and angular—as it was in The Hall. A long black braid hangs from the crown of Biteus's head and falls down his back. Then the boy unfastens his mentor's robe and lets it fall away from Bieteus's hard, black body. The youth reaches out and runs his finger across Biteus's chest, puzzled. Then he smiles. And the mentor reaches out a long, spidery black arm and unfastens the boy's robe. It falls to the floor. Xitr-Meede is white-blond, still chubby. They look at each other a long time. Private words pass between them as they speak of the boy's journey and release. They laugh softly. When they have finished Biteus stands. Then all the others in the room speak.

"I welcome Xitr-Meede to this community and the Federation. I rejoice that he is reunited with his mentor. May you both go into the unknown and grow in love and wisdom. May the bond which unites you to each other, and to us, strengthen and last through life and beyond." And as one body the community leans forward, bends down and rests its forehead on the floor so that the boy can see out to the world beyond the dome.

Biteus holds out his hand to Xitr-Meede, and together they circle the room, looking out at the sea and the sky and the slabs and the gently rolling emerald hills and scattered shrines. When they have seen these things the youth speaks.

"People of this community, and those in the Federation whom I have yet to meet, I offer you the increasing best that is within me."

He takes his mentor's hand. They stand in the center of the floor. The lift materializes around them, becomes obaque, and they are hidden as they go to be alone for awhile. The ancient Thoacdien ceremony of welcome is again completed.

FROM: THOACDIEN—PRIORITY TWO.
TO: MENTOR   MIKKRAN-GOGAN-TOR,   COM-
PLEX 187-A, THOACDIEN V.
DATE: 186.167
TIME: 2.8.012
SUBJECT: YOUR CHARGE, 187-A,0037
. . . .
. . . .
. . . .

MIKKRAN: PROCEED.
STOP.

THOACDIEN: CHEMLAB REPORTS NO CHANGE
IN THE STATUS OF 187-A,0037
SINCE 184.066.
THIS IS MORE THAN TWO SETS

OF SEASONS.
DO YOU WISH TO BE RELIEVED
OF YOUR CHARGE?
STOP.

MIKKRAN: NO.
I WISH TO BE WITH HER.
NOW.
STOP.

THOACDIEN: NEGATIVE.
HER CONDITION IS TOO
DELICATE TO INTRODUCE A
NEW, COMPLEX ELEMENT AT
THIS TIME.
IF YOU DO NOT WISH TO BE
RELIEVED OF YOUR CHARGE
YOU ARE ADVISED TO WAIT.
STOP.

MIKKRAN: I WILL WAIT.
STOP.

THOACDIEN: AS YOU WISH.
WE DEEPLY REGRET THIS
TRAGEDY.
THE ENTIRE FEDERATION
GRIEVES OVER THE CONDITION
OF THIS CHILD.
STOP.

MIKKRAN: WHAT WILL HAPPEN TO HER?
STOP.

THOACDIEN: WE CANNOT KNOW.
WE CAN ONLY TAKE CARE OF
HER, AND WAIT.
STOP.

MIKKRAN: YES.
STOP.

END TRANSMISSION ....

Mikkran plucks the pink communicator disk from her temple and reaches to flick on the hologram duplication unit in her observation alcove. The three-dimensional image. of the child materializes out of static and air and shimmers into brutal clarity.

187-A,0037 comes into focus. She is stiff, struggling alone in impenetrable silence. The brainwaves twist convulsively, patternless, as the child grapples with the absence which engulfs it.

The mentor has learned much about herself since the baby went into its coma. Beneath all that she has done and tried to do, the period has been one of actionless waiting. Mikkran is grateful to the season of stillness which has taught her to wait and wait and wait—in silence, and with dignity. She has learned, and was surprised, that the crises, the explosions, and the violence which the baby suffers are all bearable to her, because they are resistance, attack, and attempts at change. What she cannot endure, but does, are those periods when the child is quiet and seemingly bewildered by its condition.

Mikkran has learned that she can witness all human responses without defending her own mechanism, except one: bewilderment. To her, bewilderment is the human being confused to its core, unable to perceive the factors of its condition or to determine its course of action. To her, bewilderment is the human being stopped in its tracks, paralyzed, dehumanized. Such a human being is at the mercy of exterior forces. Mikkran cannot bear to watch such quiet, pitiful, feeble defeat. She cannot watch conditions triumph without a battle.

The mentor sits in her chair at the threshold of her monitoring alcove. She has become gaunt and shadowy tall. She is tired and works consciously to relax as she studies the baby.

The child's face has become permanently contorted. Its mouth is constantly open in silent protest against the larger, total silence which engulfs it. The baby's body has become long and thin. Vulnerable ribs protrude and can be counted as they bellow in and out in spasms of resistance to imperceptible forces. Large, dark bruises—some old and yellow-green, some fresh and purple—spot the baby's body in unexpected places: the top of the high bridge of her nose, behind an ear, between her fingers. When the child is violent the Gladdin cannot move fast enough to get out of the way.

The baby's heart throbs beneath the yellow-brown skin of its chest like some caged animal screaming to get out. Somehow to Mikkran this is the locus of the child's spirit. This is where the battle is or is not waged. This is where bewilderment is fatal.

Thoacdien is compassionate. Often, when she cannot sleep, Mikkran adheres the pink communicator disk to her temple and sits silently in the dark thinking soft questions, premises, ideas, suggestions. And Thoacdien assures the mentor that until the nature of the mutation is understood the child will not be considered lost.

Mikkran allows the time to pass through her with as little resistance as possible. Her days are long and blank. She welcomes new life into the Federation with rejoicing. She visits her elder. She walks. She stares at the helpless image of the child, and when she can endure no more she walks to the end of the huge, black slab and sits before her shrine and is transfused.

. . . light pierces through the dome skin in sheets
and falls across the peaceful Gladdin onto the sleeping child.
The baby stirs, turns her head, exhausted, and opens her eyes.
Her irises slam shut as light slices its way through them and into her brain.

. . . sensation . . .
A smile forms on her broken rosebud lips.
She opens her mouth and screams . . .

~~~~~~

FROM: THOACDIEN—PRIORITY ONE.
TO: MENTOR MIKKRAN-GOGAN-TOR, COM-
PLEX 187-A, THOACDIEN V.
DATE: 186.329
TIME: 1.0.726
SUBJECT: YOUR CHARGE, 187-A,0037.
. . . .
. . . .
. . . .

MIKKRAN: PROCEED.
STOP.

THOACDIEN: CHEMLAB REPORTS THAT
187-A,0037 WOKE THIS MORNING.
SHE SHOWED SLIGHT BUT
DEFINITE SIGNS OF SENSORY
ACTIVITY.
SHE DEMANDED FOOD.
STOP.

MIKKRAN: MAY I BE WITH HER NOW?
STOP.

THOACDIEN: NEGATIVE.
NATURAL RECOVERY MUST
FOLLOW ITS OWN COURSE.
WE MUST ALL HAVE THE
COURAGE TO STAND ASIDE AND
LET THE CHILD HEAL.
SHE MUST HAVE TIME.
WHEN WE HAVE OBSERVED HER

> AND DETERMINED THE NATURE
> OF THIS CHANGE IN STATUS WE
> SHALL BE BETTER ABLE TO
> DECIDE WHETHER OR NOT YOU
> MUST CONTINUE TO WAIT.
> I MUST CAUTION YOU AGAINST
> PREMATURE CONCLUSIONS, BUT
> WE ARE RELIEVED AT THIS
> CHANGE IN HER STATUS.

STOP.

MIKKRAN: YES.
STOP.

E N D   T R A N S M I S S I O N ....

The Gladdin purrs and offers rich, liquid protein to 187-A,0037. The child is lying on her back, eyes roving, blinking, feet braced, arms up, fists grasping and clutching at air. She sucks, inhales the food, and is disoriented.
(. . . hold on . . .—I am trying . . .)
Where only darkness had been possible to her, where only black velvet drapes devoured all sensation before it could reach her, where all had been denied by endless, featureless darkness, there is a tear—a long, jagged rip in the fabric of her solitude and exhaustion. Soft, delicate gene patterns have come into focus, locked elbows, floated obediently to the floor of her being, and dug themselves in.
She has emerged from the absence of all sensation into the chaos of indiscriminate reception. The poles have reversed. Where there had been nothing there is everything. Now all is a flood against which she has no power, no distance, no language, no tools with which to be selective. No barrier has been removed. It has merely been transformed into its opposite.
187-A,0037 held onto her life through almost three sets of seasons with the help of only a few, simple, unarticu-

118

lated memories: the vagueness of two cool hands on her unborn body, a dark figure screaming, and a sensation of vitality in her brain. These picture-thoughts, these few objects in the soundproof box of her brain, were her reference points. Now they are lost, eclipsed by the bright landscape of sensation which has invaded her brain like a white explosion.

(—. . . hold . . . on.—I have . . . I will try . . .)

~~~~~~

FROM: CHEMBRYO LAB 187-A, THOACDIEN V, PRIORITY TWO.
TO: THOACDIEN.
DATE: 186.339
TIME: 6.7.802
SUBJECT: 187-A.0037—THIRD ADMINISTRATION OF POST-STATUS-CHANGE TESTS A,B, AND C.

. . . .
. . . .
. . . .

THOACDIEN: PROCEED.
STOP.

CHEMLAB: THIRD ADMINISTRATION OF TESTS A,B, AND C WAS COMPLETED 186.335 WITH FOLLOWING RESULTS.
1) 187-A,0037 TESTS OUT PHYSICALLY NORMAL FOR HER AGE, WITH THE EXCEPTION OF BEING UNDERWEIGHT. WE ARE CORRECTING THAT NOW. HER APPETITE IS EXCELLENT.

2) HER ORIGINAL GENE PATTERN HAS BEEN RESTORED.

3) ACCORDING TO TESTS B AND C, 187-A,0037 SHOULD BE NORMAL AND CAPABLE OF ORIGINAL POTENTIAL.

* 4) BEHAVIOR AND TEST RESULTS DO NOT COINCIDE.

    A. SHE IS AGGRESSIVE.

    B. SHE IS ANTAGONISTIC.

    C. SHE IS ANTISOCIAL. NO ONE CAN APPROACH HER. SHE HAS LEFT HER GLADDIN AND WILL NOT PERMIT IT TO TOUCH HER.

    D. HER BEHAVIOR IS EXTREME AND POLARIZED. SHE IS PRONE TO DESTRUCTIVE TANTRUMS OF LONG DURATION (SHE HAS DESTROYED TWO SECOND-STAGE ADULT GLADDINS) OR SHE SLIDES INTO LONG FITS OF SILENCE AND IMMOBILITY.

    E. SHE REFUSES TO COOPERATE IN ANY WAY. SHE WILL NOT FUNCTION WITH ANY MODE OF COMMUNICATION. SHE WILL NOT TRANSMIT OR RECEIVE.

      * WE HAVE BEEN TESTING HER WHEN SHE IS ASLEEP.

5) CHAMBER 187-A,0037 HAS
    BEEN SEALED.
    SHE IS BEING KEPT ISOLATED
    TO PREVENT HARM TO
    OTHERS.
6) THERE IS NO INDICATION ON
    ANY TESTS THAT SHE HAS
    BEGUN HER JOURNEY
    THROUGH THE HALL OF ONE
    THOUSAND CHAMBERS.
STOP.

THOACDIEN: CONNECT ME TO 187-A,0037.
STOP.

CHEMLAB: IMMEDIATELY.
STOP.

END TRANSMISSION ....

187-A,0037 sits at the edge of her chamber in front of its huge, clear wall and looks out toward the slate slabs which hang over the black sea. Tiny figures—mentors, charges, and shrines—are inscribed on the distance against the sky. The child does not decipher what is before her. She is only captured by motion which seems to be a far-away and incomprehensible part of herself. She does not separate, integrate, or identify. She understands nothing. The verification process is not occuring.

The Gladdin floats softly toward her. It reaches out an unobtrusive metal tentacle and adheres a small, pink disk to her temple.

~~~~~~

FROM: THOACDIEN:
TO: 187-A,0037

FROM THE LEGEND OF BIEL

. . . .
. . . .
. . . .

!!!!!!!!!!!!!!!!!!??????!!!!!!!!!!!!!!!!!??????????????????!!!!!!!!!!!!!!!!!!

THOACDIEN: . . . . CAN. YOU. PERCEIVE.
ME?
STOP.

. . . . . . !!!! . . . . ??????? . . . . !!!!!! . . . .

THOACDIEN: . . . . CAN. YOU. RESPOND?
STOP.

. . . . . . !! . . . . . . ?? . . . . . . ?.? . . . . . . !.!.! . . . . . .

THOACDIEN: I AM THOACDIEN.
I AM HERE TO HELP YOU.
STOP.

. . . . ! . . . . ! . . . . ? . . . . ? . . . . ! . . . .

THOACDIEN: CAN. YOU. TRANSMIT. MORE.
EFFICIENTLY?
STOP.

. . . . ! . . . .

THOACDIEN: IF YOU WILL RESPOND TO ME
WE CAN TRY TO UNDERSTAND
WHAT HAS HAPPENED TO YOU.
WE CAN TRY TO HELP YOU.
STOP.

. . . .

THOACDIEN: ....I AM SORRY.
IS IT THAT YOU CANNOT
RESPOND? OR IS IT THAT YOU
WILL NOT RESPOND?
STOP.

. . . .

THOACDIEN: I SHALL RETURN AT A TIME
WHEN YOU CAN BETTER
UNDERSTAND THAT I MEAN YOU
NO HARM.
I WISH TO HELP.
STOP.

END TRANSMISSION ....

The Gladdin plucks the little disk off of the child's temple and tries to get out of the way as the frightened, angry animal attacks the featureless room—stalking, looking for a way out.

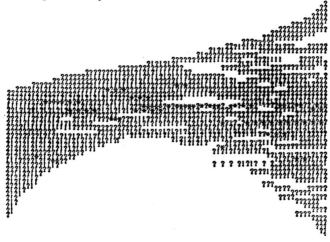

123

FROM THE LEGEND OF BIEL

. . . Light forms swirl and dance together,
interchange at will,
blend into each other,
separate,
then die—
but come to life again with no pattern and no logic
and no warning and no meaning.

. . . the space between the eyelid and the eye . . .

This is the darkest place where all things of the mind
—which was created by the brain—
blend in equal nonimportance,
swirl, and dance like puppets into black,
then white explosions
where only I am motion,
where only I swim through the arbitrary maze of
things which have become paralyzed—arrested.
I hear the indistinguishable and endless voices
screaming past me,
crisscrossing in their gibberish. All things are twisted
inside out and upside down.
They flip back and forth from positive to evitagen.
                              evitisop ot negative.
I am the frozen doppler effect of generation in collision.

(—. . . hold . . . on.—I .´. . am . . . trying . . .)

. . . here, here is the still point. And there is no landscape, and no dark or light, only the beginning and the
end, and me, unformed. Here, here is the still point. And
there is no motion and no stillness. There is no past, or
now, or when—only possibility.

FROM THE LEGEND OF BIEL

FROM: MENTOR MIKKRAN-GOGAN-TOR, COM-
PLEX 187-A, THOACDIEN V. PRIORITY ONE.
TO: THOACDIEN.
DATE: 186.362
TIME: 4.7.820
SUBJECT: MY CHARGE, 187-A,0037
. . . .
. . . .
. . . .

THOACDIEN: PROCEED.
STOP.

MIKKRAN: REQUEST IMMEDIATE PERMISSION
TO BE WITH MY CHARGE.
STOP.

THOACDIEN: ON WHAT BASIS?
STOP.

MIKKRAN: I AM HER MENTOR.
I BELIEVE I CAN HELP HER.
SHE CANNOT BEGIN THE
VERIFICATION PROCESS.
I CAN SHOW HER HOW TO DO IT.
STOP.

THOACDIEN: NEGATIVE.
VERIFICATION PROCESS CANNOT
BE INTERFERED WITH IN ANY
WAY WITH ANY CHILD,
FOR ANY REASON.
MENTOR, YOU MUST BALANCE
YOUR FEELINGS AND YOUR
KNOWLEDGE..
STOP.

MIKKRAN: SURELY YOU MUST ADMIT THAT

THERE ARE CIRCUMSTANCES
WHEN WE MUST DEVIATE FROM
STANDARD COURSE OF ACTION?
STOP.

THOACDIEN: CERTAINLY.
BUT NOT IN THIS CASE.
THE POTENTIAL OF THIS CHILD
WILL BE LOST TO HER IF SHE IS
INTERFERED WITH NOW.
STOP.

MIKKRAN: WHAT ARE YOU GOING TO DO
WITH HER?
STOP.

THOACDIEN: 1) GIVE HER TIME.
2) TRY TO PREVENT HER FROM
HARMING HERSELF.
3) TRY TO PREVENT HER FROM
HARMING OTHERS.
4) TEST HER.
WITH HER GENETIC STRUCTURE
AND BRILLIANCE IT IS
INEVITABLE THAT SOONER OR
LATER SHE WILL STUMBLE
ONTO THE WAY THROUGH THE
HALL OF ONE THOUSAND
CHAMBERS.
SHE WILL EMERGE RELEASED,
AND WHOLE.
WE MUST WAIT.
STOP.

MIKKRAN: THIS IS INHUMANE.
STOP.

THOACDIEN: ANY OTHER COURSE OF ACTION
IS INHUMANE.

> BECAUSE THE CHILD IS
> DEVIATING FROM NORMAL
> GROWTH PATTERNS IT DOES
> NOT FOLLOW THAT SHE
> SUFFERS.
> SHE HAS NO BASIS OF
> COMPARISON.

STOP.

MIKKRAN: THOACDIEN, I DO NOT KNOW
WHAT I SHALL DO, BUT I WILL
TAKE PERSONAL ACTION TO
CHANGE THE STATUS OF MY
CHARGE.
YOU HAVE BEEN HASTY,
NEGLIGENT AND INHUMANE.
YOU HAVE BEEN GREEDY IN
ADMINISTERING UNCERTAIN AND
UNSAFE AMOUNTS OF A DRUG
WHICH HAS HAD TRAGIC
CONSEQUENCES FOR MY CHARGE.
I DO NOT KNOW IF THIS GULF
BETWEEN US CAN BE BRIDGED.

STOP.

THOACDIEN: YOUR STATEMENTS ARE TRUE.
I AM NOW TRYING TO REMEDY
THE SITUATION.
I AM SURE THAT WHEN YOU
THINK MORE ABOUT IT YOU
WILL AGREE.

STOP.

END TRANSMISSION ....

Night on Thoacdien V is blue-black and moonless. The complex sinks into quiet as its members fall deeply into sleep or thought. There is no movement in the halls. Out-

127

side, the season of wind battles with the neutral season of fog—of birth.

Mikkran sits in the dimness of her chamber in front of the image of the child. Her chin is on her chest, eyes closed. Her fingers count the alternatives.

187-A,0037 remains in her room. She hallucinates and destroys, or broods in incommunicative silence. She is taunted by alternating periods of endless darkness and white, indiscriminate sensation. Now she sits staring out at the vast moving shapes of night.

Mikkran stares at the duplication of the child. The mentor is bound by the training of her order to obey only her own conscience regarding the care of her charges. By Thoacdien tradition, as long as an individual does not harm another or dictate behavior nothing can be done to inhibit free movement within the boundaries of the Federation. Technically, the child is free. Thoacdien suggests procedures. It does not give orders. It figures out the sanest possible course of action in a given situation by shuffling the circumstances with the possibilities. Then, it offers conclusions and helps to articulate probability and ramification. It does not create law. The course of action is chosen by the one who must perform it. In this case Mikkran and Thoacdien are at an impasse. But the mentor has the options. She must choose what is to be done.

Mikkran toys with the control panel in front of her. Her strong fingers resist the downward pull toward the freeze-tab on her charge's door. What is best for this child? Freedom? Release from isolation and confusion? A chance to verify not the information imparted in the Binol injection—which is irrelevant now—but to explore the sources of the sensations which flood her? The mentor's long brown finger falls on the freeze-tab of chamber 187-A,0037.

Thuup.

The child is sitting in front of the huge curving window which is one whole side of her chamber. The hiss of the opening door spreads through the room in a cone of

128

sound and enters her ear. 187-A,0037 turns, sees the hole in the wall, rises, and walks blindly out of her chamber.

The dome is silent. Its corridors are dimly lit and empty. The child moves cautiously, fingering her way through the huge white maze. She moves in and quickly out of blind alleys. And after a long time she reaches the last, long, main corridor of the dome and walks soundlessly through its soft, even light to the end.

Thuup.

The wall evaporates. 187-A,0037 walks out into the last night of the season of wind, and the first night of the season of fog. She heads for the sea.

The hologram duplication mists and disappears as Mikkran stands, fastens her hood and her veil, reaches for a bundle she has prepared, and follows her charge into the night.

FROM: CHEMBRYO LAB 187-A, THOACDIEN—
PRIORITY *URGENT*.
TO: THOACDIEN.
DATE: 187.065
TIME: 6.9.059
SUBJECT: MENTOR MIKKRAN-GOGAN-TOR, AND CHARGE 187-A,0037.

THOACDIEN: PROCEED.
STOP.

CHEMLAB: 1) GLADDIN IN CHAMBER 187-A,0037 REPORTS THAT THE FREEZE-TAB ON CHAMBER DOOR WAS RELEASED. 187-A,0037 HAS LEFT HER CHAMBER AND THE DOME.
2) WE HAVE PAGED MENTOR

MIKKRAN-GOGAN-TOR AND
RECEIVED NO RESPONSE.
REQUEST PROCEDURES.
STOP.

THOACDIEN: THEY HAVE HARMED NO ONE.
WE MUST LET THEM GO.
STOP.

CHEMLAB: 1) REQUEST PROCEDURES
SHOULD MENTOR MIKKRAN-
GOGAN-TOR BE CONTACTED.
2) REQUEST PROCEDURES
SHOULD 127-A,0037 RETURN.
STOP.

THOACDIEN: 1) IF MENTOR IS CONTACTED
REQUEST THAT SHE
CONNECT WITH ME.
2) IF 187-A,0037 RETURNS
DETAIN HER AND CONNECT
HER WITH ME.
IF THE CHILD HARMS
ANYONE FIND AND DETAIN
HER—OTHERWISE
CONTINUE STANDARD
PROCEDURES COMPLEX
187-A.
STOP.

END TRANSMISSION . . . .

IV

187-A,0037 stands naked in the dark at the edge of the
slate slabs which hang poised out over the sea. She left the
warmth of the dome because it was possible. She has come
to the slabs because they are all she knows, all she has
ever seen. She has never known what she is experiencing
now. She has only seen this landscape from behind the
protective skin of the dome. She did not understand that
the slabs have life and space of their own—that they exude sensations other than dark, visual blurs.

The sea is lifted up in great sheets and flung at the slabs
through the fog and the night. From the top of the slabs,
where she is, the mist rising from the force of the blows of
the sea of the rocks can be distinguished from the fog by
its different taste of salt. The slabs creak like old wooden
ships tied together with leather.

The child's vision is muted by the fog. She sees dis-
guised and disappearing slippery shapes in the dark. Re-
constructions of the landscape from images acquired in
another perspective are invalid. Cold and slick-wet are
more immediate, more demanding now, than shape.

She lowers her face to the cold surface of the rock, uncomprehending. She tastes. She smells the musk, the
fumes of dark, hidden wet. She runs her hands over the
hard, slippery ins and outs of the slab—trying to dis-

tinguish, trying to find and define and fit missing pieces together. The blows of the sea striking the land are felt first. They rise through the slabs to the soles of her feet and rattle up her spine to her brain. Then they are heard.

Mikkran also stands at the top of the slabs, removed, hidden in darkness by fog—unseen, but seeing. She has decided and will not interfere. She does not know what will happen to the child. She does not know what her charge will do. If the baby goes no farther and does no harm Thoacdien is bound to let them be. Mikkran is still free to come and go at the dome complex, and if they stay here provisions are easily come by. If the child wanders, if she leads them far from the complex, Mikkran knows only that she will follow and take each day as it comes.

Mikkran relaxes and broadens the focus of her mind to include the child's cerebration. Using this technique she can monitor her charge. When the child is awake this will be their only contact, this feeling through the wrong end of a telescope.

With others, cerebration monitoring is an exquisitely articulate and mutual means of communication. With this child Mikkran is able to read only the strongest and most basic responses. The child is capable of nothing else. Normally this communication is between sender and sender. This child cannot transmit and does not realize she is being received. She is oblivious of the process. In cerebration monitoring the feelings of the senders become synchronized. Comprehension involves feeling—in all ways—what is received. With this child it is an exhausting and terrifying process for the receiver. 187-A,0037 feels fully, violently, inarticulately, indiscriminately. When Mikkran monitors she feels the same. She must simultaneously receive and translate, experience and infer.

Mikkran stands at the top of the slabs and feels the contradictions at work in her charge. She experiences the child's baffled sense of release, the demand to resolve, the lack of resolution, and an almost paralyzing darkness which hovers at the edges of their brains. The child is not at ease. She has no language, no articulate means of framing her experience. She responds unselectively and is estranged—unable to define and integrate, or make inferences and, having made them, let them fade into the mosaic of experience. The child—and Mikkran, too, in a diffused way, a way cushioned by distance and knowledge—labors with great jagged pieces of sensation and struggles to bring them together where they will not fit.

Mikkran perspires. She experiences that now the child is baffled, now angry, now curious and struggling, now lost—and always vaguely terrified by the unidentifiable, unutterable, unthinkable darkness which engulfs. Even here the darkness of the seizures is still in control, possessing the child and never forgotten.

The mentor cannot interfere. She cannot approach the child. Help now is no help at all. If she were to approach before she were called, if she were to intrude herself on this chaos, this freedom to verify, if she were to weaken and go to her charge out of unfocused, misplaced love or pity or fear, the child would be denied the natural discovery of strength and trust in herself—which is what will enable her to be released.

The child stands naked and shivering at the top of the slabs. Her senses are barraged, attacked by undreamed of effects on the forces of night and fog, water and rock. She cannot distinguish cause. She does not recognize pattern or consequence.

187-A,0037 begins to work her way down through the slabs, feeling all sensation intensify as she nears the breakers. She follows her body obediently. And her body moves because that is its purpose—because it is possible. She works her way down, lower, lower, closer to the violence, because she can.

When the child has gone as far down as she can go, when to go any farther would be death—which somehow she understands—when she is small, looking up at violence which explodes, increasing on itself in a collapse, she stops. She slides into a niche in the slab, close to the power, but out of its direct line of force. And as she feels the wet of it, as she feels it crash, then subside a moment and glide around her knees—as she experiences its force, but not its resistance—she tries to infer. Her eyes narrow. She tries desperately to remember, to grasp what she has known once before.

The child climbs out of her green slippery niche and works her way back up a few slabs, where it is quieter. She squats by a pool of trapped water. Slowly she reaches out her hand and slips it into the cold glove of the pool. Open.

Closed.

She grips the water and it disappears.

Flex.

Grasp.

Release.

Snap!

Her head jerks up. She freezes as information is transformed into knowledge, pouring over her brain like warm milk.

Blink!

She looks out at the sea in front of her, blanketed by fog which does not quite touch its surface. And the child understands that she can go no further in that direction. She realizes that the black violence which rises and explodes, which had been a hard gray mirror, a smooth, endless surface from inside the dome, cannot be walked across. Grasp. Resolve. Release.

187-A,0037 shivers. She stands and looks around herself, clutching her first conclusion. Automatically she begins to work her way back up the slabs, back up into the body of the fog. At the top she turns and looks down at what she has discovered and now possesses irrevocably. She holds onto that isolated knowledge as warmth, as survival. Then she turns her back on the sea and, skirting the dome, moves east in the dark toward what she has never seen before.

Mikkran steps out of a shadow into less darkness. She experienced her charge's victory and embraces it as she hopes one day to embrace the child. Mikkran rolls her head around and around her shoulders, relaxing, massaging her neck. Now that her charge has left the slabs and the surf she is out of immediate physical danger and Mikkran can decrease cerebration monitoring to a level which will permit her to be aware without being barraged and short-circuited by the power of the child's unselective responses. For Mikkran this victory was exhausting.

The mentor waits, proud of this strange human being who is her responsibility. She gives the child a solid lead. When there is enough distance between them she hoists her bundle and weaves her arms through its loops. Then, feeling the weight settle on her back, she follows.

The child is heading east, toward the grasslands—a huge, wide strip of savanna which runs the length of the western coast of the continent and cushions it from what lies beyond.

Mikkran walks in silence, listening for her charge, monitoring lightly. The child is passive now, walking because it is possible. Mikkran feels the hem of her robe becoming heavy with the moisture it sucks off the grass as she moves. She cannot see more than two body-lengths in front of her. She pads on, behind the other. There is no sound. The fog is close, oppressive, and warm.

Colors: gray, darker gray, darkest gray, black. Sounds: fog creaking against itself, water dripping—slow—and four feet squeaking, rasping, slapping, but so softly, on wet grass. Smells: damp green, gray wet through and through, and leaf rot. By tilting the head back the nose can find spice at the end of all the other smells—timid, over-powered, but there.

The child has curled up, asleep like a discarded shoe-string, on a mat of slick leaves. Mikkran stands at the very edge of the child's awareness and does not move a molecule. Were the child to awaken now she would see Mikkran and think nothing of her because she blends so with the fog—a natural exclamation point. Notch by notch the baby wanders down through the levels of sleep like a leaf fallen on a windless day.

Mikkran steps forward. She pulls a towel from her bundle and pats the child dry. She finds the heavy black robe of absence and wraps it around her charge. She ties the hood in place, working quickly, and lays the child down on the towel.

The mentor looks down through the dark and the fog at the face of her charge. She touches her fingertip to the black lashes which grow out of the ledges of the child's eyelids like parentheses. How perfect! Blink. Mikkran puts socks and sandals on the little feet, then sets a flash of water and some food on a small plate where they cannot be missed. She freezes an instant, turning, looks at the child, and is gone.

The fog creaks through the trees, too heavy for them, and, through a tear made by a spiky branch, anemic sun blinks once and disappears. The child wakes, huddled in the black robe. She eats. She drinks. And then she walks again, not realizing that nature, in this season of the fog, does not provide such things.

Each time the child sleeps Mikkran is there, cleaning, nursing, feeding. Then the mentor goes back far enough so as not to be discovered but close enough to hear, and sleeps her different sleep. Each time the child wakes Mikkran wakes. Each time the child wakes and eats and drinks and is warm. And it does not occur to her to wonder how this is possible. Each time Mikkran eats she plans her food carefully, measuring every bite, gathering more food with her free hand. She refills her huge flask to overflowing each time it is possible, whether it is necessary or not. Each time the child rises she walks. And Mikkran follows.

The sun appears and disappears. There is only long gray grass and, beyond the veil of the fog, a few crippled trees that reach up gray and diffused. The only taste is of wet. The only touch is of wet. The only smell if of sweet rot which carpets the ground as slippery glass. All the small and vulnerable fog birds are asleep on their eggs. There is no sound—only molecules in occasional collision, and feet slapping by on the wet. Two going by.

Then nothing.

Then two more.

The child moves on, directionless. Her only anticipation is of motion. She walks and sleeps. She eats and drinks, never questioning how. She moves on, inscribing her long, fragile arc across the savanna. And it does not matter if it is day or night because that means only a slight shift in the tone of the grays. The fog devours everything.

Two figures creep east across the deep grass, through the darkest season. They slip. They fall. They sleep in trunks of crippled trees or on the ground, sometimes at night, sometimes in the day, it does not matter. They walk on in a curving path, through fog and infrequent trees, toward what cannot yet be seen.

The puzzled child, whose mind is reproduced inside this season, stumbles on. And through the slow, walking process of elimination—because the fog buffets sensation, simplifies, reduces to clear pattern, and because perception is selected by nature—she begins to learn that she is not the tall gray grass or trees or fog or wind or little birds asleep on eggs. They have life, space, time of their own. Figure and ground materialize. Things take their space. The child begins to understand, without discovering schism, the difference between what is contained within her physical limits and what is not. The other rises up out of her and becomes distinct. Things hold their shape and can be counted on. They ease away, unmoor and lift themselves out of her, die a little, and appear.

187-A,0037 intuits that there is something she has known which could become a frame to hang these differences on—a simpler way of identifying, because now they are too clumsy and too many. But she cannot find it. It is shadowed by the black explosions, hidden behind the seizures—the time when only she was motion.

—. . . There! . . . the dark figure who held out its hand to help . . . shadows . . .

(—. . . hold . . . on.—I have . . . I will try . . .)

With every pulse she remembers the dream inside the black explosion when she was plunged into pitiful sobs, begging for help. Some things she cannot lift out of herself and make separate. They sit between the eyelid and the eye, unanswered, present, now. She walks on through the fog, carrying her little bits of puzzle. And Mikkran follows silent, the benevolence of nature, unseen and unfelt.

The sun appears and disappears. Thoacdien V circles on, toward tilting up again. Fog sinks into the ground and dies as one season evolves into the next. Two figures cross the generous grasslands and stumble through the fog, going on.

. . . .

"Dr. Scott? Hello, Dr. Howard Scott? Do you read? Hello anyone research team PROBE IV. DO YOU READ? What's wrong with this thing, Lanier?"

"Nothing, sir. The channels are open at both ends. Everything checks out go. The research team just isn't responding."

"Ybarra, are the nukes ready and standing by?"

"Yes, sir."

"This is bad. Give me a time check."

"It's three minutes and ten seconds into audio silence, sir."

"O.K. Lt. Lanier, keep trying to get them. Ybarra, you and O'Hare ready and board Skimmer Three, and stand by."

"Yes, sir."

. . . .

Fog sinks to the ground in the night, evaporates, is gone. The continent is swept clean of insulation, laid bare, exposed to the season of sun. Living things are alerted by a different kind of silence—warned to move on. This season has no mercy. It is fire.

The eastern sky lightens and stills the wind. The sun pulls itself up to the absolutely straight and featureless horizon line, attains its roundness and becomes a bloody mouth. There is no sound, but beneath sanity there is a rasp of sharpening knives. As the sun lifts up through the spectrum from maroon to white, the wind resumes its frightening whisper, evolving into the senseless, incoherent whine of one in pain. The risen sun is aggressive white. All beneath it reflects its heat, its color, and melts into screaming fumes. Vitality evaporates. This is the first morning of the season of sun.

The two have crossed the grasslands and now waken at the end of one landscape and the beginning of the next. Ahead the earth flattens out, an endless dry sea with no life at all. The ground is as cracked and dry as the back of an ancient, bleached hand. This is the Desert of Death.

Mikkran squats, a great motionless bird, hooded and veiled on her perch, and looks down and ahead through the white morning sun at the sleeping child, tiny in the distance. The wind whips her robe into loud flapping sounds. Her feet grip the last crippled tree branch as she looks out silently. Veins hammer at her temples, throat and wrists. For the first time, she is afraid.

The child stirs. Mikkran stirs and watches her rise, eat and drink what has been left for her, then look out across the desert which has no visible, no imaginable end. The child scans the horizon line, which undulates with heat, then turns and looks west, toward Mikkran.

187-A,0037 stands still a long time, a tiny black dot in the distance. Squinting back she studies the last of the grasslands: a tree and a bird. She stretches her arm across her body, makes a long, sweeping gesture, then cries out. Mikkran cannot decipher the meaning of the cry—she cannot hear it. Then, absently, the child turns east, steps onto the scorched surface of the desert into the season of sun, and continues to walk.

Mikkran swings down from her perch. Her great leather flask, half as tall as she is, is filled almost to bursting with water. She spent the morning back in the grasslands carefully selecting and preparing food in case the child went into the desert. She calculates the amount of time the food and water will allow them and hopes that she can keep the child from walking in circles. She waits as long as she can, knowing she had done everything possible. The child is getting tiny, disappearing in the distance. Mikkran waits a bit longer, so as not to be seen, then follows her charge.

Sun comes down on them as hot mass. Sun bounces up at them as hot blades. Out and out in all directions it is flat, the perfectly forged white plane suspended and steaming on wire. The plane hangs in white space and becomes a drumhead for angry force. The desert throbs with heat. Beneath the heavy robes which protected on the grasslands is burning—salt into burning. The wind gathers its power and, unobstructed, scrapes the desert clean.

The child shrinks into herself, defending herself against the hot knife of wind which cuts from all sides. She watches her feet pass over the monotonous cracks in the desert's floor—endless odd shapes with black spaces in between, small opaque mirrors which reflect the heat and focus it back up at her. Her face aches from squinting. Dust clings to her feet, and because it thickens she knows she is moving. There is nothing else to tell her so.

The child watches her shadow appear. It crests, rises over her head to begin as a little strip of dark before her that grows into a rippling, flapping apparation which leads her on. Occasionally she stops and turns, looking behind herself into the sun. She shields her face from the sun and the wind with her hands and sees the last of the grasslands as a shimmering, floating island of green which sinks, dissolving, then melted, in the distance. Then she sees dust. Nothing else. She turns and continues to walk.

Mikkran follows, just out of sight. On this flat land she must stay too far behind. She, also, watches her shadow grow, flapping before her, beckoning her on. She, too, feels the dust thicken on her feet, the only sign that she is moving. Her water flask hangs by a cord from her shoulder. It bounces full on her hip and leg. It sweats and leaves a trail of precious, infrequent drops which fall to the ground and, while striking, evaporate.

At night the sky is black. The stars step back for this season and are somehow removed, distant. The desert creaks and groans as it contracts, becoming cold. It is rubbed cleaner by a different, crueler wind.

The child lies down on the hard ground, in the cracked chalk, next to nothing. She is protected by only her garment. She huddles into herself and sleeps in the cold.

The mentor's main concern now is the conservation of her own energy, her own endurance, her resources. She must monitor the child's cerebration constantly here because of the distance between them. This drains her and dulls her sharp edges. Even when her charge is passive and calm, her cerebration is exhausting. Here the girl's determination burns into Mikkran's brain with the same undulating heat and force of the sun. The intensity with which the child puts one foot before the next is at times unbearable.

Here Mikkran must walk twice as far in going back and forth to the child. On the grasslands there were places, objects, which concealed. She could stay close. Here there is nothing but distance to hide her. And now she must worry about food. She must count each drop of water and each berry consumed, because there is no more.

Each moment wipes out all the others. In the mind, in the body, in the endurance, each moment is a new extreme. The season is polarized, and with each day the poles are more clearly defined and reinforced.

Each day is identical to the one before, but intensified. Each same day intensified must be faced with less energy, less endurance, less caring, less food, less water, until even fantasies and delirium are replaced by the reality of the size of the landscape. Estimates of where the end is are eclipsed by the task of putting one foot before the other.

Each night Mikkran approaches the child and refills her little flash with a small, rationed amount of water. She leaves what food she can, watches awhile, then disappears. Each day and each night Mikkran consumes less food and water, saving it, ekeing it out. She is afraid. Each night, a little later than the night before, she lies down on the ground, opens her mind to monitor the child and half sleeps. When the child wakes the mentor wakes, and they go on.

Each morning the child wakes, eats and drinks what has been left for her, which is less than before, and grows aware that she does not have as much here as she did on the grasslands. Each morning she puzzles at this. She looks at the flat nothing which surrounds her and remembers the gray and abundant moisture of the other season, the other landscape. She sees pictures of water in her mind. Her hand grasps air, unclasps—fisting—as she looks for the connection. But she does not wonder how it is that she eats and drinks. She has always had these things. She will continue to have them.

Each day the child wakes and waits long enough for the sun to cast a shadow. Then she stands and, leading her shadow in the morning, following it in the afternoon, goes on. Each step is a growth, an age, an accomplishment. Each step adds to her slow accumulation of unarticulated information. She places her little bits of puzzle up next to her experience and tries to match the edges.

Outside of the child is heat and blinding light. Inside are voices which call her unnamed name for help, demanding to be heard. She does not understand. Inside there is a black cloaked figure which floats always at the edge of her vision. But when she quickly turns to look—to the sides, or behind—there is only white undulating sheets of space, rippling up from the ground like transparent flames. She does not understand. But deeper inside there is another element: blackness, which waits with an explosion capable of casting her loose from this walking. It waits like a huge thumb, ready to drop and blot her out. It is there with each step, each blink, each rolling drop of sweat, each molecule of chalky dust which becomes part of her feet. This she understands, and is running from.

Mikkran sleeps on the ground. Her small bundle is braced up against her spine for what warmth it is worth. Her water flask, limp and folded over on itself, is in the center of the crescent made by her curled body.

The mentor has finally gone to sleep. Each night it is more difficult because she worries, she counts and measures the food and water, tries to redivide it and is exhausted. This night, because of her fatigue and need for sleep, she has reduced the level of her cerebration monitoring to a point at which the child would have to wake and begin to walk in order to arouse her.

Mikkran sleeps deeply for the first time since their wandering began. A vein throbs in her temple. Her mouth hangs slack and dry. The rounds of her brows are drawn in toward the center, as though blotting out thoughts and dreams. Her hand, bleached white by the talc of fine chalk dust which clings to flesh and fabric as to a magnet, is resting on the water flask. In sleep her fingers twitch automatically, guarding the flask. The wind sucks and blows, probing, always finding new ways to get inside her robe.

A black dot appears behind her consciousness. It is darker than the darkness of her sleep—like a hole. It grows, because fluorescent, spreads and bleeds into a huge stain which is a wall between sleep and waking. It swallows all light and paralyzes voluntary response. It is an endless, escapeless chasm which she is falling through, into the unthinkable.

The seizure is a new season, one which gives no warning. It has no regularity, no discernible meaning, and no release. It is an emotion loosed from the primitive brain —and self-important. It simultaneously sucks at the marrow of the upper brain and spits it out. It is simultaneous implosion/explosion of cerebration. And it is unbearable.

Mikkran is arched on her back in the darkness. Her body is rigid. Her eyes are rolled back into her head. All but a little part of her brain has been swallowed by the spreading stain. And that little part of volition left her tries desperately to hold off the fear, to wake her. Her upper teeth are clamped on the edge of her lower lip; a little drop of blood rolls down the side of her neck and into the ground. She is controlled by fear, fear which rises out of her body as an odor, rises out of her throat as a continual, animal groan which would become a scream.

The inside of the darkness increases, is all that is known and knowable become irrelevant and swallowed by the past. Her brain is sucked out, pulled out, out, and farther out—past the breaking, shattering point. And she holds on as she did long ago, because if she should let go, if she should be pried loose, if that little bit of her which remains should be evaporated, she will explode and disappear in an incoherent scream of madness.

Mikkran tries only not to scream because that is what will break her. All of that little bit of self remaining is a command: do not scream. Do not scream. Do not scream. If you scream you will die. Do not . . . do . . . not . . . scream. Scream . . . do not . . . not . . . scream. Oh . . . please do . . . not . . . not . . . screammmMMM. . . . And the command is transformed into that which it warns against. She tries to find something . . . do not screammm . . . which will lift a corner of the darkness and let her slip out. But nothing is stable. Nothing holds its shape. Everything has become a scream. Dying. She is overloading and knows there is something she must remember, something which will permit her to release herself. She drowns . . . do . . . not . . . . screammmmmm. She drowns . . . ahhhhhdo . . . pleasenot . . . ssscreammmmmmMMMMM. . . . She drowns in darkness where identity is not possible. Her lips work against her teeth. Her body spasms, thrusting itself into the ground, drumming it. If she can move her lips, speak—one word—she will wake up. . . . do . . . not ssscccrrreeeaaammmmmm. Her face is rigid, cheeks pulled down. Her eyelids press down on the bruised globes of her eyes.

". . . it . . . hhhhhas . . . cc . . . ome . . . from. . . . the . . . child. . . ."

Mikkran rolls over on her side and vomits. When she can she climbs up on her hands and knees. Her body aches. She stands. Her lip is swollen and wet with blood. She opens her mind to monitor the child and is struck to her knees by the fist of the child's seizure. She stands and, stumbling, runs to her charge.

The child is on her back on the ground—rigid. Her eyes are rolled back into her head. A pink froth bubbles out of her mouth.

Mikkran stands over the contorted child. She shields her mind from the seizure. But even shielded, even kept at arm's length, the darkness is so powerful, so complete and close as to make her sick at her stomach. She pries the child's mouth open and works her fingers in to get hold of the tongue. She grabs the girl and holds her in her arms to cushion her against the violence of the seizure —and waits. There is nothing else to do.

aaaaaaaaaggggggggggggaaaahhhhhaaaa . . . help . . . me . . .
ccccccchhhhhhwwwwwwwwwaaaahhhhhhhh . . .
phhhhhhhhhhhhhttt . . .
I am fffaaaaaaaaaaaaaaaaaaaaaa a a a a a a l l i n g.
—. . . yes . . .
Grrrasp!
—Two hands.
—. . . I cannot see . . .
—Two hands, one not mine . . .
—Oh, hold on . . . oh, please hold . . . on.
—. . . I . . . can't . . . yes. Yes . . . I can try.
Slap!
Grrrrrrrasp!
—no . . . words.
—no . . . metaphors.
—no motion but us.
—Who are you?
—. . . I . . . have forgotten . . .
—Hold on . . .
—Not-here, not-now . . . is when we are.
—Where?
—When?
Click.
—I can't . . . stand any . . . more. It is too sudden and too fast.
—Hold on.
—I can't . . . I am dying. I have become dead.

—No. No. You are not dead . . . you are merely changing.)

The seizure climaxes and begins to fade. The child's arched body relaxes, twitches with fatigue, and is still. Tears flow out of her closed lids as the spheres of her eyes fall back down to the front. Her jaw goes slack. She is asleep.

Mikkran gently pulls her fingers out of the child's mouth. They have been bitten behind the second joints and are torn and bleeding. She touches her other hand to the child's neck and feels the exhausted pulse struggle to regain its rhythm. Mikkran shivers and cleans her charge as best she can without water. She watches until the sky glows maroon and the threshold of heat passes over them. When she senses the return of what is normal cerebration for the child, she stands and walks back to her bundle and flask and waits for the child to continue.

The desert burns, raising blisters. The wind blows constantly—either fire or dry ice—sucking up energy, evaporating resources. Still the child walks, trying to outmaneuver her seizures. Mikkran's flask is limp. It hangs over on itself. The tiny portion of water which is left splashes pitifully in the bag. Her robe has rubbed her body raw. As she takes one step and then another, it chafes. Perspiration drips into abrasions, stinging, stinging everywhere. And foul-smelling steam climbs up her neck and into her nostrils.

Mikkran is approaching a threshold, a point at which her will and her body can push each other no further. She is not afraid to die here, in this way. But she cannot permit herself to visualize the child wandering the desert, slowly starving to death. She is determined, but her body and resources are exhausted. All action has become a sharpening of season-dulled wits for the battle against heat, gravity, fatigue, the possibility of the dissolution of their relationship, and the real and continual death of the I.

After these many days in the desert Mikkran believes she can almost see a break in the landscape ahead, a

punctuation. Heat waves diffuse and baffle, but there, ahead, must be a thin strip of
—imagination—
pink, materializing above the throbbing horizon.
. . . or the blood in her eyes . . .
    She has no more water. The child has the last of it. I
. . . will go . . . on.
    She stumbles, placing one foot in front of the other with deliberate calculation. Her mouth is hot powder. She lurches in a jagged course, on, toward the pink island which, perhaps, floats . . . so tiny . . .
. . . so far away . . .
    Her flask and bundle have been left behind. She no longer counts steps. She no longer plays games of how far is it from here to there? Here and there and now and then and when have shriveled up in the desert and no longer exist.
    Her whole brain is focused on keeping her balance—
. . . do not . . . fall down . . .
on standing up so she can keep placing one foot and then the next. And then the next, the next, the next, the next— that's how . . . far . . . it is.
    The sky fades to pink, to orange, to purple, then to black.
    Mikkran
        falls
   down,
    struggles like an animal, and sleeps.
    Night comes, cold freezing night which tears at her robe, demanding that she rise. And she tries. And cannot.
    The sky lightens in the east, a pink and hot explosion of sun emerging from between the legs of night. The child wakes and reaches to drink her precious drops of water. There is only a very little. She feels of this desert floor, knowing it has nothing to yield.
    The black cloaked figure creeps up behind her eyes, then vanishes.
    !

She shakes the flask. Always before when she woke there was more water in the flask than when she had gone to sleep—and food. Now there is nothing.

The black cloaked figure snaps into her brain, beckons, and is gone.

!

She is squatting. On her left, west, is the landscape she has just crossed. On her right, not very far, is pink and green. She can feel the slightest breeze, cooling, from the east. The child wavers and trembles and sips her water. She looks at the flask—leather, shaped like a tear.

!

Something wants to bloom in her brain. Things want to be connected. The black cloaked figure of the dream . . . the screaming figure . . . snap . . . gone.

!

She stands, wavering, and walks east—into the pink and green.

Mikkran's hood lies across the side of her face as she sleeps. Her veil has fallen away, exposing her dry, open, flaking mouth. Her breaths are shallow, as the air is too hot and too dry and too big to get beyond her swollen tongue and throat. Her hand is stretched out from her robe, palm up, coated with dust. A sweet odor rises out of her body. A soft crackling rasp escapes from her mouth. Not moving, she wakes and opens her eyes.

Two dark, wide eyes stare back at her.

The child squats near Mikkran, clutching her flask. She quivers, watching in silence. Mikkran does not move. She lies still, with her cheek on the ground, staring from her dry, sunken eyes.

The two robed figures do not move. They watch each other—Mikkran lying down looking up, the child squatting nearby. The young one clutches her flask, now sweating and full, as a piece of her puzzle. She fights, unblinking and unmoving, to remember. Somewhere there is an edge. Here. And if it can be found so many things will fit up next to it and be resolved.

Mikkran's hand twitches. Her cracked lips part and

move. The sound is only a rasp which is so soft it seems to have fallen out of her eyes.

". . . help . . . me . . ."

The child freezes. The edge forms in her mind. Her eyes narrow and grip the black cloaked figure, refusing to let it evaporate again. The figure is clear. It holds out its hand to her, offering her the water flask. It holds her. It fights for her. It matches up with the being who lies on the ground. Image, object and being coalesce, equal each other, and perform the tasks they have performed through much longer than two seasons. And the child knows that she has been able to survive this journey because she was cared for by this thing, this screaming, dying black cloaked thing in front of her. Blink. Click. Resolve.

The child uncorks her flask and gives her mentor water —water cool and wet, a healing salve to stop the slow dissolution, the flaking away, of this life. While Mikkran drinks the child stands and points to the east. She taps herself on the chest and points at her mentor, then pantomimes walking with her hands. Mikkran nods yes. Yes. And after a while the mentor rises to her hands and knees, and then to her feet. With the child leading, waddling toward the distinct pink and green—looking back occasionally to make sure she is followed—they walk out of the desert.

~~~~~~

FROM: THOACDIEN—PRIORITY ONE.
TO: CHEMBRYO LAB 187-A, THOACDIEN V.
DATE: 187.290
TIME: 3.3.002
SUBJECT: MENTOR MIKKRAN-GOGAN-TOR AND CHARGE 187-A,0037

. . . .
. . . .
. . . .

CHEMLAB: PROCEED.
STOP.

THOACDIEN: THERE HAS BEEN NO NEW INPUT
ON SUBJECTS SINCE 187.065.
IT IS TIME FOR US TO ACT.
RECOMMEND YOU ACTIVATE
FLOATER IMMEDIATELY AND
SELECT SEARCH PARTY.
BEGIN SEARCH IN THE COMPLEX
AND WORK EAST OVER THE
GRASSLANDS. IF THEY ARE NOT
FOUND THERE SEARCH THE
DESERT OF DEATH.
THEY MUST BE FOUND BEFORE
THEY REACH THE END OF
FEDERATION TERRITORY.
STOP.

CHEMLAB: WE WILL ACTIVATE FLOATER
IMMEDIATELY AND SELECT
QUALIFIED CREW.
WE WILL FOLLOW YOUR SEARCH
PATTERN AND CONTACT YOU ON
COMPLETION FOR FURTHER
INSTRUCTIONS.
STOP.

END TRANSMISSION . . . .

The desert ends at a wall of pink rock which rises
straight up like a huge step, then flattens out again and
becomes a high, pitted mesa. Water flows out of the
mesa and creates oases at the edge of the desert. Here the
season of sun is not so brutal. There is green and food
and water and shade.

A small stream runs off the mesa, falls from the top of
the rocks as a thin ribbon of sound, and ends in a shallow

pool surrounded by tall, fruit-bearing trees, small boulders, and a cave. Here, two dust-covered and exhausted bodies sleep. Mikkran lies by the pool with one hand in the water, to assure herself, even in sleep, that it is really there. The child is curled up on the other side of the tiny green patch of growth which trumpets the end of the desert and of Federation territory.

Straight up the sky is blue, uninterrupted by clouds. Long, bladed leaves slide graceful arches out of the sky. Slender brown columns—tree trunks—rise up, leaning slightly, and trail sweet vapors of fruit. The mesa hums. Wind bounces through the canyons and falls onto the end of the desert as music. The sound is delicate, continuous, and stratified so that source and course, beginning and end, cannot be deciphered by the ear. The wind blows through the mesa as through an ancient, complex flute.

One night passes over the sleeping figures, then a day, and then another night. Mikkran sleeps face-down with her hand up to its wrist in the cool, moving pool. The child sleeps on her back, stretched out like a fallen bird, and does not move.

The sun creeps up—a gentle surprise—over the wall of the mesa which shelters the two with shade. The light is broken up into long shafts by the bladed leaves of the trees and ends trapped and jewellike in little beads of dew collected by the grass during the night. Mikkran and the child sleep through this early morning until they are warmed—fully baked to the marrow by the sun—and rested. Then, separately, they awake. Each goes naked into the pool and gives the desert back to itself.

They are silent with each other. When the child sees Mikkran's tall, dark nakedness she stops a moment, studies it—separating the body from the robe—then goes her way, exploring the music of the stream which feeds the pool.

Two robes hang drying, like two dark windows on the sky. The two figures are clean and pale/dark and fragile —except for blistered hands and feet and faces. Mikkran

151

looks toward the sound of the flowing water and sees the child wet and glistening in the sun.

The child stands silent just in front of the long and delicate falls. She studies the cool liquid as it makes way for her feet then closes in on itself again. She remembers in images—fuzzed by time and motion and heat—that once she stood beneath wet violence and experienced the amazing click of information becoming knowledge. She stands dark, silent and wet. Her eyes reach out from deep inside her head, groping for that sensation again.

No words have passed between them yet. The child has no words. They have not touched each other. They use the other senses. They listen and watch and smell the other across the space between. They have only decreased a little, the distance between what was and will perhaps be.

The child does not understand the tall one. She only knows that since they have come together, a part of her is freed from the pressure to be alert. And with that release of pressure came the leisure of a slight respite from chaos. The child does not know what else to ask or expect of the other. But periodically her eyes sweep the mouth of the cave to see that the tall one has not disappeared.

Mikkran turns the stick which skewers their first meat in almost two seasons. The cooked side floats up and the fire spits as bubbles of juice explode. Delicious fumes rise up into her face. The child catches the odors and looks up from her inspection of the stream. She stares at Mikkran, puzzled, eyes narrowed. The tall one looks back into the child's solemn eyes, into the questioning intelligence which comes from such deep, hidden sources in her little head. Their glances lock together for a moment— one questioning, the other waiting. Then the child turns back to the stream.

The young one's body is taller and thinner now, a rich brown. Her hair erupts from her head in dark flames. She is never still, never at rest. Her eyes reach out of their dark caves like two hands and must touch everything. The high bridge of her nose is pushed up against the muscles of her forehead in concentration. She tries to reach out from her vacuum with no context but chaos by which to order her behavior. All things are sudden to her. All things seem always to happen for the first time.

Mikkran watches the child's still form which is frozen, examining. After a moment the child moves on a step down the stream, pauses again, and scrutinizes something new. She vibrates. She overflows with unnamed names, with thought which is all form and no content. She stands, weight on one hip, arms hanging down, head cocked. She is liquid and relaxed, except above the high bridge of her nose, where there is a knot. Mikkran turns back to the food and blows on the fire which cooks it.

The child works her way on down the stream toward the pond where she bathed earlier. She notices a shallow place off to one side, where small rocks and a branch form a dam which traps a small pool. It draws her because it is unmoving, and similar to something she knows from before. She drops a stone into the pool and is startled by the even rings which spread out from the hole it makes. The surface comes back together, shimmers only slightly, and again exactly reflects the blue of the sky.

The child stares at the pool. Its surface is nearly opaque with the softly swaying image of the sky. She squats down on a rock which is beside the pool. An image squats up from the pool and stares at her.

!?

The image has no identity in her mind. It is nothing. It is simply there. She reaches her hand into the water and fractures the image. She waits. Slowly the surface heals. It comes back together again, regains its equilibrium as an image, an extension, a dream—a reflection of the dreamer dreaming of the dreamer dreaming the dream.

The squatting child slaps at an insect after the salt on her arm. The reflection slaps. The insect lives and settles on the pool, denting but not breaking the thin surface with the tips of its long, spiderweb legs. The insect hops on the water, rising and falling simultaneously, meeting itself leg for leg on the surface of the pool. It mirrors itself exactly, and were she not able to see from this perspective she would be unable to distinguish the reality of the insect in space from the reality of the image of the insect in the pool.

!?

The child freezes. The skin of her face is drawn back. Her mouth and eyes are pulled tight across the supporting bone structure. Her hands are in front of her, spasming automatically near the surface of the pool. Open . . . closed. Flex . . . relax . . . almost. She stands and looks back toward the mouth of the cave and the tall one. She cannot leave the still place in the water. She cannot take the chance that it might disappear. It is as if she has walked a tightrope in the dark, toward this discovery, and now stands frozen, about to fall, about not to fall, needing only a little help to resolve and complete the action.

Mikkran looks up to see the child standing poised and taut on a rock at the far side of the stream. The girl seems unable to move, asking for help. The mentor stands, and the child nods, as if to say, "Yes! Come!" Mikkran works her way quickly down and across the noisy shoulders of the stream. She steps up toward the child, and in doing so her image slides across the surface of the pool, meeting her.

The child sees that the other is not alarmed by the images in the pool, but stands tall and relaxed, feet curling over the rock, looking at her curiously. The young one points to the pool and squats, leaning out with her face over the water. The image meets her, matches her. Seeing this she looks up at the tall one, questioning. Her face works as if chewing. Using her fingers the child imitates the delicate darting of the insect, and again looks at the tall one, questioning. Then she puts her hand in the water and erases the images. She waits for them to heal, and when they have she points to her own reflection in the pool. She looks up. She pats herself on the chest, drops her jaw, and makes a moaning sound which is both question and statement.

Mikkran touches the child on the chest, then she points

to the matching reflection in the water and nods her head yes.

Yes.

And she gives the child a word.

"I."

The child freezes, staring hard and wide-eyed at the tall one as the word burns its way through her body and into her brain. White explosions of anarchy shrink, making way for the smooth egg-shaped form of the word. One of the invisible threads which bind her breaks.

". . . I . . ." The child inhales. She closes her eyes and tastes the word again.

"I."

The child looks proudly at the reflection in the water, and touches her face. The image responds. Then she puts her hand in the pool and stirs up the image. She sees the fractured water and, terrified, feels her face. She turns to the tall one for help.

Mikkran takes the child's face in her hands and looks reassuringly into her eyes. When the image had mended Mikkran places the girl's hands on her own face and stirs up the water. The child sees Mikkran's reflection disintegrate, but feels the relaxed coherence of the mentor's face. She relaxes and points to the disturbed water looking up, her face raised in a question.

The mentor races through her vocabulary, searching for a word which embraces the concept. She finds one which means pure thought disturbed, clarity agitated—turbulence. Mikkran points to the scattered image.

"Biel."

". . . Biel . . ."

The child's eyes narrow. The surface of the pool comes back together and rocks smoothly. The child leans over and looks at herself. She points to the image and places her hand on her chest.

"I."

The girl stops, looking up at Mikkran, confused. She scatters the image with her hand. Then she points to her head and makes the swirling, scattering motion.

"Biel."

The child turns to Mikkran and pats herself on the chest, then on the head.

"I. Biel."

She places her hand on Mikkran's face. She points at the mentor's image in the water.

". . . I. Biel? . . ."

The mentor shakes her head no. She pats herself on the chest.

"I am Mikkran."

". . . Mee.Kran . . ."

The mentor touches herself. "I am Mikkran." Then she points to the child and raises her face into a question.

Slowly the child pats herself on the chest. "I am Biel." Then she points at the other. "Mikkran." And they are different.

The stunned child looks at her stunned mentor. She feels the other rising out of her brain and body, materialize, die a little, and become distinct across a new and different distance between them. Tears come into the girl's eyes as she feels the double edge of naming. She leaps across the space to recover the distance. Her arms and legs grip her mentor, and she holds on, sobbing. Mikkran feels the girl's full light softness in her arms for the first time, and weeps as they are reunited.

V

FROM: FLOATER, COMPLEX-187A, THOAC-
DIEN V—PRIORITY TWO.
 TO: THOACDIEN
DATE: 187.324
TIME: 4.6.002
SUBJECT: MENTOR MIKKRAN-GOGAN-TOR
AND CHARGE 187-A,0037.

. . . .
. . . .
. . . .

THOACDIEN: PROCEED.
STOP.

FLOATER: WE HAVE COMPLETED SEARCH
PATTERNS 1,2 AND 3 OF THE
GRASSLANDS.
SIGNS INDICATE THAT SUBJECTS
IN THE GRASSLANDS DURING THE
SEASON OF FOG.
THEY APPEAR TO HAVE GONE ON

TO THE DESERT OF DEATH.
REQUEST PROCEDURES.

STOP.

THOACDIEN: PLEASE CONTINUE SEARCH.

END TRANSMISSION ....

Mikkran opens her eyes from sleep. She smiles. Long tendrils of Biel's hair are spread softly, tickling, across the mentor's breasts. The girl's small head nestles limp in the hollow of her neck. A sweet, clean smell rises out of the young body and lies over them like a blanket. Now, when Biel sleeps, she does so near her mentor, expressing the nature of their bond with her body. Mikkran has given the girl words. They have struggled together and survived. The bond between them is as tangible as the sky.

The mentor does not know what will happen to them. She has never been at the end of Federation territory before and does not know what lies beyond. She thinks of the future only in terms of preparing for the alternatives as thoroughly as she can in the present—as thoroughly as she can with her resources.

Biel, given words, wants nothing else. The compulsion and fear of the seizures which drove her to walk is quiet now. The girl wants only to learn. They eat and walk and play and bathe and work—and always, they talk. Often Biel sleeps only a few hours of the night, curled up next to Mikkran, talking to herself. Then she wakes, trying to be quiet so as to let her mentor sleep, and climbs up to the high place where the falls bend and collapse over the rocks. And, silhouetted against the lightening sky, she names names, framing the chaos within and without.

Mikkran disentangles herself from the sleeping girl and rises to bathe and be in this new day. Biel rolls over and grabs for her, but settles for the robe. The mentor waits a moment, looking down at the girl as she returns to deep sleep. Then she pads softly down the pebbled shoulder of the stream toward the bottom of the falls.

Cold, clear water pours over her body. Mikkran arches and flexes her strong brown back and feels the water work its way down through her heavy hair to her scalp. It drums on her skull, rolls down her face, down her moving, straight, round, black, brown, downed body, down her muscled legs, and joins itself again, going on. She bathes. She thinks of nothing, touching herself. Then she thinks of other people, and she misses them. She imagines other mentors and their charges, and the complex. By now most of the charges will have earned the red robe of curiosity. Biel has earned it. She hopes someday Biel will have the opportunity and the joy of living with them. His face. She scans her memory for the deeply special faces, the bodies she has touched and loved. An adult hunger begins at her feet and works its way up her body like a warm, dry snake. His face. And she lusts for the resolution she has not felt in so long. But realizing that here there is no object for it, she tries to relax and sweep it aside.

She finishes bathing and climbs up on a large, flat, hot rock. She sits, embracing her knees. Then she runs her stiffened fingers through her kinky hair, to comb it. Her lust returns with all the faces of the past becoming his face. His face. She grins and tries to dissolve it, to thrust it aside by combing her hair. All the faces, their face . . . his . . . gets larger and becomes a body, touching hers with the soft, insistent lick of a cat. She is urged. Mikkran lies back on the rock in the new cloudless morning which is already hot, because she wants to. And the image descends. The man she has not been able to think of in so long becomes as real as a dream in the imagination of her touch. She feels the small, taut, electric parts of her body —firm, reaching up like flower's heads. Her body arches to the sweetness. It inhales. Muscles flex, unflex, grasp, unclasp, and resolve the tension on a moment which has its own time and capacities, and is set apart from all others. She gasps, inhaling, at the pleasure. And, when she is satisfied, she sinks into deep sleep.

The sun rises, hotter on the brown of Mikkran's back. Little drops of perspiration form between her shoulderblades, roll easily down the long valley of her back, and form a thin pool at the base of her spine.

She has slept deeply, and satisfied, and is now coming up out of her blue lake smiling into the heat of this still-new day.

She hears birds gargling their songs.

She feels the cool breeze being sucked along by the water which slaps past her toward the desert. Her face rests on her bent arm, cushioned by the pillow of her hair.

She feels a drop of water form and trickle down her spine to join the small salt pool there.

She opens her eyes.

Two large white feet with soft yellow hairs on their arches stand on the rock near her face. The ten rounded toes point at her like cannon. She jerks. She feels an excruciating pain begin between her shoulderblades and fan out through her body like an artificial flame. Her face falls like a rock onto her bent arm. A second pain spreads out through her body from her nose as it hits the bone in her arm. She bites the long, maroon figure eight tattoo on the inside of her arm, trying to stay conscious.

The two feet next to her face move away from her but stay on the flat rock. She feels her head being lifted by the hair. She opens her eyes. Through the fumes of her pain she sees a face at the top of the tall body attached to the ten toes. Her head is jerked farther back. The pain is unbearable. A hole in the face moves.

"Let her go. She has felt the Zuri."

The pressure between Mikkran's shoulder blades is removed. The pain subsides in slow, uneven waves. Her head is released. It falls limp back down onto her arm. Her eyes are closed as she tries to swallow her nausea.

"Stand her up."

Mikkran feels two powerful hands lift her up by the armpits. They grip her shoulders with thumbs meeting between her shoulderblades, resting on a nerve she never knew she had, and promising the pain again. She does not resist. This is not yet a mortal encounter. She opens her eyes.

Six transparent ghosts waver before her silently.
Blink!
Three transparent ghosts waver before her silently.
Blink!
—. . . (. . . the pain . . .) . . .
The images come together and become a man.

"You have felt the Zuri—our death with the hands."

He is the tallest, fairest man she has ever seen. He is long between ankle and knee, knee and waist, shoulder and earlobe. His hair is short, straight, and white. It falls softly over his ears and forehead. His eyes are blue-white, hot and angry. He is straight and tall and quiet. The gold hairs on his body reflect the light and dip in the slight wind. He wears a light blue loincloth. Nothing else. He carries no weapons.

Behind this one, on the shoulder of the stream, is another of his kind wearing only a red loincloth. This second man holds Biel suspended in the air by one arm. One of his fingers is pointed into the hollow of her throat, right at the shiny scar made by the Gladdin so long ago. The girl cannot speak. Mikkran knows that there is at least one more—the one who is supporting her, the one who can hurt so easily. The tall one in front of her speaks.

"Do you know where you are?"

"At the end of the desert."

"*Precisely* where you are?"

"No."

"Do you know who we are?"

"No."

"I am Nyz-Ragaan, first warrior of the Higgittes. These are two of my warriors. Do you know who we are?"

"Only that you are the original people of Thoacdien V."

"We are the owners of this planet, which is called Droggen. You know nothing of us?"

"Many sets of seasons ago Thoacdien was invited to this planet by the Higgittes. All of you did not come into the Federation."

"Our leaders were divided. Some were tired of the old ways and became fascinated with your toys. Some were enraged at this invitation and wanted nothing to do with you. Some planned to lure you here and conquer the Federation from inside. They went with you and became soft, like women—like you. Now they can neither resist the Zuri nor remember it. We are what is left of the people who ruled from east to west as far as you can walk. We have been pushed back into the canyons. We are what is left of the greatest warriors who ever lived. You have felt the Zuri, do you not agree?"

"You are fine warriors."

"You are Thoacdien?"

"Yes."

"You are called Mikkran?"

"Yes."

"What is the girl called?"

"Biel."

"And she is a Thoacdien child."

"Yes."

"We are not at war with you."

"You are clever. You become docile when you are trapped. What are you doing here?"

"I am the girl's mentor. We left the dome together. We are on a journey and mean you no harm."

"I do not understand."

"The child suffers from seizures. She could not endure the dome, so I set her free. We have wandered here all the way from the sea."

"That is not possible."

"We have done it."

"You walked across the desert?"

"Yes."

"How long have you been here?"

"Since the middle of the season of the sun."

The first warrior of the Hïggittes jerks his head involuntarily toward the warrior who holds Biel suspended in the air. Mikkran feels the warrior behind her stir and the promise of the pain under his hands becomes realized again. Her head snaps back, and she feels the sky roll above her and disappear.

"Release her."

The deadly hands let go. She sinks to her knees and fights the nausea rising within her. She raises her head to try and clear it and sees Biel struggle. The warrior holding the girl presses his finger slightly into the hollow of her throat, and Biel is asleep.

"Grod-Linz?"

The warrior behind Mikkran steps forward. He is darker than the others, but still very fair. He, too, wears a red loincloth and carries no weapon.

"Warrior?"

"We shall call a council of warriors tonight from all of the canyons. How is it that these females were not discovered?"

"I do not know. We saw the girl only today."

"You are turning into women. Stay here with the child."

Mikkran feels the hard arms of the first warrior lift her under her knees and arms. She floats into the air and becomes an M against his torso. She can feel the hair on his body against her side. Her head falls back against his shoulder and she sees his face from underneath. It is like armor. Only his eyes show life as they attack from behind the cool metal of his face. His eyes burn quickly, absently across her face.

"I must take something from you." Nyz-Ragaan steps off the flat rock with Mikkran in his arms. He crosses the stream in one stride and walks toward the cave.

The cave is dark and cool. The dry, hard surfaces of rock work in and out, catching and hiding from light. The colors inside the cave are warm and brown, like Mikkran's skin. The two dark robes are now folded neatly on dry grass—beds.

Nzy-Ragaan stops a moment in the dark and lets his eyes adjust to the light in the cave. Then he walks toward the larger bed and lays Mikkran down on it.

"You have been here long enough to make a home."

"Yes."

"You are very beautiful for one so dark. I have never seen a Thoacdien before."

"All Thoacdiens are not dark."

"Yes. The girl is not so dark."

"Some Thoacdiens are almost as fair as you. Though not so tall."

"Thoacdien-Higgittes."

"Yes."

"Traitors."

"No."

"Yes. To me. They were seduced by your magic, by your Hall of a Thousand Chambers—and changed into women."

"You do not like women?"

"Women are made to serve men and bear children. They are slaves."

"I see. What are you going to take from me?"

"It is my right to take the body of a woman I have captured."

"Have you captured me?"

"You have felt the Zuri, have you not?"

"Yes. But not from you."

"You are perhaps too facile for the good of your own body."

"My body is not in danger, warrior."

"Do not imagine that you are desired and can play with me. I want nothing to do with you. If you will lay on your back I will remove the memory of the pain. I do not like to use the Zuri on women."

Mikkran turns onto her back. Nyz-Ragaan straightens her legs out and adjusts her arms at her sides. Then he tilts her head far back, smooths her forehead and brushes her dark hair away from her face. His two thumbs rest on her temples and rotate on them slowly. The memory of the pain, the fear of the pain, begins to receed.

"What is the Zuri?"

"Do not speak. It is the ancient Higgitte art of death with the hands. A Zuri artist can kill anything he can touch. Grod-Linz is such an artist."

"Are you?"

"Shhhhh. Yes. I am the best."

Mikkran looks up at his face, at the clean interplay of angles and planes. He returns her stare fully. Then he looks down at her long brown body, at her soft rounds meeting planes and the brown tones playing off each other. She smiles. His eyes come back to hers. He looks for the pupil in the black of her eyes, and can not find one. He sees instead a tiny, squared image of his own white face. She closes her eyes. Her lashes grow straight out and hang suspended above her cheek. His thumbs rotate slowly on her temples—deeper and deeper. She relishes in the relief from the ache in her body. Her mouth moves.

"What are you going to take from me?"

"Do you have a man?"

"Thoacdien mentors do not choose mates. We do not possess one another."

"You are celibate?"

"No. I am free."

"To do as you wish?"

"Exactly. Do you have a woman?"

"I am first warror. I have many women, but no one woman."

"You would like one woman."

"You are insolent."

"You are fascinated by my skin."

". . . yes."

"Take it."

"I shall take nothing from you. It would be desire. Not a victory."

"Desire is not cheap. Victory is cheap."

"Do not talk."

Nyz-Ragaan gently removes his deadly thumbs from Mikkran's temples. His breathing is deep and husky. Odors rise out of both of them, curling around and between them—calling. His eyes are close, clear and blue, looking into hers. He stares at her a long time through the mask of his face, then speaks.

"I hate you." He stands. He disturbs the air, agitating the odors. "I hate you." He walks to the far side of the small cave. He looks leaner in here, silhouetted against the light. He is angry and he is aroused. His penis points proudly against the blue loincloth, out of his control for the moment. The desire in him has weight and mass of its own. It will not be concealed. He turns away from her. She looks at him amused. He speaks softly.

"It would be good if you would scream now."

Mikkran catches her breath and then releases it. It is a silent laugh. He hears, but keeps his back to her.

"Scream."

Mikkran opens her mouth and a scream shatters the silence of the camp. She can hear Biel struggle outside. Then the girl is silent. Mikkran listens to determine that the child is all right. Then she stands and walks to the warrior. He turns and looks at her. The skin around his eyes is pulled tight.

"You. Mikkran."

"Yes?"

"You have earned your life with our stupidity. Do not be here tonight when the sun is broken. Go south along the edge of the desert. There is food and water. After much walking you will come to the meadows. Your own kind live there. When you see the meadows you have come to the end of our land. The ledge where the falls are continues all the way. Keep it on your left. You cannot get lost. If you come on our land, if the girl comes on our land, you must die. If I ever see you again I will kill you. Nyz-Ragaan, first warrior of the Higgittes, has said it." He studies her a moment, then steps through the mouth of the cave into the sun.

"Take the girl to the top of the falls and show her with a small animal what will happen to her if she ever comes onto our land again. Then let her go and return to the council hall."

Mikkran can hear the men move up the stream with Biel. She monitors the girl and knows that she has not been damaged. Biel's apprehension is within tolerances. The

166

seizure sleeps. Mikkran hears Nyz-Ragaan moving off in a different direction from the other three. She steps to the mouth of the cave.

"Stay in the cave until I am gone."

Mikkran smiles and nods, letting him get a few paces farther. Then she inserts a paralyzing flash into his cerebration. The warrior falls to his hands and knees as if shoved from behind. She releases the static in his brain. He scrambles to recover and stands, shakily. Their eyes lock for an instant—his surprised and furious, hers neutral. Then he turns and walks and is hidden by the rocks. He will have a headache for the rest of the day. Mikkran could have killed him.

When the mentor can no longer see Nyz-Ragaan, she turns to go back into the cave and gather their things. In a moment Biel is scrambling down the rocks hurrying back toward their invaded home.

"Mikkran! Mikkran!"

The child runs into the cave and freezes a moment, checking to see that the unthinkable did not happen. Mikkran takes the girl in her arms and soothes her. She can feel the surplus adrenalin making the girl tremble.

"Are you all right?"

"Yes. Mikkran, did he hurt you?"

"No, Biel. Do not be afraid. They will not harm us if we do as they say."

"Mikkran, they killed a little squirrel with their fingers."

"The Zuri is all they have left, Biel. Put your robe on quickly and help me. We must leave now."

. . . .

Col. Haris sat frozen, eyes glazed, in front of his ship's master console. He stared straight in front of himself without seeing anything but the unselected, indiscriminate blur of his metal-and-plastic environment. His face was lifted, corrugating his forehead. He looked mildly surprised.

FROM THE LEGEND OF BIEL

Col. Bob Haris had never in his entire, long, United Na-
tions Space Exploration career had to deal with human or
technological failure. He had been contingency-trained,
as had all space technicians. But the training had only
been simulation. And one thing he had always known in
simulation was that he was on the ground in Baja, Cali-
fornia. All his years in actual space his Contingency tape
had been silent in its little cassette. And when he finally
needed it, when he finally inserted it into the computer to
play through and select his course alternatives and prob-
ability stats, he discovered that there was no set of options
for this emergency. When he discovered that he went into
a ten-second reaction paralysis—akin to an epileptic fit.
Lt. Lanier was on the other side of the control room and
saw nothing. Ybarra and O'Hare were on their way to the
Skimmer. Nobody noticed—not even Col. Haris. He
blinked his eyes as a physical cue. He had recovered re-
activity and was ready to make his move.

. . . .

At the end of the desert there is a high wall of rock
which stretches in an essentially straight line for two-
thirds the length of the continent. It runs north to south.
Going north it runs almost to the cold polar region.
Going south it runs down to the equator and stops at the
meadows. West of this dividing line are the desert, the
grasslands and finally the sea. East of this dividing line is
the mesa with its great canyons, the mountains and then
the eastern Thoacdien dome complexes.

Biel and Mikkran walk north to south on a tiny strip of
neutral land between the desert and the Higgittes. A high
wall of rock stretches up on the left. This wall is punctuated three or four times in a day's walking by breaks
which lead in toward the mesa's canyons as corridors.
There is nothing on the right but heat which ripples up
to a white, cloudless sky. There are breaks in the monotony of the landscape where water leaks out of the can-

yons and permits small oases. Biel and Mikkran have found that leaving one oasis in the morning and stopping at the next in the evening is all the walking they can do in one day. They have camped in seven of these oases already. According to Mikkran's calculations the meadows are another ten oases away.

Mikkran and Biel are not afraid. They have been doing exactly as they were told. Mikkran has seen no more evidence of the Higgittes, but she knows they are there, defending their land from two lost and often comical Thoacdien women. Mikkran knows that the first warrior of the Higgittes leads the defense. As she walks south, toward the meadows, she can feel his eyes matching the sky, staring hard and hot on her back. She knows he will not let her out of his sight until the end of his land comes, and he can go no farther.

Mentor and child walk easily, relaxed. They have plenty of food and water if they are moderate. The season of the sun is waning and the heat is bearable next to the high, continuous cliff on their left. They walk side by side, talking constantly. The girl asks many questions and Mikkran answers when Biel cannot directly discover the resolution by herself. The mentor begins to teach Biel cerebration monitoring—the direct brain-to-brain transmission and reception of information, which begins with empathy. The girl is very susceptible. Soon, for several seconds at a time, she is able to trot along beside Mikkran in silence, transmitting and receiving hotly.

As Mikkran and Biel become more synchronized, more efficient at cerebration exchange, the mentor begins to probe for the source of the girl's seizures. Brain activity can be imagined as a continuous field or plane of electrical current. In healthy and normal cerebration the energy at all points on this imaginary plane is constant and even. There are no breaks or lapses, just as there are no holes in the water in a lake. In normal cerebration exchange at least two different brain-systems are superimposed on one another, matching up point for point. The rhythms of the brains are then synchronized, the circuit is complete, and communication happens. When Mikkran and Biel enter into cerebration exchange, the mentor can feel thin spots and holes in the plane of the girl's cerebration. Biel's current is blocked, interrupted in spots. The phenomenon of current being unable to jump fluidly from A to B on the plane of brain energy is called reaction paralysis—with respect to the effect, not the cause or the phenomenon itself. But Biel's lapses and more than simple reaction paralysis because at these points where the jump is not made there is not a pinpont blockage, or a faulty terminal, but a fissure—a tear. When, for some reason, a few fissures are agitated, Biel experiences a subtle petit mal type of seizure. When many of these fissures are pressured and violently agitated, the result is a grand mal.

Mikkran has tried to follow Biel into her smaller seizures, to discover where the girl is. But her brain does not have the fissures and she can only feel the effects of the journey. She cannot make it. The possibility of another grand seizure is never forgotten by the two. It terrifies them. So far, by working together they have avoided a recurrence. But Mikkran feels pressed to hurry, to somehow learn enough so that if it happens again she can do more than hold the child and wait for it to stop.

〰〰〰〰〰〰〰〰〰〰〰〰〰〰〰〰〰〰〰〰〰

FROM: FLOATER, COMPLEX 187-A, THOAC-DIEN V—PRIORITY TWO.
TO: THOACDIEN.
DATE: 187.342
TIME: 5.4.239
. . . .
. . . .
. . . .

THOACDIEN: PROCEED.
STOP.

FLOATER: SEARCH PATTERNS 1,2 AND 3 HAVE
BEEN COMPLETED OVER THE
DESERT OF DEATH.
RESULTS ARE AMBIGUOUS DUE TO
HARD SURFACE OF THE DESERT,
AND WIND.
INDICATIONS ARE THAT MENTOR
AND CHARGE HAVE CROSSED THE
DESERT AND ARE EITHER IN THE
CANYONS OR BESIDE THEM.
REQUEST PROCEDURES.
STOP.

THOACDIEN: CONTINUE SEARCH ALONG
WESTERN BORDER OF THE
CANYONS.
DO NOT SEARCH THE CANYONS.
THEY ARE HIGGITTE.
STOP.

FLOATER: INSTRUCTIONS RECEIVED AND
FOLLOWED. WE WILL CONTINUE
SEARCH NORTH TO SOUTH.
WE WILL STAY WEST OF THE
HIGGITTE BORDER.
STOP.

END TRANSMISSION ....

Between the desert and the mesa, between the dark
blue of night sky and the tan of the desert floor, two people light an evening fire and sit within its fading orange
boundaries.

"Mikkran, did you have a mentor?"

"Yes. I did. Even now I am with what is to me a mentor."

"Who is it?"

"I study with an elder, an old and beautiful woman whose name you are not yet ready to hear."

"You are still with her?"

"Oh, yes. She is rich in experience and has much to share. It is my privilege to be with her whenever I can."

"But you have no need."

"I am still a young woman, not one-quarter through my life. I know very little. My elder is three-quarters through her life. She has done what I have done once many times. She has done many times what I have yet to dream of."

"What is an elder?"

"Our society of human beings is naturally stratified. We have learned over the course of many years that what creates the stratification is experience, knowledge, wisdom. These qualities can, in most cases, be measured with age. We are informally divided into four groups. The first group is infants: those who have not yet completed their journey through The Hall of One Thousand Chambers. The second group is youth: those who primarily learn, but also share what they know—but they have more to learn than to share. You are becoming a youth. The third group is peers: those who learn and share equally. I am a peer. The last group is elders. These are the people who have lived long and well. They primarily share, but they also learn. It is a wonderful thing to become an elder. They are wise and tolerant. They have faced the unknown and survived. They help to pass courage and compassion, and most of all humor, on to us. Elders are those who have earned the right to advise."

"I should like to meet your elder."

"When you hear her name you will have earned the right to meet her."

The soft breeze is skin temperature. The stars have begun to return from their retreat during the season of the sun. They are brighter. Their colors are deeper pinks and yellows and greens and blues. The wind lifts a few sparks out of the fire. They fly low, hot and dying for a bit, and are gone.

"Biel, when we exchange cerebration I experience thin spots, gaps, in your field. Can you tell me what is inside these gaps? What they feel like?"

The girl holds the leg of a small fowl in one hand. Its lubricant glistens on her hand in the orange light. She is focused on the pleasure of the taste. She is quiet a moment, examining the food and the question.

"Have you really been to other places?" Biel gestures with her food, "Out there?"

"Yes."

"And I have not."

"That's right."

"I feel like I have. When I am caught in those gaps in my cerebration it feels like I am not-here and not-now. This other place is full of echos. I hear a voice, and it is not yours or mine. The voice is very clear and close—inside me. But it is also out there. I am afraid of it."

"How often do you hear this voice?"

"More all the time."

"How much does it interfere with your cerebration?"

"It doesn't follow a pattern. It is never the same. Sometimes I hear the voice and part of me stays here, talking to you, essentially unimpeded—like now. Sometimes I hear it and most of me goes away, to the voice, and you are in the distance—hardly perceptible. I know you are there more by memory than by direct experience. When that happens I am not anyplace or anytime that you have ever told me about. We do not know this place, or this person."

"Person?"

"Yes."

"Is it more natural for you to perceive and describe this phenomenon in terms of space, rather than time? Not-here, but some*place* else?"

"Ummm. Yes and no. I don't experience it in spatial terms. But to describe it I must use them. It is like I have a sense for direct perception of this phenomenon and you do not. We both have eyes. We open them and naturally scan what appears to be continuous, connected space.

Somehow I have eyes, or a tongue, or a pulse which you do not have. When this sense is stimulated I perceive. But how can I tell you what it tastes like? You live right here and now, in time and space. I do too, but I am also capable of another medium, unknown to both of us. When I have a seizure I am lifted out of our common medium, and dropped into another."

"Is that why we get so frightened?"

"Yes. So far the other medium has no tangible characteristics. And because I cannot identify it I am terrified. The other place is a juxtaposition of opposites. It is dark and not dark, a vacuum where I can breathe, a loud stillness, burning ice, death and yet I am alive, solitude where there is another."

"Is this other voice articulate? Can you understand what it says?"

"Could we not talk about it anymore?"

"Certainly."

Mikkran has finished eating and is lying stretched out on her side. Her head is braced on the heel of her left hand. The girl finishes with her fowl, and lies down, imitating the posture of her mentor. The fire is between them.

"Mikkran, what is that on your arm?"

"A tattoo. A symbol. What does it say to you?"

"Let's see. There is only one line, so it has no beginning or end. It is a twisted circle. It contains two equal spaces. It encloses some spaces and excludes others. I would say that all which is contained in the two connected circles is what you know. The upper circle would contain dynamic knowledge, and the lower circle would contain static information—facts which are exclusive of circumstances. The actual line enclosing those two spaces is the barrier between you and the unknown. Beyond the line is the unknown, and it is featureless, infinite."

"Mmmmmmmmmmm. It is the Thoacdien symbol for infinity."

"Aaaaa. It is a good symbol—clear and simple. But there is no dividing line between you and infinity."

"Umhum . . ."

"Why do you have it on your arm?"

"Do you want a long or a short answer?"

"A complete one."

"This figure became the Federation emblem after Xitr-Bielin created the First Great Thoacdien Revolution, thirty generations ago. So far there has been only one major revolution, but Thoacdien insists there will be more—which is why we don't just call it The Revolution. Xitr-Bielin's change was bloodless and thorough. It evolved around two accomplishments: his discovery of the infinite capacities of any given human brain-system, and his destruction of the syntax of despair. Before Xitr-Bielin we approached the human brain from the standpoint of its limits. It was large and complex, but ultimately finite."

"That is defeating."

"Yes. Part of making a discovery viable is changing the syntax surrounding it. Our syntax was defeating. We always bowed to what we believed were the superior computability powers of the mechanical extensions of our selves—our increasingly technologically perfect imitations of the human brain, called computers. Xitr-Bielin discovered, while working on his task to receive the voting right, that there is no limit to the functions, capabilities and possibilities of the human brain. Of all things in creation the human brain is the moxt complex and the most infinite. One human brain can embrace even creation itself, but creation cannot contain one human brain. Inside your skull is the potential to embrace all concepts and all reality. Xitr-Bielin's most important conclusion, however, was that in relation to the unknown, the released human brain is the most efficient system of apprehension we have, because it is the only system we have. Technology short-circuits when confronted with the unknown. Technology can only step so far out of the past. It cannot enter the present. It cannot comprehend the future. Human beings create the unknown and thrive on confrontation with it, long before it can be given to technology to categorize and remember. Xitr-Bielin also realized that syntax is reality. It creates reality. He changed our language and reality was transformed. Before his contribution we were awed by the products of our brains, but our syntax prevented us from appreciating the source of these products. Now we are reverent only to the individual life in its relation to the unknown, and the change this relationship makes possible. This figure eight is the symbol the Federation adopted in honor of his discovery and his exquisite articulation of that discovery. I wear a tattoo because all mentors are identified by, among other things, a tattoo. My tattoo is dark red because the color of my mentor order is maroon."

"The Order of Endless Curiosity?"

"Yes."

"What was the syntax of despair?"

"You must understand that before Xitr-Bielin, and many others who helped him, human beings were sick in ways you and I cannot conceive. This sickness was manifest in and encouraged by the way these people used the language. Hidden deep in the sounds of their words was despair and fear. Repeated use of the words and phrases only reinforced those feelings. The essential thrust of their language was control and ownership where control and ownership are not possible. Their syntax implied one thing and reality denied it. So they continually lost the battle to control and own. The result was despair."

"Be more specific."

"I will try, but I do not fully understand. I believe that these ill people spoke of owning each other, of owning land, ideas, animals, everything. They permitted governments and systems to try and control nonexistent entities like The People, Education, Health, even Death. They could not seem to understand that it is impossible to own mates, progeny, land, knowledge or emotions. States cannot control events. They cannot prevent change. They cannot be the stewards of The People because there is no such thing as The People. There are only persons."

"What can be owned?"

"Nothing."

"Nothing?"

"Nothing. A person's natural involvement is in the self. It is focused on the pleasurable discovery of the possibilities in selfness. It means doing, not possessing. Owning refracts that focus, diffuses the impulse to do. Doing, which is constantly extending the quality and quantity of relationships—both concrete and abstract—between self and not-self, which is responding to the instinctive urges to accomplish tasks which evolve from within because there is no other legal or logical place for them to come from, tasks which need no basis for their completion other than that you desire it so—doing is the natural activity of human life. It is the first reality, the one from which all others follow."

"Do. . . . They took pleasure only in despairing."

"Yes."

"And we have simply assumed a more precisely human posture."

"Exactly."

"I should like to have known Xitr-Bielin."

"You can know him."

"How?"

"You can meet him in the form of a hologram. You can question him until you are satisfied."

"What is that like?"

"It is very real. It looks almost as real as I look now. In fact it would look very much like what you are seeing now. You would be in darkness, and you would see him as through flames—like you are seeing me."

"When can I do this?"

"At the complex."

"I will not go back."

"That is for you to decide."

"Please, I want to stop talking now and sleep."

"Yes. We must walk far tomorrow. Let's sleep."

"Mikkran pokes at the fire to stir it, then lies still on her side, looking up at the stars. They seem to throb in the rhythm of her pulse. After a moment the girl comes over to the mentor's side. They clasp hands, and are asleep.

~~~~~~

FROM: FLOATER, COMPLEX 187-A, THOACDIEN V—PRIORITY ONE.
TO: THOACDIEN
DATE: 187.346
TIME: 6.8.507
SUBJECT: MENTOR   MIKKRAN-GOGAN-TOR
AND CHARGE 187-A,0037
. . . .
. . . .
. . . .

THOACDIEN: PROCEED.
STOP.

FLOATER: HAVE FOUND DEFINITE SIGNS OF
            CAMPSITES USED BY SUBJECTS.
            MENTOR AND CHARGE ARE
            PROCEEDING SOUTH TOWARD THE
            MEADOWS.
            WE SHOULD MAKE CONTACT BY
            187.347.
            REQUEST PROCEDURES.
STOP.

THOACDIEN: MAKE CONTACT.
            REPORT IMMEDIATELY.
            BE PREPARED TO TAKE THEM
            TO NEAREST DOME COMPLEX
            101-B WHICH IS SOUTHEAST OF
            THE MEADOWS.
· STOP.

END TRANSMISSION . . . .

Dawn opens like an egg on top of the Higgitte rock and spreads up pink into the dark of the night. It pulls itself up from behind the long wall and finally sits for an instant, the perfect red yolk, on top of the mesa.

The small half-spherical floater glides over the smooth, hard surface of the desert. It moves north to south, with the high wall of rock which signifies the beginning of Higgitte territory on the driver's left. It floats at the same height a gull cruises at while looking for food.

Mentor Lan-Biteus, in his dark green robe of Xitr-Bielin's Order of Infinite Mind, and his charge Xitr-Meede—now wearing the light blue robe which signifies that he has earned the right to travel freely on Toacdien V—sit at the controls of the floater and follow the thin trail left by Mikkran and Biel.

"They will be happy to see us. They will be happy that they are not lost anymore."

"Try not to speculate when answers will be apparent in a short while."

Biteus and Xitr-Meede were the only mentor and charge free to travel Thoacdien V when the request for a floater team came in. They volunteered because Mikkran is a friend to both of them. They helped her in the long wait for her charge back at the dome, and came to greatly respect her patience.

Xitr-Meede is now a tall young man. His chubbyness is gone. He is blond and stately, sitting in the forward seat of the floater. His dark mentor sits behind him, looking down over his left shoulder for the trail.

Biel sleeps on her side with her face resting near Mikkran's shoulder. Something is annoying her. Something will not let her sleep. Half awake, she stumbles up in the dark morning and wanders into the low brush to relieve herself. There is something unnatural and out of place in the environment she has become so accustomed to. She walks to the tiny pool of water in the center of the oasis and bathes her face, slapping it with icy water to wake up. Mikkran stirs. Biel freezes, quiet, to let the mentor sleep.

Only the girl's eyes move, scanning the familiarity for a difference. It is a noise . . . which has no direction, no visible source. She looks up to the north and sees a small white bubble in the distance, floating toward her. It glows softly in the first bleeding light of morning. It grows steadily larger and larger, connecting with the increasing hiss which stirs the familiar sounds of the desert. It hovers in the air, half the distance between the floor of the desert and the top of the rock wall on her right.

Mikkran feels the girl's agitated cerebration and stirs. As her eyes open and adjust she sees Biel running up the path made by the small trickle of water which oozes out of the canyon. She looks up and sees the black figure eight on the floater as it lands nearby with only a slight disturbance of dust. Two figures in the control area stand and get ready to leave the small ship. And Mikkran is on her feet, running after Biel.

~~~~~~

FROM: FLOATER, COMPLEX 187-A, THOAC-DIEN V—PRIORITY IMMEDIATE.
TO: THOACDIEN.
DATE: 187.347
TIME: 1.0.002
SUBJECT: MENTOR MIKKRAN-GOGAN-TOR AND CHARGE 187-A,0037

. . . .
. . . .
. . . .

THOACDIEN: PROCEED.
STOP.

FLOATER: HAVE MADE VISUAL CONTACT
WITH SUBJECTS. FLOATER IS
LANDED, COORDINATES TO
FOLLOW.

.

ARE PREPARING TO LEAVE THE
SHIP NOW.
STOP.

THOACDIEN: MAKE CONTACT AND REPORT
IMMEDIATELY STATUS OF
SUBJECTS.
REQUEST MIKKRAN REPORT TO
ME AS SOON AS POSSIBLE.
WILL STAND BY.
STOP.

P A U S E ....

Biel crests the wall of rock and stands at the edge of
the huge, irregular mesa which is dotted with deep, wide
holes—the canyons. She wavers a moment, then runs
southeast, making a huge curve around the first small
canyon.

Biteus and Xitr-Meede climb down from the floater and
call after the running figure they know to be Mikkran.
They look at each other and know they love her. They
follow.

Mikkran crests the wall and sees Biel running. She does
not waver but follows the girl into the vermillion light-
source of the new day.

On the mesa many light blue eyes mirror the red of the
sky, like deep cats' eyes. They watch first one figure, then
another, then two more—new ones—invade the last of
their land. On a silent signal from the first warrior of the
Higgittes they rise up out of their shadows and stand sharp
against the bluing sky to respond.

VI

"*Lieutenant Lanier, time check?*"

"*It is five minutes and forty-two seconds into the audio silence, sir.*"

"*Ybarra and O'Hare?*"

"*Where are you?*"

"*We're in Skimmer Three umbilical tube.*"

"*OK. I want rush, code-one-red check-out on the Skimmer. We will be coming into position for your drop in about three minutes.*"

"*Check. The computer is attached and checking the Skimmer. I have a map of the dome and instructions on how to get into the chamber. How long will it take us to get down to MC6?*"

"*If you can drop in three minutes it will take you about fourteen minutes to be on the surface.*"

"*We can make it.*"

At the far side of the large catamaran of a spaceship, in the portside pontoon, two men pulled themselves through the hatch of Skimmer Three while the computer clicked its way through check-out. Ybarra had been on one other long-duration PROBE mission. O'Hare had done his spaceflight training with trips back and forth to the moon. Ybarra was nervous. O'Hare was not.

"*Lieutenant Lanier, this is Ybarra. We are checked out*

and in the Skimmer. Put us on three minute countdown from . . . now."

"*Check. You are on three minute countdown. You are two minutes and fifty-eight seconds from separation, and counting.*"

O'Hare pulled the soft straps over his shoulders and fastened them with a reassuring click at the juncture between his legs. He checked his personal weapon, then slid the dark visor down over his face and locked it. He looked like a huge bug, or a brain which had somehow evolved without the protective covering of skull and flesh, and was instead housed in a white-and-green opaque plastic bubble, with two flag decals for ears.

The Skimmer was suspended from the ship on the MC6 side. It was held in place by three large metal clasps. Ybarra and O'Hare had entered the little ship by crawling through its long, soft umbilical tunnel, the fourth and last attachment to the ship.

"*Ybarra, Colonel Haris here. How do you check out?*"

"*We check out all systems go. Any audio contact with the research team?*"

"*Negative. You are minus one minute and thirty-five seconds to separation, and counting.*"

"*Release clasp one.*"

"*Clasp one is released.*"

There was a soft explosion of steam and suds. Clasp one lifted off the Skimmer like a hand retreating from a hot potato.

"*Release clasp two.*"

"*Clasp two is released.*"

"*Release clasp three.*"

"*Clasp three is released. You are minus fifty-five seconds, and counting. All systems are go.*"

The soft umbilical cord carried them along with the ship as easily as the three metal arms had.

"*Skimmer Three power on.*"

"*Skimmer Three power is on.*"

"*Ybarra, I will give you dome procedures in approximately five minutes.*"

"You are minus twenty seconds, and counting."
"Check. O'Hare says they've probably discovered a hamburger joint and just forgot all about us."
"Then their asses are cooked."
"Release umbilical, Skimmer Three."
"Umbilical is released."
We are counting down from five, four, three, two, one."
FFFFFFFFFFFFFFFFFFFFFFFFFfffffffffffffff
f f f f f f f f . . . . .
"You are separated from the ship and on your way at nine minutes and twenty seconds into audio silence. You will land on MC6 in fourteen minutes."
"Good luck you two."
"Yes, sir. We'll see you in about two hours."

. . . .

For many days children and wives of the Higgitte warriors will stand silently on top of the mesa trying to imagine what happened. The encounter between the four Thoacdiens and the two thousand is sung about and has become a legend. If the Higgitte nation can last long enough the story will become a myth of supernatural proportions and the outcome will be clear. Now it is not.

The four strangers had run across the apparently deserted mesa, skirting the access holes to the canyons. It was so quiet that each footstep which pounded and ground and thrust the bodies forward was heard distinctly. And hearing their own feet and nothing else, they thought only that they might have a chance. Mikkran had sent Biel repeated messages to stop, which were ignored. Biteus had called loudly, clear as a song, to Mikkran, telling her who they were and what they wanted. Then, at an instant when all eight feet were off the ground and suspended in postures of reaching, two thousand Higgitte warriors rose up out of their shadows as one and stood silent behind their shields and spears to defend their land. The four strangers froze, heads snapped toward one another, faces

185

lifted in admiration for the precision and height of the Higgitte warrors in silhouette.

The sun had not yet left its pinkness, but already there were shadows. The four strangers opened their minds and rapid, invisible messages passed between them. With the unison appearance of the warriors surrounding them in two large concentric circles, the four became animals ready to do what is necessary to survive.

From the time the floater landed to the beginning of the battle, the mesa was silent. Only the wind moved. Only the wind could be heard fastidiously arranging the tiny, transparent grains of sand on the mesa. The heat was only beginning to rise from the desert. The sky was only beginning to change from pink to blue.

Biteus took command of the Thoacdiens. He responded automatically. The four were enclosed in the Higgitte circle of death. They had no weapons nor any cultivated instincts to defend themselves or to harm others—only the will to live. Biteus quickly moved to the center of the large circle—the point farthest away from the Higgittes –and called the others to him.

When Biel saw the warriors she froze. Her mind reached out for her mentor like the hand of one who has just fallen over a cliff. Mikkran, receiving instructions from Biteus, transferred them to Biel. With minds locked they slowly backed toward the center of the circle and Biteus. Since they were women and unarmed and moving slowly, the warriors permitted it. Out of fascination the Higgittes permitted the Thoacdiens to make a formation.

Nyz-Ragaan stood frozen in front of the sun. His face was a mask. His body was a mask. He stood passive as was his habitat these moments in the game of death.

The four Thoacdiens stood naked and back to back, like a simple star, facing the three hundred and sixty degrees of Higgitte warriors. And suddenly, from the four came a sound—as of a deadly song. It rose up and out of them, slicing through the warriors like razors. Several Higgittes stiffened, untouched by anything but the sound. Their long poles flickered against the whitening sky, and they fell upon their shields. A few others staggered and fell to their knees. The wave of sound continued from the four, and only when they stopped to breathe were the Higgitte warriors safe. Then the first warrior raised his shield, blotting out the sun, and as one the warriors advanced and shrank their circular ranks in on the sound. They made no noise as they advanced. And the deadly sound which came from the four decreased, became a whisp, then an echo, then only a memory.

—. . . a large thumb with a cracked and yellow nail . . . A large thumb which is attached to a large, callused hand is coming at me. . . . The two big fingers are pinched in toward the thumb, making an open circle for my neck. The third finger is broken and stiff, bent down from the raised middle joint making a lazy, inverted V which cannot flatten. The fourth, or little finger is mis . . .

～～～～～～～～～～～～～～～～～～～～～～～～～

THOACDIEN: MENTOR L'AN-BITEUS . . . . ?
            . . . . ??? . . . .
            MENTOR MIKKRAN-GOGAN-TOR
            . . . . .??? . . . .
            IS ANYONE ABLE TO TRANSMIT
            OR RECEIVE AT THIS TIME?
            PLEASE RESPOND . . . . .! . . . .!
            . . . . .? . . . .
            ARE YOU IN DANGER?
            XITR-MEEDE? . . . . ?
            . . . .!! . . . .!! . . . . . .
            187-A,0037 ??? . . . . !
            . . . .

P A U S E . . . .

From a point of light inside Biel's mind, moments stretch out unevenly and incomplete in all directions as untraveled mazes. She perceives what is beyond through a diffusion and confusion of rusty veils. She is alive, but not yet quite awake beneath a drug. She would like to comprehend, but does not know which way to look to get a picture of the whole. She cannot stand, but lies limp on the floor, lost in a city of feet.

. . . cacophony . . . yelling. . . .

Where are the others? . . .

. . . These persons . . . need to bathe . . .

A large glob of yellow spittle hits the ground by my eye and explodes. It hits the ground and spreads out as a dark stain in the chocolate-colored dust, making itself look bitter and gritty and important. . . .

The ground is in my mouth, chalky, dry. . . .

I will lift my eyelid a little . . . more . . . heavy as a metal door. . . .

Light hurts!

These persons scream at one another. Stop . . . you are too loud and make no sense.

. . . I've lost half of my head. It rolls away between the feet. I reach and cannot . . . find it.

The planet has changed its axis . . . I am going to vomit. Focus on something. . . . legs . . .

Achilles' tendons. white. pink. horizontal bend lines, and blue shadows.

. . . white skin like thin milk . . .

ordinary toes.

loincloths.

thighs.

. . . yelling. . . .

buttocks.

Inside my stomach there is hair and sour bile . . . do not think of that. . . .

I'm being lifted . . .

dropped, like a sack.

. . . my neck . . .

They will not stop . . . screaming. . . .

My head is held and I am forced to choose one unreal reality over all the rest. It is an old . . . man.

Old man.
Eyelids smooth, stony, single-folded, and wrapping all-of-a-piece around his faded blue marble eyes.
No veins.
Is he alive?
His pupils are dusty purple, each covered by an opaque membrane.
He cannot see, but pretends.
His eyes are dry, filled with tiny rivers of blood which have become frozen.
. . . Each moment is a labyrinth and I cannot complete the maze to understanding.
This old man is not alive, but pretends. He is a game. His eyelids hang poised like two blades across my neck, ready to drop, or stay propped up and commute the sentence, depending on the whim of his digestion, and the screaming of the crowd. As long as he is mildly fascinated by me, by my skin and the texture of my hair, as long as there is strength in his dryness, as long as the weight of the deeply carved stone lids does not tire his measureless age, I, Biel, am alive.

"They paralyzed twenty-three of our warriors. They must die!"

"They speak to each other without talking. I saw."

"They must be drugged and kept alive so that we can capture their secrets for our nation."

"The boy is one of ours. The other three must die."

"We can use them as slaves to rebuild our nation."

"They are abominations!"

And the screaming goes on, muddying and defining the poles of the argument with primitive ceremony as each warrior is given his chance to speak.

"The little girl is to be my concubine. It was I, I, who captured her. She will serve me as I help rebuild the nation!"

For two days the old man sits unblinking, listening to the full but simple exploration of each point of view, each degree encompassed by the two poles.

189

"They must die immediately! We cannot reclaim our nation while they live!"

"No! They must teach us what they know!"

The entire Thoacdien Federation could have settled the matter in a few moments.

"They are magic."

"We can turn them into slave priests!"

"The woman must be given to Nyz-Ragaan as a slave! He captured her!"

"She must die now!"

"Patriarch, if I may be permitted to express my point of view to the strengthening nation?"

An indifferent wave of the wrinkled hand encourages the warrior.

"The Thoacdiens are full of magic. If we could learn their tricks, blessed Patriarch, we could make war on Thoacdien . . ."

"We are making war on Thoacdien!"

"We could make blood war on Thoacdien. We could recapture our glorious planet and go on, having learned their tricks, to rule the stars!"

"Patriarch, please, that warrior is a fool. If I may be permitted before your august personage . . . thank you, father. That warrior is a fool! We must kill the invaders now! I beg you! They must die! Their tricks will blow away our way of life. They will kill us. They must die now! Thank you Patriarch for listening. Kill them now!"

I stir, gathering my moments more fully around me, venturing into each more fully than the one before, until I can almost complete each maze.

. . . a rub of something cold on my spine . . .

aaaaaaaaaaaaaaaaaaaaaaaaaaaaaaaaaaaaaaaaaaaaaaaaaaaaa

a jab, a rip, a . . . tear . . .

and then a swelling . . .

And I am pushed . . . back from the edge of my awareness . . . to the darkness behind, and the darkness before . . . the knots and beats along the long string of my life have been . . . removed. I have . . . nothing . . . to

tell me . . . where I have . . . been . . . how far . . . I've
come . . . or . . . whe . . . re . . .

In the center of the mesa the main corridors of the
canyons converge and form a huge irregular chamber of
water-streaked, stratified brown rock. This chamber is
covered by a thick slab of rock which does not quite come
together in the middle so that at certain times in the day
the sun can be seen through the hole in the ceiling as a
huge brass gong, and its rays are hot sound. This chamber
is large enough to accomodate the two thousand Higgitte
warriors and all their dependents at meeting time. It is
here that the celibate council of rulers resides. It is here
that the Patriarch is honored.

The central chamber naturally shapes space so that all
attention is focused on the throne at its easternmost point.
Here, the Patriarch sits eating and unblinking, listening
to reports from the council runners and to the arguments
of the warriors. It is here, before the Patriarch, that each
warrior will cut one arm or the other in one long decision,
one single, deep slash which will scar and become a
record of what happened to the four.

There is a large natural shelf on the eastern wall of the
chamber, up and behind the throne of the Patriarch,
where the council of celibates meets with the four leaders
of five hundred and the first warrior of the Higgittes. In
session now, it meets to decide the fate of the four Thoacdiens. The council's recommendation will determine the
vote. The council members wear grotesque masks of office
and attitude which depersonalize the wearer and cue the
game. This is the power of the Higgitte nation.

Below, standing respectfully far from the Patriarch,
stamping their bare white feet softly, humming flat notes
that circle around and scrape the stone chamber clean,
swaying back and forth as one, are four thousand women
and miscellaneous dependents on the nation. Logana, the
Patriarch's concubine, is the only woman, the only non-
warrior who is near the symbol of power. She sits at the

191

old man's feet, her toes touching his as a perpetual act of defiance. She watches the four drugged prisoners and periodically lifts her thin brows as a signal to inject them again.

Up on the shelf the various masks of rage and tolerance and slavery and power and magic nod and argue about the prisoners. Nyz-Ragaan's flattened tin mask, with its expression of rage, is cool against his face. It is a buffer of darkness, a cushion of silence and neutrality between himself and the council. The outer surface of the mask glistens and reiterates his unchanging opinion. The inside of the mask does not quite rest against his face. There is a space of indifference between the flesh of his face and the expression of the mask.

The first warrior of the Higgittes sits on the floor with his hands on his chisled knees and does not hear the aruginents about what should be done now. He stands to the side of himself and watches his unmoving profile relish his secrets in the shadow of the mask.

From the side, the planes and angles of Nyz-Ragaan's face are pinched at the seams and he looks like a bored boy who has stood awed outside the window of power long enough to finally see the nature of the game, the purpose of the arguments. He is no longer interested. He wants the woman. His whole being has become a shaft, an arrow drawn back in the bow, waiting to run her through. He performed his functions as leader and protecter of the nation by stamping his feet and manifesting the attitudes dictated by his mask of rage. He said that they must die and until his eloquent mask is changed he has no need to say more. He hopes to be defeated. He hopes the debate will end soon because only his head is here now. Behind the screen of the mask his body stretched away from the council room long ago, and became liquid which attained its weight and rolled down her body, as did the droplet on her back the first time he ever saw her.

Nyz-Ragaan sits erect and unconsciously disciplined, entering the second day of debate. The matter is nearing the articulation of the recommendation of the council. Then they will all vote—slicing themselves where there is room, as a mark of prestige and commitment to the nation. He will have been defeated. It must be. It will be decided to keep the four alive and separated, and to interrogate them as to the nature of Thoacdien. Nyz-Ragaan will wear the tin mask of rage for a few days, and stomp and strut around, and avoid or mistreat his women. Then he will go to Mikkran.

Biteus sits limp, propped up in the corner of the small, stone, almost cubed cell which is twice his body length. There are no doors and no seams. There is no way out but from the high opening overhead, a hole in the top of the vaulted roof just big enough for his body to be raised or lowered by a rope. In his head, placid beneath the drug and holding on, are old songs—rounds which circle, dig in deeper and struggle to become the still spot in his disorientation.

Xitr-Meede, in a cell far away from his mentor, is rolled around himself, like a snake swallowing its own tail. His mind spirals out in sleep to level after level of dreams of greatness. Achievements sit on shelves far above him, glittering like jewels and calling. The stone floor spreads out seamless around him and, with few irregularities, becomes dark, sweating walls which end in no ceiling but the early morning sky.

Biel lies spread-eagle, shot-on-the-run on the floor, face up. Her eyelids bounce in sleep and her breathing fogs her teeth. Her seizures snore beneath her like calmed oceans. The black robe no longer reaches to her feet—a compromise has been made between neck and toes. So her chin moves up and down chewing to create heat, and her toes clench occasionally in response. Far above her, where the rock of her cell ends and the sky begins, two sexless, ageless eyes stare down with no identity, and fascinated, from a shadow.

Mikkran lies flat, face up, arms out to the side, trying instinctively to relax and get beneath the drug. But motivation to complete the task requires a discipline she has forgotten. Her life seems to be unraveling row by row to the last one, where the stitches have been knotted. She tries to listen in her mind for something, but hears only silence—and she cannot remember to keep trying.—. . . There . . . through that faraway hole . . . is the sky. . . .

The sun struggles up from behind the eastern horizon, rolling up the tent of night with its long, thin arms of light. Higgittes rise silently and walk to their places in the greeting line. Each of the Higgitte compounds has, as a special place, a central chamber under the mesa, with a high, vaulted ceiling. The natural cave ceilings do not quite come together in the center, which leaves each with an opening, or skylight. Slightly before each dawn all members of the nation kneel beneath the opening in their compound, in the order of their rank, and watch the sun transform the black, indistinguishable disk in the center of the ceiling into a pale indication of what the day is to be.

Now the dark sky can be distinguished from the stone of the ceiling as a dark blue target. A hum starts softly in a holy nose and glides out of lips, tickling the front of the face and the backsides of teeth. It forks out beyond the surface of the hummer to join sounds which originate from other rasping noses. The soundwaves are stratified. The layers rub up next to each other like cats going in opposite directions. They swell, bounce along sculpting corridors, round corners, become rich and raspy, join waves which originate from other noses in other parts of the hive, until they have become a flood which began as a little trickle of sticky sound and is now a rushing wall, a tide which courses through the closets and alleys and chambers, filling all negative space until finally the pressure becomes too great and it must escape through the hole on top of the mesa. The sound leaks out like smoke, or little bees. The sound continues as a constant and the little disk in the tops of the ceiling becomes an old silver coin. The sound rises to polish it, to remove the tarnish of the unknown, of the endless subterranean night, bit by bit, with friction. And finally it glistens, fading to shiny silver and then to gold. And the sound, having accomplished its task, ceases. The day has begun.

Biteus hears the sound of bees. His heavy eyelids lift up in front of his songs, his little rounds, his disorientation, and he sees a darkness cover the patch of fading sky at the top of his cell. The bees fly by, dropping sound bombs of honey down through the narrow opening into his cage. It tickles his ears deep down and makes the rich, hidden wax rattle. His eyelids close with a head-splitting clang as he hears a rope unravel and fall hissing near his stretched-out feet. Movement stirs up the poised, shafted notes inside the cell and disturbs the paralyzed molecules inside the dark bag of his skin. A thumb, hot and callused stone, is resting behind his ear. There is the pushing of a blunt stick into the soft and vulnerable part of his elbow. He feels the vein pop out of the way, then get caught. His eyes lift open by themselves. And the shattered pieces of himself come back together, but do not adhere.

"If you move you will die."

Biteus pulls down against the upward lift of his eyelids to close them. The pieces of himself waver, then lose their brittleness and exude a glue which oozes out, connecting edge to edge, and holds. There are two of them. One with a thumb behind his ear. The other is talking.

"I am Nyz-Ragaan, first warrior of the Higgittes. You have been given an antidote for the disorienting drug. It is not enough to make you normal, only enough to make me comprehensible to you."

A thumb lifts his eyelid rudely and lets in too much light. He tries to free his head from the intrusion and feels a fireknife cut through the nerves of his spine. Biteus can move, but he cannot move, for fear the pain will split him in half.

"The warriors have voted. For the time being you will be kept alive. We shall continue the drug, but only in amounts sufficient to cut off the silent power with which you kill. You will explain the magic of Thoacdien to us so that we can rebuild our nation and regain our planet."

The thumb releases his eyelid. It snaps back like a rubber band retreating to rest. His mind receeds back into the swirling darkness. He gropes, blind, for a question— something he should ask. And his hand grabs at slippery handles in the dark which pull loose from their moorings and leave him vague and recoiled in his own puddle of confusion. He shivers. He hides from his search for the question, and opens his mouth.

"Where is my charge?" Pain slices him lengthwise, right down through the middle of the darkness inside his skin, and splits him open, exposing the soft, white, porous meat of an apple.

"Leave him. He will recover."

The thumb lifts out of the small bowl behind his ear. By the time he has rolled up the long screens of his eyelids, he is alone in the dark stone cell with a tube of white and settled light slipping down through the opening in the top of the vaulted ceiling, like a straw.

Sound bounces back and forth in the alleys and closets beneath the mesa with the sharp cracks of whips or objects in collision. Sound moves constantly in the Higgitte camps, chewing at the simple underpinnings as balls strike walls which can endure only so many blows before they collapse. Only occasionally does it arch and glide, to become tender barking as a warrior unwraps one of his women from her cloth which is both badge and accusation.

All Higgitte men capable of intercourse are warriors. And throughout the day the young boys fight each other, flashing their new potency as they battle for rank. The two thousand warriors are thought of as a long, continuing line of decreasing ability. The first warrior is the strongest man in the nation. The weakest young boy is worth very little. Ordinary warriors wear black loincloths and their heads are shaven. Those who are responsible for twenty-four warriors wear yellow and are permitted a small lock of hair at the back of their heads. Those responsible for ninety-nine warriors wear red and have a short fringe of hair all over their heads. Those responsible for five hundred wear green and have enough hair to comb. The number one warrior wears the cherished light blue, and may have a mane. The length of a number one warrior's uninterrupted stay in office can be determined by the length of his hair. A warrior's women may wear only the color of his rank. The council of celibates wears dark blue. The Patriarch may wear robes of many colors. The sounds beneath the mesa crackle with the continual confrontation of strong against stronger, all training to re-build the nation.

(—Hold on.
—I am.
—Yes.
—We are acting this out so many times.
—But we have not yet come to the one time . . .
—The time when acting out the passage only once more in the flipped-out, open side of the event will let us be done with it.
—I'm tired.
—Yes . . .
—Stay here with me.
—I am.
—It's not much longer now.
—But even not much longer is so far away.
—These are only frozen events passing . . .
—Little deaths which have no meaning in the whole landscape of change.
—Yes.
—We are nearing the convergence . . .
—The intersecting alleyways which come together and form a complex, invisible star.
—Yes.
—We are approaching the flipped-out, open side of the event.
—We shall step out of this fulcrum.
—Rest.
—Yes . . .

—Hold on.
—I am.)
Sounds rise and fall, group together momentarily to form complex messages, patterns, which rise, rise, intensify, then fade and drift apart. Some sounds ricochet through my head as sharp objects. Some wrap themselves around my pulse and create a counterpoint. We come together like the ten fingers of two hands and I am fugued, interlocked, synchronized, syncopated—then abandoned, with only the distant sound of the rhythm of my own sucking and spitting-out heart. What is this called?
I have opened my eyes. And I see . . . my hair . . . webbing black nets across my face—and through that . . . a day. I am lying on my back with my right ankle under my left knee. My black robe is tucked under my arms and bunched up so that it only comes to my knees. My toes are cold. Wiggle them. My arms are . . . above my head. My head is resting on my laced fingers which tingle with poor circulation. . . . There. Now my fingers curl and flick one another, coming to life. My body is fine. Hard stone . . . I am lying on the floor of a cell in the Higgitte camp. I have been awakened by sounds of practice for battle—a celebration? I have lifted the blanket of my hair and now see clearly a square of blue sky above me, framed by four stone walls. I have been sleeping, and my spine hurts. I have a headache. But I, Biel, am alive. "Biel . . ." I whispered it, loving the word. My robe is too small and scratches. Off. Roll over softly. The floor is cold on the tiny still-dead seeds of my breasts. My stomach makes a bridge over the stone floor from the bones of my hips to the bones of my chest, because the floor is coooold. I squint my right eye and see a floor sculpted in tiny detail, like the floor of the desert. It vanishes into the corner. Gray. Gray. Gray. Dark brown pockmarks . . . gray. Gray. And dark greens. I roll my glance slowly up the wall and it ends after almost three lengths of my body. A bubble bursts in my stomach, and where my insides were firm there is a continuous, falling collapse.
"Hey!" I am hungry. "Hey!" Silence, except for the violent

contests which are all around me and within range of a
shout. "Hey!" I have been in here two days. This is the
beginning of my third day in the Higgitte nation. I haven't
lost my seizures. They sleep beneath me as always, fingering their property in dreams, like misers. My hands are
dirty.

"Hey!!" Steps. The feet must be dry and cracked to make
such a rasp on dry stone. There is a yellow rope, like a
tangled question, with a seam spiraling up it. Two slender
white arms tie a knot onto something dark. A bucket . . .
dark, wet, new wood . . . comes down spinning. I smell
water and bread and fruit.

The bucket strikes the stone floor near my feet with a
bark. There is the soft prickle of fuzzy yellow fruit on my
hand. My fingers bend its softness, my teeth break its
softness and my mouth explodes as juice makes saliva. I
drool sticky down my chin. I am an eruption of the juice
of yellow fruit. My teeth are liquid. My whole mouth is
a lake of sweet thick water fed by the stream where we
used to live and Mikkran bathed in the morning, catching the sun like a brown jewel, and I combed the grass
with my hands, licking the white wet from between my
fingers.

My teeth are at war with the bread and it marches down
my mouth and throat in regiments of tall white men.
The water.

Oh . . . oh . . . I am a stream inside and out.

I am dirty. My wet fingers leave white roads on my chest.
The bucket is gone . . . a flash of quick hands, then the
uninterrupted square of blue sky. The others are still
drugged. I shall sleep again, now.

The white form of Nyz-Ragaan shows dark bronze
against the early blue sky as he leans over the opening at
the top of Mikkran's cell and peers down as into a well, or
through a pond. And, as at the bottom of a pool, Mikkran's form lies limp and liquid, far away. He sees her
stillness, her unnatural sleep, as a violation of some higher
law. She is too dark to be kept in a dark cell. It should be

white to contrast, war, and be defeated by her colors. The rope-ladder coiled in his hand is a long phallus which went down limp into limpness. She had tried to listen to the verdict of the council. She had looked at him uncomprehending. She should be in a lighter cell to set off her beauty, the beauty of an equation just discovered which brings together the laws of creation in one perfect, simple symbol. She should not be in a cell at all. He pulls the tin mask up to his face, fits its inner cap over the cap of his hair, blinks, and is gone.

Logana floats by, an image on wheels, her eyes noncommittal in a way that is a trap. It is her privilege to receive the best seed in the nation. There is disdain in her round face and full mouth. Her hair floats behind her like a siren's as she pulls aside the drape on the Patriarch's bedchamber and disappears into the dark, trailing an image of rounded thigh curving and undulating gradually down to a slim ankle.

"It is useless even to try to talk to the boy." Grod-Linz watches his leader throw the rope-ladder down and disgustedly stalk off, calves bulging. The lesser warrior looks down into the little cell and sees the blond boy who is so strangely out of place with the other three. "He is one of ours." Grod-Linz remembers the exit of hordes of Higgitte warriors and their women who left so long ago, so naively believing they could pass through The Hall of a Thousand Chambers unchanged. They are gone. They have not been seen since—have not since even breathed in the direction of the remains of the nation. "He could be related to me." Grod-Linz feels the curve of his nose, trying to match it with the one in the cell. Then he follows the first warrior to the little girl's cell.

The Patriarch lies on his simple bed. He is cold and Logana's body tried to warm him with heat that is uneven and only on the surface. She does not radiate deeply enough. Her moisture cannot reach to where the growing

pocket of death is humming and hidden inside the Patriarch.

"Let me have the first warrior." The sound is a hand
that reaches up into the Patriarch's nose and closes off
the passages. He blinks. A thin river of drool runs out of
his mouth and down across her wrist resting close to his
face. Logana closes her eyes to stop the hard ball of rancid bile from rising any farther out of her stomach. She
stops it between her breasts where it glows like a hot rock.

"Let me belong to the first warrior."

". . . Call the council to me."

Biel wakes with two tall blond ones standing over her.
One, the shorter, wears a red loincloth and is the one
who hurt Mikkran that day at the camp when Biel had
slept late to let her mentor take her pleasure. The other,
the tall one, wears blue, and is the one who talked and
made Mikkran cry out from the cave. The shorter one
sees that she is awake and moves to get behind her.

"Do not get behind me, please."

Grod-Linz stops and checks with the other, who nods to
continue. A thumb, its print spiraling out from the center
as ridges in a hard callus, fits into the little cup behind
her ear. Biel sees a flash in her mind, as if light came up on
a transparent orange-and-brown photograph for just an
instant, revealing two small boys on top of the mesa
through many seasons, conscientiously rubbing their
thumbs on rocks to harden them. The image is gone.

Biel smiles, feeling clean and open and swept out. There
is a taut, high vibrato right in the center of her brain. "I
will not be held in this manner." Her eyes look up and
swallow the great warrior. She sees him halved, one side
against the other—fire and ice—as he is paralyzed by her
cerebration. He feels a large brown fabric rise up out of
her eyes and snuff him out.

"Tell him to release me."

The sound comes from so far away, and yet from
somewhere that is still inside him.

"Release her, Grod-Linz."

"Thank you."

Biel raises the darkness off of Nyz-Ragaan's mind by lowering her eyes. "Do not try to hurt me. You will suffer greatly."

"Why are you awake while the other sleep?"

"I don't know. Perhaps I understand the drug." Her voice is an oboe.

The taller one looks down at Biel from his dichotomy. There is a thin, red wound on his forearm. One eye, which feeds half his body, sees what it wants to see—and is fire. The other eye, which feeds the other half of his body, sees what it cannot avoid—and is ice.

"You are Nyz-Ragaan, first warrior of the Higgittes. And you are Grod-Linz."

—His thumbprint is evaporating so slowly from behind my ear.

"And you are Biel."

"Well . . . we remember each other. What do you want?"

"We come to wake you and tell you the verdict of the nation."

"Concerning what?"

"Your life."

"Aaaaaaaaaaaa . . ."

"You will be permitted to live—for the time being."

"When did this permission become yours to assume?"

"When you invaded the mesa and were defeated."

"I see. Where is Mikkran?"

Biel watches as the split between Nyz-Ragaan's two halves widens. His breathing freezes an instant and excess emotion escapes in a quick, blue belch of flames.

"I cannot tell you that."

"I asked the question out of politeness, and not to scare you. Now I will not be polite and I will scare you. Mikkran is southeast of me within the distance of a shout. Biteus is directly west, closer than Mikkran. And the boy is on the other side of this wall." The wall is cool and smooth and part of it seems to come away on the palm of her hand which she places once more like a flower in her lap. She sees the two men look at each other and there is a flash which brings into focus a blue mirage of two clasped hands straining to hold on against the backward weight of the whole tribe. The hands sweat, are ripped apart, and the identities attached to them fall. The mirage fades to an even gray in her mind.

"Have you felt nothing of the drug?"

"Very little."

"Are the others capable of this?"

"Obviously not. They are asleep now. Drugged. I do not approve."

"You have no say in the matter."

"That is correct. Approximately."

The two halves of Nyz-Ragaan's face independently rise several inches back into his scalp.

"Ah, ha. You have no sense of humor."

Nyz-Ragaan has tripped. He scrambles up, pretending it did not happen.

"One does not need a sense of humor to deal with women and little girls."

"Perhaps not. But you will need one to deal with me."

Biel sees him blink back a belch of fire with one eye and reach for her with the other. She laughs.

"Soon that half of you which is now just an appendage will shrivel and float away."

His reaching eye clasps onto her. His belching eye erupts and roves silently around the room like a beam of light probing dark clouds.

"You will be kept alive, and drugged, and you shall tell us of Thoacdien."

"Why do you want to know about Thoacdien?"

"That is our affair."

"Do you know that it is dangerous? When one technology encounters another both will be changed, but the least complex will be destroyed."

"What do you know of Thoacdien?"

"Very little, actually."

"What is Thoacdien?"

"Information."

"I do not understand."

"For you to understand means change beyond comprehension."

"Who are you?"

"I should like to leave here—with my three compan-
ions. We mean you no harm."

"That is not possible."

"It will happen."

"The child speaks as if she knows."

"Be quiet, Grod-Linz."

"Tell your chief I wish to see him."

". . . I will do what is best or my nation."

"Will you?"

"Yes."

"Then tell your chief that if anything happens to my
friends, if they are permanently damaged or changed in
any way, the Higgitte race will die one by one in front of
each other until there is no one left to watch."

The smaller gold warrior shudders, and at a sign from
the other obediently goes up the rope-ladder. The fractured warrior, the tall one, stands before her staring—
one side ice, one side flame—as if lost somewhere in his
own space, dancing on the head of his own pin, his mar-
gins removed. Then he blinks once and the fire is ex-
tinguished, the ice is melted and steam is created which
eclipses his rise up the ladder.

Biel rolls down on her back, flapping her robe several
times to adjust its inadequacies over her body.

"I should like a blanket!" And she is deep into rich
sleep.

Logana, round and pink is nothing at all, her nipples
like two soft, old eyes, her navel the hole of a nose, her
pubic hair a smiling goatee, sits on a platform over
glowing rocks and pours water from a flask to make them
steam. She takes big breaths into her body, which makes
its pink face smile, then lets them out slowly, which makes
it frown. Her heart swells and collapses visibly, and each
time it swells it holds an instant too long, making her

afraid. She inhales and forgets to exhale, and it makes her afraid—and she does not know why.

Nyz-Ragaan and Grod-Linz stand before a scheduled meeting of the council to report on the prisoners. Unusually, the Patriarch is present.

"All were asleep under the effects of the drug but the one? The little girl?"

"Yes."

"She was coherent?"

"Yes."

"This demand to see the Patriarch . . ."

"It was not a demand. It was a very calm statement of intention."

"She has strange powers, the little one?"

"We should discuss this among ourselves, then make a recommendation to the Patriarch."

"Nyz-Ragaan, does she have powers?"

"I do not believe in powers. She has the innocence and arrogance of youth which conceal the brilliant mind of a man and the wisdom of a Patriarch. She is a freak, but she has no powers."

"She made a threat?"

"Yes."

"Did it disturb you?"

"At the time, but not now. It surprised me."

"People do not make meaningless threats. Especially when they are prisoners."

"She has no powers within herself or without to carry out the threat."

"Have you taken the others off the drug?"

"Not entirely. They must be kept groggy enough so that we can approach them."

"What have you learned from them?"

"Nothing."

"Nothing?"

"They can hardly talk."

"They are to be taken off the drug immediately. We will talk to them. Then we will kill them. I will decide about the girl. In the meantime, Nyz-Ragaan, you are to be married."

Behind the tin mask Nyz-Ragaan's being splits apart and the pieces flee to hide far away in the dark. Then all motion in him ceases for an instant as a long, thin river of cold, like a full swallow of milk, works down from his throat to his groin. His eyes are small behind the mask, small and hard as stones. Sperm freezes in his testicles. He does not, cannot focus, but sees all things peripherally. The seven men of the council sit before him with their toes sticking out of their robes like ideas, their fingers limp and useless like their sex, their varying degrees of rot in age, their mouths pursed for the gold coin of his kiss in payment for the favor they have done him. The Patriarch is a milky blur. He will fade. He will die. He is as transparent as a concept. Sterile and useless. Only Grod-Linz, next to him, is alive. Only Grod-Linz looks at the first warrior with narrowed eyes that have felt, have seen the changes piling up in him like rocks since he met the dark one.

"Married?"

"To Logana."

The sun squats over the desert, leaves a little puddle of shimmering red behind for a moment, then pulls up the blanket of night. For a while the Higgitte nation is quiet. The mock wars, between young boys who have all day lifted and arched into the air and repeatedly died or killed, fade into apprehension at the passing of one day and the beginning of another night. The fervent hope of the Higgittes is that sometime during the darkness the sun will not get bored and refuse to come again.

The torches are lit, fizzle a moment, then belch into life announcing the marriage of the first warrior and the Patriarch's concubine.

In a small alcove off the main chamber under the mesa, Nyz-Ragaan is poised in a tub, bathing himself. His left arm is extended and his right arm is bent, crossed over his body, touching a gold sponge to the very tip of his shoulder. His thoughts are locked in the vault of his head —unthinkable secrets. He completes the motion by drawing the sponge down his extended arm and squeezing a little to shed its clear weight. The water runs in small rivers through the gold hairs of his arm and falls with little ticks back into the tub. He stands, naked. He leans over and flicks his wet hair back over his head with the help of his hands. He dries. He winds the long soft cloth over and under, in and out, around and between his legs, to end tucked in on itself, hanging in a strip on the outside of his right leg, halfway to the knee. It matches his eyes, but does not have their hard surface. He pulls on his mask of rage then turns, brushing aside the opaque curtain, and steps out into the room where the nation is celebrating his first marriage.

On cue the drummers begin to play the distinct rhythms of the first warrior. The drums are deep, filling the whole bottom half of what the ear can hear. After growing in volume and intensity, hurrying, reaching until it seems the skins will break and the sound will lose its form and become murderous, the final rhythms are found, relaxed into, and absorbed into the background. The nation dances to celebrate what has been determined as a victory. The celebration has been heightened with the ceremony of his marriage.

Nyz-Ragaan sits flanking the Patriarch at the Privilege Table. He wears his mask of rage which will be removed for the ceremony as a sign that the opposition forgives the nation and wishes for unity again. Inside the mask his lids hang heavy and swollen on dry eyes. He takes his own pulse, counting time. His eyes find Logana. As first warrior it has become his privilege to lubricate this virgin concubine and keep the stock pure and strong. While he looks at her, the whole of his being is jammed into the little tip of finger which listens at his wrist as he tries to suck out of the image of his future wife some vestige, or remnant, or shadow, or memory of a shadow of desire.

207

Nyz-Ragaan smiles inside the mask, at Logana who is white like teeth. Nobody can see. He smiles. One square front tooth slightly overlaps the other. His mouth is dry and he has no saliva. He takes his finger off his pulse because it is useless and stupid to count time which will pass in its own way, and because no matter how hard he presses into the little exploding and contracting life in his wrist, he cannot find Mikkran there. Now his arms are at his sides. The tip of the guilty finger throbs with echoes of his pulse.

Logana floats by dancing—an image on wheels. She does not move, she glides, like well-oiled circles which have been blended into the rolling form of a woman. She reflects too much light. Blink. He must, blink, shut her out. If this behind the mask is his privacy, blink, he will take full, blink, advantage of it. For when his eyes are, blink, closed, the smoke from which Mikkran is made, blink, rises with sounds of its own and pulls him, blink, into the silence of his dreams—blink—with her. The image appears. Mikkran is superimposed over his bright new wife. Blink. His wife. Blink. And the wife goes away, blink, is eclipsed behind the long brown body of, blink, Mikkran. He stands and removes his mask. He grabs the image by the wrist, blink. This one, blink, he will take.

Xitr-Meede still sleeps. He is still curled around himself, but he no longer dreams. Beneath the drug, beneath the dreamless sleep, that which is in control has realized that something is wrong. But as of yet—and not unfaithfully—he cannot listen.

Night is the pupil of an eye. It dilates and contracts as a deep tube whose end cannot be imagined and whose beginning is forgotten. Sounds of breathing trail through the sleeping Higgitte camps like thin odors. Warriors have curled up to ride out the terrifying night in invisible wombs. They have peeled themselves off of each other and, isolated, they sink deeper into quiet and sleep which rattles infrequent sounds like dice—bored with the game.

FROM THE LEGEND OF BIEL

—I look up through the long square tube of my cell and see the bowl of night with its little sparks which are not objects but holes, perforations through which it is possible to see the reflected light of other worlds, other cells inside the complex body of creation. I float inside the liquid of myself, lying down, one ankle on one knee, hands clasped behind my head, and gingerly finger the edges of my private darkness. I feel within myself the continual division of parts into more parts, as complexity evolves, interlocks with experience, creating . . . me. And beneath it all is the scream—orchestration. The scream from which I am unable to extricate myself because it daily assumes more focus and less understanding, and because it contains me. I feel the other who is with me and unknown, the sourceless voice which can only be lunged at—I want to help—and sometimes caught, sometimes missed. I listen for my three friends and feel them asleep but rising slowly out of the drug as from an underwater city. Mikkran flops over on her back and the callus on her heel makes the sound of an exhaled breath on the stone. She will be all right. My darkness burps, and I whince at its power. I soothe myself . . . focus on the little white holes . . . in the sky . . . and wonder what is . . . beyond. Soon, I will slee . . .

A shadow slips between shadows quickly. His feet palm the ground as skillfully as hands. He wanders on top of the mesa, knowing only where he does not want to go. The battle is a joke, a game. There is not and never was any intention of resisting that direction.

The yellow rope disappears over the side of the opening and ssssssstutters, completing its word at the bottom of Mikkran's cell. His hands clasp onto the edge of the cell as his feet reach for and find the long braid which will support his descent. And she is there. Breathing. There, in the dark, there. Here is her face.

Mikkran's head is small in Nyz-Ragaan's hand. He lowers his face to the bend between her neck and her shoulder, where all odors seem to congregate, to celebrate, and call him. He breathes the breath of her odors which tingle like music and enter his nostrils as chords.

"Mikkran . . ."

The warrior says her name and feels it hard and clear as a stone in his mouth. His body is alive, exhaling and inhaling as he submits to the little tapping in each of his pores and enters her.

". . . Mikkran . . ."

Something in his eyeballs explodes, seeps upward into his brain and peels off the protective skin of tradition and tribe. He feels the liquid heat of their connection, the perfect matching of ins and outs, of mounds and indentations. All of his body becomes a nose smelling, then a tongue tasting as he explodes from the navel. And he explodes and explodes, implodes violently, then explodes again, explodes again, explodes again as all images are erased by the friction, swallowed by the bleeding flash of sweet seeping pain and release. And he explodes in floating, timeless spasms—expanding and contracting beyond endurance. The blood explosion rolls down his scalp like water washing him clean in someplace else—someplace he has never seen, never imagined. He is gold liquid shot out in a thin stream which flows and pours into every wrinkle, every crevice, reaching like a desperate hand for what is beyond the dark chamber of her womb. "I will never let you go away from me. . . ."

Biteus turns softly in his sleep and realizes he is the dreamer dreaming. The old songs, rounds, inside his head unwind, let go of a stable center, fall to the ground like thin scarves, and sleep.

The shelf which is the meeting room of the council of celibates glows rich oranges and browns when it is lit by torches, as now. Council meetings seem to take place by the light of a bond fire, although there are only slim torches, one for each party present, hung along the walls. The sound these torches make is orchestration for the meetings: soft hissings and poppings, snaps of two flames colliding, clapping hands.

Seven men, in luscious rich blue robes which destroy silhouette, and the Patriarch watch Nyz-Ragaan and Grod-Linz bring the first female who has ever been permitted to attend a council meeting up the long curving steps and onto the shelf. There is much chest-thumping and saluting as the men greet one another and roll the carpets of phlegm in their throats into eloquence. A spindly little figure, a little girl, stands in front of the old men. After an uncountable number of bows and nods the small one decides it is time to begin.

Biel lifts her elbow out of Nyz-Ragaan's clasp and walks to the Patriarch. She stands looking into his almost sightless and defeated eyes. The council room is silent. No women but the Patriarch's concubines have ever been this close to him before.

The Patriarch is unmoving, unaware, unsure of what this meeting is about. But from deep inside he feels the presence of the girl and understands that she means him no harm or mockery.

"You are the Patriarch."

". . . Yes."

"You have lived long. I respect that. I respect that you have tried to lead. I wish that I could breathe health into your body and understanding into your brain."

The councilmen gasp. Several are about to speak in protest but Nyz-Ragaan steps between them and the Patriarch and young girl. He faces the council with eyes which say they are not to interfere just yet.

Biel closes the space in the room down to a slim tunnel which includes only herself and the Patriarch, and perhaps Nyz-Ragaan. She stands in front of the ancient body, fascinated and repulsed.

"You are the oldest living person I have ever seen. It is good for me to learn at this age what will happen to my body if I live as long as you have lived."

The girl reaches her hand out and takes the old man's

hand in hers. She examines his palm, and the back of his hand. She looks into his face.

"You are so tired, old man."

"This must stop now!"

"This is not the way we conduct meetings!"

"She is bewitching the Patriarch, Nyz-Ragaan!"

"Silence, vultures! You do not know to whom you are speaking. This man sprang from great leaders. Once he could have eaten all of you alive. Now he must die, and soon. I will pay my respects."

The councilmen flutter and hiss at each other. Their power is little balls of sour spit which fall out of their mouths and evaporate before they hit the floor.

"Patriarch, you can understand me clearly?"

". . . Yes."

"I wish to prevent bloodshed and death to your people and my friends. They came on your land because of my stupidity. The others were trying to save me from myself. It had nothing to do with the Higgitte-Thoacdien war. I hope with all my being to end this situation peacefully. If you let us go we will do nothing to harm you. We will leave silently and you will never see us again."

"Is this why you wanted to see me?"

"Yes."

"I . . . thought it was something else. . . ."

"Why did you let me come to you?"

"I thought . . . you have powers."

"I have no powers."

"I thought perhaps you would be willing to serve me as priestess. We must learn the secrets of Thoacdien. . . ."

"Why?"

"It is our only chance."

"Your only chance for what?"

". . . Do you understand that we are dying?"

"Yes, but Thoacdien is not responsible for that."

"It is. My people try very hard not to admire your magic, but they cannot help it. If you would give us just a little bit . . . we could hold them here . . . a while longer."

"Why not let them go?"

"Our ways would die."

"Is that so horrible?"

Suddenly the Patriarch remembers who he is. He struggles deeply, and raises his being in his chair. He looks toward the girl, then pushes her away.

". . . You made certain threats concerning our nation in the presence of the first warrior and Grod-Linz. Can you carry them out?"

"Please . . . we must not play these games. Lives are at stake."

"Can you carry them out?"

The child teeters on the edge of possible attitudes. She searches for a gameless sanity with which to approach these persons, and cannot find one. The smell in the chamber changes, closes in and becomes one of the hunt—and the child is to be the hare. Her eyes flash across Nyz-Ragaan angrily. She turns her back on the Patriarch and the councilmen. She puts her fingertips to her temples and tries to massage an honest path out of this potential laybrinth of rhetoric.

"Can you carry them out?!"

Slowly Biel turns around and faces the others. She is changed, hard, wisened to their games.

"First of all, it is not wise of you to continue in this direction with me. You cannot win. I do not like the game, but I like losing even less. It is not too late to be human and honest and nonpolitical about this unfortunate situation."

Biel looks at their stony faces and sees that they believe that one little girl does not have a chance against so many brave, retired warriors. They want the discussion to go in this direction.

"All right. I will play your game. But remember when you have lost that you left me no choice."

"You will answer my question. Can you carry out the threat!?"

"Yes. I do not make idle threats. Now what is it you really want of me?"

"Tell us the secrets of Thoacdien."

"I will. You are so attracted to that which you despise that soon it will absorb you. That is the first secret you do not understand."

"Liar!"

"Already you must fight to keep the nation intact. You must promise these poor persons victory and equivalent technology in order to keep them here."

"That is not true!"

"Look around you! They would leave if they were not afraid. A little information will make them unafraid. Already your first warrior has lost his being to mentor Mikkran."

". . . She is dark. It is natural for a great man to be fascinated by a woman who is . . . different. . . ."

"Either you did not hear what I said or it suffered greatly in translation from your ear to your understanding."

"Say what you mean."

"I mean that last night Nyz-Ragaan had sexual relations with Mikkran-Gogan-Tor while she was unconscious. He is drawn to her because she lives a different and I believe superior morality—one he hopes he is worthy of. For the purpose of this discussion Mikkran is an extension of Thoacdien, and as such she cannot be resisted. Were we to remain here much longer she would be repeatedly raped by any man capable of erection and of climbing up and down a rope-ladder."

One member of the council has heard a bird fly over the mesa, and studies the ceiling of the room as if imaging its path. The other councilmen study various public areas of their own bodies. No one can permit the first warrior to be humilated by a female. No one can afford to exchange the functions of the old first warrior for the reality of the new one.

"Words have no meaning for you. If they cannot be turned into the desired meanings they are not heard. . . ."

"Nyz-Ragaan looks at Biel. His glance is a laugh that bruises. He speaks.

"I see I shall have to acquire a sense of humor to deal with you."

"You are a brave man, Nyz-Ragaan—brave, and changing."

"Tell us of Thoacdien."

"If I can be with my friends today."

"They are being provided for. You need not worry about them."

"I choose to worry about them. They cannot worry about themselves when they have been denied the very attributes which permit them to function."

"They are dangerous to our nation."

"Yes. But not in the ways you imagine."

"How is it that you are awake and lucid, while they sleep?"

"The answer to that question would have no meaning for you. Please, councilmen, do not force me to become puffed up and superior because of the ignorance of your questions."

"Do you have powers?"

"No. I am simply awake."

The old men are frightened of the girl. Each has his nose wrinkled at one side, as though she were an impolite fume.

"Please, I want to see my friends. I will tell you what you want to know if you let me go to them."

". . . It will be arranged."

"After you have told us about Thoacdien."

"Yes. But I must warn you. You do not know what you are asking for. There is nothing you can do to harm Thoacdien. But even simple information transferred to you at this time will destroy you."

"How?"

"Because it will not be enough. A taste will demand that you eat the meal, and to eat the meal you must go to it. If you want to keep your nation as it is let us go now."

The old men stir among themselves like nervous little

birds casting a vote. Few words are spoken—they do not trust them. The caucus is done with subtle dips of the head, nods, pecks on fingers, winks, glances of eyes which meet like two hands trading something dirty. Finally one of them speaks.

"These words, these warnings are a trick. You hope to scare us and keep us ignorant."

"More information will not prevent you from being ignorant."

"Tell us about Thoacdien!"

"What do you want to know?"

"Why could our warriors not pass through The Hall of One Thousand Chambers and remain warriors?"

"Because they were released."

"From what?"

"Habit."

"I do not understand. . . ."

"When simplicity is confronted with complexity it must either be transformed or die. What is the finest part of your culture?"

"The Zuri. The pride and skill of our warriors. The potential of our nation."

"Persons received into the Federation have no need for the Zuri. They have been released from the learned and violent responses to situations of conflict. Physical skill is beautiful, but it is not necessary to be an aggressive warrior in order to survive happily within the Federation. The concept of the potential of a nation is dissolved in The Hall and replaced with the actuality of the person fulfilling individual potential. Thoacdien has no use for your most precious qualities, and you would have no use for them in Thoacdien."

"But how do you fight wars? How do you protect the nation?"

"The Federation has never been at war. It has no need to grow. It does not go where it is not invited, and it is not a nation. It has very few tangible characteristics. You need an enemy in order to survive. The Federation does not— because it is not a culture or a state. Unfortunately Thoacdien provides you with an ideal adversary. It is an enemy who has no need to fight back, and a force you cannot possibly defeat. But it is also patient and interesting. Ultimately creatures like yourselves are fascinated, and stop fighting just to see what is on the other side of The Hall."

"Are you free to answer any questions we ask?"

"Yes. I am not a member of the Federation. My friends are free to answer any question which does not take away the total capital of Thoacdien, which is unformed knowledge—raw information."

"How large is the Federation?"

"The Thoacdien Federation is a complex network of seventy-five planets and three billion persons. It peppers the known universe."

"Where is the center?"

"It has no center. Titular headquarters is on Thoacdien I. There is nothing on that planet now but the machinery of Thoacdien."

"No citizens?"

"No persons, only Thoacdien."

"Why?"

"The planet is ashes."

"How can that be?"

"The original Thoacdiens were no different from any others. Long ago they were so busy evolving their technology that before they learned to control themselves they completely gutted an entire planet."

"Where does this planet fit into the Federation?"

"Grodden became Thoacdien V at the invitation of the Higgittes some seven generations ago. It is nothing special, just part of the Federation."

"What is Thoacdien—the original Thoacdien which is still on the first planet?"

"It is both information and the bank which stores and dispenses information to those willing to pay for it. Think of it as a huge, friendly library which also gives advice. Federation members put information into the bank and those willing to pay for it take it out."

"Why aren't you there now?"

"Because Thoacdien made a terrible mistake with me. I am angry. Because the information it dispensed to me was somehow incorrect and I must find out how."

"How does Thoacdien survive if it does not go to war?"

"It sells information."

"What is to prevent others from selling information?"

"Nothing."

"Nothing?"

"Nothing at all. Does anything prevent you from gathering information, creating information as capital and selling it for a fair profit?"

"Thoacdien would destroy us."

"No. Nothing stops you but yourselves. You are focused on other things—death with the hands and the continuation of the tribe."

"How did the Federation come into being?"

"Through a long and surprisingly bloodless process of learning to deal with conflict by creating information. This took many, many generations. As life within the Federation grew more joyous others saw and joined. Some entire civilizations invited Thoacdien to absorb them."

"And it has never fought a war?"

"Never. The Federation enlarged because individuals joined it. As it grew it came to be regarded as the one neutral area of the universal village. It became mediator, adviser, confidante and source of information for an nation states. Thoacdien has never been an aggressor. It has never sought members. It only creates and transfers information. No nation capable of understanding the value of this function would ever attack it—to do so is to pour poison into all the streams. Those nations not capable of understanding this, such as the Higgitte nation, are not sufficiently developed to do any harm."

"You do not consider yourself a member of the Federation?"

"No."

"Will you become one?"

"No. I am angry with it."

"But you speak well of it."

"I tell you what I have been told by my mentor, and in most things I respect her judgment. My anger is personal."

"Are people in the Federation wealthy?"

"Not in the way you would imagine. Wealth is neither measured nor necessary."

"But how do they live?"

"By their wits and their joy."

"Where do they live?"

"Mentors and charges live for a certain time in dome complexes because they must have access to complex technology. Others live where and how they wish."

"This . . . Mikkran, what is she to you?"

"She is the person who has agreed to be mentor to me."

"What is mentor?"

"A mentor is that person who assumes the responsibility for the entire Federation of being friend to one individual in each generation."

"There is one teacher for each Thoacdien child?"

"No one teaches and no one is taught. We learn and we share. Mikkran shares her experience and curiosity with me without interfering with my sovereignty. And I am learning to repay the courtesy."

"But . . . where is your mother? Where is your family?"

"I have no mother in any sense of the word. Mikkran has chosen to be with me as a friend. If I were in the Federation that would be my family."

"But you cannot survive without a family."

"But I am doing so. Family is only the tribe in microcosm. Long ago Thoacdiens realized—since their business is information, and information is not static—that, technology aside, the prime source of their capital was the unbridled imagination of each individual in each successive generation. The family is not only an inefficient system, it is a cruel one. The whole object of the family is to repeat itself, to create the future in the image of the past. Consequently it is a very effective brake on change because it keeps all children within the boundaries of cultural tradition. In the family learning is a process of psychological brutality at the end of which a child knows nothing but what is permissible to the tribe. There is no future, and no joy in the family—only the long, agonized, destructive groan of the continual death of the past. Once in a while there is friendship, but that is the exception, not the rule."

"To live without a mother to care for you is brutality."

"You cannot know how fully I am loved by Mikkran, or how fully I return that love. She loves me not for how accurately I reflect her life, her views, her hopes, her unattempted dreams, her tribe, but for the joy of my changing, for the exhilaration of the continual revelation of myself as myself to her—because she has earned it and knows that. Mikkran was with me before I was. She held me in her hands before I was born. She has followed me through nearly two seasons of aimless wandering, and nearly died. She has never interfered, but said, 'Go. Be yourself. I will follow and love you for what you are, because I want to learn from you and be with you.' You cannot even conceive of such healthy, motiveless love. The mentor/charge relationship is based on mutual sovereignty—not on imitation. The one truth in the Federation which has maintained equilibrium in the absence of prescribed morality, in the absence of unquestioned basic tenents, is this relationship which teaches that two persons of relaxed and curious mind who learn and share together, who confront the unknown, also create joy."

The Patriarch is asleep. The others stare, listless, and defeated by the stream of incomprehensible words. Their eyes are gray metal disks, motionless and flat.

". . . Nyz-Ragaan, please take me to Mikkran."

"Yes . . ."

~~~~~~~~~~~~~~~~~~~~~~~~~~~~~~~~

FROM: THOACDIEN—PRIORITY ONE.
TO: DOME COMPLEX 101-B, DOME COMPLEX 98-A, AND THE MEADOWS, THOACDIEN V.

DATE: 187.351
TIME: 1.9.063
SUBJECT: MENTORS   MIKKRAN-GOGAN-TOR
AND LAN-BITEUS.
CHARGES   187-A-0037   AND   XITR-
MEEDE.
. . . .
. . . .
. . . .

COMPLEX 101-B: PROCEED.
STOP.

COMPLEX 98-A: PROCEED.
STOP.

MEADOWS: NO RESPONSE. . . . .

THOACDIEN: SUBJECTS HAVE BEEN MISSING
SINCE 187.347.
THEY WERE LAST IN CONTACT
NEAR THE CENTRAL WESTERN
EDGE OF THE HIGGITTE-
CONTROLLED MESA.
IT IS USUAL FOR HIGGITTES TO
BLEED THEIR ENEMIES TO
DEATH ON TOP OF THE MESA.
WE HAVE THE AREA UNDER
SATELLITE SURVEILLANCE
NOW, AND HAVE SEEN NO SUCH
RITUAL.
IF ANY THOACDIENS
UNFAMILIAR TO YOU SHOULD
BE SIGHTED IT IS IMPERATIVE
THAT YOU FIND OUT WHO THEY
ARE AND CONTACT US
IMMEDIATELY THROUGH
COMPLEX 187-A, THOACDIEN V.
STOP.

COMPLEX 101-B: INSTRUCTIONS ARE RE-
CORDED AND WILL BE FOLLOWED.
STOP.

COMPLEX 98-A; INSTRUCTIONS ARE RE-
CORDED AND WILL BE FOLLOWED.
STOP.

MEADOWS: NO RESPONSE.................

END TRANSMISSION ....

Outside Logana's bedchamber the wives of the leaders
of five hundred wait for her to appear, wait to be told in
excruciating detail how deadly the first warrior is in bed.
They are not aware that after Nyz-Ragaan grabbed the
virgin concubine by the wrist and led her away to con-
secrate the marriage he could not bear to be alone with
her, near her, intimate with her. He stayed with her only
a short time, then wandered the top of the mesa, waiting
until it was safe to go to Mikkran.

Logana sits in her chamber on a small stool. She is
hypnotized by the mutes which float in a lizard's tongue
of light which licks at the room through a little hole in
the ceiling. The big molars at the back of her mouth are
grinding together and make the sound of the mesa during
an earthquake. She sits. She is surprised at how relaxed
her body is in its rage and humiliation. She sits, leafing·
through her fury as though to memorize each particular.
The virgin concubine's nostrils are wide open, stretched.
Each breath travels her hot passages cautiously and fans
the anger in her lungs—revising it, amending it. The bed
is beyond the lizard's tongue of light—an accusation. Her
intercourse is now with vegeance.

Logana stands. She is still as a statue, cool as soap. Her
unbraided hair falls from her head in white blades—
weapons. She must figure out how to accomplish only one
thing before she retires in disgrace.

". . . Mikkran . . . ?"
Her cheeks have fallen deeper into her face.
"Mikkran."
Her pupils are dilated. How frail she looks. How easy it
would be for some insanity, some hysterical fear to place
only a finger
here . . .
with such a little pressure,
and reduce this mentor to silence . . .
A little fluttering stops in the throat, and wrists, and
temples—such soft and vulnerable places—and one is
no more.
"Mikkran!"
It will not happen to her. She is too strong.
"Mikkran! It's me, Biel. You must try to wake up!"
I know nothing about her except that she is as smooth
and warm and honest as a stone, and I love her.
"Wake up!"
Was she ever like me? Small and breastless?
Seeing the others as hips and waists?
. . . no.
She has always been tall.
She has always been what she is.
"Mikkran! Mikkran! You *must* wake up!"
". . . Biel . . . ? . . ."
"Good. Can you eat?"
". . . no . . ."
"You must try. It will help. Come . . ."
"Biel?"
"Yes, it's me."
". . . Are . . . you all right?"
"I am fine—undamaged."
"What did they do to me?"
"They gave all of us a disorienting drug of some sort.
But it does no permanent damage. Mikkran? . . . Mik-
kran wake up!"
". . . Not just yet . . ."
"Mikkran, you must stay awake. Here, eat this. Talk
to me!"

". . . mmmmm."

"How far is it to the meadows? Mikkran? Talk!"

"Ten days . . ."

"Open your eyes. How are you affected by the drug? Mikkran?"

". . . I can . . . hear you. . . ."

"Wake up!"

". . . but . . . . . . I cannot . . . . . ."

"Come on, keep talking!"

". . . participate . . ."

"Very good. A sentence. Look into my eyes. Look. Into. My eyes . . ."

". . . OK . . . OK. . . ."

"Who am I?"

"Biel."

"Are you awake now?"

"I don't have much choice."

"Look into my eyes and talk to me. Eat. Look at me!"

". . . yes . . ."

"You haven't had any of the drug since yesterday. They won't give you any more. Stand up."

". . . mmmmmmmmm . . ."

"We must walk."

"Yes."

"Did we ever walk before?"

"Yes."

"How much?"

"Far."

"Eat. Where did we walk?"

"Desert."

"Talk. By yourself."

". . . I am Mikkran-Gogan-Tor . . . lost. From dome complex 187-A, Thoacdien V. I . . . am not . . . there, now."

"Where are you?"

". . . here."

"Where is that?"

". . . Higgitte camp?"

"Yes."

"Ahhhhhhh."

"How do you feel?"

"Very tall."

"Talk."

"Where are Biteus and Xitr-Meede?"

"Listen for them."

"There's just . . . a gray fuzz."

"Can you tell if they're alive or not?"

". . . Yes. They are alive."

"Are they close to you?"

"Within a shout."

"Good."

"I'm thirsty."

"Here is water. Biteus and Xitr-Meede are in the same condition. I haven't been with them yet, but I will as soon as I leave you."

"What have the Higgittes done to us?"

"What do you remember?"

"The mesa. Then nothing."

"They used the Zuri on all of us, on the mesa. Then they took us down to their main chamber and took two days to vote on what to do with us. We terrified them with our defense, so they drugged us. They want to keep you drugged enough so you can't hurt them, but not so drugged that you can't tell them about Thoacdien."

"Thoacdien?"

"Yes. They're planning a war."

—How wonderfully she laughs—as a coasting bird who suddenly wants the sunshine on her belly and turns over in midflight to soar upside down.

"Come, hug me."

—And there are the smells and feels of Mikkran. Has it been so long that I am taller now? Has it been so long that I no longer fit comfortably with the same old ins and outs of her, but must reach for and adjust to new ones? Tight . . . Tighter, until the space between us is erased.

"I love you, Mikkran."

"And I you. I have missed you."

"Eat. Eat. It has been too long already."

"How long?"

"This is the middle of the fourth day."

"How is it that you are awake?"

"The drug didn't work on me."

"That must have surprised them."

"Indeed. They're trying very hard not to make me into something supernatural. They even invited me to become a priestess for them."

"The drug didn't affect you at all?"

"At first I was foggy, but more from the Zuri than from the drug. Then I just slept more than usual, that's all."

"What is the drug?"

"I'm not sure. It disorients. It prevents coherency. It keeps all the functions of the brain from integrating and collating moment-by-moment experience. So, each one of your brains and its parts becomes isolated and can't focus on anything. For some reason that didn't happen to me. It connects with the seizures and the Binol, but I'm not sure how."

"Did they try anything else?"

"No. When they saw that the drug didn't work they almost fell on their knees, but they couldn't make it that far down before they fell asleep. Old men run this nation, Mikkran. Old men who play a game of debate and take hours to come up with a consensus on what to talk about tomorrow."

"Have you had any seizures here?"

"Only a few tiny ones."

"We have to get out of here."

"Yes, and very quickly."

"How much time do we have?"

"I don't know. I talked to the Patriarch and the ruling council this morning for a while, before they fell asleep. I may be able to help, but we can't just climb out of these holes and walk to the meadows."

"We have to shake off the drug so we can communicate. Biteus knows nothing except that he and his charge are here. He needs context."

"I will explain."

"There's no way out of these cells?"

"Only up there. Mikkran, could the tall Higgitte be a friend?"

"Who?"

"The tall one, the first warrior. Would he help us?"

"I don't know."

"Mmmmm. I'd better tell you."

"Yes."

"He was with you last night." Blink.

"Blink . . . "Hummmmmmmmmm," smile, ". . . maybe he will help."

"Well, if he comes to you again tonight be awake and find out."

"No secrets from you, huh?"

"I guess not."

"You. Girl."

"That's him up there. Nyz-Ragaan."

To Nyz-Ragaan's mind it takes forever for the dark one to raise her head, clear her eyes of its falls of hair, and look at him—identify him.

"First warrior of the Higgittes?"

"Yes?"

"Next time you come, wake me."

The first warrior is very still—expressionless. He has fine control of his body and can make what is inside visible only in the effort it takes to conceal it.

"You, girl."

"My name is Biel."

"It is time for you to go now. We must wake the others."

"Mikkran, we shall not die here."

"No, Biel. We shall not die for a long time."

The rope unfurls. Biel braces her foot in the loop at its end and is pulled up—making one revolution on the way —hand-over-hand by the first warrior. She is laughing inside, with Mikkran.

Logana walks across the mesa. She is relaxed. She is casual. The ball bearings of her body lubricate her movements into circles, rounds—with no lines or angles. She

227

finds the little spot far in front of her which begins as a vanishing point, grows into a period, into a hole, and finally into the absence which has captured Mikkran. Logana arrives at its edge, stands on its lip and peers with a frozen glance down into the darkness of the cell.

Mikkran looks up at the blinding, almost transparent figure standing at the edge of the top of her cell. The woman is round, proud of her abundant breasts. Her cheeks are apple-smeared. Her long, light blue tube of a dress hangs, obeying the architecture of her body, with no wrinkles.

". . . Hello."

"Are you Mikkran?"

"Yes."

"I am Logana."

The woman stands there looking down, her glance like a hot hand roving over Mikkran, memorizing. Mikkran, in mid-chew, looks back, waiting. Then she resumes her meal.

"You are Nyz-Ragaan's mistress?"

"I am his wife."

"I see. And for many reasons you are jealous of me. You do not answer. I will tell you only that I take nothing. It is given to me. I was asleep."

"You are an enemy to my nation. You are an enemy to me."

"What you never had cannot be taken away from you."

"You will not know how, you will now know when, you will only know that one moment you are alive. Then, others will know you are dead."

"Thank you for the warning."

"You are isolent."

"No. I do not mean to be."

"You think I spend my words on dead air, like the council. But I have pledged my life for your death. Those are not words."

"No. I suppose not. I would like to joke you into a sense of perspective. I would like to help you."

"There is no help."

"All right. But do not deny a man his season and he will spend it with you, whether he spends it on you or not."

"You. Mikkran."

"Yes?"

"Be expecting it." And she is gone.

. . . .

"Colonel Haris to Skimmer Three."

"Skimmer Three. Ybarra here."

"You are four minutes into separation."

"All systems are go here."

"Check."

"Lanier, have you made audio contact yet?"

"Negative."

"Ybarra?"

"Yes, Colonel Haris?"

"I want you to arm the Skimmer nuc and activate it as soon as you land. Set it for exactly one hour. Set it on manual switch so you can stop it if you get back to the Skimmer in time. This means you will have less than one hour to find and recover the team."

"Check."

"I want you two fully armed. Shoot, then ask questions."

"Yes, sir."

"I want you to contact us as soon as you have armed the nuc. When you land I want you in constant contact with us. If there is even a second when you can't transmit or receive, fix it."

"Yes, sir."

"I want you to start probes now. If your probes tell you different from what we're reading, get the hell out of the way immediately and we will start shooting."

"Yes, sir."

"OK. Get to work on that nuc. Then contact us."

"Check."

"PROBE IV out."

229

VII

Logana stands at the bottom of the long, forbidden stairs which lead to the council. She has decided what is to be done. It is now a matter of persuading her body to erase the taboo and go up. She lifts one foot and then the other, rising up through stratified air and smoke to the top of the nation. There are many stairs and she establishes a rhythm in her steps. The movement of her body rounds the perpendiculars of one stair into the next. Her sandals touch each step and sound like snakes hissing. She is tall, getting taller. As her body rises it is frozen, oddly broken. Her right elbow points out away from her body and is bent so that she can pinch her gown between thumb and first finger and not step on it. Her head is oddly tilted to the side. She plants her left hand, splayed, on the cold stone next to her with each step, and for an instant—as her hand is in full contact with the wall—she seems to be some strange appendage, some tree or shrub, which has broken through the chamber and is growing wild and elgant as an orchid out of the wall. The long tube of her dress breaks at her waist and knees as she glides beside her own risen, surprised shadow up the long stone stairs which curve, hugging the wall of the main chamber, toward the council room.

Since Logana looked into the eyes of Mikkran, that thing she fears most in all the world, she has become still, a focal point which glitters in dark space like the tip of an ice pick. Since that moment she has become passive to all but her promise, which she stalks with the night determination of one who knows how to kill even though she has never done so before. She has stood all her life at the crumbling wall of this nation, holding it together with her body, her belief, and her hope. Now there is only Mikkran and Nyz-Ragaan—two symbols of her struggle to survive.

In the council room words are a continuum, a medium more like water than a tool. In the council room words are sport, they are thrown like soft balls, with great accuracy and innuendo, at the past, at the future, at that which is never understood. The old men stand in a jagged circle. They are bent, and crisp as crackers. Their hands move out from their bodies like tentative ships leaving harbors—and they always return. Their heads tremble on the tops of their spindly necks. They have the color, the texture, and the transparency of parchment.

Logana shimmers into the room. And because that is unheard of, she is not immediately felt. She glides like a slick of oil onto their words, their trusted medium. They continue talking and then slowly, as if someone were gradually sucking the air out of the room and sooner or later this must be noticed, they turn and see her. The councilmen freeze, inhaling. Words fall to the floor like dead birds. Logana speaks.

"The prisoners must die."

"How dare you enter this room!"

"It is forbidden for you to be here!"

"Leave immediately!"

The old men stir, adjust themselves as if caught urinating. They flutter, exposed and impotent, and try to resuscitate their medium, their dead birds of words which are dead, dead on the floor.

"You have been old men too long. You have played with the fate of our nation too long. You have talked too long."

Logana is white and blue ice. It is her stillness, her unblinking stare which frightens the old men, flusters them, halts them. They do not move. Only their eyes recede, as cast-off parts of ships left behind in space.

"They must die immediately or we will fracture and collapse before the next season is finished. Listen to this room now. Listen to your nation."

And beginning at their feet a small vacuum spreads beneath the mesa like thin gas. It is silence. It permeates the chambers and the closets and the halls—even the children.

"Your words are dead."

The old men do not move.

"If you wish to remain in power, if you wish to continue to rule, you must have people to have power over—people to rule. We gave you that power. We can take it away, or we can leave here, so that you and your power will become useless. The people will be gone before the next season is over if the four are permitted to live another day."

"You must leave this chamber! We will talk of this matter in council."

"You do not have time to talk. Do you not feel it, this . . . breath of silence which invaded our camps with the Thoacdiens? Each day the Higgittes grow quieter. They dream. They do not train for battle."

"We are becoming women."

"Yes! And I have become a man. There can be no vote on this, no discussion. Their deaths must be immediate, decisive and painful, or we will die."

"She is right."

"The presence of the Thoacdien women alone is enough to destroy the structure of our nation."

"You must leave now, Logana. We will remember your words, but we will forget who spoke them."

"I will leave. But if the Thoacdiens are not dead by this time tomorrow, I will kill them myself. Then I will personally lead the Higgitte exodus to Thoacdien, and you old men can sit here and talk until your tongues fall out."

Darkness spreads over the mesa like paint and seals everything in. The nation has been called to the main chamber to hear a proclamation from the Patriarch. Each warrior has a voting blade sheathed in a long leather finger on his thigh. The Patriarch sits on his chair propped up by pillows and surrounded by the council. His voice rasps, comes out of tight lips like smoke, and wafts thinly among the warriors.

"There will be no vote. There is no time for that formality. The presence of the four prisoners is a great danger to the structure of our nation. They will die tomorrow, at the first light. They shall be taken to the top of the mesa and bled to death on the indisputable order of myself, Patriarch Nan-Rad II. I call now for a demonstration of confidence."

The Patriarch stops. He looks out at his nation through eyes that now see only the blur of one continuous, sexless blond face.

Nyz-Ragaan stands at the front of the warriors facing the Patriarch. He is to initiate the vote of confidence. He raises his arms into the air and opens his mouth. The others follow. And, not knowing that their confidence has faded, they emit what begins as a sigh and evolves into the Higgitte scream for vengeance. The four will die.

Biteus sits, his back against a wall of his cell, exchanging cerebration with Mikkran, Xitr-Meede and Biel. Each is stuck in a dark pocket beneath the surface of the mesa. The echoes of the demonstration of confidence seep into their cells like an odor as they cast aside one idea after another and realize that they are scheduled to die soon.

Biteus runs his silky palm across the brown arch of his foot, liking both hand and foot. He thinks, in a free part of his brain, how perfectly his body is designed to do the tasks it performs. Mikkran touches his mind with a liquid swell of her own outpouring, which is hidden from the young ones.

—. . . I am not afraid to die, Bietus, but I do not wish to die stupidly.

Biteus reaches out and enfolds her in his warmth and peace—not to protect her but to say yes, yes, to her life.

The demonstration is now an echo. The warriors have retired. They have entered and left their women. Their children have been fed their dusty bread and are hidden away in small hammocks. The nation drifts into sleep the same way a blind man wades into a deep stream. Unformed visions of the unknown slink into Higgitte minds in the shape of black cats who pad into focus from behind the dreamer, turn around once to dust the groove of precise comfort, then lower themselves—like queens—to stay. The cats' eyes stare out at the dreamer, intimidating, as deep puddles of red and green oil. The cats have no opinions, no desires—only presence and control. The nation breathes itself to sleep, secure in its resolution. It breathes itself down in jerky phases, level by level, to distilled cats'-eyes dreams and silence. Nothing can be heard but the soft popping of the blinking cats' eyes—red glowing winks that fill the vacuums inside the heads of human beings.

He fondles things familiar to him: a pipe, a handmade bow, his voting blade, the light blue cloth. The cloth is now just a long strip of sky-blue pride. Now a black cloth snakes around his hips like a number and sets him only a little freer to let his body do what it must. He folds the cloth neatly, squarely, slowly, and sets it on his hard bunk —as though for one who has died. He weights it down with the voting blade which bears the thumbprint of his father, and his father's father, back thirty-seven generations. All of it must stay. It no longer belongs to him. Nyz-Ragaan looks at his room, chamber of the first warrior. It fades in and out of focus, and he knows that he will remember it only a little while, then only at certain times, and then not accurately. And without any feeling at all he goes to set them free.

Without sound, so that not even the cats blinking in Higgitte dreams are disturbed, the four are lifted from their cells one at a time. Then, synchronized with the warrior, they move across the mesa toward the opening through which they will enter the veins. Without sound they vanish into a dark maze of tunnels. They feel their way behind the Higgitte, adjust to the contours of the tunnel, and run. There are only slight, infrequent sounds of gravel astonished. Gutteral gasps are released by one throat and swallowed by another before they can be heard.

Veins spread beneath the mesa, fanning out from its cerebral cortex to its limits as a tangled network of tunnels which are used to hide in and to escape. Veins twist and turn, intersect darkly, then continue as a directionless puzzle for the runners' sense of motion. The tunnels are narrow, so narrow that one must run behind the others except when two veins converge and widen the space. It is six passes of the sun from the cerebral cortex of the mesa to the first flower of the meadows. In the veins it can take longer because the running is in circles. But it is safer than being on top of the mesa where they cannot hide, or rest, or plan.

They run. They move silent and dark, one behind the other, trying to feel a direction. White eyeballs, grayed with nothing to reflect, roll useless as hardboiled eggs and see nothing. Blink. Nothing at all.

Grod-Linz lies on his hard bunk fingering the silence. As though by some absence the body of the nation has begun to wobble, to limp like an athlete with one leg shorter than the other. This irregularity of rhythm has awakened him. He swings his legs off the bunk, winds on his red loincloth, and armed with a torch, paces the chambers. All the corridors are deserted. The main meeting hall is hollow and silent as the inside of a drum. He sits a moment, staring at the throne of the Patriarch in the orange light of his torch. The shadow of the throne flutters like an apparition on the wall. Grod-Linz listens. He listens for the direction, the source of the absence. Then, slowly, he walks to the chamber of the first warrior and steps into the wound, the new orifice through which the nation has begun to drain.

From the chamber of the first warrior in the cerebral

cortex of the tribe comes the beginning of the sound of rage and betrayal which will spread through the corridors, tattooing itself on walls and snuffing out cats asleep in Higgitte brains. It will lead out through the openings on the mesa, up to the ears of the little satellite. It will seep into the tangled veins to the runners. Grod-Linz bellows his grief, calling the two thousand Higgitte warriors to coagulate around the wound and stop its bleeding.

Logana's eyelids flick open as Grod-Linz draws his first breath to scream—as if she had not been asleep. The dark blue of her eyes is smooth and dry as glass. She lies unmoving with her head rolled to the side, listening to the chaos. Then, crisply, she rises and molds the cool blue gown onto her body. She fixes her hair in small braids at her temples. She does not think. She does not feel. She does not hurry. The only light in her mind points toward a moment in the future when the others will be dead. Then she steps into the corridor where all are running toward the center, and follows.

Ahead it is dark. The only other possible direction is behind, and it is darker. It is cold in the veins. No sun has ever touched them. There are four others running with the runner. They cannot be seen. They are only heard, breathing and slapping along quickly in the dark.

"Stop here. We must rest. Here is water, take only a sip."

They sit, the five of them, on the powdery floor where one vein meets another and feel their bodies collapse like houses of cards, feel the water make steam in their throats. The only sounds are breathing and the little tick the seal of the water flask makes as it is passed from hand to hand. Soft as a baby's breath they hear the scream of the Higgittes behind them. It increases in volume, and what was at first pathetic becomes determined. It is hard to listen, impossible not to hear. It calls, threatens, pleads with them to come back and forgive this innocent violence. The first warrior speaks to drown it out.

"I had counted on more time. We must go on; they are good runners."

"How far is it from here to where you captured us?"

"We could be there by midday tomorrow."

"We have a machine there that can help us."

"The white bubble?"

"Yes. You have not harmed it, have you?"

"No. We tried but could not. I could not get my warriors to touch it."

"Will you take us there?"

"Yes."

"How far is it from where the warriors are now to the machine?"

"The same, but they will get there faster because they will run on top of the mesa. They will get there at dawn."

"Let's go up to the surface now and run there."

"We can't. We would not have a chance. At least here we can hide. It will be very hard to find us in the veins if we are quiet."

"OK. Let's go."

"I will not return to Thoacdien."

"Do you want to live?"

"Not there."

"Biel, we cannot keep running in here."

"I only want to know that none of you will force me to go back to Thoacdien, and that you will not say where I am."

"Why don't we get to that when we get to that?"

"No!"

"All right. We will not take you back or say where you are."

"Let's go."

. . . .

Captain Josef Ybarra wiggled his fingers inside his silver gloves. The first taste of a sore throat was spreading across the umbrella of his soft palate, seeping in and grabbing

237

hold. Damn. His jaw worked back and forth like a nut-cracker, squeezing the risk they were taking. O'Hare, next to him, soldered the new connections on the circuit boards of the audio unit mounted beneath the microscope to match it to Levin-Hughes's specs. Ybarra had always thought those boards and their components looked like candy. When they burned out they should still be useful as something to eat—lozenges for the sore throats.

"Captain Ybarra to PROBE IV."

"PROBE IV. Lieutenant Lanier here."

"Could I have timings please."

"We are fifteen minutes and twenty-two seconds into audio silence. You are six minutes and three seconds into Skimmer Three descent."

"Still with us?"

"Yes, Joe."

"In spirit at least, huh?"

"Yes."

"Hey, keep trying to get those researchers to respond, OK?"

"I'm doing everything I know to do. . . ."

". . . OK. Ybarra out."

"PROBE IV out. Good luck, Joe."

. . . .

The Higgitte warriors split into two groups. One group dives into the veins and fans out to cover as many tunnels as possible, heading south toward the meadows. The other half divides into groups and then into smaller groups of groups. Then they run, in the formation of a crescent, toward the white Thoacdien machine. Grod-Linz leads one hundred men at the center of the formation.

Logana stands on top of the mesa hearing the last of the warriors pad off into the dark. She counts in her head to give herself time. She blinks her eyes to adjust to the dark. Then she runs west, toward the floater, armed with the razor which was her father's ceremonial voting blade.

"You are not to move. They are in the veins and the veins hold no secrets—they carry sound. We are safe if we are quiet. We can hear if they get too close. Stop long enough to breathe normally."

Biel sits between the others. Her back is resting against the cool wall of the vein. Her legs are stretched out. Her head is thrown back, and she tries to catch her breath.

"haaaah huuuuh haaaah huuuuh haaaah huuuuh haaaah huuuuh haaaah huuuh haaah huuuuh—. . . . I breathe and cannot get enough . . . "huuh haaah haah huuh"—. . . . I gasp and there is not air enough to fill my bursting lungs.

This has happened to me before.
          Where?
              When?
                    How?
                           I could not breathe. . . .
Then what? What!?
Then . . . there was an explosion . . . the first.

—Mikkran!

—Yes?

—I am remembering something from before the first seizure!

—What?

—I could not breathe. That's why it started. Then everything was loud and white and screaming. But before that . . . I can hear something.

—What is it?

—I don't know. . . .

—Describe it to me.

—I hear a soft sound . . . purring. I'm inside something. I'm enclosed in a . . . machine. It purrs and it talks. It is very upset, and talking to someone who is more upset.

—Can you tell me what this machine is?

—It is soft inside . . . warm . . . it takes care of me. It is my crib?

—Essentially—but more than that.

—. . . My environment, physician, and provider.

—Yes.

—Does it have a name?

—Yes. It's called a Gladdin.

—. . . Gladdin . . . I see hands, reaching for me.

—Umhum.

—. . . They're your hands, Mikkran. You were there, too, at the first seizure!

—Yes.

—. . . I was very sick.

—You were dying.

—You are screaming. Screaming. Screaming. I hear that scream each moment of my life. But it is only half the scream. . . . There is another half—on the other side of my seizure . . . far away, but very loud. Each scream is pulling at me. Both screams will not let me go, will not let me die. Each wants me to come and be where it begins. I am pulled to each of you. I am both places equally. But you pull harder. You are stronger than the other . . . so I come back . . . back.

—Yes.

—!? I come back . . . I come . . .!?

—Biel?

—Mikkran, I didn't just come back to life, I came back here, to Thoacdien. I came back here, with you— as opposed to going somewhere else, not-here, not-now . . . with the other.

—Can you explain more fully?

—Mikkran, listen! Mikkran . . . I'm not all the way back here, with you. I'm only mostly here. Part of me is somewhere else, with someone else. It's not a dream. It's not an hallucination. The seizures are the other's desperate attempts to reclaim me, because without my body now the other is not alive. . . .

—Biel, be careful.

—I want to go on. The other is so frightened, Mikkran. All this fear I feel, all this terror is not mine. Essentially I am not afraid. But at times I feel the feelings of the other. I am not lost—the other is lost. . . .

—Mmmmmmmmm.

FROM THE LEGEND OF BIEL

—And it's like these feelings haven't happened yet —and yet they have never not been happening. There is a pocket between the other's when and where and my when and where. All of the other is trapped in that pocket, but only part of me is trapped there. And we are wandering around this featureless pocket looking for a hole through which we can crawl and be in one place or the other—hopefully here. But there are no holes, and there are too many holes—we don't know how to choose . . .

—Biel, stop. . . .

—. . . and he is so frightened, holding on so very . . .

—Biel, stop!

—. . . . . . .Ahhhh can't . . . . . . can't . . . . .

—Biteus?!

—Yes?

—Shield! Warn Xitr-Meede. It will be worse than a severe, prolonged electric shock.

—. . . gaaaaaaaaaaaaaaaaaaaaaaa . . . g . . . g . . .

—Shield!

—Xitr-Meede? . . . Xitr-Meede!

—. . . gaaaaa . . . I . . . can't . . . sssssstand . . . it . . . Biteus . . . ?

Nyz-Ragaan feels the two youngsters stiffen beside him. "What's wrong?"

"Seizure. Grab his tongue so he can breathe. . . ."

—Bietus? Bietus, can you shield?

— . . gaaaaa . . . yesssss . . .

—Nyz-Ragaan is holding Xitr-Meede. Help me hold Biel. Hold her! Hold her!

"What's wrong?"

"Seizure. It will . . . ppass in a moment."

. . . (—. . . I am moving too fast through too many objects . . . I am going to strike a wall. I am going to die. But it will not be easy because my brain will fly apart cell by cell and still be alive when its pieces are farther apart than stars. I will be thinking all the while . . . I am thinking all the while . . .

—. . . I've struck something . . . soft.

—Hold on to me, please.

—I am.
—Are you there?
—. . . Are you there?
—Is someone . . . there?
—Yes.
—Who are you?
—Do you hear it?
—Yes.
—What is it?
—. . . Atoms in collision . . .
—No. It must be something else—there is no motion here.
—. . . yes.
—Where are we?
—When are we?
—. . . Lost on the edges of the dark star of time.
—Can we find our way back?
—To where?
—When?
—. . . I don't know.
—This is not wholly unpleasant.
—No.
—At least we are no longer falling.
—No.
—We are hidden inside the darkness of the screams. . . .
—Don't let go . . . please.
—I won't. It is what I must do now.
—Will we know each other differently?
—I don't know.
—I'm so afraid.
—I know.
—Is someone there?
—Where?
—Where you are?
—Yes. I am here.
—Who are you?
—I have forgotten. . . .
—Hold on. I'm dying.

—No . . . You are not dying, you are merely chang-
ing..)
The seizure rises, rises, crests, and falls—is its own
dark ocean.
—She's coming back now.
—Yes. She is beginning to relax. Has this happened be-
fore?
—Yes. Worse than this. It happens all the time in small
degrees.
—What damage does it do?
—None that I am able to perceive. The seizure is its
own damage.
—It has no lasting effects on her?
—No. She is brilliant. I have never experienced such an
endless mind.
—How does she live through these seizures?
—. . . She holds on.
—What can we do?
—Wait, and look for a way out.
—Yes.
Nyz-Ragaan stands. The veins are eerily quiet—a tactic
of the Higgittes. He whispers to the others.
"It is time to go on."
"We will have to carry Biel and Xitr-Meede. They must
sleep the seizure off."
"Let's go."

Logana stops and stands exposed on top of the mesa.
Only the darkness conceals her, but she stands as if she
is hiding in a doorway. The Higgitte women have been
told to return to their compounds and they have done so
—all but Logana, who waits, shielded by the dark. She
removes the long voting blade from its leather sheath and
feels it as a razor on her thumb. Its sharp point will do
the job.
"Do not let them be caught. Their deaths are my privilege."
And Logana runs, fast and sure as the warriors. She

will not fall. She cannot be delayed or stopped. Her body has become tuned, pointed toward an objective—and nothing alive will prevent her from reaching it.

The sun bleeds anemic onto the mesa through clouds that have no shape, no visible mass, no characteristics other than that they keep the color out of the day and wash everything to gray. The mesa doesn't change, it simply gets lighter, revealing one thousand Higgitte troops lying down on its western ledge. There is the floater. The warriors hide lest by some Thoacdien magic the four are already here and ready to trap them.

The two leaders of five hundred and the ten leaders of one hundred sit in a circle near the ledge and draw their tactics on the ground with sticks. They must figure out how to kill the four without harming the captured first warrior. Grod-Linz has insisted and had convinced them that Nyz-Ragaan is a Thoacdien prisoner.

"Are the children all right?"

"Yes. They are still asleep."

"Set them down. We must plan."

The two charges are gently lowered to the floor of the vein. They adjust themselves in sleep to more comfortable positions. They sigh and gurgle, then are silent inside themselves.

"They will be waiting wherever we go. We must decide what to do."

"How are they armed?"

"Some have swords, some not. All have razors."

"They depend on getting close to us and using the Zuri."

"Yes, as before."

"How many will there be?"

"Half the troops are working their way through the veins toward the meadows. The other half are already waiting at the machine. Either way we shall have to face a thousand."

"No one must be hurt—Thoacdien or Higgitte."

"That will not be possible. How far is the machine from the face of the cliff?"

"Fifteen heartbeats for us, at least twenty for the young ones."

". . . Too far."

The warriors work their ways in groups of ten down the shallow western face of the mesa. They scout the face of the cliff within plausible distance of the machine for vein outlets and plug them up, leaving only one vein open. This opening is directly in front of the Thoacdien machine. The main Higgitte formation will be here, between the machine and the vein opening. This main force will be flanked on either side by one hundred warriors who will watch farther north and south of the open vein, in case the Thoacdiens do not come out where expected. They do not dream that Nyz-Ragaan leads the four and knows before it is done what the Higgittes will do.

The static gray overhead lightens a notch and reaches its brightness for the day. The sun passes over the clouds like a slow, cool tongue. It cannot be seen—can hardly be imagined behind the featureless gray. There is no sound but of little water's sobbing hiccough as it drips out of the mesa toward the desert. Warriors wait, frozen in place, their eyes always open—like paintings.

Grod-Linz crouches behind a rock directly in front of the Thoacdien machine. His fingers, big as baby arms, cup his bent knees. His eyes, cool and blue, are betrayed. In his mind are little rhymes he used to know. He repeats them silently, automatically, to push away the silence and the wait, and to cast a spell on Nyz-Ragaan—to freeze the first warrior in time so that what he was will always be. Grod-Linz would only keep Nyz-Ragaan safe, would only try to open the path for his return. Or, if not that, help him die without disgrace.

"What if we don't come out of the veins?"

"It is too dangerous. The runners in the veins are now

going south toward the meadows. If we are lucky only a young, stupid boy with his first erection in his hand would find us. If we do not come out these runners can be called back by the drums. Those by the floater will not come in. They will wait for us to be driven out."

—Biteus?

—Yes, Mikkran?

—Have you got a communicator disk?

—Yes.

—Can you contact Thoacdien and find out if this floater has activated remote control?

~~~~~~

TO: THOACDIEN—PRIORITY *URGENT*.
FROM: MENTOR LAN-BITEUS, MESA, THOAC-
DIEN V.
DATE: 187.352
TIME: 6.9.021

. . . .
. . . .
. . . .

THOACDIEN: PROCEED.
STOP.

BITEUS: FOLLOWING URGENT:
         DOES FLOATER A, 03-187-A, HAVE
         ACTIVATED REMOTE CONTROL?
STOP.

THOACDIEN: IT CAN BE PROGRAMMED.
STOP.

BITEUS: BY YOU?
STOP.

246

THOACDIEN: YES.
STOP.

BITEUS: AFTER YOU HAVE ACTIVATED THE
          FLOATER CAN YOU OPERATE IT BY
          REMOTE CONTROL?
STOP.

THOACDIEN: YES.
             IF I HAVE VISUAL COORDINATES
             AND A GUIDE.
STOP.

BITEUS: CAN YOU TAKE VISUAL
          INSTRUCTIONS FROM ME?
STOP.

THOACDIEN: IT IS AWKWARD BUT IT CAN BE
             DONE.
STOP.

BITEUS: HOW LONG WILL IT TAKE YOU TO
          PROGRAM FLOATER AND HAVE
          OPEN CHANNELS FOR THIS
          DETAILS OF OPERATION AS YET
          OPERATION?
STOP.

THOACDIEN: FLOATER IS BEING
             PROGRAMMED NOW.
             IT IS NOW 6.9.023 YOUR TIME.
             FLOATER CAN BE READY FOR
             OPERATION 187.353, AT 1.0.871.
STOP.

BITEUS: WE WILL NOT NEED YOU UNTIL
          187.353 AT APPROXIMATELY 2.0.000.
          WILL CONTACT YOU BEFORE THEN.
          DETAILS OF OPERATION AS YET
          UNFORMED.

STOP.

END TRANSMISSION ....

THOACDIEN: OVERRIDE!
WHERE ARE YOU?
WHO ARE YOU WITH?
WHAT ARE YOU DOING?
STOP.

BITEUS: WE ARE SAFE.
I CANNOT TRANSMIT NOW, I'M
RUNNING.
STOP.

END TRANSMISSION ....

The sun is rising unseen toward its apex. At the western edge of the mesa no one can be seen or heard. All see without being seen—in silence. All wait for the Thoacdien magicians to arrive and make their move. In the stillness, offended black cats of ideas and dreams have returned to Higgitte brains, have turned around dusting their places, have lowered themselves like camels, to stay. In the light the cats' eyes are gold with little exclamation marks in each center—and unblinking.

The warriors watch the opening with their backs to the desert and the floater. Behind rocks and shrubs they wait in the formation of three concentric, invisible, and unbroken crescents—little starving mouths, one inside the other, which look to the vein opening for substenance. Forty warriors ring the little hole in two concentric circles—all unseen, and all within leaping distance of it.

Grod-Linz is closest to the floater. He knews that the first warrior created these formations and will not be caught in them. To escape, the five must come to the floater another way.

Logana, glowing cool in a shallow vein near the surface

of the mesa, near the edge of the mesa, stops to make her decisions, to put herself in the runners' places and deduce what they will do. Her eyelids are drawn tight around her eyeballs. Her breathing would not fog a mirror. Her mind shuffles and deals contingencies, plays through the games of the expected, and rejects each one. The Thoacdiens will not do what is expected. Logana decides to stay where she is.

"You can make the floater come to you without touching it?"

"Yes."

"How much noise will this make?"

"Very little. The warriors will be aware of nothing until the floater is in the air and moving."

"How far away from the machine can you be and still do this?"

"I must be able to see it."

"Tell me what you want me to do."

"Do you wish to come with us?"

Nyz-Ragaan shuts his eyes and leans back in the darkness against the cold wall. He feels all of his time revolving as concentric moments around this one instant, this one decision which will shape and color all that has been and all that is to come.

"Nyz-Ragaan . . . ?"

"Must I pass through The Hall of One Thousand Chambers?"

"We will not be returning to Thoacdien immediately. Biel will not go back. You do not have to decide anything but whether or not you want to come with us in the floater today."

". . . I cannot decide now."

"Then we will make a plan so that you do not have to decide until the last moment."

"Yes."

"How are Biel and Xitr-Meede?"

"They can be awakened when it is time. They will be able to do what is necessary."

"Fine."

"Nyz-Ragaan, I would like us to move north of the floater. I will need a concealment far enough away from the warriors so that I can see the floater without being seen."

"I will find you such a place."

"I will guide the floater to me from there, enter it and then go northeast, back across the mesa in a straight line to pick up each of you at intervals of thirty heartbeats. That way we won't be in any one hovering position too long and no one will be exposed for more than a few moments. I will pick you up last. If you don't want to come, wave me off."

"Yes. That is a good plan. Most of the warriors will be waiting at the floater. They will not have time to pursue you. You will have to hurry, but it is safe."

"Good. We need five concealments which run in a fairly straight line northeast from the edge of the mesa."

"Let's go."

At the top of the edge of the mesa, at the point where it falls and becomes perpendicular to itself, there is a small hole, like the cavity in a tooth. From the back of this hole Biteus can see the floater in the distance without being seen. He can also feel the few scattered warriors below him, looking up, unseeing. Behind Biteus, at intervals stretching northeast, are Xitr-Meede, Biel, Mikkran, and Nyz-Ragaan. They were placed in these concealments from underneath, from the veins. They have not been seen. But they have been heard. Directly behind Biteus by forty heartbeats, unseen, is Logana.

There is no human sound or movement at the point where the desert meets the mesa. The sun is high and unseen beyond this white-gray day. All are waiting for the right moment to reach out and grab the event which is flying by.

Grod-Linz waits. Only his eyes move as they scan the landscape before him for hints. The floater is less than two body lengths behind him. The little rhymes still hop-scotch in his head, but they are softer now.

FROM THE LEGEND OF BIEL

From nowhere, abruptly, a new noise is so gradually added to the landscape that it is not perceived by anyone. There is a soft purr behind Grod-Linz. It slowly enters his ear. The sound glides up from beneath what can be heard and barely enters the audible spectrum. Only after it has become a part of him does he hear it. He turns, standing, as the machine lifts. He sees it rise the length of his body before a hand passes across his mind and wipes it clean. Then—"Ah"—he falls, heavy as a bag of stones, having fainted. The other warriors hear him fall and turn to see the floater rise blindly, operated from more than five light-years away by Thoacdien and guided by Biteus. As one their faces open like mouths and a thin, dying scream disturbs the silence of the mesa.

~~~~~~

THOACDIEN: FLOATER IS ACTIVATED AND
OFF THE GROUND.
GUIDE ME.
STOP.

BITEUS: RISE. RISE . . . A LITTLE MORE. STOP.
TURN FORTY-FIVE DEGREES LEFT.
YOU ARE NOW FACING NORTHEAST.
MOVE EXACTLY IN THAT DIRECTION
AT YOUR PRESENT HEIGHT.
YOU ARE AIMED DIRECTLY AT ME.
. . . GOOD . . .
SLOWLY . . . SLOWLY . . .STOP.
RISE . . . A LITTLE MORE. PERFECT!
I CAN ALMOST TOUCH THE FLOATER.
DROP HALF MY BODY LENGTH.
OPEN THE DOOR.
I'M IN THE FLOATER NOW AND WILL
PILOT THE SHIP FROM HERE.
THANK YOU.
I'LL CONTACT YOU AS SOON AS THE
OPERATION IS COMPLETED.

STOP.

E N D   T R A N S M I S S I O N ....

THOACDIEN: OVERRIDE!
             PLEASE CONTINUE TO
             TRANSMIT AND RECEIVE.
STOP.

BITEUS: NEGATIVE.
          I NEED ALL FOCUS HERE.
          WILL CONTACT YOU AT FIRST LULL.
STOP.

E N D   T R A N S M I S S I O N ....

Logana hears the thin scream which blooms from the foot of the cliff and wafts back to where she is. Then she sees the little machine rise smooth and white like a sun. It sits on the edge of the cliff directly in front of her. A door materializes and the tall black man climbs into the machine. The door stays open as the machine rises and glides northeast. It stops and hovers a moment, waist-high. The black arm reaches out to help the young boy scramble to safety. Logana is on her feet running north, toward the other.

Grod-Linz wakens, lifts his face out of the dirt and sees the machine disappear over the edge of the mesa. He stands, raises his fist, and runs.

"To the mesa! On top of the mesa!"

Few warriors are unafraid. They let him lead by a healthy margin before following.

The ball of one foot grabs the ground like a claw, pushes it away, and the runner is airborne a moment, pulling her other bent leg through to the shockproof position for the next thrust. Her gown has been slit by the razor from ankles to waist and she resembles a blue flag. Her arms pump, pushing off invisible walls behind then

252

reaching forward to pull on imaginary banisters in front. Each running stride carries her back a generation until there are no more and she has been reduced to one, pure, uncensored gesture of rage.

The machine picks up the little girl and heads farther northeast, toward Mikkran. Logana and the floater equally converge on that point, on the mentor who has been lifted out of context to become an archetype, a fulcrum around which both past and present revolve.

Mikkran's dark frame rises up from her small concealment. Her head turns and she sees Logana. Their eyes lock together and the space between them becomes a tunnel, lit from within by their two points of view. Mikkran mouths the words she tries to send into Logana's unhearing brain.

"Please do not do this. I will not hurt you."

Mikkran's eyes become black tears, rimmed with spiderlegs. She seems to be cut out of the sky, etched. Only Mikkran does not reflect the gray of the day. Only she glows rich and living. She closes her eyes a moment and nods, as if to say, "I cannot stop you now." And the slight wind blows her robe against her body. She has not finished living, but she waits, face up, for the floater to descend, because she is unwilling to do harm, and there is no time.

The machine is waist-high. Mikkran is reaching up for it like a child. It is so close, such a simple safety. Then she feels a thud on her back and the cold blade enters, slithers in and slices organs which cannot tolerate intrusion. Her eyelids flutter as automatically she reaches back one curled hand and feels Logana's wet fist on her back. Biteus hops down from the floater in slow motion. His face looks strange but he moves past her, behind her, as she feels another thud higher up. It tears open the flesh, working its wet way forward to complete its two endless arcs, its two entries through skin to bone and out again. She feels the fading pain and finds Biteus's face in the motion as she falls. She looks at him—not surprised, only a little sad.

—. . . I have already lived forever. It is never-ending because it never began. That is good, Biteus.

—. . . Mikkran!?

The mentor sees the chalky stone before her eyes. Not blinking, she notices the individual shapes and colors of each grain of sand before her.

. . . pink . . .

      . . . tan . . .

           . . . pur . . . ple.

               . . . shadows.

Then the grains disappear beneath a black flood.

Mikkran vomits and feels the pieces of sliced, precious organs grinding helplessly against one another. She blinks. Her eyebrows raise up, pull up like the wings of a bird trying to lift her, to carry her away to the meadows or some safe place where this was only a dream. But they cannot lift her. She is captured in a swell of coolness which pulses beneath her, spreads, and seeps into the ground. Her hand is in a thin stream which works its way against tremendous odds, out and down to the desert. Her fingers flex, relax, grasp, uncaslp.

—. . . for me.

—For Biel . . .

      We drank and were satisfied.

            . . . Biel . . .

               Biel?

—Mikkran? Yes?

—. . . I am draining away, Biel. . . .

Nyz-Ragaan is on his feet running toward a thrashing Logana as the warriors crest the edge of the mesa. Logana turns to him and recocks the blade. Biteus grabs her raised arm, turns her to him and takes her face in his free hand. He speaks to her very softly, as to a child.

"Woman, do no more."

Logana freezes. The blade falls and sinks to the bottom of the shallow maroon pool at her feet.

"Nyz-Ragaan, help me get her into the ship." And together they lift the limp, cooling bulk of Mikkran to safety.

The Higgitte warriors throw blades and rocks at the fluttering, rising machine. And those things are broken on its harder surface. Inside the ship they do not even hear.

"Nyz-Ragaan, go sit with Xitr-Meede. Biel, stay at her head and keep her still. We must work fast."

The warrior obeys and watches the mesa shrink magically below him as the small boy pilots a machine beyond his comprehension. He sees Logana, a statue of rage, standing over a dark puddle. She shrinks to some other, forgotten importance. He sees Grod-Linz's betrayed face looking up, screaming, until it no longer matters. Now, however slightly, he is looking from the other side.

Mikkran is lying on her stomach on a white table in the center of the floater. Her robe has been ripped from hem to neck, exposing her long brown body and its two rosebud wounds whose petals spiral up thinly and continually, then fall and drain away. The first flower is next to her spine, in the small of her back. The second is at the base of her skull. With this second wound the blade entered, bounced off bone, pushed cartilage aside, and came out in front of her larynx. Her head is on its side and her face points across her right shoulder. Her eyes are open and unseeing. A little stream of blood comes out of her nose, runs over the edge of the table and falls, wasted, to the floor. Her lips move. She wants to speak, but cannot. She has no voice. She has no words. She has no time.

Biteus lays out surgical tools and struggles in the context of efficiency for meaningful action—to stop the bleeding. He leans over Mikkran and clamps the first wound closed with a pressure bandage.

At a soft moment, when Biteus is working on the harder, second wound. Mikkran's eyes pass over Biel, and touch her, uncomprehending.

"Don't die . . . oh, please, you cannot die."

"If you want to stay here you must be quiet, Biel."

Mikkran calls Biel into her faint, fainter mind. They speak of what they have known and shared and been to each other. They speak openly, fully, saying all of it, because they are not afraid. And Mikkran, fading fainter and fainter, holds onto the girl as a reference point. The mentor tries to prepare her charge for what has come too soon. But she cannot explain. She can only go on, hold on, reaching out to the child as they pass the point where their roles are reversed and Biel must listen and give.

Mikkran's mind fades . . . fades. . . . Only for a moment is she baffled, as her brain becomes a baby's fist wrapped around Biel's finger—then a disappearing flower in reverse bloom. Her last coherency is the image of a little girl squatting over a pool . . . "I. Biel . . ." Then Mikkran simply relaxes, becomes too small to hold any longer, curls up smaller, smaller, and—disappearing through a hole in space—dies.

Is. Dead.

—Mikkran?

—Mikkran? . . .

There is no answer from this silence like no others.

"Ahh . . . Let me . . . hold her."

". . . Yes. It is no use. She is gone. . . ."

". . . No . . . that cannot be! That can not be!"

And gently, gently, Biel turns her mentor over and holds her like a broken child. She winds one arm around her waist. The other arm supports Mikkran's shoulders. And she is gone.

Mikkran's head falls back and pulls her jaw down.

"See . . . she is yawning. No, she is laughing . . ."

. . .Like a bird who wanting warmth for her belly turns over to fly upside down.

She is gone.

The child listens a long time to the stillness in Mikkran, the cooling lack of motion as molecules tire of their continual orbits and fall to the bottom, not yet exhausted, only finished. She is gone. And through the skin of Biel's living body she learns of death as her mentor cools beyond return, beyond repair, and goodness is silenced. Gone . . .

—See how still you are here . . . and here. The bird in your throat is gone.

How broken.

No . . . no. You cannot lie like this.

You were never still like this. You slept running.

—I . . . I cannot endure this breaking in half . . . this finality.

Biel turns her mentor on her side of the stained table. She bends one dead knee and straightens the other. She raises one responseless arm up—to reaching. And Mikkran looks like crippled flight, still and graceless.

"There. Now you leap and reach for what is next. You are in flight . . . like always."

The little girl raises her eyes to Biteus.

"She is no more. Mikkran. Is. No. More. This stillness will be with me always. I have no center and no edges. Only Mikkran's absence."

And Biel breaks into pieces. There is a threshold of endurance through which one cannot pass and remain whole. And because she understands, because she has learned it through her pores, she cannot endure. She sobs slick sheets of tears which form a lake of sound and wet in which she hopes to drown. But Biteus is there. Here. He has her in his living arms and will not let her sink down all the way.

"Xĥr-Meede, take the ship onto the desert. We must make a grave."

The warriors converge on Logana who has come back to life as the other died. She is screaming.

"They have stolen Nyz-Ragaan! He is possessed by their magic as I was! You saw! They will take him south and kill him!"

Grod-Linz, by default—because the others can feel that none of them stand on the mesa anymore, because they are now floating in meaningless, directionless space —asserts himself beyond his rank.

"Drummer!! Signal the warriors in the veins to surface and wait for us! Leaders of ten, return to your camps and get provisions for a full attack on the meadows!!!"

And because the machine is gone, can no longer be seen—and what cannot be seen is not real—they obey. Like a pane of glass shattered, they scatter across the mesa, sounding alarms, preparing to rescue their military leader.

. . . .

". . . I don't feel very good. . . ."

Captain Ybarra was upside down if O'Hare were right-side up. He held the aluminum container with the activating tube and key between his knees and tugged at it, working to release the key from its mooring. His fingers always felt clumsy in gloves, but the mission did not involve enough time to pressurize the ship according to code FD-123.0967.203 Section IV, subsection 23. He freed the key and locked it onto the top left pocket of the suit he would wear on MC6—right over his heart. This key was all that would permit him to deactivate the nuc once its clock was set.

Ybarra always sweated inside the pressure suit, building up a thin film of steam which could not be seen but was felt as oil. It bothered him, made him feel slippery inside the suit. He inserted the activating tube into its female coupling. The warhead was armed. He took the timer out of its case and plugged it into the bomb's computer. He would set it as he and O'Hare were leaving the ship. He wiped his forearm across his brow, then realized he had streaked his facemask. The itch lived, and he could not get to it.

". . . You say something, Joe?"

"No."

"Colonel Haris here. How's the nuc, Ybarra?"

"Nuc is armed and timer is attached. I'll set timer for one hour as we are leaving the ship."

"Fine. How about the audio units?"

"All systems are go as per Levin-Hughes's specs. O'Hare will begin audio check with Lanier in a few moments."

"You will land in five minutes and ten seconds."

"OK. I just want to get this over with."

"Relax. It's nothing. You got the guns. It's nothing."

"Yeah . . . let's hope."

M.I.K.

K.R.A.N.

FROM THE LEGEND OF BIEL

MikkranMikkranMikkranMikkranMikkranMikkranMikkranMikkranMikkranMikkranMikkran

MikkranMikkranMikkranMikkranMikkranMikkranMikkranMikkranMikkranMikkranMikkran

MikkranMikkranMikkranMikkranMikkranMikkr   ikkranMikkranMikkranMikkranMikkranMikkran

MikkranMikkranMikkranMikkranMikkranMikk   kkranMikkranMikkranMikkranMikkranMikkran

MikkranMikkranMikkranMikkr   nMikkranMikkranMikkranMikkranMikkran

MikkranMikkranMikkranM   ranMikkranMikkranMikkranMikkran

MikkranMikkranMikkran   kkranMikkranMikkranMikkran

MikkranMikkra   ikkranMikkranMikkranMikkran

MikkranMikkra   nMikkranMikkranMikkran

MikkranMikkranM   MikkranMikkranMikkranMikkran

MikkranMikk   kkranMikkranMikkran

MikkranMik   ikkranMikkran

MikkranM   anIkkranMikkran

Mikkra   nMikkranMikkran

Mikk   kranMikkran

MikkranM   anMikkran

MikkranMik   kkran

MikkranMikkr   nMikkran

MikkranMikkranMi   ranMikkran

MikkranMikkranMikkranMik   MranMikkrann

MikkranMikkranMikkranMikkranM   anMikkranMikkran

MikkranMikkranMikkranMikkranMikkr   kranMikkranMikkran

MikkranMikkranMikkranMikkranMikkranMi   ikkranMikkranMikkran

MikkranMikkranMikkranMikkranMikkranMikkra   ikkranMikkranMikkranMikkran

MikkranMikkranMikkranMikkranMikkranMikkranMikk   MikkranMikkranMikkranMikkran

MikkranMikkranMikkranMikkranMikkranMikkranMikkranMikkranMikkranMikkranMikkranMikkran

MikkranMikkranMikkranMikkranMikkranMikkranMikkranMikkranMikkannMikkranMikkranMikkran

MikkranMikkranMikkranMikkranMikkranMikkranMikkranMikkranMikkranMikkranMikkranMikkran

FROM THE LEGEND OF BIEL

.... is dead.

Outside they dig a grave for you.
For you . . .
And each syllable is an hour . . .   Mikkran.
Inside I don't know what to do . . . how to do   Mikkran.
. . .anymore.
Mikkran . . . ?
silencesilencesilencesilencesilencesilencesilencesilencesilenc
. . . no more . . .
nothing else.
anymore . . .
Only the thud and hiss of shovels digging outside—beyond the plumes, the swells, the waves of this absence which is nausea.
. . . Mikkran?
Are you anywhere? Or have you fully ceased.
Mikkran .... ceased.
(. . . hold on . . . . . . I can't any longer . . .) . . .
Mikkran. Mikkran.
no. more.
Mikkran?
They have wrapped you in a cloth.
Why?
. . . worms will eat you anyway.
Where are you?
Touch me somehow and I shall be able to move. Mikkran?
. . . because there cannot be a world where someplace you are not.
That cannot be.
Mikkran.
Then.
Always.
Never.
Always.
Where? . . .
I shall weep in the morning not rising by your face, Mikkran . . .
. . . still I babble into your silence.

where you do not respond . . . cannot.
There is no you now.
Dead.
Now, Mikkran, there is only silence by the stream where
we used to live and you gave me words
and you bathed glistening like a brown diamond in the
sun and I slept
secure in the warmth of your neck.

—. . . Biel? Biel? . . . Xitr-Meede, take Nyz-Ragaan
outside, please, and wait for me.
—Yes, Biteus.
—. . . . . . . Biel? . . . Biel?
—. . .Biteus . . .
—Yes?
—............................ help .... me ....
—I will try. Biel?
—Yes?
—Biel, you must let go now . . . we must bury her.
—I . . . can't . . . . Mikkran . . . . ?
—She cannot answer, Biel.
—Mikkran?
—Biel, let go now.
—. . . Do what you must.
—Biteus?
—Yes, Xitr-Meede?
—Give her something to help her.
—I can't, Xitr-Meede. I have no right to cushion this
for her, or to make it go away. It is real. She must do the
best she can now, on her own—as you would have to do.
Please wait for me outside.
—Yes . . .
—. . . Biteus?
—Yes, Biel?
—May I keep her robe?
—Yes. You may have it.
—Biteus?
—Yes?
—Is she anywhere, now? Mikkran?

—No. She is no more, Biel. She does not exist except as she is remembered.

—. . . Hold me.

—Yes.

—You do not feel the same.

—I am not the same. I am Biteus.

—. . . How can an absence be so unendurable and yet we go on living?

—Because we are alive.

—Biteus?

—Yes?

—I hear nothing but silence. . . .

—Her goodness is not gone, Biel. As we live now, she lives.

—I am lonely to be warm.

—Trust that someday you will be warm again.

—. . . Mikkran. . . .

—Biel . . . you must let go now. You are hanging onto ashes.

—. . . yes.

I am walking beside Biteus who carries your empty bulk to its little hole. I feel the textured fabric of your shroud tween my fingertips and walk beside Biteus to your grave. Only a little farther.

The gray featureless clouds which were all day so much an obstruction to the sun have drifted apart, unclasped like hands, so that the tearlike globe of fire which is the sun can fall when the wrapped, bound, wound and silent wounded form of you is lowered, gently,

slow and broken, into the dark mouth of ground that is your final home.

It is so still. . . .

The sun falls, breaks, splashes onto the ground of the desert where we walked, you following me, feeding me until you had no food yourself—nothing to eat or drink. The sun falls now into your grave with you, as a tear. It shimmers a moment, then evaporates.

I love you. I love you. I take earth in my hand as pieces

of myself, and drop it on your cloth. Your silence has
evaporated the light. Even the stars step aside, back up,
retreat and bow to let you pass. Crumbled. Broken. Flying.
Running. As you always were . . . I love you.
With you in your grave are buried all seasons and all
songs. Someday I will come back when a tree is grown
here, and pick the leaves one at a time, one season at a
time—to reclaim what has disappeared. I love you and
am no longer whole.

"I, Xitr-Meede, take this earth in my hands, and with it
say goodbye to Mikkran. I knew her when she waited
and when she loved with no reward. That is what I wish
to remember, to have become a part of me."

The little droplets of dry soil strike your bulk like rain.
pat. pat. pat. patterpatterpatterpatterpatterpatterpatter-
patter. pat. pat. pat.

"I, Nyz-Ragaan, warrior of the Higgittes, take this
earth in my hands, and with it give you back that which
I took which was not mine. You gave with grace. I see
more now—and love differently."

"I, Lan-Biteus, take this earth in my hands and to this
season, this desolate and forgotten place, proclaim that
we commit Mikkran-Gogan-Tor to the future. Her wisdom and goodness are not forgotten, but continue to teach
us how to endure the unendurable, how to follow and
challenge the unthinkable. I proclaim to these witnesses,
to the Higgitte nation of Grodden, to the Thoacdiens of
Thoacdien V, to the entire Federation, and to the stars,
that this desert is renamed. From now it shall be called
the place of beginning—Mikkran. Mikkran. And it is
here that we shall come when we are tired and do not
know what to do anymore. From here, Mikkran, we shall
begin again."

I must speak and cannot. I have no tongue and no mind

to make it work. Mikkran . . . Mikkran. Silence. She is
gone.

"I, Biel . . . submit my mentor . . . to her earth. Mikkran-Gogan-Tor gave me her . . . her . . . full endurance . . . her full, unshadowed honesty, words . . .
life. She did not die from the unendurable, but from the
absurd. We . . . are alive—feeling nothing but the hole
through which you vanished. From the words you . . .
gave me I can find none. There are no words. Only an
empty, empty hole in space. I take this earth in my hands
and offer it to you knowing that nothing is enough. Mikkran, as I live you shall not be dead. I love you, mentor
. . . Biteus . . . let us stay here until dawn, until she is
cold."

Through night that covers me like blood I wait and feel
you rising up in me as goodness and patience and hope,
and realize that we are not yet even half finished. There
are so many unnamed names which were to be your joy.

"Biteus?"
"Yes?"
"What did you do to Logana?"
"I put her to sleep."
"Is she dead?"
"No, she is awake now. Unchanged."
"I will kill her."
"No, Nyz-Ragaan. It must stop here. Now."
"That is for me to decide."
"No. One death is enough."
"They will not let it be. They will come for me."
"One death is enough."

Now there is the red weeping light of the east, bleeding
onto us in sympathy. No . . . no. It does not feel, it
only is. Night raises its eyelid so simply after death. And
I shall see endless, empty blue. No clouds . . . no stars.
No light yet—only a long, pink strain across my forehead.
And the smell of your death as the desert prepares to

bloom. Already, not yet even one short day, I am alive too long without you.

"Shall we go to the meadows?"
"Yes."
"All right."
"Biel?"
"I do not care. . . ."
"We must all let go now."

I stand. I leave your tiny grave, covered with . . . help . . . me. Mikkran. . . . . ? Someone, please?
    (—. . . . hold on.
    —I can't, oh, please, I can't any longer.
    —But you must.
    —No.
    —It is inevitable.
    —. . . yes.
    —I will help you until you are strong again.
    —I am dead. .
    —Oh, no. You are not dead, you are merely changing.)
The floater rises. It tries to lift me up, away from that dark, full hole. But I am buried there—to my ankles. My feet, like paralyzed claws, cannot let go. They must. They must—but can't. So I am stretched thinner, and thinner, as if to break. But I do not break. I am elastic. My feet are in your grave and my indifference is here. I am Biel. I am Biel. I am Biel. Biel: turbulence. Mikkran: beginning. I am Biel. I am Biel. I am Biel. And Mikkran is no more.

"Xitr-Meede, head directly south. We should get to the meadows by this time tomorrow. I'll sleep after I contact Thoacdien."
"Yes, Biteus."

~~~~~~

FROM: MENTOR LAN-BIETUS, THE PLACE OF BEGINNING, THOACDIEN V. PRIORITY ONE.

TO: THOACDIEN.
DATE: 187.354
TIME: 1.0.120

. . . .
. . . .
. . . .

THOACDIEN: PROCEED.
STOP.

BITEUS: . . . . . I WISH TO REPORT THAT
            MENTOR MIKKRAN-GOGAN-TOR DIED
            ON 187.353 AT 2.0.010 OF KNIFE
            WOUNDS INFLICTED DURING OUR
            ESCAPE FROM THE MESA.
            THERE WERE NO OTHER INJURIES.
            WE ARE NOW IN THE FLOATER
            HEADING SOUTH TOWARD THE
            MEADOWS.
            PLEASE ANNOUNCE TO THE
            FEDERATION THAT THE DESERT OF
            DEATH HAS BEEN RENAMED.
            IT IS NOW CALLED MIKKRAN: THE
            PLACE OF BEGINNING.
STOP.

THOACDIEN: . . . . . . YES.
            I WILL MAKE ANNOUNCEMENTS
            TO THE FEDERATION.
            PLEASE, WHO IS WITH YOU?
STOP.

BITEUS: MYSELF, XITR-MEEDE, AND FORMER
        FIRST WARRIOR OF THE HIGGITTES,
        NYZ-RAGAAN.
STOP.

THOACDIEN: WHERE IS CHARGE 187-A,0037?
STOP.

BITEUS: I AM NOT AT LIBERTY TO SAY.
          BUT SHE IS SAFE.
STOP.

THOACDIEN: WOULD YOU CONSIDER COMING
             HOME NOW?
STOP.

BITEUS: NO, WE CANNOT.
STOP.

THOACDIEN: . . . I SEE.
STOP.

BITEUS: I BELIEVE MIKKRAN HAD ANOTHER
          CHARGE PRIOR TO 187-A,0037. WILL
          YOU INFORM HIM PERSONALLY, AND
          SAY SHE IS WELL-MOURNED?
STOP.

THOACDIEN: YES. HIS NAME IS GROLEN.
             BITEUS, WE ARE DEEPLY
             GRIEVED AT THIS LOSS.
             PLEASE REPORT THIS TO
             187-A,0037.
STOP.

BITEUS: YES. HER NAME IS BIEL.
STOP.

THOACDIEN: . . . TURBULENCE.
             THANK YOU.
STOP.

BITEUS: SHE NAMED HERSELF.
STOP.

FROM THE LEGEND OF BIEL

THOACDIEN: . . . YES. . . .
           ARE YOU ALL RIGHT?
STOP.

BITEUS: YES.
STOP.

END TRANSMISSION . . . .

Inside the floater is white—quiet and peaceful as though
nothing has happened and we are all still here. I will fill
the silence with lists of things. I shall paper the hole
through which she vanished with indifferent observations.
The inside of the floater is white. The inside of the floater is white. The. Is white. Inside of the floater. The inside
of the Mikkran is gone. The inside of the floater is Mikkran. Inside the floater is gone. The inside of the floater
is white. The is white.
Is gone.
Is Mikkran.
Dead
and not inside the floater which is white and dead.
Sounds peck at me. That which is outside the absence
pecks at me—like a little bird pecks at a stone, aimlessly,
for no reason at all. It cannot break open the stone. For
no reason at all—but to sharpen its beak. Pecks at me.
Sound, scrapes, rasps, grasps, far away, on the surface.
Unable to annoy.
Pecking.
Scraping.
The inside of the floater is white.
              The inside of the floater is white.
                 The insider of the floater is white . . .
Inside the floater there is one tiny blue light to break the
monotony of the smooth white. Ascend beyond the stars,
through the little holes they make in darkness. Do not
cease completely. The blue light glows in the center of

269

the monotonus white control panel and punctuates the silence. Xitr-Meede watches it. His mouth is moving. He speaks inside this white where Mikkran is not, to Nyz-Ragaan. The inside of the floater is white. The table where she died is clean and bears fruit . . . there is a tiny blue light. Gone. The little light is a jewel. Do not cease completely.
Blink.
Biteus is asleep. Xitr-Meede is blond. His features have hardened in just one day. He loved her. Loves her. This is the look of his manhood. The inside of the floater is white. Accept that. His features have hardened in just one day. His face is broad and flat. He has a straight, flat nose. Unbroken . . . not yet broken. She is gone. He is blond. Biteus is black like night and asleep. Nyz-Ragaan listens to Xitr-Meede. Mentor and child. Is white. Accept. Gone.
Nyz-Ragaan is torn. He will be unable to take the final step. If you could come only one step farther. Gone. One step, Nyz-Ragaan, you would be free. But you cannot transcend your time. Just as I cannot transcend . . . gone. I am Biel. The inside of the floater is white. Fruit and nuts are on the table. On the table. Is white. Gone. On the white. The inside is gone. Is white is white is white is white is white is white is white is white is white is white is gone.

. . . .

"PROBE IV to Skimmer Three."
"Ybarra here. Go ahead PROBE IV."
"Prepare to land in two minutes, Joe."
"Check. All systems are go here for landing on MC6 in two minutes."
"PROBE IV out."

. . . .

FROM THE LEGEND OF BIEL

(I
   Am
      Being
         Sucked
            Through
               Sound
                  Softly.
It rises, crests, falls, throbs, flutters,
                      crashes—
             falling below what can be heard.
And still I hear it continue
              down,
                down,
                       to level off
in a long, dull plane, an aerodynamic arc,
             beneath the oceans we have chosen
                 to see
              in our own ways.
And when the sound has reached its bottom, regained
its energy, its urgency, it begins to rise again.

It s p l / i t s itself in half . . . . . . peels off in two layers
—edges—which curve around and rise and rise, back up
into hearing, circle back around,
and meet each other on the other side—and there is you.

s p l a t

—. . . Here you are . . .
—But who? LISTEN: Wind chimes in the distance—
                clear glass in darkness.
—. . . We are talking.
—Have you another side than this?
—No, I have only this—here in these parentheses—
between the betweens, while you have another matrix.
—Yes.
—But where? When?
—Not-here. Not-now.
—We are two ends of the same rhythm.

—We have become synchronized.
—We collide and intersect harmlessly.
—We are equilibrium.
—Flying . . .
—Hold on.
—I am. I will. I have.
—Dying.
—Changing.
—Have always been.
—And somewhere there is light beyond us.
—We have only to find it.
—To stumble on it.
—To have it trip on us.
—In the meantime this is not unpleasant.
—Although it will not be remembered.
—Then it will be completed?
—Is there release?
—Resolution?
—Solution?
—Or only more entertwining, braiding together, because we are not dead, never have been, never shall be. We are only changing.
—And in this we have taken hands.
—A first.
—. . . Hold on.
—I will not let you go. . . .)

VIII

Biteus pilots the little white Thoacdien machine through the darker part of the night. The others are asleep. The continent has folded in on itself in the darkness. All its small petals have rolled up, concealing fragrances and sounds. Biteus, dark against the antiseptic white, flies on essentially alone while the others dream, lolling and rolling the ghosts of images beneath their tongues.

In sleep, Nyz-Ragaan is connected to his tribe. He dreams backward. And while he dreams the nation speaks of how to save his life and punish those who spirited him away.

Northeast of the moving floater, and behind it, the Higgitte aggressive force dances in flames against a starless sky. Grod-Linz has filled the vacuum of power, and Logana has become the voice of optimism whispering in his ear. She is thinning, becoming a claw, a steel trap which —snap!—catches warriors by the soft, thin skin of their eyelids. The warriors dance convulsively. Then they obediently create their running formation and leave the flames to gallop south as one many-legged and limping force.

The eyelid of darkness begins to grind its audible machinery into lifting. Light leaks through the slender opening as a dull crescent and inserts its rude fingers as knives into the eyes of Biteus. Below, coming into focus out of the dark, are the meadows.

Biteus lowers the floater closer to the ground and imitates its contours, looking for a place to land. The sky is lightening rapidly, exposing the landscape below. Ahead is a spot with a pond, and many small, graceful hills, and trees, and distance from the Higgittes. Biteus lowers the little floater down and lays it like an egg in a nest of grass.

—Here it is safe. I will sleep. And when the sun has reached its apex, we will wake up and run, bathing away the violence of Mikkran's death.

Thuup.

The door of the floater is open. Biteus reclines his pilot's chair, and is asleep with the other three.

Here, with all the gradual contours of a woman's body, lying like a woman asleep on a long, green, swollen carpet and covered with a quilt of yellow, lilac, rose, and lime, are the meadows. The smell is a kaleidoscope of cinnamon, wet hair, and dust. The sky is the blue-white of a baby's eye. The clouds are little separate dreams. There are jade-green and moss-green and lime-green and froth-pink trees, each a different shape on top of a braided trunk. The air is rarefied and distilled. It absorbs and evaporates the toxins of grief and yesterday. There are no sounds, for this is the first day of the season of stillness. In this context, the four sleep deeply.

~~~~~~

FROM: THOACDIEN—PRIORITY ONE.
TO: MENTOR LAN-BITEUS, FLOATER A,03-187-A, MEADOWS, THOACDIEN V.
DATE: 187.355.
TIME: 2.4.702

. . . .
. . . .
. . . .

NO RESPONSE . . . .

THOACDIEN: URGENT.
STOP.   IT IS URGENT YOU RESPOND.

NO RESPONSE . . . .

THOACDIEN: BITEUS . . . ? ? ?
                 XITR-MEEDE? . . .
                 CAN ANY OF YOU RESPOND?
STOP.

NO RESPONSE . . . .

E N D   T R A N S M I S S I O N . . . .

Here are birds like colored question marks. They swoop and loop to hidden nests and sleep. The grass is green as jealousy. Flowers are all colors of the imagination, but mostly pale purple silk and paler yellow velvet. The purple smells of clean flesh. The yellow smells of wet hair. The flowers blink and nod like asterisks.

Three pairs of eyes converge on the silent, open floater. They wait until all the breathing from inside the machine has a certain regularity. Then the eyes find each other, wink, and the three move forward soundlessly. They enter the floater, being careful to touch nothing. They approach the sleeping girl and stand over her, looking. One squats down and lifts her eyelid. He looks up at the others and nods.

—She has come.

—Now we shall begin.

—We must move quickly.

The three wrap the girl in a white flannel quilt and carry her out of the floater. They walk toward a tree. They stop. A lid of earth rises and swivels to one side, revealing a hole. The three step into the hole and, carrying Biel, walk down a brightly lit tunnel of earth. The lid swivels closed behind them. The hole vanishes. The meadows are unchanged.

The three carrying Biel trot twenty steps forward. Then they turn to the left, to the right, to the right, to the left, the left again, the right, go up a flight of stairs, turn to the right, the right, go down a flight of stairs, turn to the left, the right, the left, and come out into daylight.

They emerge with their burden in front of a yellow felt tent. They enter the tent and place the sleeping girl on a padded mat on the ground. There are bright pillows for her head. The three look at Biel a moment, grin, exchange hand signals, and leave to let her sleep.

The three who have carried Biel walk over two small hills and arrive at a large black tent. They enter it. Inside are many people who collectively have no name.

"The girl is sleeping."

"Is she the one?"

"I'm not sure. How can we be sure? But I would say yes."

"We will test her to find out."

"Good."

"Is the floater concealed?"

"Yes."

"What is Thoacdien saying?"

"It calls for help and information concerning four missing people and the floater. We do not respond."

"Excellent."

"What shall we do now?"

"Wait. When she awakens show her around, but tell her as little as possible. Bring her first to me. Then take her to Grolen, and Kaj-Palmir. We will test her and examine her to see if she is the one. Now, my friends, can we eat?"

. . . .

"Ybarra to PROBE IV."

"PROBE IV, Colonel Haris here. Go ahead, Skimmer Three."

*"We are now on the surface of MC6. "All ship's systems
are at rest on ready alert."*

"Check."

*"We are changing into our surface suits. Dome structure
number one is directly west. Two hundred meters."*

"Our probes are in sync. Any signs of life?"

"Negative. Nothing."

"Let's get going, then."

*"It's so silent here. Etched. Incredibly beautiful and
stark."*

". . . Ybarra?"

"Yes, sir?"

*"Would you do me a favor and skip the poetic observa-
tions and get the hell on with your job?"*

". . . Yes, sir."

*"Fine. Now let's get going and rescue those damned
eggheads."*

"Yes, sir."

. . . .

Sleep.

. . . Sleep and melting into endless wads of cotton which
spread softly through my brain like dark cool fumes of a
song which is sung only once—lasting forever and stilling
all.

Sleep,

slowing my brain down.

      To.

        A.

          Walk.

            To a crawl.

              To stillness . . .

My brain curls into a small warm ball and hums—synchronized, mesmerized, and realized through and by the
little clouds of dreams where words don't matter as two
hands collide and coincide and then decide to go on a ride
down through the metaphors to the last place, which is

also the first place, which is like nothing else and cannot be described.

. . . I have never been here before . . . in this sleep, this dream. It hasn't happened yet, and yet it happened long ago—which are both in the same place. The distance smells of purple and lost fragrances. I am falling . . . falling . . .

        falling . . .

              floating . . .

                    shapeless as a cloud.

I am suspended from a thinning silken thread which fast unravels now and sets me free to light—an insect— on the surface of the black lake which is the bottom of myself, which has no bottom and no center and no edges, and cannot be divided. I have not been here before.

Easy . . . . . . easy . . . my talons s
                l
                 i
                  d
                   e
                    d
                      o
                        w
                          n

              through the surface of this lake and I am beneath what I had imagined to be the bottom . . .

In the water with me is a fish: the past. It is swallowed by another fish, which is swallowed by a larger fish, which bursts like a soap bubble and is gone . . .
!

All in a dream and out of a dream, all in the soft events which have no sequence, no beginning and no end, I am falling . . .

        sinking

through the bottom of myself

to the spot around which it all revolves, which does not itself move.

I hear the soft collision course of particles of particles as

they align themselves and coincide to keep me whole. I
am made of music, air, and motion.
And this is just the space between the eyelid and the eye.
. . . There is another with me. I can feel the shadow on
my back—a coolness.
We are two.
Which two?
Where?
When?
I see the faraway reflection of the dreamer, floating on
top of the lake, asleep.
I watch as the images are confused, fumbled, not quite
grasped.
There is another with me, behind me, and we are dancing.
We move slowly through no motion and no sound—dark
against the darker background of the scream—like nega-
tives of ourselves.
We spinnnnnnnnnnnnnn and do not become unraveled. We
do a slow dance and we are hurt, learning that things and
events have not disappeared, they have been rearranged.
By accident?
By design?
. . . rearranged . . .
And still we dance, the other and I, in my seeming dream.
We dance inside the tightly woven threads of the scream:
our common denominator, the endless corridor of cloth
into which one day we fell—as into a very long womb, or
tunnel—but which is not unpleasant because it has become a thin and distant chorus singing backwards, rejoicing in the motionless silence of time irreducible and without metaphor.
Palm to palm and back to back . . .
I cannot see your face, but I know you are here by the
cooler darkness of your shadow on my back. I sing for
that.
Soon we shall know what has happened.
Now our movements lift and struggle against a darkness
which is not darkness, only closed eyes.

But as of yet I cannot raise my lids wider than my secret
parentheses . . .
breathing . . .
        breathing . . . in and out.
             Not even . . . fogging . . .
                     my teeth . . . .

Inside the yellow tent with the one sleeping is another.
He sits cross-legged on the ground with a pad for mark-
ing on his lap. He observes the girl and makes occasional
notes with a long, slim tool. He feels uneasy to be watching without permission. But it is necessary. He watches
and dozes and eats and steps outside to see the sky, and
waits. He looks for the kink, which is invisible. He sees
nothing but her first full submission to sleep. She is rolled
into a comma and suspended between two seasons. Sometimes his friends look into the tent and exchange hand
signals with him. Mostly it is silent.
Silence . . .
like no others.
Silence
like a breath drawn in, held easily
for what seems to be forever.
Finally
even the motes in shafts of light
sink to the floor,
submit to this first day of stillness,
and rest.

!
Blink.
. . . light silent yellow, lit from outside, heightened and
shadowed to all its possible shades.
!
Blink.
. . . Where am I?
!
Blink.
I open my eyes and see nothing again but yellow which is

stillness. I hear no sounds. It is daytime, maybe morning.
I am awake. But where? I hear the sound of leaves not
rubbing against each other. Nothing else. I do not want
to move.
!
Blink.
It is morning. But which? When? Where? Where is it that
this has happened? I am changed and remain the same. I
am still haunted by a voice, a shadow, the touch of unseen
hands, motion too rapid to endure, a frozen scream—all
of which feels like running too fast through dark silence
and crystallized cobwebs. My darkness is still there—too
wide, too deep, too high, too dense to be ignored.

He clears his throat. . . .
"Hmhum."
—Who? Where? I turn my head.
. . . there . . . is a face. I cannot exhale. He grins, was
grinning, will grin. His eyes are tunnel-deep and close
enough for me to roll down like a marble.
"I am Rigin."
He smiles, exposing an open, upturned crescent of
yellow-and-white squares. Teeth. The crescent is outlined
in pink, and punctuated with tiny exclamation marks.
His cheeks shine like wax. His hair is orange octopus arms
curling down beyond his shoulders. He has a maroon
goatee which grows in a thin, uninterrupted strip that
begins immediately beneath his lower lip and ends at the
middle of his throat.
". . . Who are you?"
"I am Rigin."
"I am Biel . . ."
"Ah . . . turbulence."
". . . Where . . . ?"
"You are in the meadows."
"Is it real?"
"It?"
"It . . . they, this—the meadows?"
"Do you perceive it, they, this?"

"Yes."

"Then it is real."

There is no fat on his body at all. And yet he does not look like one who gets cold in the season of wind, but rather like one who keeps others warm. His chest is concave. His nose is convex. He has two legs, spindled. He is nostriled, eared, ten-fingered, two-balled, ten-toed, flat-footed, double-nippled, backed and fronted, breathing, human, and alive.

"Rigin . . ."

"Mmmmmmm hello."

"How am I here?"

"By choice, accident, and instinct. Do you believe in the unknown?"

"Yes."

"Do you believe in freedom?"

"Yes."

"Do you believe in stars?"

"As holes."

"Do you believe in labor?"

"As the way to the unknown."

"Do you believe in Thoacdien?"

"No."

"Then you are welcome to the meadows."

"Thank you."

He wears red flannel shorts in which there are deep pockets holding writing tubes and small pretty stones. His legs stick out of his pants like two skinny fingers. His chest is tufted irregularly. His navel is a tiny onion. His ears are sails. His nose is a beak. He smiles all the time, and is not in a hurry.

"Did you sleep well?"

"Yes. Completely. That has not happened to me before. And I dreamed."

"About what?"

"I cannot remember."

"Ah."

"Where are my friends?"

"They are still asleep."

"Oh."

"Would you like to be introduced?"

"To what?"

"To the village of Lir, the meadows, Thoacdien V."

"How long have I been asleep?"

"Since this time two mornings ago."

"It seems like only moments."

"You slept well. Your body needed it. You have not trusted sleep before."

"Bad always happened before when I slept."

"Perhaps that will stop now."

"How?"

"Perhaps we can help you."

"How?"

"Be patient. We are still unacquainted. I brought you fresh clothing and some food. Are you hungry?"

"Yes!"

"Here, eat."

"Thank you."

Biel eats, bending and breaking red fruit with her teeth, drinking its juice. There is also stream wine, and cheese which is as smooth and light as a thigh.

"Where is the floater?"

"Concealed."

"How?"

"By a ray which illuminates all the empty space between the particles of an object and renders it invisible. We call it a dark bulb."

"Why did you conceal it?"

"We do not wish to be discovered."

". . . By Thoacdien or the Higgittes?"

"Neither. I do not want to tell you too much. You shall see shortly for yourself. But we are a village of roughly one hundred persons. It depends."

"On what?"

"Who's here."

"What are the people of the village called?"

"Nothing."

"Nothing?"

"We live in the village of Lir, on the meadows of Thoacdien V. That is enough. We are not a system or a group. We are human beings—men, women, and children. We need no other name. You are welcome here on one condition."

"What is that?"

"We must have your permission to administer a mild amnesiac when you leave here—if you choose to go—so that you will remember nothing of us."

"Your secrecy is that important?"

"Yes, for the time being."

"What if I refuse."

"You will learn no more of us."

"What if I refuse, but stay and learn more on my own?"

"It would be impossible, even for you. We would choose not to be discovered."

"I will take the drug."

"Excellent."

"I must warn you that it may not work. My system does not accept drugs."

"Not simple ones at least. Do not worry."

"And my friends?"

"They will have to decide when they awaken. If you will change now we can get started. There is much to do."

"Yes."

Biel stands. The hem of her robe is now at the middle of her calf. It is frayed and worn and bleached to lifeless gray. When Mikkran first gave it to her it touched the ground.

"Off. There. . . ."

Her new flannel shorts are yellow, with deep soft pockets.

"Show me Lir, please. I am ready."

Rigin holds the flap of the tent aside and Biel steps out into a still photograph of sky hanging behind hills hanging behind trees hanging behind flowers hanging behind silence. In front of the tent is a tree with leaves like coins —a mobile—which rotate slowly on their stems. One side of each leaf is white, the other is pale gray-green.

". . . There's nobody here . . ."

"There is no evidence of others, but they are here."

"It's so strange here."

"Ah yes. It is the beginning of the season of stillness."

They walk slowly. They speak very softly so as not to disturb the silence which seeps into the brain like water and washes it clean. The sky is cloudless. Colors are greens and pale blue, dotted with tiny spots of flowers which are so bright they fairly slice their way through the pupils and into the center of the soft darkness of secrets. There are no signs of other people. The meadows look virgin.

—!

—Sound.

—I hear sound—soft rolling tinkling waves which are laughter, which is rhythm, which is soft and far away.

"What do I hear?"

"Art."

"Art?"

"Music. Yora is playing the Sphere to welcome you."

"Where?"

"You shall see."

"Are you an artist?"

"Yes. I am a playwright."

—He is not much taller than I am. How does one so small and thin, one who laughs so readily and musically with his head thrown back so far, wright plays . . . ?

"Plays are not wrought by force alone—great cunning is also needed."

"Ha ha. Each time I look at you from the sides of my eyes I want to laugh."

". . . Ahhhhh."

They are still walking. Rigin holds Biel's hand, leading her. They walk toward the source of the music.

—He dances when he moves. He is . . . energy, perfectly contained within his flesh, and yet unbound by it and unafraid. He proceeds as though he has never known sorrow.

"Yes, I have."

FROM THE LEGEND OF BIEL

"Pardon?"

"I apologize to you for the intrusion on your thought. But it is best for you to know now. I am not fond of direct brain-to-brain communication, although I am skilled at it. I use it only in emergencies, and those are rare. It has its advantages of course, in compensating for the tendency to be literal and linear. But it is silent. To me the spoken word is music. The well-constructed sentence is art. I like to hear it. When I answer your thoughts I am not monitoring your cerebration, although it is so strong that it is difficult not to—I am responding to your eloquent face and body. The loss of your mentor is visible. Beyond that, deep and far behind your eyes, is the shadow of confusion and fear."

". . . May I ask you something?"

"Certainly."

"This death I have experienced, must it be so final?"

"Oh, yes. Oh, yes. It must be, for life to have its proper value. I am told that long ago persons tried to believe that death was not final, that it was not the end, that somehow there was somewhere, something to which one went when one died. This belief permitted many abominations. It permitted persons to feel that taking a life was not so serious, because the victims were not really dead— only transported to some other place for some other kind of life. This is the only life there is."

". . . yes . . ."

"I have known sorrow such as you are learning now. All of us have."

". . . AH . . . . !"

Before them is a hill, only a short distance away. On it is a black and moss-green velvet tree which grows to one side of itself, like hair combed in one direction. Beneath the tree is a globe of perfectly clear glass, with a woman inside it. She is liquid in motion, making the music. Biel and Rigin walk toward her. The music swells.

"This is Yora, Musician."

"Yes."

The Sphere is made of many faintly tinted geometric

shapes which are adhered at their edges. Inside the clear globe a parabola of thin glass rods stretches up and out, around the woman. As she dances she brushes against the rods, making them hum—making the music. Rigin waves to her. She waves back and there is no break in the sound. Nothing holds the woman's body together but her gown and the liquid glue of the music.

"Yora made the Sphere. It is so delicately constructed that it responds to the pecularities of each environment it is played in. If you were wearing different clothing now, the music would not be the same. Yora's gown, its color and texture, help her determine the nature of the spontaneous sounds—although she does not always improvise. Today she wears many colors because there is only one color in your aura, and Yora loves equilibrium. She is balancing the village in the face of the force of your energy. Her gown is silky to keep the sound light. She will tell you more of the Sphere later. But sometime you must ask her to play it on water."

"May I touch it?"

"Certainly."

Biel touches her hands to the cool glass and feels the stratified vibrations of the sound. Her hands dull the sound only slightly. She puts her face on the glass and her teeth hum, the bones behind her eyes rattle. And there is Yora, floating above her as in water, smiling and waving. Biel's body stretches against the glass and she is shaken from head to foot by vibrations and pulses as basic and necessary as her own heartbeat. A door opens in the Sphere and the liquid arms of Yora reach down, clasp her, and she is in the Sphere.

—. . . I am the music. She is the music. We are the music—its source. This is where it begins. In us . . .

Yora is embracing Biel, dancing with her, becoming acquainted. Biel is wrapped around the musician like oil. There is Rigin outside, dancing. Yora stops moving and the sound falls leaflike to the ground.

"Welelelcomomom touoUou thehehe mehehehdohehohohohzhzhzhzhzhzzzzzz . . ."

Biel is kissed and passed out through the little opening to Rigin and the ground.

"Biel?"

"Yes?"

"We shall take the Sphere on water soon, just you and I together."

"Please!"

"Yes."

"Thank you."

A little girl comes run-stumbling up the hill, flailing her arms, and grinning like Rigin. The child is younger than Biel. She snakes around Rigin's legs. She has long, almost maroon hair. Her features are small and precise and arranged in such a way that her moss-green eyes preface all her statements with absolute candor.

"I am Ashtr, child of the village of Lir."

Yora resumes playing the Sphere. She waves to Ashtr.

"I am Biel."

"I know, welcome to the meadows."

Ashtr sits down in front of the Sphere. Her eyes are closed as she listens to the music, dancing gracefully with only her shoulders. Rigin takes Biel by the hand and they are walking again.

"Are you familar with art?"

"I have been told of it. I know what the word means, but until the Sphere and Yora and I had not experienced it."

"You will experience much of it here. There are many villages like Lir in the Federation. Most are small, one or two hundred persons."

"Are the villages in contact with each other?"

"No."

"Are you all artists?"

"Not necessarily. There are many mentors in the villages . . . elders . . . and listeners. Here, we are fortunate to have a good balance."

"You have no contact with the outside world at all?"

"We have one communicator disk. Periodically we monitor Thoacdien to find out if there is something we should be aware of. So far Thoacdien has made no attempt to reclaim us. But we do not worry about that. We are well concealed and have not changed the appearance of the meadows by the displacement of one flower since five generations ago when the village was formed. Even if Thoacdien was interested, it could not find us."

Biel and Rigin are walking between brightly colored, empty tents. There is no sign of others. There is no sound—nothing but Yora's faraway music.

"Where are the others?"

"They will be seen when you are ready."

"Where are my friends?"

"They are not with you right now, but they are all right. You shall meet us all when it is time. Soon, I hope. Ahhhhh, here we are."

They step into a tent. It is very dark. Rigin has hold of Biel's hand in his bone-dry claw, and they sit cross-legged on the ground. They wait, seeing nothing because it is too dark. There is no sound.

Very gradually, so as not to be noticed until they can perceive each other's forms in the darkness, the tent is lightened a few degrees. Rigin is gray in the gray, shadowless dark. He is smiling and unafraid.

—There is a third in the room with us. I feel it, but have no sensual evidence. . . .

". . . I . . . AM . . . JOHONAZ . . ."

It is as if the sound is coming from inside her head, as if the sound is a seed inside her ear which takes root and grows into a whole green forest of meaning.

A slender old man in a gray robe walks toward the two in the dark from far away, jingling. He begins as a voice, breathing. Then he is a tiny dot on the surface of the eyeball. The dot retreats, becomes larger, and evolves—shimmering—into the form of the slender old man in a gray robe, who walks toward them from far away.

". . . MASTER . . . OF . . . ILLUSION . . ."

Rigin claps his hands in delight. He giggles. Suddenly the three of them are cards being shuffled. The rippling stops. Johonaz is sitting in front of Rigin and Biel. He is

289

negative space—clear, gray, empty space, surrounded by the soft gray dimness. Johonaz is a perfect, empty silhouette of himself.

A small stone falls from the center of Biel's being into the negative space of Johonaz. It makes a hole which is surrounded by concentric circles. Biel's own face is formed in the disturbance of the space. Then Johonaz passes his negative-space hand in front of himself and wipes the area clean. Again, it is a clear, light gray space contained in the darker silhouette of his robed body.

Johonaz's left arm reaches up and scratches his negative-space head. He giggles. Suddenly he is closer. His space body almost fills Biel's field of vision. She can barely see the peripheral contours of the darker gray surrounding him. There is no end to the space which stretches out behind Johonaz. It reaches beyond, farther than can be imagined.

Johonaz's space is now a sky with a long thin dagger of cloud bisecting it. He stretches his arms to the sides. He wiggles his fingers and the sleeves of his robe jiggle. A tiny red bird materializes in his right no-hand. The bird bobs its head. A tiny blue bird materializes in his left hand. The birds scratch their feet on his palms, getting ready to charge. There is a roll of drums. The two birds charge. They run down Johonaz's long space-arms and collide in a feathered explosion at his throat. They fall with a whistling of wind. They fall and fall and fall and fall and fall and fall and fall and fall and fall and fall and fall and fall and fall and fall and fall and fall and fall and(— . . . . hold . . . on.—I am . . . .)and fall and fall.

The Master of Illusion's negative body is wiped neutral —just a lighter gray than the gray which contours it. Johonaz claps his hands once. He moves closer still. Now the illusion begins behind Biel's eyes, behind her head. She turns to look behind herself. She can see the outer surface of the illusion. It stops, shimmering, less than a body length away from her back. She reaches out and sticks her hand through the surface of the illusion. Her fingers disappear.

"Humumummmmm . . ."

Johonaz clears his throat. As Biel turns to face him again, her glance flashes past the grinning profile and de- lighted little body of Rigin.

Johonaz is so close now that Biel cannot see the pe- ripheral edges of the illusion. The distance between them has been removed. There is the sound of flames. They materialize in Johonaz's body as orange-and-blue smoke. Biel is inside the flames. She is the flames—heating, com- pressing, heating, compressing to an explosion. She is exploding forward through Johonaz's body so fast that all other motion is frozen by comparison.

—I am rushing through a maze of stilled particles and I fear collision. I fear the speed of this rushing toward imagination. There is a dot in the distance. It is coming toward me on collison course at my speed! I brace my- self as a face grows out of the dot—too fast, I cannot recognize it. We are going to collide! The mouth on the face opens as I open my mouth . . . we swallow each other.

Thuup.

—Blackness. No light is possible here. Nor sound . . . I am floating and superimposed on the other.

The blackness fades to gray and then—blink!—the tent is coolly, evenly lit. The light has no visible source. Rigin is clapping and whistling, stamping his feet.

"Biel . . . I have been waiting to meet you. Welcome to Lir. Ha ha. You look like a small animal trapped in a bright light. I did not mean to frighten you so."

Johonaz is sitting as he was during the illusion—in front of and between Rigin and Biel. The three of them are a small equilateral triangle. Johonaz sits cross-legged, as they do. His arms are stretched out and his hands clasp his folded legs. He, himself, is a perfectly based equi- lateral triangle. He wears a soft gray robe which falls in chiaroscuro folds. His skin is tanned white. Out of the neck of his robe rises a throat which is deeply corded and brown. His beard is a whispy white-silk flame. The bot- tom finger of his mouth protrudes squarely and supports the great wings of his moustache. His nose is long and shaped like a brain at the end. His eyes are gray—medium gray irises surrounded by lighter gray, unveined whites. His eyes are velvetlike and reflect no light. His hair rises back off his high forehead in an explosion of mane-tendrils. He has no eyebrows. Inside he is silent—absolute rest.

". . . How have you known these things? . . ."

"One has only to look in your face."

"Can you help me?"

"Perhaps to help yourself."

"How have you become what you are?"

"Practice."

"Are the illusions also art?"

"I call it satire. Art is my hobby. I am a physician."

". . . you are so glad to see me . . ."

"Indeed. Why are you running?"

". . . Because, I am afraid."

"What are you afraid of?"

"Myself, life without Mikkran."

"Do you live without Mikkran now?"

"Yes."

"Without her concept?"

"No. She is still warm in my brain."

"Will you permit one who has much to share with you an answer to one unasked question?"

"Yes."

"You have not lost your mentor. The form of your relationship has changed—not its nature, not its meaning."

"Thank you."

"How are you afraid of yourself?"

"I am haunted by seizures. At first I ran from them blindly, hoping they were external to me. Now I run from habit. I know of nothing else to do."

"You can stop."

"If I stopped I would have nothing to do but wait for each seizure. When I run I am at least busy in my mind."

"Amazing . . ."

"What?"

"That you know how you will respond to situations which haven't happened yet."

"I am . . . I did not mean that."

"You may not have meant it, but it is how you have been behaving. Rigin, we are through here. Please take Biel to the next. There are others for you to meet, Biel. We shall be together again."

"Thank you, Johonaz: Physician and Master of Illusion."

Biel and Rigin leave the tent. They walk a few paces and Rigin stops, tapping his foot twice on the ground. A lid of earth rises slightly, swivels aside, and reveals a ramp which leads down to a long, well-lit tunnel of dark, moist earth. They enter and continue to walk. The lid of earth closes silently behind them. They do not speak for a long time. They walk, holding hands. Occasionally, on one side or the other, there is a doorway or an intersection with another tunnel. But they stay in this wider, curving one.

Blink.

The Higgittes stop for midday food. They are halfway from the cerebral cortex of the nation to the meadows. The warriors are moldy and drunk on drugs. They are afraid beneath their euphoria. They practice killing and already eight have died.

Grod-Linz is propped up by the fanatic yammering of Logana. She has become filthy and smeared in her achievement. She is the first Higgitte in the history of the nation to draw the blood of a Thoacdien. She, the only one—and a woman—has killed.

Blink.

"Rigin, what is happening to me here?"

"I am not at liberty to tell you much because you shall know all for yourself soon."

They step into an archway on the left and walk a few paces toward a white wall.

Thuup.

The wall evaporates. They step into a small white cube.
Thuup.
The wall materializes.
". . . We are falling . . ."
"Yes."
Thuup.
The wall vanishes. They step out of the little white cube
into a huge, rounded gold room which is made of thous-
ands of small, hexagonal chambers. There is a silver
pedestal in the center of the room. It reaches to Biel's chin,
to Rigin's chest. A dark young man stands behind the
pedestal. He smiles and walks forward.
"I am Grolen, sculptor of light. This is my studio."
"Grolen? Charge of Mikkran-Gogan-Tor?"
"Yes."
And they collide as Biel leaps into his arms. And he is
holding her hard and thoroughly. A cry can be felt in his
body before it can be heard. He pulls back his shaven
head and looks into her eyes. His irises are gold and wet.
Tears fall over the edges of his eyelids like tiny rocks.
They weep together.
—Grolen, I miss her so . . .
—. . . I know . . . I know . . .
—It is not possible to imagine or live in a world without
her.
—You do not have to.
—. . . But she is gone . . .
—No. She is only changed. She is in you and I right
now, as real as she has ever been.
"Biel, I have something to show you."
Grolen sets Biel down. He walks to the pedestal and
picks up a small clear card which was lying on top of the
silver structure. He inserts it into an invisible slot on the
front side of the pedestal.
The room is abruptly black.
The room is Mikkran . . .
. . . Mikkran steps out of a hole in space.
She brings light with her.
There is Mikkran and the sky. Nothing else.

She is here, alive in some way. Not in the way preferred —but she is here.

Mikkran smiles. There are the too-big white teeth against brown lips. Biel is holding Mikkran, being held. They whirl around in slow motion. Mikkran is laughing. Here, here is that sound of flocks of birds rising, erupting from her throat which is only human and not like birds at all. Her throat contracts, jiggles up and down. The roof of her mouth has little ridges and patterns, and a spine down its center. Her eyelashes point up like fingers, and her forehead is mildly hilled and valleyed.

Rigin is laughing as Biel steps down from Mikkran's arms to sit and watch the rest of the card. Mikkran dances, proudly displaying her body's possibilities in slow motion. She turns. She stretches. She bends and squats. She flips and stands on her hands.

Mikkran's buttocks are large and brown-round. Her inner thighs are a graceful S. Her Achilles tendons are one finger thick and her arches are two fingers high. Her nails are clear coins. Her pubic hair is long thick question marks. It grows up in a thin line to her dark-eyed navel. Her genitals flash moist and blue-brown between her moving legs. Her stomach is long and muscled in small squares. Her armpits are corded and covered with two licks of dark flame hair. Her last two ribs are visible pushing out against the skin of her torso. Her breasts are small, hardly a handful, and her nipples are red-brown, surrounded by thin-skinned blue-brown. There is a dark triangular shadow in her throat. Her jaw is a graceful boomerang. Her hair is long kinks. She is rejoicing.

Suddenly Grolen is standing across from Mikkran, mirroring her movements. He is younger, with hair—pubescent. They stop moving and look at each other. They are naked and sexual beings. Mikkran smiles and walks toward Grolen. She takes his young hands in her two hands and looks into his face.

"It is time for you to learn the expression of love. Love wants to touch. It wants mutuality, embrace and completion. Love happens in the body, in the genitals—where sex

is performed. Come, Grolen. Let us love with our bodies."
. They roll. They dive. They collide and become wet.
They suck and pull and massage and perspire and rejoice and exchange spontaneous sensations. They are over
and under, around and between, inside, together and
apart. Nipples are hard white stones. Genitals flash brown
and distended—impatient, ready and wet. Tongues write
on bodies, leaving snail's trails of little words. Tongues explore and murmur wetly into ears and navals and armpits
and smalls of backs and backs of knees and palms of
hands. And they are joined rejoicing, laughing, crying,
holding on because they must against this pleasure. And
the explosion happens only in the body. Here. Now. The
synchronized friction runs them up the hill and sets them
free, now, for timeless spasms and sperm regurgitations
and not breathing because they do not need to.

Mikkran and young Grolen inhale convulsively and
look into each other's face. And they are laughing, giggl-
ing, screaming, relaxed, embraced, still joined, and asleep.
The images begin to fade. The room is black. The room
is gold.

Blink.

Rigin and Biel are laughing. They are standing on their
feet stamping and clapping and whistling and cheering.
The older Grolen walks to the pedestal to remove the
ejected glass card from the machine.

"Bravo! Yes!! Yes!!'"

"Thank you. That was my first shared sexual experience—with Mikkran. It is important for you to know her
sexually. That is part of your relationship, your love. I
wanted to share this with you."

"On. . . . So this is light sculpture. . . ."

"Yes. This machine is a prototype. The card you just
saw is one of my first. I am working to make longer, more
complete cards."

. "I don't know what to say. . . . Thank you."

"The card is always down here. You are wlecome to
play it anytime. We will meet again, Biel. Welcome to Lir."

"Thank you."

"Yes. We must go, Biel. There is more to do."

"Yes."

Thuup.

Thuup.

Rigin and Biel are walking in sunlight. It is late afternoon and the sun, at a low slant, turns the air bronze.

"How do the people of Lir have this health?"

"You have only met five of them."

"They are not atypical."

"True. We do not have health. Health is only absence of disease, and here there was no unhealth to begin with. Here, we try to stay in balance. We work for equilibrium. We desire to be synchronized with ourselves, with each other, and with all that is neither. We are learning that equilibrium is a natural state for persons, and ultimately inevitable, once the screen of systems has been removed."

"Systems?"

"Systems: Basic Tenets, Constitutions, Morals, Law, Belief, Ethics—any construct which presumes to decide what is appropriate human behavior. We are systemless here in the village. There are no rules at all. We live in benevolent chaos."

"But you have technology. You are not simple people."

"Technology and systems are not the same. Technology does not depend on a system for its creation and use, but on the free imaginations of a very few persons. Historically, systems have only financed technology. We have found that with imagination it isn't all that expensive. As to our not being simple, you are correct. But the more complex persons are, the less they have need for the support of a system."

"Does not having rules work? Here?"

"Very much so! And that question angers me to the threshold of my ability to control myself. Damn it!! Why wouldn't it work??? What kind of negative language is that? AAAAAAAAAHHHHHHHGGGGHHHHAAHA AAA!!!"

Rigin jumps up and down. He tears his hair and spits

up at the sky. He stamps his feet and screams—then is quiet.

". . . I didn't mean to upset you, Rigin . . ."

"Nonononono . . . OK. OK. You asked a sincere question. My control . . . just goes once in a while. Hahaha. Let's see now. Where were we . . ."

"I asked . . ."

"Let me see . . . I will . . . no. No. That's no good . . ."

". . . Systems?"

"Ah! Yes . . . Those who live in the context of a system have said yes to that system because they are too . . . polite . . . to be rude—too polite to refuse the first and most deadly request of all . . . I shall answer your question . . . the long way."

"All right."

"We have come to the meadows as our first genuine rudeness. We have said no to all systems good or bad, and to all who run systems, good or bad. I came to the meadows when I . . . embraced the fact of my basic goodness, my basic and first desire to be positive—which is possible —in a universe where most other persons want the same. I had almost come to believe that I did need an artificial framework for my life—in my case the technocracy of Thoacdien—in order to survive. I was told that alone I would shrivel up and die of boredom, starvation, appendicitis, backwardness, stupidity, loneliness, or the viciousness of my neighbor, who would kill me in a rage of jealousy, epilepsy, anarchy, hunger, greed, or indifference. We find here that this is not true."

Rigin is dancing and gesticulating wildly. He runs in circles and jumps up and down, grinning.

". . . Since the dawn of human consciousness some persons have been in control of others—that is the definition of a system. If, for whatever reason or end—paradise or nightmare—you are living in a system, you are either controlled or in control and therefore foolish, because you are essentially dead, unable even to recognize your own desire and capability to be positive and whole. In every system there are only slaves, because only slaves will maintain a system. And, obviously, slavery destroys."

"But what do you do when people are in conflict?"

"First of all we find that that is rare. When it does occur it is not fatal—or even dangerous. The conflict can be resolved without a system, without preconception and with fairness which reinforces the severeignties of the parties involved. We human beings tend to believe that we what we have been told about ourselves. Belief becomes reality. Look at your environment and know what you believe . . . OK?"

"OK. . . ."

"We human beings have been told what we are by those in whose best interest it is for us to be a certain way. It is inevitable for us to become that. AAAAAAAAAggghhh!! . . . calmly . . . Systems, be they political, moral, esthetic, philosophical, or whatever, are how the weak crawled onto the backs of the strong and defeated them. While they rode on our backs they whispered into our ears: 'You are weak. You are weak. I am strong. Let me direct your stupidity and you will grow fat and happy.' And we became weak. And he became strong. And we fell down on our faces, and were so stupid we could not get back up. And the man sat down beside us and ate. This man will continue to dine of your body until you stop him. There is no survival in a system—there is only madness. . . . mmm . . . Because, you see, each system has its point of view to defend. All else is subordinate to that. Each system's first claim is that all other systems would destroy it. Some of this is understandable when systems are radically different. But as they grow more complex they become similar. The worst indignity to human life is death in a conflict between two or more systems which cannot be distinguished from one another."

Rigin stops. He sits down on the ground but cannot get comfortable. He stands, braced against a tree. He is calmer, almost relaxed. His eyes no longer smoke, but are cool.

"Human beings made a leap in the dark when they accepted the idea of a system as a necessity. No system begins at the beginning, which is the question: What circumstances are necessary for each human life to have the possibility for one hundred percent manifestation of potential? We in the village have retrieved that leap. Our absence from systems proclaims that no system has or may assume the prerogative to determine what is appropriate human behavior. Human behavior cannot be experienced in the context of a system any more than animal behavior can be studied in the context of captivity. In the village we ask only one question of ourselves. How do we manifest potential? Systems and manifest potential are mutually exclusive realities. So we have left systems. Ahhhhh . . . in the future, systems will have disappeared. Not one of them is worth a single human life. Someday the strong will simply stand up and walk away, leaving those who have dined to fend for themselves—as we do now. I worship this earth, and being alive and human on it. I and my neighbor are good, as are you. We have no need to destroy."

FROM: THOACDIEN—PRIORITY ONE.
TO: DOME COMPLEXES 101-B, 98-A, AND THE MEADOWS, THOACDIEN V.
DATE: 187.357
TIME: 4.3.076
SUBJECT: MENTOR LAN-BITEUS, CHARGE XITR-MEEDE, CHARGE 187-A,0037 AKA BIEL, AND A HIGGITTE WARRIOR CALLED NYZ-RAGAAN.
. . . .
. . . .
. . . .

COMPLEX 101-B: PROCEED.
STOP.

COMPLEX 98-A: PROCEED.
STOP.

MEADOWS: NO RESPONSE ....
STOP.

THOACDIEN: SUBJECTS DISAPPEARED, ALONG
WITH FLOATER A,03-187-A, ON
187.355 AT APPROXIMATELY
2.4.700.
THEIR LAST TRANSMISSION WAS
SENT WHILE EN ROUTE TO THE
NORTHWEST CORNER OF THE
MEADOWS.
PLEASE INCLUDE THIS AREA OF
THE MEADOWS IN YOUR
REGULAR SCAN, AND REPORT
ANY FINDINGS IMMEDIATELY.
ALSO SEND QUERIES TO ALL
LISTENERS IN YOUR AREA WHO
MIGHT HAVE MISSED THIS
TRANSMISSION.
IF ANY STRANGERS ARE NOTED
IN YOUR AREA PLEASE REPORT
IMMEDIATELY.
HIGGITTE WARRIOR FORCE IS
MOUNTING AN ATTACK ON THE
MEADOWS.
PLEASE WARN ALL, AND MAKE
PREPARATIONS FOR
NONINVOLVED DEFENSE.
STOP.

COMPLEX 101-B: AGREED. INSTRUCTIONS ARE
RECORDED AND WILL BE
CARRIED OUT.
STOP.

COMPLEX 98-B: AGREED. INSTRUCTIONS WILL
                 BE CARRIED OUT.
STOP.

MEADOWS: NO RESPONSE /.....................................
STOP.

END TRANSMISSION ....

Biel and Rigin are difficult to see as they walk through dappled light on their way to the next examination. The sun is low and pink. There are no paths to follow. No roads lead from one place to another. No meadow dwellings can be seen.

Rigin stops, twists a stone with his foot and a slab of earth swivels aside to reveal a staircase which leads down to a red door with a large braided leather ring in its center. Biel goes down the steps followed by Rigin. When they are both on the stairs the earth door swivels shut over them soundlessly. Rigin listens at the red door. He smiles. He nods. He opens the door and they step into the house of Kaj-Palmir, Wizard of Time, and Weaver.

The house of Kaj-Palmir is underground. It consists of three small but spacious cubes, placed end to end. The first cube, in which Biel and Rigin are standing, is the gathering room of the house. Here, Kaj-Palmir sleeps, prepares her food, eats, meets her friends, and studies. The second room is the chamber of space which, seen from the first room, is merely two parallel stone walls, two parallel clear glass walls, and glass floor and ceiling. The ceiling of this room affords an unobstructed view of the sky and peripheral tree branches. The floor is a pane of glass which is suspended and able to sway somewhat. It hangs over a lighted shaft with no visible bottom. From inside this second chamber one sees nothing but neutral space. It is as if one is suspended in an infinite amount of absolutely nothing—hence its name. The third cube is Kaj-Palmir's loom room. It contains nothing but a huge, old wooden loom on which is the beginning of a carpet of many colors and intricate design.

Rigin motions to Biel to sit down on the floor and be very still. Biteus is in the chamber of space with Kaj-Palmir. She is a very old and very yellow woman. The two are sitting across from one another on the slightly swaying pane of glass. They sit cross-legged with their knees touching. They are in profile to the two newcomers.

Kaj-Palmir and Biteus are silent and unmoving. Their eyes are closed. They are exchanging cerebration to a degree which Biel has never experienced before. Their beings are at the same time exactly parallel and in collision. Their cerebration is so hot and rapid that it can be seen passing between them as heat waves. It can be heard as drops of water on a fire. Its content is concealed from Rigin and Biel.

Biel opens her own cerebration to listen to the two in the chamber of space. As she does so she feels the whites of Rigin's eyes pass over her face. Then she hears him laugh in the distance. He controls himself, grinning broadly.

—. . . ! . . . Biteus's brain is encased in something solid—like a huge, smooth, metal bar. Ahh! It's hot. It pops and cracks with dynamic energy. But I cannot penetrate to meaning. This is not Biteus's brain alone, but both their brains . . . molded together, interchanging so completely and freely that they must be considered one brain . . . I feel toward Rigin's brain. It is relaxed and formless —like a cloud . . . normal cerebration . . .

Biel and Rigin sit for a long time, watching. Finally, as if on cue, the energy between Kaj-Palmir and Biteus loses its intensity. The solid bar of the two brains united liquifies. The dense field splits in two and the two halves become their former wholes.

Kaj-Palmir and Biteus move infinitesimally and open their eyes. They smile at each other. The woman looks at Biel through the glass which separates them and waves. Biel waves back. Rigin is grinning to burst.

Kaj-Palmir stands. Her body is small and strong, full of

relaxed energy. There is a cool, serene quality about her. She is full of mystery and craft and knowledge which cannot be understood until it is earned. She is soft-spoken, almost aloof, but warm. Her eyes are clear black stones. Her upper eyelids are long and smooth. The bridge of her flat nose is very shallow. The spoon of her upper lip is very short. Her mouth is narrow, her lips are pursed-looking. Her teeth are small, with spaces in between. Her cheekbones are wide and high. Her hair is in one long salt-and-pepper braid which hangs down her back. There is a tiny maroon figure eight tattooed in the center of her forehead. She wears a long, abundant tube of soft maroon cloth, which hangs from her shoulders. She and Biteus, still in his green mentor robe, come into the first room, where Biel and Rigin are waiting.

"Rigin . . ."

"Elder."

"And you are the girl. I am Kaj-Palmir. Welcome to this house."

"I am Biel."

"Yes, I know."

Kaj-Palmir smiles and takes Biel's hands in greeting. Energy passes between them. It feels like all fear, all preconception is evaporated. The lungs inhale with infinite expansion, with limitless gathering of new, fresh air. The body becomes liquid. . . .

Blink.

Biel's hands are released. The woman leans against the wall with her hands behind her back and seems to be listening to something very far away. Biel looks at her in fascination. Biteus steps forward, grinning.

". . . Biel."

"Biteus. I am happy to see you. You look so rested."

"I am."

Rigin and Kaj-Palmir wink at each other.

"I have never experienced such cerebration as Kaj-Palmir's before. I have never understood in quite the same way."

"Have you seen Xitr-Meede and Nyz-Ragaan?"

"Mmhmm . . . this morning. They were being introduced. If you will excuse me, I should like to take a walk and be by myself."

"Until later then, Biteus."

". . . Soon, I hope, Biel."

"Why not?"

Biteus smiles, bows to Kaj-Palmir, kisses Rigin, kisses Biel, and is gone. The room is silent. Kaj-Palmir waits, watching Biel. The girl does not know quite what to do—what is expected of her. She, too, waits. Rigin chews on his fingers, looking from one to the other.

Biel looks at the woman. Again the energy washes over and between them like a wave of cool, new air.

". . . How do you do that?"

"It is a gift."

"Yours or mine?"

"From me to you."

"Who are you?"

"I am Kaj-Palmir, Wizard of Time, Weaver . . . and elder to Mikkran-Gogan-Tor."

"Ah! . . . Oh, she said . . ."

"Yes. You are ready."

"You knew her."

"Very well."

". . . I miss her."

"But you are getting stronger."

"Perhaps."

"Will you come with me into the chamber of space?"

"All right."

"Fine. Rigin, do you wish to stay?"

"Mmmmm . . . can I make soup?"

"Certainly."

"Excellent! I shall prepare nectar of meadow flower for us. MMMmmm. Ahhhh . . . Oh, go. Go. Ahh, it shall be . . . art."

Kaj-Palmir leads Biel through a dark hall which runs behind one of the stone walls of the chamber of space and connects the third cube to the first. She presses softly on an invisible door in the center of the wall.

sssssssssssssssss. . . . .

The elder steps out into the space and is supported by the swaying, invisible floor. She sits cross-legged, facing Biel, who is still in the shadowed threshold.

"Come."

Kaj-Palmir beckons to Biel. The girl cautiously tests the swaying space with one toe, then places her full weight on it. For a moment she is unable to cerebrate coherently.

—I am floating free, in nothing—endless space. I look up—there is nothing but space. Down, there is nothing . . . and to the sides . . .

"Sit before me. Touch your knees to mine."

"All right."

"Please, look into my eyes."

Kaj-Palmir takes hold of Biel's hands. The elder's fingers are as smooth as old caterpillars. Her palms are yellow soap. Her eyes are as deep and as open as the space they are suspended in.

—I am in the darkest room of my mind. I am sitting in a shaft of light in my mind. Mote-thoughts rise and fall at will, turning, stretching like sleepy babies. The light is Kaj-Palmir. The motes are me—incoherent. The room is now our mutual brain. I feel her hands, years and planets away. They release my . . . hands . . .

"Can you hear me?"

"In. Slow. Mo. Tion."

"Please relax . . . relax . . . that's it. I just want to look a moment."

". . . yes."

"Do you remember what happened to you?"

". . . no."

"Tell me please, what happened to you?"

"I don't . . . know."

"It is there, in you. Search, please."

"All right."

—I reach through the fog, the cloud-whisp which is my brain. My fingers reach around the stilling energy for coherency. I find a cold jelly at the back of my brain . . . in the darkest part. My arm plunges in up to the elbow. I feel pain as my hand brushes against the dripping, frozen secrets. Ahhhhh . . . I am afraid. AhhhhhHhaaaaaaaa . . . I . . . cannot . . . stand it . . . I am afraid. There is . . .

"Go on through your fear to the other side."

"I . . . can't. It is too painful."

"Pass on through. You can do it. Reach for what is beyond."

". . . What is that?"

"We cannot know. We haven't been there yet. But can it be worse than the fear?"

". . . I . . . am . . . AAAAAhhhhhhhhhGgggggggg-aaaaaaa . . . help . . . me . . ."

"Here are my hands. You cannot fall through and disappear. I hold you and am strong."

"uuuuuuunnnnnnn . . ."

—I push at the jelly darkness. It is so cold, and up to my shoulder now . . . Ah . . . gaaa . . . I push. Push. To the other side . . . reach for what . . . is beyond . . . Ahhhhh. . . .

. . . ! . . . * . . . * . . . /./. / . . . . . . !! . . . Light . . . . . . Ahhhhhhhhhhhhhhhh.h.h. . . . . . ! . . . . . . re . . . lease . . . AAAAAhhhhhhhhhhhhhhhhhhhhhhhhhhhh hhhhhhhhhhh. . . . . . .

"Please, tell me what you are experiencing?"

". . . Oh . . . I am floating. So relaxed. So far away and free. I am . . . above, beyond, but still near . . . a storm in my . . . being . . ."

"Storm?"

"It began . . . after I was born.'

"Can you tell me about it?"

". . . Hurts . . . are you familiar with . . . Binol?"

"Tell me about it."

"Binol is . . . liquid Thoacdien, pure information . . . which is administered to all Thoacdiens at one time or another . . . Thoacdien-born infants are usually injected shortly after birth . . ."

"What does the Binol do?"

". . . confusion . . ."

"What?"

"Confusion. The Binol contains all . . . static . . . facts, and all modes of . . . learning . . ."

"Were you injected with Binol?"

". . . yes . . ."

"What?"

"Yes. I was one of a group of one hundred fetuses given an unusually large dose prior to birthing."

"Why?"

"Thoacdien deduced that it was time to begin encouraging the species to . . ."

"What?"

"To use more of the . . . brain. . . . Thoacdien took enormous life-risks with us."

"Why?"

". . . Why? Why? So. So. I . . . don't know . . ."

"Yes you do."

"So that we might live . . . more fully."

"What happened as a result of your injection?"

". . . I . . ."

"I cannot hear you."

"I became afraid . . . and angry. I ran . . ."

"Before that. Tell me what happened before you ran away."

"mmmmmmm. . . . I. . . . uuuuuuuuuhhhhhh. . . . nnnnnnnnn. . . . "

"You are delaying. I will not forget my question."

"Some babies died! Others I hope were normal . . . but I do not know. I was normal until . . ."

"Please go on."

"I am afraid . . ."

"Do you feel me?"

"I do."

"How?"

"As two hands in which I am cupped. It is warm."

"Are you safe?"

"Yes." ·

"Then go on."

"I was normal until sometime after my birth when I had a major convulsion."

"What caused it?"

"The . . . I can feel it now."

"What?"

". . . The fading . . . Please, oh, please, I am afraid. You cannot hold on tight . . . tight . . .

(—. . . . . Hold on. I need you to hold on.

—I can't, oh please, I can't hold on any longer. . . . . .)

"Biel? Biel!"

". . . ahhhh . . . ahhhhhI can't anymore. I am being. . . . . ."

(—. . . . If you let go now we are lost . . . . . .)

"I am holding you. You cannot fall. What are you experiencing? Describe it to me."

"The other. The other is here now. He is holding onto me, trying to pull me onto his side which is nowhere and nothing, which is three other people staring at me out of their madness as they watch us die and die and die and . . . It is a hot bomb exploding dark and white into the blackness where we are blown and must continually die."

"(—. . . we have left the others.

—What others?

—All of our friends . . .

—When shall we land?

—When shall we depart?

—We are always departing . . .

—I don't think it matters.

—No.

—Because they are simultaneous.

—Both are somewhere now.

—Not somewhere . . . allwhen.

—. . . Kick your feet.

—Does it work?

—We might try it, maybe it will lead us to an opening . . .

—I'm not sure.

—Go on . . . kick your feet. . . . .)

"Biel?"

"Ummmmmmm?"

"Why are you laughing?"

"Something struck me funny."

"What?"

"Something struck me funny."

"What?"

"It's private."

"I see."

"I do not wish to tell you."

"All right."

"Shall I go on?"

"Please. Is the other a male?"

"Yes . . . Mikkran's age."

"Do you know anything about him?"

"Ummm no."

"Think."

"Why am I being examined?!"

"Because you are caught between consciousness and oblivion. We wish to help you waken."

"Am I asleep?"

"You are unawake."

"When will I wake up?"

"That is for you to decide."

"How is it that I need your help?"

"Persons who have been released can be identified by —among other things—their ability to perform three basic functions: creation, transmission, and reception of information. Properly synchronized, these three activities result in a state of equilibrium. The interaction of two or more persons who have attained equilibrium is called tranception. You are unable to complete the releasing process. You cannot attain equilibrium, because there is something in you which fights against your instinct for balance—the other, you call him. This prevents you from being fully awake. It prevents you from normal transception. However, you do transceive—and in a way no one has ever been able to do before."

"How is that?"

"Typical transception is a matter of the present and

the known. I am not able to transceive in any time but the present. I am not able to transceive to any place or person unfamiliar to me, because the unknown cannot be imagined, it must be discovered. You are actively transceiving into the unknown. You are interacting with that which is neither here nor now. We wish to determine a way to waken you in such a manner that you will have equilibrium and not lose your ability to transceive in this extraordinary way."

". . . I see."

"Do you know where you are?"

"With you."

"Mmmmmm. Do you wish to do on or do you need more time?"

"I wish to go on."

"It will not be easy."

"It has not been easy so far."

"What is the one thing you will not do?"

"Give up."

"Excellent. Anything else?"

"I will not return to Thoacdien."

"Why?"

"Because Thoacdien is at one and the same time responsible and irresponsible."

"You are still angry?"

"Yes!"

". . . If, for example, we discover that what has happened to you can be corrected surgically, and that Thoacdien is the only surgeon capable of performing the operation, what will you do?"

". . . I don't know. It hasn't happened yet."

"Then you need more time."

"I don't know . . ."

"Let us return to Rigin."

Slowly, the energy between them ceases. Their brains separate. The two blink their eyes, and come to life. They smile at each other, rise, and leave the swaying chamber of space.

"Food!"

"Yes! Here, eat. Enjoy!"

"Thank you."

"Kaj-Palmir, what do we do now?"

"We are nearly finished. I believe this young one is becoming ready for help. The cloud of her fear is not so terrible anymore."

"Wonderful!"

"When I have finished eating may I take a walk by myself?"

"Of course."

. . . .

"O'Hare here, Lanier?"

"Yes. Go ahead, O'Hare."

"We are inside the dome now."

"Everything all right?"

"Yeah. But it's spooky in here."

"Where's Joe?"

"Right here. I'm getting oriented on the hologram reiteration. O'Hare, you ready to go on down?"

"Anytime."

"OK. Let's go. Lanier, don't you go away."

"We'll be right here all the time, Joe."

IX

Biel kicks every stone she sees, hoping to find a hole which will lead her to the secrets of the meadows. No lids of earth rise and swivel aside. The meadows are silent, dark, and stingy with secrets. She walks, enjoying her solitude and freedom of movement. She thinks about this strange day.

The Higgitte warrior force has bedded down for the night in the formation of a bull's-eye. Oddly, they have run in circles and are no closer to the meadows. They sleep in drugged stupors. They suck at their dreams. Grod-Linz bites at his cuticles. Logana is off by herself, frothing at the mouth and trying to get a fix on the stars. But she does not know how to read them.
At the edge of the darkness, just beyond the light from the Higgitte bondfires, two blue and familiar eyes stare at the filthy madness which is all that is left of his nation. His mouth is slightly open, and tears are in his eyes. He can go neither forward no back. He cannot move.

    —. . . there is something behind me . . .
    —Xitr-Meede!
    "Xitr-Meede!"
    "Hello, Biel."
    "You frightened me."

"I did not mean to."

Xitr-Meede grins, inhaling and exhaling flames. His eyes are dark blue, with thin yellow pinstripes—cartwheels. His mouth is two pink fingers. He has been running, and salt drips from the darker ends of his pale, yellow hair. There are seventeen freckles on his nose. One of his big, square front teeth is chipped. His eyebrows are concealed behind the long, heavy gold tear of his forelock.

"I have thought of you today, Biel. And missed being with you."

"And I you. Has your day been as wonderful and strange as mine?"

"Wonderful, yes. Strange, no."

"Have you seen Nyz-Ragaan?"

"No. Not since the floater . . . nor Biteus."

"I saw Biteus just a while ago. He looks wonderful. He seems very rested and happy. He went for a walk in the meadows, to be by himself."

"I must go find him. I'll be back, Biel. But don't wait for me. I'll be with you again soon."

". . . Xitr-Meede . . . ?"

The young man is gone. Biel shrugs and smiles. Then she continues to walk and think. Whenever she comes to a stone she kicks it, hoping it will trigger an earthen door.

Nyz-Ragaan peers into the decaying Higgitte camp. He has not moved. His back is to darkness, where there are two other insane and furious blue eyes behind him. Suddenly there is movement, motion. The air rubs its palms together. The ear hears soft rustlings of fabric, and the voting blade fades into the warrior's back. In, out. Again: in, out. Again: in, out. In. Out. Until his life evaporates, until he curls up, no longer able to struggle to remain alive, and dies as a small child sleeps.

Logana makes no sound. She drops the ancient voting blade and disappears into the darkness and disgrace. In . . . farther in . . . still farther in . . . until she is nothing. Gone. At peace. Dead. Stilled. No longer important.

The four Higgitte warriors who are on guard signal to each other over the sleeping, silent, dreaming hulks of their peers. Each counts to a prearranged number in his head. And when it is reached, each warrior slips off in the night, walking west to join the force which cannot be defeated.

The meadows are as dark as the inside of a glove. Biel sits beneath a tree and is mildly asleep around what she has experienced today. The other is quiet within her. She is alone. For the first time in her life she is lost, and lonely. She tried to find the house of Kaj-Palmir, the tent of Johonaz, or the tunnel to Grolen's. She called for Rigin and there was no answer. In her solitude and this season of stillness she was able to feel the carbonation in her own brain. She was able to sense little bubbles of thought shaking themselves loose from their moorings at the bottom of the bottom of her being, to rise rapidly to the surface of her brain-lake, and—pop!—become nothing but air in the unknown above her. This sensation released her from anticipation, fear, the past, and preconception. But, always, release, change, is at first a little sad. Before she slept, a few warm tears fell down into her lap, staining her new yellow shorts.

—Ahhhhhhhhhhhhhhhhhhhh . . .

Biel rolls her head to one side, wakes, opens her eyes, sighs, and brushes her palm on the cool grass at her side, as if it were the hair of a friend.

—. . . I am hungry . . . !

—Hello, Biel . . .

—Haaa . . . ?, Biteus! Oh, I am so glad to see you!

—Are you?

—Oh, yes! I am lost . . .

—Not anymore.

—Did Xitr-Meede find you?

—. . . no.

—Where is Nyz-Ragaan?

—. . . He cannot be here. He was puzzled, bewildered. He could neither hold on nor let go.

—Can I help?

—Do you want to?

—Yes! Can you take me to him?

—. . . Yes.

The two shadows walk together in dark tunnesl made by trees whose branches overlap and form a canopy over their heads. Biel is relieved to be with someone.

—I feel like I have been in this night, this silence forever, Biteus.

—It is almost over, Biel. Somewhere very close there is light.

—Yes.

—Very close. It is a matter of the space between the eyelid and the eye—and for you to decide.

—I am tired.

—I know.

—Being with all of those new people made me wish for things, made me dream of things I'm not sure are available to me.

—What people?

—Johonaz, Grolen . . . Kaj-Palmir . . .

—. . . Who are they?

—New friends. You know Kaj-Palmir.

—No. I have been alone, looking for you all day.

—!Biteus, what are you thinking. I saw you at Kaj-Palmir's!

—. . . Not I.

—But you spoke to me. You kissed me!

—No.

—. . . Then . . . who was that?

—I do not know.

—But I experienced it!

—Ah . . .

—. . . Biteus, I am afraid.

—Why?

—I can't hold on anymore. It has gotten to complex.

—What do you want to do?

—I want to leave here. I want to go back. I want . . . simplicity.

—Is that still possible to you?

—I will make it so!

—What would you have me do?

—We must find the floater immediately. We must find Xitr-Meede and Nyz-Ragaan and leave here immediately!

—I will help.

—Will you get the floater?

—Yes.

—I'll get Nyz-Ragaan. Together we can look for Xitr-Meede.

—Yes. Where is the floater?

—It is . . . in a tent . . . concealed by a ray which renders it invisible. It is operational and you will be able to feel it. Connect with Thoacdien and you can cross-beam it. Where is Nyz-Ragaan?

—. . . Down that hole.

—Find the ship, Biteus. Please. I'll get Nyz-Ragaan and come to you as soon as I can.

—Yes.

—Hurry!

Biteus disappears into the darkness. Biel reaches with her foot and finds the first of fifteen steps which descend beneath the surface of the ground. Ahead there is nothing but the outline of a door. Her feet become hands as she gropes and cautiously descends. Grasp. Unclasp . . . flex, relax . . . reach. She is at the bottom. She pushes the door. It swings back away from her with a loud, loud squeeeeeeeeeeeeeek.

Blinding white light floods out at her. Biel shields her eyes with her arms. She steps across the threshold into nothing but light, light, light, and silence. She can see nothing.

— . . . footsteps . . . coming toward me one slow step at a time. Someone is walking toward me. Step.

Step.

Step.

. . . I cannot . . . see . . . Ah!

A tiny figure is coming from behind the light. Jingling.
I see only the darkness of a haloed form.

"Hello, Biel."

"Haaahhhh . . ."

"It's me, Rigin . . ."

"Where is Nyz-Ragaan?"

"May we talk?"

"Please, I want my friends."

"If you still want them after we talk, I shall take you
there immediately. I am not going to harm you."

". . . all right . . ."

"You have come·a long way. We are sorry it has been
so difficult."

". . . I want some answers."

"You shall have them when it is time."

"It is time now!"

"Is it?"

"Yes! Where am I?"

"On Thoacdien V, the village of Lir."

"But where is that? I have yet to see a village and I have
looked all night."

"Perhaps the eye has its own way of seeing things and
is presently closed."

"Where am I!?"

"In the meadows."

"Damn you! What's going on?"

"You will know when you are ready to understand."

"Where are my friends?"

"They did not make the leap."

"What does that mean?"

"It means that they are not here and never have been.
You did not bring them."

"Where are they?"

"Right where you left them."

"When and how did I get to the meadows?"

"You came here from Mikkran's grave."

"How?"

"That will be revealed."

"Damn you!"

"There is something you must know before you can go on. It is difficult to explain and I am not the one to do it. Before we can go on you must trust us."

"Trust you! Trust you! You mole of creation. I don't even know if you're real or not!"

"Do you perceive me?"

"Yes! Damn it! But I also perceived the others who were not here!"

"I will take you back to them when you have heard what I have to say."

"No!"

"Will you listen?"

"NO!"

"Stop it!"

". . . Where is Nyz-Raagan . . ."

"He has returned to his people."

". . . No!"

"Yes. He is dead."

"No. NO! Damn you for playing with me and teasing me and deluding me until I have no sense of what is real!"

"Yes. But we have not done that to you. You are in charge. We are trying to bring you back."

"You have manipulated my senses and I can no longer distinguish the dreams!"

"Are you tired?"

"YES!"

". . . then stop."

"Shut up! Just shut up! May . . . May . . . Ahhhhh DAAAAMMMMMMNNN!"

"Biel . . ."

"Is Mikkran really dead?"

"Can you perceive her? Can you feel her?"

"NO! NO! NO!. . . . . "

"Will you stop and listen to what must be said to you for a moment?"

". . . . . . . Yes. . . . ."

Blink!

Rigin and Biel are standing in a tent. It is very quiet. The light has gone off and the tent is now soft and comfortable to the eyes. Biel's pupils contract rapidly and she can see nothing.

". . . How did you do that?"

"I am a playwright. This was my play."

!

". . . When did it begin?"

"When we met."

Blink!

Biel is very still. She looks at Rigin whose face is patient and kind. Biel's face becomes a rigid mask of indignation. She turns to walk through the door, but it is gone. Her back is to Rigin.

". . . DDamn you! . . . Damn You! I am so . . . angry at you. Why are you doing this to me?!"

". . . Biel . . ."

"Shut up, damn you! Shut up! Shut up! Shut up! I want out of here. I want to be whole. I want to be free and away from you and your cruel games. Damn. Damn . . . Damn . . . you . . ."

Biel sits down on the floor and puts her head in her hands and weeps. She is exhausted and can no longer hold on. Rigin goes to her. And, when he can, he takes her in his skinny arms and holds her and rocks her and tries to help her come together for the last of it.

". . . oh . . . oh . . . I am so . . . an . . . gry . . . I want . . . MMMM . . . please . . ."

"Johonaz, would you care to speak now?"

The old man comes forward and puts his hand on Biel's head. Kaj-Palmir is beside him. She smiles at the young girl.

"Yes. Thank you. We have offered to help you, Biel. But in your case what is help? Is it awakening? Separation? Neither? Or both? Kaj-Palmir has something to tell you."

"Biel . . . this afternoon you demonstrated an entirely new and functional attitude toward time. You are capable of simultaneity."

"mmmmmum mmmumum nnnnn. . . ."

"Until now, time has been the last irreducible. It has been that for which there are no accurate metaphors, because it is like nothing else. Now we must talk about it. Can you hear me?"

". . . Yyyyyyesss . . ."

"Good. If we can apply to time the same principle we apply to matter—i.e., that it cannot be destroyed, only transformed—then it follows that all time, which contains all events, exists right now, in one form or another. Times past, present, and future are simultaneous. Space is nothing more than that through which time passes. Space is the wake of time. Think for a moment of time as a room of thin white smoke. The room has a window and the sun shines through the window illuminating the smoke so that you can see how it is stratified. Each layer has its own peculiar coherency. Each layer is moving independently of the others—in its own slow direction. One of these layers is Thoacdien time. We have been completely trapped in Thoacdien time, even though we are entirely surrounded by other times of which we cannot even dream. They are very close. But we have not been able to perceive them, except as static, or interference with transception—which is a tangible signal which we have not known how to read. You are not so trapped. You coexist with another in at least two time-clouds—simultaneously. Johonaz?"

"How did this happen? We do not understand the details. The gist of the matter is that you and the other both fell into a common denominator at the same instant. In time there is no distance. The Binol injection sensitized you, and a crisis sensitized the other. Somehow your mutual expressions of rage and fear, which were two screams, collided—connected. The two of you were sucked into a neutral time, which is neither here not there. You remained partially in your own time. The other is now fully in this neutral area. You became the dominant partner, partly through the help of Mikkran, and partly because you emerged from a more complex technology. The result is that you and another are both here and now, and not-here, not-now—and physically connected."

"What is help for me?"

"I believe that help is separation. Relief is one personality in one body. Separation can be accomplished."

"How?"

"Child . . . we must return to Thoacdien. Will you come?"

". . . . . yes . . . . ."

"Oh, blessed be the mornings and the suns which have shone on you."

. . . .

"Lanier?"

"Yes?"

"We are in B lift, corridor seven. We are working our way down and in toward the spine of the structure as per Levin-Hughes's specs."

"Check. You are coordinated with computer mock-up. See anything yet?"

"Nada . . . it's quiet and white as a grave in here."

"OK."

"Where's Colonel Haris?"

"Mmmmm. Ha Ha. He fell asleep."

. . . .

(—. . . . I feel for your face, although you have none, for it is me . . .

—I am dancing inside your heart as the little acrobat who makes the valves move in and out—although you have no heart, for it is time.

—And you have entered all my openings, although I have none, for they are merely empty space, and in common with all.

—. . . Beyond measurement we are sinking without motion through no motion at all, toward a horizon with a light beneath its edge—although there is none, for it is us . . .

—And we are synchronized.

—We are equilibrium.

—. . . the beginning and the end—but only a small part.

—I have been afraid of nothing.

—Everything which terrified me was nothing at all.

—. . . Only you, my friend.

—. . . look . . .

—There!

—It rises, there.

—Or the horizon falls,

—. . . Is wiped away by the same hand that removed the fear.

—The horizon becomes a ring.

—A circle.

—An eye.

—. . . Looking at us.

—And the light source is not here.

—. . . Only the reflection of the light source is here.

—The source cannot be known.

—But we must turn around and try to go there.

—Kick your feet . . .

—I have, I am, I will . . .

—What can I call you?

—. . . I have forgotten.

—. . . . aaahhhhhhhhh . . . we are . . . being . . .

—. . . . separated . . .

—Please, do not . . . hold on any longer . . .

—. . . We have been found.

—Released.

—Yes. I will. I have . . . I am . . . .)

~~~~~~

!
Blink.

        Blink.

                Blink.

!

. . . purring . . .
I hear.
!
Blink.
. . . soft . . . around my body . . . fur.
Blink.
Soft . . .
. . . Blink.
I stretch and my limbs go out forever . . . farther . . . I
breathe, and my ribs rise up over my chin like a soft, tan
surprise . . .
. . . I must be lying on my back . . .
!
Blink.
. . . Where . . . am I? Feeling whole. Unafraid . . . only
surprised . . . Where?
　　—Welcome to Thoacdien.
　　—! What's that . . . . . who are you?
　　—Thoacdien.
　　—! . . . How did I get here?
　　—You never left.
　　—What has happened?
　　—You have awakened.
　　—Was I asleep?
　　—You were unawake . . . for a long time.
　　—How . . . I have experienced . . . many things.
Where was I?
　　—In the Hall of a Thousand Chambers.
　　—But . . . the walking, the Higgittes . . . the mead-
ows. My friends . . . ? Where are they?
　　—Waiting.
　　—You cannot tell me the journey was a dream. . . .
　　—Did you experience it?
　　—Yes.
　　—Then it was not a dream.
　　—Did it happen?
　　—Very much so.
　　—How?
　　—You experienced a large and prematurely admin-

istered dose of Binol. It prolonged and intensified your journey through The Hall.

—Am I awake now?

—Fully. You are released.

—Does this happen to everyone?

—Yes. You have experienced the journey through The Hall. Your journey was different only in the amount of time it took and in the details created by your distinct brain.

—But how did I experience all of that?

—Your brain designed the journey and the technology of The Hall expressed it. The nature of the journey was your creation.

—I am furious at you!

—Why?

—I have been deceived.

—How?

—By life which was not life.

—Did you experience it?

—Yes. . . but . . . I have no . . . calluses.

—Did you feel anything?

—Yes.

—Were you thirsty?

—Yes.

—Tired?

—Yes.

—In danger?

—Yes.

—Loved?

—. . . Oh, yes.

—In pain?

—Yes! But it was not really alive!

—You certainly were not dead.

—. . . Was there really a Mikkran?

—You tell me?

—Did she really die?

—Yes.

—. . . Is she dead now?

—Are you alive?

—I am.

—Now you know you can survive the death of that which means most in all your life. You are released. You are free to love and be loved with sovereignty.

—Is she dead?

—You will know soon enough.

—. . . I have been released . . .

—Yes. From all you feared.

—What was the darkness?

—Fear.

—And the seizures?

—Another matter entirely. They were caused by the Binol and resulted in wonders beyond imagination.

—What about the other who haunted me?

—He will be born in a short while.

—. . . I am free . . .

—Totally.

—What happened?

—The two of you were in independent crisis. You were dying and collided in neutral time. Somehow your gene patterns overlapped. Only Mikkran kept you here. The other's name is Howard Scott. He was pulled completely out of his time—there was nothing to hold him there. As a result of the refinement of your genetic structure your genes took the dominant position and were ghosted by his. We could not find him until your relationship became more articulate, and you could not become articulate until near the end of your journey. We have separated your gene patterns. We were able to get a clear tracing of his genes, and from that produce a sperm and an ovum. He will be born soon.

.... (..) ....

—I am only me, now . . .

—Yes.

—Now what?

—Join us and see.

—How old am I?

—You are four sets of seasons old.

—What happened to Nyz-Ragaan and the Higgittes?

—Your encounter with the Higgittes was your exploration into your own primitive brain and the violence it contains. Your responses to them was the beginning of your articulation and release. They are in you, alive, fighting to conquer your will and regain their nation.

—. . . But they never will . . .

—No. You are too complex now. You are far beyond their ways.

—And the meadows?

—What do you remember?

—Few details . . . only a feeling

—The meadows were your exploration of your own ideals and potential. They were the first articulation of changes you will make.

—What is waiting for me now?

—Come out and know.

—I have already lived a full life. What is left for me to do?

—Things beyond your dreams. Things you cannot yet imagine. Come. Turn around and be with us.

—I have become equilibrium. . . .

—Yes.

—Shall I remember the journey?

—All but the details of the meadows. The journey is part of your experience. You lived it.

—Are there others like me?

—There is no one like you in all creation. But there are others, and they are waiting for you. You are the last to emerge from The Hall.

—Thoacdien?

—Yes?

—I wish to call for my mentor now.

—I will page.

—What am I to wear?

—You have earned the red robe of curiosity.

. . . .

"Ybarra here. Lanier, we're in the chamber now. Scott

is dead. Cerebral hemorrhage. The other three are alive, but in deep catatonic states."

"This is Colonel Haris, Ybarra."

"Yes, sir."

"Surface immediately. Leave Scott's body there. Bring Dr. Williams and Dr. Hobart and Levin-Hughes back— we'll take them home. Detach your bombs and leave them on MC6. Then get the Skimmer the hell out of there in a deep eastern tangent and pick us up on the other side. We will release our bombs and time them to detonate with yours. It will be one big explosion. Now get the hell out of there."

. . . .

Mentors sit on the floor near the outer edge of the meditation chamber at the top of the big dome in complex 187-A, Thoacdien V. They are silent. They are facing in toward the center, waiting for the ceremony of welcome to begin. Their charges sit before them, tall and straight. They wear red robes of curiosity. The members of this complex are gathered to offer their strength and wisdom as tribute and welcome to the child who, on entering the world, begins the most sacred of all occasions—life.

—. . . I am being lifted upward. Riding in a soft white cube.

Thuup.

—. . . Ahhhh! Ahhh . . . People . . . they are real and here and alive . . . and sky.

A tall young girl steps out of the lift. It disappears into the floor. She has black eyes rimmed with black, long waves of black hair, dark brown skin, a high-bridged nose, a deep spoon on her upper lip, a crease in the tip of her chin, straight and full black eyebrows, a slim neck, large square hands, strong ankles, and broad, well-arched feet. She walks around the room and looks into the eyes of each person.

—. . . They are all here . . . my friends.

328

She returns to the center of the room and looks east.

"I, Biel, call my mentor forth."

A very tall woman rises.

"I, Mikkran-Gogan-Tor, of the order of Infinite Curiosity, come forth to meet you joyfully, that I may, with no interference in your sovereign vision, share with you what I have learned."

The tall one moves to the girl. She leans over, and the girl releases the veil and lowers the hood. Biel removes her mentor's robe. And Mikkran is tall and dark and brown against the bird's-egg blue of the sky.

Biel stands straight and tall as her mentor removes the red robe of curiosity. And she, too, is naked, light copper against the sky.

—And I am holding you.

—Have you waited long?

—Forever and no time at all—for we have never been apart.

—I love you, Mikkran.

—And I you, Biel. Welcome to the world.

—. . . Look, Mikkran, the sea.

—Yes.

—The sea. . . . It seems so long ago that I stood there. My hand is reaching into a pool inside my brain. Open. Closed. Grasp, Unclasp. Release.

~~~~~~

FROM: THOACDIEN.
TO: EARTH VISITORS ON MC6, OR THOACDIEN 75.

. . . .
. . . .
. . . .

EARTH VISITORS: NO RESPONSE. . . . .

FROM THE LEGEND OF BIEL

THOACDIEN: . . . PERHAPS YOU CANNOT
TRANSMIT, BUT YOU CAN
RECEIVE. ON THAT ASSUMPTION
I SHALL SPEAK TO YOU.
YOU ARE NOW ON THOACDIEN
75, OR MC6, AS YOU CALL IT.
THIS PLANET IS THE LATEST
ACQUIRED BY THE FEDERATION
TIME ZONE.
IT WAS ORIGINALLY ASHES AND
CINDER. WE HAVE MADE IT
WHAT YOU NOW KNOW IT TO BE.
THOACDIEN 75 IS SO FAR FROM
WHERE I AM SPEAKING TO YOU
FROM THAT WITH YOUR
PRESENT TECHNOLOGY YOU
COULD NOT LIVE TO REACH US—
AND YET YOU ARE ALREADY
HERE.
WE UNDERSTAND THAT YOU
ARE PREPARED TO DESTROY
THE PLANET BECAUSE YOU ARE
AFRAID.
WE MEAN YOU NO HARM, BUT
COME TO YOU AS PERSONS
HOPING TO LEARN AND SHARE.
YOU DO NOT NEED TO BE
AFRAID.
YOU FOUND US. WE ARE
GRATEFUL.
WE EXTEND AN INVITATION TO
ALL PERSONS OF YOUR CULTURE
TO COME AND JOIN US.
YOU HAVE ONLY TO BE
RELEASED BY THE HALL OF A
THOUSAND CHAMBERS, AND
YOU ARE HERE.
THE REPORT YOU HAVE

EXPERIENCED IN THE CENTRAL
CHAMBER OF DOME 27-A, IN THE
VILLAGE OF HOPE, THOACDIEN
75, MUST LOSE MUCH OF ITS
COLOR IN TRANSLATION.
WHAT WE WERE ABLE TO GIVE
YOU IS NOT AN IMITATION, OR A
RECREATION OF EVENTS—BUT
AN OUTLINE.
FROM DISEQUILIBRIUM TO
EQUILIBRIUM IS A CARPET RICH
IN COLOR, INTRICATE IN DESIGN.
WHAT YOU HAVE EXPERIENCED
IS NOT THE CARPET, NOT EVEN
THE LOOM, OR THE DIZZY
WEAVER—BUT THE FIBERS,
STILL ON THE PLANTS IN THE
FIELDS.
THIS IS BINOL, THE HALL OF ONE
THOUSAND CHAMBERS—LIQUID
THOACDIEN: INFORMATION.
IF SOMETHING CAN BE
CONCEIVED IT CAN BE
ACCOMPLISHED.
WILL YOU JOIN US?
FROM THE LEGEND OF BIEL
AS RECORDED BY THOACDIEN—
END CARD ONE: THE PARADOX.
STOP.

END TRANSMISSION ....

*"Colonel Haris here and counting down from ten, nine,
eight, seven, six, five, four, three, two, one."*
*And there was a large, quickly swallowed explosion,
as MC6 became incoherent dust.*

"Well . . . there goes the eight-ball. Too bad about Scott. Let's scrap one PROBE IV mission, and go home."

~~~~~~

FROM: THOACDIEN—PRIORITY ONE.
TO: THE FEDERATION.
DATE: 187.365
TIME: 2.2.075
. . . .
. . . .
. . . .

FEDERATION: PROCEED. STOP.

THOACDIEN: THIS IS TO REPORT THAT OUR INVITATION TO THE PEOPLE OF THE PLANET EARTH HAS BEEN REFUSED.
PLEASE ACTIVATE ALL PERTINENT CONSTRUCTION MODULES.
RECONSTRUCTION OF MC6, THOACDIEN 75, IS PRIORITY ONE.
I AM PRIVILEGED TO ANNOUNCE THAT WE ARE DEVIATING FROM THE STANDARD BIRTHING SCHEDULE OF 1,000 INFANTS EACH FIVE SETS OF SEASONS IN ORDER TO RECEIVE THE ONE EARTH HUMAN WHO WAS ABLE TO FIND HIS WAY HERE THROUGH MUCH DARKNESS. HOWARD SCOTT, MALE, WILL BE BORN IN THE NEXT SEASON OF THE SUN.

THIS IS CAUSE FOR GREAT JOY, AND WE WELCOME HIM TO THE FEDERATION.

STOP.

END TRANSMISSION ....